The sabotage was bad enough...but now the bodies were piling up.

As they drove out of the parking lot, Lyle was mulling the options for spending the night and thinking about which direction to turn. When they paused at a stop sign a few blocks away, a light-colored sedan sped toward them from a side street. It didn't stop. Just before it smashed into the driver's side of Lyle's car, the driver hit the brakes. The sedan skidded and spun up alongside them. Two men were inside. "It's them," Lyle's passenger shouted.

The man closest to Lyle pointed a pistol at him. He motioned for Lyle to pull over.

Lyle nodded to the gunman then slowly slipped his car into reverse—and jammed down the accelerator. The Chevy Camaro jerked backward. Lyle spun the wheel, turning the car around abruptly. As he shifted forward and picked up speed, he glanced in his mirror. Traffic was keeping the other car from turning around. From the darkness behind them came a flash. And a gunshot. Almost simultaneously, a bullet slammed into the trunk of Lyle's car.

Lyle took a sharp turn and hoped he lost the gunmen. He came to the end of the block and turned again. Headlights spun quickly around the corner behind them. Lyle tried to recall the faces of the two men. He had seen them for only a second or two. Was the driver wearing funny glasses? What was it about his face? He looked familiar.

Lyle slid the Camaro out on to a busy, well-lit commercial street. He kept up his speed, racing through a stop signal on yellow. He looked in the mirror again. The light sedan was a block and a half back. They had a little cushion of space. Before he could relax, traffic suddenly stopped in front of them. A semi-truck was turning into the street from a parking lot.

The signal behind them changed. The light-colored sedan was moving. Lyle couldn't wait. He veered off into the opposing lanes. He had to get around the truck. He swerved back into his lane, just missing an oncoming van. Behind them, the gunmen swerved out of the lanes, too. They were closing. Another flash and another gun report. This time the rental car's taillight shattered.

He thinks he's on edge now…then people start getting killed…

"Stressed out" has been ex-cop Lyle Deming's default setting for years, but his new job, driving a cab in a theme park, promises to cure his chronic anxieties. Nostalgia City is the ultimate resort for anyone who wants to visit the past. A meticulous recreation of an entire small town from the early 1970s, it's complete with period cars, music, clothes, shops, restaurants, hotels—the works.

The relaxed, theme-park atmosphere is just what Lyle needs—until rides are sabotaged and tourists killed. Then park founder, billionaire "Max" Maxwell, drafts Lyle into investigating—unofficially. As the violence escalates and employees get rattled, Lyle gets help. Kate Sorensen, the park's PR director—and former college basketball player—becomes another incognito investigator. Except that she's six-foot-two-and-a-half-inches tall and drop-dead gorgeous. So much for incognito.

Together, Lyle and Kate must unravel a conspiracy of corporate greed and murder.

Death in Nostalgia City

Wanda — Warmest wishes,

Mark S. Bacon

Mark S. Bacon

Nov '14

A Black Opal Books Publication

Black Opal Books

BECAUSE SOME STORIES JUST HAVE TO BE TOLD

Chapter 1

Whose idea was it to replace the chrome knobs and push buttons on car radios with *touch screens*? Lyle had no clue. He eased off the accelerator of his 1973 Dodge Polara taxicab so his passengers wouldn't miss anything. The sedan lumbered past an appliance store where a dozen identical images of the Fonz—leather jacket and all—were speaking unheard words from 24-inch, picture-tube TVs in the shop window. Lyle's passengers gaped. A common reaction. Lyle had been at his new job for six months now, so the time warp didn't faze him. He liked it. The new job brought him back to happy days.

"Oh, baby, I'm in love," cried the DJ on the car radio. "That was a new one by Roberta Flack, 'Will You Love Me Tomorrow?' You're listening to Big Earl Williams on KBOP. Next up, the latest from Three Dog Night, but first—"

Lyle turned the radio down so he could talk to his fares, a wholesome-looking sixtyish couple, probably from the Midwest. "This your first time?"

"Yes," the husband said. "First time."

"We've heard all about this place," his wife said, "but we had to see for ourselves. It's amazing."

Lyle glanced at the couple in the mirror. "Just your average town."

"You got good cell phone coverage here?" the husband asked. "I'm having problems with my iPhone."

"What's an iPhone?" Lyle said.

"What, are you nuts? A *cell* phone!"

"Don't be a cynic, Warren," his wife said. "It's part of the experience here."

"Okay. I get it." He held up two fingers in an awkward peace sign. "Far out, man. Groovy."

Lyle smiled. He didn't mind. He tried not to let little things bother him anymore. If people didn't want to get in the spirit to relive the good old days, that was their choice. It just puzzled him why anyone would spend the money to visit Nostalgia City, one of the most elaborate theme parks in the world, and not enjoy the masquerade.

Nostalgia City was the brainchild of billionaire developer Archibald "Max" Maxwell. The re-creation of a town from the early 1970s was as complete as billions of dollars and Max's ceaseless energy could make it. Aimed at baby boomers, or anyone who wanted to go back in time, Nostalgia City was the size of a small town. Rides, shops, restaurants, hotels—everything—was constructed from scratch in northern Arizona near a reclaimed stretch of Route 66. To Lyle, a baby boomer himself, it was part resort, part theme park, and very much an escape. His new job gave him the chance to meet people not because they were robbed or assaulted but because they were on vacation.

Lyle steered the cab into the curb lane to give his passengers a closer look at the storefronts. He loved his big, old '73 taxi. His parents had driven a Chrysler Cordoba with "soft Corinthian leather." His Dodge wasn't as fancy—after all, it was a cab—but it was fully restored. You could almost believe the 7,000 miles on the odometer. Like everything else in Nostalgia City, the cab didn't look like an artifact. It looked new.

Rolling through the reproduction of a decades-past downtown, Lyle and his passengers came to a stop light. At the corner, Lyle's guests stared at a Flying A service station with its white-uniformed attendants. Each gas pump was a sculptured red tower with one long hose and side-mounted nozzle, like a fashion model with one hand on her hip. As the tourists gawked, something moving drew Lyle's gaze up a hill to the left. He saw a white 1970 Ford Torino moving toward the cab, picking up speed. Instantly, Lyle saw something missing—a driver.

In seconds, the Torino would smash into the driver's side of Lyle's cab. He stomped on the gas pedal and yelled for his passengers to hang on. The taxi's rear tires chirped. Then the rubber took hold. The Dodge lunged forward as the Torino rushed toward it. Lyle escaped the runaway car—almost. The Ford scraped along a corner of the taxi's rear bumper, catching the edge of a metal advertising sign on the back of the cab. It ripped off the sign with quick, metallic popping sounds.

Streaking forward, the driverless car headed for the gas station. It ran up the drive and caromed off a column supporting an awning over a row of pumps. The heavy metal awning trembled, tilted, then crashed to the ground. Slowed but still unchecked, the Torino reeled on. It plowed into a stack of motor oil cans, sending them flying. Finally, the Ford rammed into a gas pump, giving up the last of its momentum in a resounding crunch.

Gasoline gushed from the damaged pump while the motionless Ford straddled the concrete island like a ship stuck on a shoal. The sharp gasoline smell pierced the air. Lyle stopped his cab away from traffic. He bailed out and barked at his passengers to get away from the station. Seeing a customer standing near the flowing gas, he motioned for him to back away from the growing, flammable lake.

Everyone waited for the explosion.

But it didn't happen.

Lyle dashed up to an attendant who had jumped out of the way of the car and was lying on his back, stunned and trembling. "Shut-off."

The attendant pointed to the side of the building. Lyle found the emergency shut-off and punched a fist-sized button.

"You all right?" he asked the attendant.

"Think so." The young man stood and dusted himself off. "We gotta call for help."

"Already being taken care of." Lyle saw another uniformed attendant in the service station office with a phone in his hand waving toward them.

The gasoline contained itself in the station's parking area. An asphalt berm became a dam creating a small gas lagoon a few inches deep. Avoiding the gasoline, Lyle trotted over to the Ford. Its front bumper, grill, and the right side of its body were shredded and crushed, but the driver's side looked relatively untouched except for long scratch marks from Lyle's cab. Lyle glanced at the Torino's driver's side front door for a second, then pulled it open. He knew the engine wasn't running, but he wanted to make sure the ignition was off. He stuck his head in, careful not to touch anything he didn't have to. His right hand rested on the smooth vinyl seat as he leaned in farther. Then he felt someone tapping him on the back.

"Don't touch anything," said a deep voice. "Step back, sir."

That was a little difficult because a large man in a shirt and tie stood right behind Lyle. The man had a badge holder hanging from his pocket and a holstered semi-automatic clipped to his belt.

"Clyde Bates, chief of security," the walking impediment said. "What happened here?"

"Looks like someone tried to top off his tank."

Bates scowled. "Okay, comedian, were you driving?"

"Yes—but not *this* car. No one was driving the Ford. That was the problem."

Lyle recognized Bates from a staff meeting a couple of months earlier. He noticed the prematurely gray hair trimmed in a crew cut and the expression that said smiling was off limits. The park security chief looked as if he was once in shape but that recently his center of gravity had been moving south.

Lyle stepped away from the Ford and pointed to his Nostalgia City ID badge. "Deming. Lyle Deming. The car's in neutral. I was just looking to see if—"

"Where'd it come from, that hill?"

"Yes, it—"

"See anyone around?"

"No. Just the car, no driver."

"You didn't see anyone on the sidewalk?"

"No. So I looked inside the car to—"

"Okay. We'll take it from here."

Since Bates was alone, Lyle wondered who the "we" referred to. Then he heard a siren and knew reinforcements were on the way. A black-and-white early '70s Plymouth with "Nostalgia City Security" painted on the door rolled up, followed by two fire engines of the same vintage.

Bates started giving orders, and Lyle walked a few steps away to pick up his yellow cabbie hat that had fallen off. He ran his fingers through his dark, wavy hair and set the cap on the back of his head.

"Think it was an accident?" Lyle asked. "Maybe something slipped."

"An accident?" Bates said, looking away. "Dunno. Make a report. We'll handle it."

Lyle didn't like his attitude. "What makes you think it *wasn't* an accident?"

"Nothing."

"Could this be related to the ride someone vandalized? Or the bridge—"

"That's *our* business. Not your concern."

Just walk away, Lyle told himself as he touched the rubber band on his wrist. Leave the make-believe policeman alone. *He's right, not my problem.*

Lyle inspected his cab. The rear bumper was twisted and scratched. The mangled advertising sign lay on the pavement and the trunk lid now sported several jagged air holes. Lyle was about to round up his passengers when someone yelled at Bates. A firefighter knelt at the edge of the toppled awning. Lyle ran over to see if he could help. Right away, he knew no one could. A middle-aged man had been standing under the awning when it collapsed.

"Dead," the firefighter said.

Chapter 2

Kate Sorensen sat in the twenty-seventh row of an otherwise empty Las Vegas showroom and edited news release drafts on her tablet while occasionally glancing at the rehearsal.

"Two, three, four..." A choreographer in green slacks and baggy T-shirt shouted at the handful of dancers aligned across the stage. "Kristy, you've gotta get your sea legs, honey. This stage sloshes around *all* the time."

Behind the dancers were huge brass dials, switches, and controls designed to look like the bridge of a Navy ship. The broad, nautically themed stage floated in an enormous Plexiglas water tank spanning the front of the theater. As the dancers marched left, the deck dipped to one side. Waves splashed the stage. Kate could almost feel the rolling of a ship. Couple the undulating movement with flickering lights, ocean sounds, and a fine sea spray and the audience might need Dramamine. Would the dancers?

Obviously more work was necessary before the show would become flagship entertainment for the SS Las Vegas Hotel/Casino. Kate looked down at her work and then wrinkled her nose. Something smelled like rotting seaweed. It certainly wasn't her perfume. That came from Saks. Did this mean the show was a stinker?

When her cell phone whined inside her suit pocket, she reached for it, expecting to hear the voice of her secretary. She brushed her long blond hair away from her ear. "Max, what a surprise. How are things in Nostalgia City?"

"First, congratulations. Saw all the publicity you got for your hotel's anniversary. Tie-in to naval history was clever."

"You have to find a new approach every time, stuff to catch the imagination."

"You do that pretty well—come up with great ideas."

"Hope so. In a few days, we're launching a new extravaganza. Ha, no pun intended. I'm going over the stories my staff
has written. So far I don't see many new ideas."

"You'll make it come together. You usually do."

"Why all the flattery, Max? You must be in a good mood."
The founder and CEO of the giant retro resort was not the kind of
person to call for idle chitchat, especially at work. "Everything
going well there in Arizona?"

"Doing okay. Attendance is up."

Kate leaned to one side to get comfortable. Her long legs
sometimes made her feel cramped sitting in one-size-fits-all theater seats. "I read that the Indian casino and your excursion train
through the reservation are behind schedule."

"A little. We'll work it out. So, you still like it there in Vegas?"

"Why do you ask?"

"Would you be interested in joining us here?"

"Go to work for you? You've *got* a public relations VP."

"As of now."

"Move to Flagstaff?"

"Why don't you come out here for a couple of days and
we'll talk."

Go back to work for Max? Several thoughts fought for attention in Kate's head. Although it paid well, Kate's job as com-
munication director for the SS Las Vegas Hotel, "The Cruise Ship
of the Strip," was becoming routine. Bruce, her boyfriend, room-
mate, and possibly future husband, might throw a tantrum if she
asked him to move to Arizona. And Max could be a tyrant to
work for. He interfered. On the other hand, the innovative billionaire had enthusiasm and a stomach for risks. Working for him
was never dull.

"Come for a visit," Max said. "I'll send the corporate jet."

"I don't mind flying commercial. Let me think. Call you tomorrow."

As Kate put away her phone, Mario Danova slipped into the
seat next to her. His expensive suit and capped-teeth smile said
"show biz."

"Looks like it'll be a great show, eh, Kate?"

"Yeah. It really rocks. Hope no one gets seasick."

"Seasick?" Danova's nametag read, Executive Vice President – Entertainment. "Oh, you're kidding, huh. Think you can get us on the *Today Show*? We really need to rev up our publicity machine."

"Sure, Mario. The campaign's on track. We'll make sure everyone knows about the show."

"Okay, but we need to get moving. Jack Stegman wants plenty of interviews. He's the star. You'll headline him, right?"

"I will."

"And he wants you to retouch his publicity photos."

"We did that already."

"Did you? He said the shots make him look like Wayne Newton. You'll fix them, right?"

Maybe Max wouldn't be too difficult to work for at that. Promoting a theme park could be an interesting change after ten years of hyping Las Vegas casinos. But Max always said he would never offer a job to someone who had quit working for him. Why had he changed his mind?

Chapter 3

Watching a body being scraped up, dumped on a gurney, and hauled away was not a new sight for Lyle, but that didn't make it any more appealing. He took deep breaths as he felt the adrenaline wearing off. Firefighters had found the victim's wallet, so security officers headed out to check the park's hotels to see if they could locate family. Lyle was glad this was one death he didn't have to deal with. The people left behind—loved ones—made lasting impressions on him.

Driving home that afternoon in his own car he tried to think of other things. He turned his Mustang down the central street in Timeless Village, a mixture of new houses, single-story condos, and upscale apartments just outside Nostalgia City. The home styles were generic southwestern stucco. Pinon pines and sage figured prominently in the landscaping. Not all the homes were occupied yet, and the village was always quiet.

Lyle *thought* he was going home, but when he got to his street, he continued straight ahead toward Gilligan's Island. A half mile later, he was pulling into a small strip shopping center. Sitting between a hair salon and a Chinese restaurant was Gilligan's Island, a neighborhood bar. It wasn't Lyle's normal quitting time, so his dad wouldn't be expecting him. He'd have a beer and unwind.

He left his hat in the car, pulled off his dark glasses, and wandered inside. Ducking under faux palm fronds, he saw a few patrons at the far end of the bar, talking to the bartender. Lyle took a seat close to the door. Reedy wallpaper covered the walls and tropical fish swam in lighted blue tanks. Somewhere, a bubbling pot of chili sent its aroma into the bar. Lyle loosened his bow tie and let the ends hang down the front of his white shirt.

The bartender looked up. "Lyle, howya doin'? Want a draft?" Lyle nodded. The bartender, also bar owner, had bushy dark hair, a long, thin face, and inquisitive eyes behind wire-rimmed glasses. He wore a yacht cap and told everyone to call him *the skipper*, even though he didn't look any more like Alan Hale, Jr.—the actor who played the role in the TV show—than Raquel Welch looked like Flipper. He handed Lyle a frosty mug. "I heard there was excitement at the park today."

Lyle put his hand around the beer. "Bad accident. How'd you find out so soon?"

"Somebody who works on Main Street was just in here. Said he saw fire trucks at the Flying A station. You see it?"

"Yes."

"What happened?"

"A car smashed into the pumps." Lyle saw no sense in spreading the sad details. Everyone would hear about it soon enough.

A couple strolled into the bar and the skipper had to walk down to wait on them. Lyle was off the hook. He took a swallow of cold beer then rested both arms on the bar. He could feel tenseness in his shoulders, so he relaxed into a slouch. Before he could take another sip, his cell phone rang.

"Dad, you okay?"

"Lyle, I need my meds."

Lyle sat up. "Your pills were...on the kitchen counter this morning. Yes, I made sure they were sitting where you could get them."

"Oh, I have them all right. But I'm going to need a refill soon."

Lyle let out a breath and leaned against the bar. "Okay, we'll get one next week."

"You have to ask the doctor about this. I think that maybe I need a new prescription. Something stronger."

"Sure, Dad, we'll talk to him." Lyle swiveled his stool away from the bar so everyone wouldn't hear his conversation. "Dad, remember, I had to get special permission to carry a cell phone in the park? You're only supposed to call me in an emergency."

Hank was silent.

"Dad?"

"You got a reject from that insurance company today. They denied your claim for your stepdaughter's therapy. Sounds like that insurance you're paying for is no damn good."

Son of a bitch, Lyle thought, his mind traveling to the stack of medical bills and insurance forms on his desk at home. His stepdaughter, Samantha, had been in a serious accident three months before, but her recovery was going well, thanks to continued medical care. Although he was divorced from Samantha's mother, Lyle remained close to his stepdaughter, helping her out financially and emotionally as she worked her way through college.

Samantha's extensive medical bills might have made Lyle happy that he paid for full coverage. Trouble was, Federal Patrician Insurance Company was full of excuses for delaying or denying payments.

Thanks for the good news Dad, he thought. And thanks for opening my mail.

"Your friend Marko called this morning," Hank said. "He thinks you can get reinstated if you just see one more counselor."

"Another shrink, you mean."

"Now, Lyle."

"Okay, Dad. Thanks for the message."

When he hung up the phone, Lyle sat staring absently across the room. The bow of a wooden boat, made to look as if it had just crashed into the barroom, stuck out from a corner. Painted on the nose was the name, *SS Minnow.*

"So, how's your dad?" the skipper asked.

Lyle spun around in his seat. "You don't miss much, do you?"

The skipper put a hand on the bar. He looked hurt. "I was just—"

"He's okay," Lyle said with a wave of his hand. "As good as he gets."

"You get along?"

"Before his last heart attack he spoke to me maybe once a year or so. Now he lives with me *and* he calls me all the time."

"Maybe he's lonely."

"Maybe."

The skipper was silent a moment then said, "You work tomorrow?"

"You bet. Saturdays are the most fun." How long had it been since he'd used *that* word to describe work?

Lyle finished his beer, paid the tab, and walked outside.

When he reached for the door handle of his car, he froze. Something he'd seen at the crash site hadn't registered at the time. Now it appeared in his head like a Polaroid picture developing. Not all the damage on the driver's side of the runaway Torino had been made by the back end of Lyle's taxi.

"Wonder how that happened?" he said aloud.

Chapter 4

Driving along Interstate 40 in northern Arizona, Kate Sorensen watched Nostalgia City billboards flash by as she wondered what in the world she was doing. It was just curiosity, she told herself, that prompted her to fly out to Flagstaff, rent a car, and head toward Max's metropolis.

The next billboard said she was approaching a *Blast to the Past*. A few miles later a sign heralded, *The Living Time Machine*. Clever? Almost. If Max's PR was as mediocre as his advertising, no wonder he needed help. When she reached the exit for the small town of Polk, she pulled off the interstate and drove south. She passed through Polk, traveled several more miles, and was soon entering Nostalgia City's massive parking lot. The lot wasn't full, but rows of cars stretched on for acres. A dry, mid-April breeze whispered to her as she got out of her car. The air smelled fresh, like it did in Vegas before a million cars took to the streets every day. She heard a humming and the sound of voices. Turning around, she saw a tram waiting for her. She nestled herself into a molded bench seat, angling her legs to the side. As the tram started, a recorded voice said, "You're about to step back in time. But before you do, remember where you're parked. You're in section T for teenybopper."

Kate scanned the passengers. On the row behind her were two couples, perhaps in their late fifties. She could see few children on the tram. The demographics weren't quite Sun City, but this was no Sesame Street crowd, either. Except for a few teens, everyone was a gen-Xer, like Kate, or older.

Kate's Nordstrom blazer and camel skirt made her more formally dressed than the other visitors. Her blonde hair tied up tight and her makeup subdued, she sparkled under the desert sun. She did look dressy for a theme park, but what the heck, this was a job interview, even if it was with Max.

As the tram reached the park's main entrance, the recorded voice resumed. "When you leave the tram you can either go directly to a ticket booth, or stop at one of the automated information stations."

Kate stepped from the tram and saw a dozen oddly shaped kiosks. Some looked like jukeboxes. Others were in the shape of space capsules, stacks of huge phonograph records, old-style TV sets, and other bygone cultural icons. They were scattered across a broad concrete square like giant toys on a playroom floor. Kate chose a kiosk in the shape of a pudgy carhop on roller skates. The carhop's food tray held the flat video screen. Kate pushed a button. A twangy guitar played a song she recognized but couldn't name then a man's voice began. "Are you ready for a trip back? Welcome to Archibald Maxwell's Nostalgia City. Everything you see and hear is just as it was back then."

So Max *did* flaunt his name here and there, just like the news reports she'd seen. Kate had to bend over to read the screen. "Notice there are several ways to enjoy your trip to the past. If you'd like to stay in one of our hotels, touch the green button. Once inside the park you can catch a taxi or shuttle bus. If you'd like to rent a car, touch the red button."

Rental cars in an amusement park? That was a twist. Kate touched the screen and watched a video of an old car driving toward the camera. Was it a Pontiac?

"This beautiful 1972 Chevrolet, or one of a variety of other classic wheels, is available for your stay in Nostalgia City."

As the announcer spoke, names of car models and typical rental rates crawled across the bottom of the screen. The prices! In Vegas, anyone could rent a new Italian sports car or a limo *and* driver for the same price as these automotive relics. But then lots of people liked old cars. Kate touched another button.

The screen filled with an aerial view of Nostalgia City, and the reason for the rental cars and taxis became obvious. The park covered several square miles. In the middle was the "city" portion of Nostalgia City, subtitled Centerville, a re-created town from 40 years ago. Arranged around it in a semicircle were other themed areas, all connected by roads that radiated out from Centerville like spokes on a wheel.

The areas included an amusement park called the Fun Zone, a cluster of hotels and restaurants, a golf course, and a small dude ranch. The entrance where she stood was at the end of another spoke. A remarkable accomplishment, Kate thought, in light of the resort's checkered past. Owing to Max's unfortunate decision to build a multi-billion dollar development just before the recession hit, construction stopped for at least two years. Max had the advantage later, however, of a cheap labor market during the most intensive building phase. Derided by the media at first because of the on-again, off-again nature of its construction, Nostalgia City became a sensation when it was finally finished.

Kate remembered the glowing TV news stories. One over-enthusiastic network reporter had worn wide bell-bottoms and a tie-dyed top to cover the grand opening. Kate had a good idea of who the park's prime market was, judging by the ages and prosperous look of the tourists flocking in. Why, she wondered, *did* Max want PR help—especially hers?

To enter the park Kate had to go through a security check. It looked like the checkpoints at airports, except the uniformed personnel smiled more often. This kept weapons out of the park, without dampening visitors' spirits. She looked past the gates and saw lines of taxicabs and small buses. All the vehicles looked old fashioned, yet new.

Their gleaming chrome, shiny paint, and other details said they must be recent models, but the styles were obviously decades old. Advertising signs, promoting park attractions, decorated the sides of the buses. One sign said, "Hustle your bones over to the Graveyard Grill. Try our Ghoulash."

Kate grimaced at the puns. She decided to check out the Fun Zone amusement area and headed for a shuttle bus.

e/ɔe/ɔ

Two and a half hours later, after exploring part of the park and going on a few rides, Kate stood before an office building on a side street at the edge of Centerville. The bronze sign set into the stonework said only, "Maxwell Building." Inside, Kate gave her name to a guard who directed her to a bank of elevators.

Kate found Max's office on the top floor. The brightly colored, squared-off waiting-room furniture was obviously accurate for the period. The receptionist's suit could have been from the 1960s or contemporary, but her hairstyle was something Kate

remembered seeing in old movies and in one of her mother's photo albums. Almost before Kate could give her name, Max came
out a doorway to greet her.

Chapter 5

You didn't call from the VIP entrance," Maxwell said. "Had a car waiting."

"I wanted to look around," Kate said, "so I got here early." Her height made her used to glancing down to meet people's eyes but, in Max's case, he was nearly a head shorter. Unlike many men in their seventies, he didn't have an ounce of fat on him. His wiry frame was almost always in motion. Fat didn't have time to stick. Some people called him beady-eyed, but Kate knew his look was just intense. His sharp eyes sat on either side of a hawk nose. He eschewed a comb-over and had his thinning hair cut short.

Maxwell's penthouse office was roomy; Kate remembered he liked lots of space. The carpet featured a wavy geometric pattern, like colorful amoebas dancing across the floor. Max's huge Danish modern desk and his other furnishings looked dated but new, a contradiction Kate was getting used to. From the office windows she could look out over the park. Railroad tracks ran through Centerville and stretched off to the northeast. She sat in a low chair in front of Max's desk.

"You've looked around. What'd you think? Is there enough here for you to promote?"

"You've done an amazing job. As usual."

"Try some of the rides?"

Kate nodded. "What about the Indian casino? Is that still under construction?"

"Yup. Decatur Group thinks they're moving full speed ahead. *I* could have had the place *finished* by now. They only ordered their slot machines recently. Hell, it's supposed to be open by July."

"You didn't bid on the casino development, did you?"

"No. Since I sold the Vegas property, I'm out of the gaming business. Decatur will run the casino for the tribe. We'll be linked to it with the train."

Maxwell seemed to have a hard time sitting still. He got up and moved around the office as he talked. "This'll be a huge marketing plus. It's the main reason I bought the scenic railroad. We offer a thirty-minute train ride to a full-blown casino and it'll add another dimension to the park."

"And no doubt you'll get something in exchange for pouring Nostalgia City tourists into the casino." Max knew all the angles—or thought he did. For what it must have cost to build Nostalgia City, Kate thought, Max needed angles.

"We've got lots to offer, lots of things in the works. Need someone to publicize it. Did you try the Living Dead ride?"

"The zombie one? The line was too long."

"Too bad. It's a hellava ride. 'Cept we're not supposed to call 'em rides. They're *adventures*. This one's based on the '68 George Romero movie, *Night of the Living Dead*."

"Sounds gruesome. I read about it. You've had mostly good publicity, except for the accident last week."

Over the past few days, Kate had checked the Internet and used her media contacts to collect as much information on the park as she could.

"Got lots of PR when we opened. But we want to build a long-term name, not just get ink 'cause we're new."

"So, you're not satisfied with your media coverage?"

Kate assumed that Max's present public relations VP would be history soon. She wanted to know the point of contention. Max had a habit of firing PR people.

"Publicity? That's part of it. But I want more from my PR department. I want someone to do the same thing you did in Vegas."

"As I recall, you weren't *getting* good publicity when I started at your Vegas hotel. We had a little troubleshooting to do."

Maxwell walked back toward his desk. "There's always a hitch or two. Nothing's perfect."

"Max, is that car accident a big problem? I read about that guy getting killed. But it was a small item in the Vegas paper."

"Accident? Yes, terrible. Horrible accident. That man's poor family. We're trying to help them now."

"It's not the only problem you've had, is it? I read about trouble with the railroad construction. A bridge collapsed before it was finished. And possibly some ride vandalism?"

"Where'd you read that?"

"The bridge story was in the papers. The thing about vandalism was rumored on a theme park website."

"Good girl, you did your homework. Knew you would."

Calling her a girl would not insult nor sidetrack her. She knew Max too well. "Is something going on, Max?"

"Wish I knew."

Kate was silent.

"Okay, we've had some bad luck. No question. And every theme park has to deal with vandals. So do we. But you know how the media is. I don't want the stories to get out of hand."

Kate sat back in her chair and turned her gaze directly on her former boss. "I understand. You want Kate Sorensen, spin doctor, in case there's another accident."

"But there won't be. What I need, Kate, is for you to kick our publicity campaigns into high gear. With your contacts—"

"With my contacts I can try to keep a smiley face on the park's image, no matter what."

"And do your usual fine job of generating stories with great promotion ideas."

This was far more demanding than Kate had anticipated. Working for Max—a sometimes ill-tempered meddler who didn't always keep his mouth shut—was one thing. In addition, she'd have to play spokesperson for an accident-prone theme park. It sounded exciting. She hadn't come to Arizona to say *yes*, but now she wanted the job. Besides, Vegas glitz was wearing thin.

"I don't know, Max." No reason to agree right away. "I'll have to talk to Bruce."

Before he called her a cab, Max told her what he was willing to pay. She hoped he didn't hear her intake of breath.

Chapter 6

Lyle had an idea why the president of Nostalgia City had asked to see him. But maybe Archibald Maxwell really did just want to thank him for his actions at the gas station. In any event, it gave Lyle the chance to see the executive offices. He'd never been above the second floor. When he reached the inner sanctum, he first noticed the silence. Thick carpet soaked up all sound. The heavy decision-making probably went on behind the large, wooden double doors with chrome-plated handles shaped like Route 66 highway signs.

Lyle wondered what the receptionist with the beehive hairdo did when she went to the grocery store or the movies. Venturing outside Nostalgia City was an occupational hazard for those who styled their hair to match their jobs. The people in Flagstaff and nearby Polk likely were used to seeing beehives, flips, and flat tops. Lyle's tonsorial concession to the period was his sideburns. They were somewhere between Elvis and Walter Cronkite.

"I'm here to see Mr. Maxwell."

"I'll tell him you're here."

"Don't you want my name?"

She pointed at Lyle's shirt. He glanced down at his badge and grinned then turned away and headed for a chair. "She can read your badge, dummy," he mumbled to himself.

The reception area's spare '60s modern decor with brightly colored pop art paintings—such as a collage of yellow stars and Marilyn Monroe's face—made the room feel like a museum. Lime green and orange vinyl furniture completed the impression.

Lyle settled into an uncomfortable, low-backed chair and picked up a magazine with Steve McQueen's picture on the cover. A minute later, the solid wooden doors opened and the most stunning woman he'd seen in a long time walked out. She had to be at least six feet tall. Business clothes didn't completely hide her curves. And those legs. She reminded Lyle of a taller, older version of Susie Lopresti, the cheerleader he lusted after in high school. Lyle pushed his cabbie hat back on his head to get a better view without appearing to stare. He didn't need any subtlety, however, because the woman walked right up to him.

"All set," she said. "Are you parked downstairs? I appreciate the service."

Lyle stood and looked up. *Damn*, she was well *over* six feet. Her blond hair, knotted up to look businesslike, drooped a little as if it wanted to be unfastened. "I, ah, my cab's downstairs."

He dropped his magazine and turned to the door. Just then, another cab driver walked in.

"Does someone need a lift?" the driver asked into the silence of the reception area.

The beehive looked confused. She glanced down at her desk and then looked up. "Mr. Deming? You have an appointment with Mr. Maxwell."

"That's right. Is it 4:30 already?" He turned to the blonde. "I'm sure my colleague here can help you."

"Sorry," the blonde said. "It's your hat. I thought you were waiting for me. Thanks anyway."

As she turned to go, Lyle thought he caught a hint of a smile.

He sank back in his angular chair. Had she really been that spectacular, or was he just horny? Since his wife divorced him, dates had been few and far between—zero in fact since his dad moved in. It wasn't that Lyle was unattractive. Some people said he resembled George Clooney—okay, maybe a slightly *older* George Clooney. Lyle didn't have time to consider this further because Archibald Maxwell came out to greet him. He ushered Lyle back to his office and they sat opposite each other in chairs next to a window.

"Want to thank you for your quick work last week. One person was killed, but it could have been much worse with all that gasoline around."

"I just reacted, that's all. Somebody had to. Wish I could've helped that guy." Lyle didn't really want to be reminded.

"The pump that broke shouldn't have spilled gas. It malfunctioned. We're replacing them."

"Let's hope nothing like this happens again."

Max nodded. After a moment he said, "You like driving a cab?"

"Yes, I do."

"You used to be a policeman," Max continued, "a detective sergeant in Phoenix." It was a statement, not a question.

Lyle thought he knew what was coming. He glanced around at the unconventional artwork in the office. On one wall hung a painting of a rural landscape surrounding a spark plug the size of a Saturn moon rocket. The painting next to it featured a full-color Spam can label. Lyle remembered that one. Must be a print.

"Our security chief tells me you were a good investigator, solved a lot of cases. Right now, Nostalgia City has a situation we need to solve. I think you could help us."

"Mr. Maxwell, I appreciate the compliment. I know we had some problems, but even with the car accident last week I didn't think it was too serious."

"It's damn serious, and we have to stop it right away, before it gets worse. That's why I hoped you could help."

Maxwell's eye contact was hard to avoid. Lyle glanced at the Spam can again but found his gaze quickly pulled back to the president.

"Sorry," Lyle said. "I don't want to be disagreeable. I do like working here. I worked for the Phoenix PD for years, but now *this* is the kind of job I want." He touched the name badge on his breast pocket. "I like visiting with the tourists, showing them around."

Maxwell stood up, looked out the window for a moment, then faced Lyle. "We would—of course—offer you additional compensation, and you'd report directly to me. Clyde won't like that idea. Tough for him."

"I appreciate the offer." Lyle lifted his hands, palms up. "I do. It's not the money. I'm retired from being a cop. It takes it out of you. I came here because I wanted a change. Besides, security is pretty good. Bates's people should be able to handle it."

Maxwell snorted. "I like to have back-up plans. Thought you'd be just the person. You were a detective *and* you know your way around the park." He stared at Lyle.

"But if the runaway Ford just lost its brakes or something..."

"Hell, it was no accident. Done on purpose. This is the third act of sabotage in two months." Max shook a finger at Lyle as if it were his fault. "First a ride, then the railroad bridge, now this. Trouble is, we don't know *why*."

"What's the sheriff doing?"

"Not much. Besides, we don't need that kind of publicity."

Lyle hadn't realized the accidents represented a serious threat to his newly adopted home. His new job meant more to him than most people knew, but going back to being a cop wasn't an option.

"We've got to stop this, now," Maxwell said. "Would you please think about it, Mr. Deming?"

Chapter 7

I t looks worse than it is," Joann Nye said. "Most of this has blown over."

Eighteen days after her talk with Max, Kate Sorensen, the new Nostalgia City VP of public relations, was asking herself what she'd gotten into. Her new secretary waved a hand over a small sea of newspaper clippings and a few website printouts covering the public relations department's conference table. Bold headlines shouted, *Theme Park Crash Claims Life of Tourist, Nostalgia City Shocked by Death, Houston Man Dies in Theme Park Accident.*

"This is about two weeks' worth of clips," Joann said. "We usually lay them out so everyone in the department knows what kind of media hits we got. Bob, your predecessor, used to review the clips with staff every Monday."

"Kinda focused on print media, wasn't he?" Kate scanned the clips and discovered the tourist's death had been front-page news all over Arizona and the West. Many major U.S. papers ran at least a small story. "What about social media?"

"It was bad too, for a while," Joann said. "But tweets from visitors are all back to positive. People love to take pictures of themselves with the old cars and stores and post them."

"Anyone post pictures of the gas station crash on Facebook?"

"I don't think so. We don't monitor that too closely."

"We'll have to start." Kate said. "Did the crash affect attendance?"

"Not much. Weather's been good. People forget, or they don't worry about it."

Joann was a slightly overweight woman in her thirties. Her business dress and makeup were more Flagstaff than Vegas. She looked like a soccer mom, but her voice had authority.

Kate picked up a clipping. "I see the sheriff called it a 'one-in-a-million accident.' Things must have quieted down after that." She gathered up a handful of the clips and took them to her office.

Kate couldn't decide if she liked the office décor or not. Her desk, credenza, and a bookcase had a dull, brushed aluminum finish. Sleek, new, and retro, they felt cold. She'd warm the place up with books and plants. When she had time.

She sat at her desk and started reading the accident clipping from Arizona's largest paper, the *Phoenix Standard*. The story carried comments from witnesses and a description of the crash scene.

Another paper focused on interviews with the sheriff and included a cost estimate of the damages. In all, bad press about an unfortunate accident. But she could deal with it. Did it really warrant Max's offer to nearly double her salary? Max's projects always had ups and downs. Maybe he was just worrying more as he got older. Regardless, the offer had made Kate's decision to leave Vegas an easy one.

She set the clipping aside and glanced at the framed picture on her desk. The tanned face of an athletic-looking man smiled out at her. Bruce had surprised her by not arguing over a move to Arizona. Was it the size of her salary? She hoped Bruce could find something to do in Arizona. He was sales manager at a fitness club in Vegas.

Joann stuck her head in Kate's office. "Max's assistant just called. He wants to meet with you at *11 o'clock* instead, *before* your program for new hires this afternoon."

"Thanks, Joann. Max wants me to hit the ground running. That's fine. What's the afternoon program all about?"

ↄ⃝ↄ⃝ↄ⃝

"One of the things they asked me to cover in orientation today," Lyle Deming said, "is what we *didn't* have back then." He stood on a riser and scanned the theater-style classroom looking at the rows of new employees. A few were his age or thereabouts, although many looked like they were younger than some of his sport coats.

"*Back then* means the Nostalgia City time frame. Essentially, we're in the early 1970s—up to 1975—but we include a lot of stuff from before then. In the early 1970s we still had lots of 1960s cars, music, clothes, stores, you name it. One decade drifted slowly into the other. Sometimes we just refer to the park's '60s and '70s time frame as NC time or the NC era."

"Why that period?" asked a scholarly looking young woman in the second row.

"Nineteen seventy-five marked the fall of Saigon and the end of the Vietnam War. That period, roughly from President Kennedy's inauguration until the fall of Saigon, was a definitive time—a transition for America. I think marketing to baby boomers also has a lot to do with the park's focus.

"Now I'm not an historian, just an NC employee like you, but I was in school in the '60s and '70s so I can tell you the things we definitely *did not* have during that time. First, we didn't have CD players. And there was a good reason for that. No CDs."

The new employees chuckled. Lyle had their attention. For the time being.

"And, we did not have: DVDs, MP3s, or even PCs. There were no laptops, no flat screens, no video cameras, no digital cameras, no digital music, no digital TV." He held up a hand, spreading his fingers. "These were the only digits we knew about.

"Macs were hamburgers, a tablet was a yellow pad with lines on it, and blackberries were fruit. No Web surfing, only ocean surfing. And let me emphasize, we did not have smart phones.

"Now, why do you think I mention all this, particularly the cell phones?"

A young man with long hair and freckles raised his hand. "We're not supposed to use our cell phones here at work."

"Right on, man. Back in the day, if I saw someone having a conversation with his hand—" Lyle held his hand to his ear. "—I'd think he was nuts. Closest thing we had to cell phones was the Bat Phone. Or the shoe phone. Remember *Get Smart*? No, never mind.

"Anyway, dig this: Do not use *any* electronic gadgets like cell phones, or iPods, Kindles or whatever in the park. Leave them in your locker. Questions?"

Lyle looked across the rows of people and noticed the gorgeous blonde he'd seen weeks before in Maxwell's office.

"Remember," he said, "music was a big part of NC time, so

try to learn some of the artists' names. You hear their songs play-ing all over the park. Back then, everybody had transistor radios and they listened to groups like The Doors, Led Zep, The Rolling Stones. I know." Lyle held up a hand. "The Stones are still around. They're even older than *I* am!"

One of the training coordinators signaled Lyle that his time was running short. After a few minutes, he asked for final ques-tions.

A young man in his twenties raised a hand. "You mentioned the Vietnam War. That was a big deal wasn't it?"

"Yes, it was. Bigger than Afghanistan or Iraq. It lasted for years and years."

"How come there's nothing in our handbooks about it?"

"Lots of things happened in the NC era: Vietnam, assassina-tions, riots, Watergate, the Cold War. But Nostalgia City's de-signed for fun. Our guests pay a lot of money and they want to just chill and enjoy the good old times. They want to relax and unwind, not fight the Vietnam War all over again."

Chapter 8

After he finished his talk and the training coordinator announced a break, Lyle watched as the tall, shapely blonde strolled up to the podium and stood below the platform. She looked up at him with deep blue eyes, perhaps one of the few times she ever needed to look up at anyone. Judging by her tailored jacket and dress, Lyle figured she didn't sell sodas and hot dogs.

"If you're looking for a cab," he said, smiling, "I'm off duty."

The woman gave him a puzzled look. Obviously, she didn't remember.

"I was kidding." Why was he nervous? He'd met beautiful women before.

The puzzled look faded from her face. "You really think there's no place for Vietnam in Nostalgia City?"

"Why dramatize a war?"

"It shouldn't be dramatized, but from what I've seen, Vietnam is ignored. Isn't that unrealistic? And what about the social unrest, marches, sit-ins?"

"What's the point? I mean, yes, Vietnam happened in the '60s and '70s, but this is a theme park. People want to be entertained, go on some rides, and maybe dance a little."

"Seems like avoiding any mention of what was really happening turns NC time into a fairyland. Sort of a fantasyland for adults."

"What's wrong with that? What should we have? Vietnamland? Anti-warland? Hand out souvenir protest signs? Rename a hotel the Hanoi Hilton?"

Lyle knew instantly he'd overreacted, even before the woman's surprised look registered with him. He wanted to bite back his last words.

He stepped off the dais. "Sorry. Didn't mean to be sarcastic. I like it here. I like the park, and Maxwell's vision of it is fine with me."

"I guess so."

"Hey, you're on a break. Can I buy you a cup of coffee?"

To Lyle's surprise, the blonde, who introduced herself as Kate Sorensen, agreed. In a few minutes, they were seated at a table in a large employee cafeteria that had obviously depleted Arizona's entire supply of Naugahyde and Formica.

"I'm usually not that negative," Lyle said as they sat facing each other. "Well, not always. In fact, I'm trying hard to relax and get rid of my cynicism."

"A *little* cynicism is okay," she said with a thin smile. "By the way, I enjoyed your talk. You made the younger employees really think about all the things that weren't around then, stuff we take for granted."

"I like doing it. And it's a break from driving my cab."

"So that's what you meant about a cab ride. How did you get the job speaking to new hires?"

"My big mouth. I made a couple of smart remarks when I went through orientation. The guy briefing the kids must've lived through a different period than I did. Sounded like he'd read it in a book. I just corrected him once or twice."

Did Kate raise her eyebrows a fraction?

"Don't get the wrong idea," he continued. "I didn't make fun of him. I went up later and apologized. A week or so after that someone from training called and asked if I'd be interested in doing this. I only do it once in a while. For fun."

Lyle was now certain he had pegged himself as an antagonistic know-it-all.

He tried a different tack.

"Lots of this I remember 'cause I had an older brother who was into cars and bands. I remember hearing The Beatles back when I was in early grade school. Guess you could say I'm a baby boomer too, but a late boomer."

"As opposed to a late *bloomer*?"

"Yeah, that too." Lyle was pleased to see Kate smile. "You're obviously new. What do you do here?"

"PR. I'm the new VP of public relations. I started today."

VP, huh? Lyle looked into her lively, expressive eyes. She had a slender nose and wide mouth that on a smaller woman would have seemed too large.

"Do we need to revamp our image?" he asked.

"Recent publicity hasn't been good, has it? We need to handle accident problems. And the vandalism," she said, lowering her voice. "I heard that someone tampered with the Yo-yo ride. It was a clumsy job and was spotted right away."

Lyle wondered what to say. The tourist's death—and what Max said it could mean to the park—had stayed in his head despite his efforts to ignore it.

"It's okay," Kate said. "Max told me everything. It's one of the reasons I'm working here. Max—Mr. Maxwell—decided he needed a new PR person. No one else knows about the problems besides you and me and the security chief, Bates.

"And half the people who work here."

Kate nodded. "Guess you're right. That's one reason why Max asked you to look into the accidents. To see what's going on."

"I told him I'd think about it."

"He said you turned him down."

He tried his "I'm only a cab driver" routine, but she'd obviously been told he was a former police detective. He affirmed his faith in Bates's abilities and explained how he just wanted to drive his cab.

"I know Maxwell," Kate said. "I worked for him in Vegas. If he says he needs help, he means it."

"So he told you to come over here and persuade me to go back to being Sergeant Friday."

"Not exactly. It was partially my idea since you were going to be at the orientation."

"Maxwell used to build hotels in Vegas, didn't he?"

"Are you changing the subject?"

"Trying to. That okay?"

"Sure. Max was in Vegas a long time. I did PR for him at the last hotel he built."

"This is a bigger project."

"Bigger than I realized. They even built a residential community."

"Timeless Village. That's where my dad and I live."

"Your dad?"

Lyle explained his father's health conditions and the fact that he'd moved in with him recently.

"I'm in Timeless Village too," Kate said. "Sort of like up-scale company housing, isn't it? My boyfriend and I thought about buying a house there. But we're also going to look in Polk and Flagstaff. He's trying to sell our condo in Vegas."

That told Lyle that Kate was not married but also not available. Not that he had anything in mind. She was probably too young for him anyway. It was amazing, when he thought about it, how women who were "too young for him" were getting older.

"I think I'm going to like it here in Nostalgia City," Kate said.

Chapter 9

Lyle left the training center, having managed, again, to avoid becoming an NC cop. But why had he reacted to Kate's comments about the park's lack of controversy? He didn't mind talking about Vietnam and all the shit that happened back then. Not at all. Some people just didn't understand how a tranquil fairyland job was just the tonic for stress. Come to think of it, so was *gin* and tonic. He thrust his hands into his pockets. The rubber band he wore twisted and pulled the hairs on his wrist. It helped him focus.

He paused at a street corner and glanced at the retro-style signs above the shops. Most were made of neon tubes bent to form letters. On the opposite street corner, under an orange Rexall Drug Store sign, sat a trolley. Lyle hopped on, and it took him to the Fun Zone amusement area. His badge got him quickly through the employee entrance, and a five-minute walk brought him to the front of the large K-BOP studio trailer.

Inside, the main room of the portable broadcast studio was a comfortable office. Poster-sized photographs of The Beatles lined the walls. The pictures told the story of the singing group from their fresh-faced, mop-haired days to their bearded Hare Krishna period that ended when the group broke up in 1970. When Lyle asked for Earl Williams, a technician pointed to the next room, a glassed-in broadcast booth partially obscured behind potted plants. Lyle leaned over and saw his friend Earl behind the glass. Williams was talking to an animated young woman who appeared much smaller than she probably was—compared to Lyle's friend, who could double for an NFL linebacker. Williams saw Lyle and motioned for him to come into the booth. Above the door, an old-fashioned "On the Air" light was lit, but Lyle stepped in.

Lyle had first met Williams at a Phoenix radio station when Lyle was police spokesman for a neighborhood crime-watch program. Lyle wondered how NC had lured Earl away. Williams had become the leading oldies DJ in Arizona and even had his own nationally syndicated weekend program.

"'Scuse me, Drenda," Williams said. "This is an ol' buddy of mine."

Taking his earphones from around his neck, he stepped away from his console. The DJ's hair was long but not quite an Afro. Williams' smile and child-like impulsiveness contrasted with his imposing size. He wrapped his large arms around his friend and lifted him off the ground momentarily. At 170 pounds and nearly six feet tall, Lyle rarely considered himself small. Next to Big Earl, he felt like Billy Barty.

"Lyle's a buddy from Phoenix. Lyle, this is Drenda Adair."

Drenda *was* as tiny as she first appeared. Lyle took in her short auburn hair and simple makeup. *Cute*, he thought, though her dress and bearing meant business.

She greeted him then turned back to Williams. "Okay, Earl, please remember. NC era only. The station is part of Nostalgia City and in Nostalgia City, it still *is* 40 years ago. I'm sorry to be the one to remind you." Before she left she turned and added, "It's great to have you here. I've been listening."

With that, she bustled out of the booth.

"They warned me 'bout that lady when I started this gig," Williams said. "I shoulda known better."

"I know who she is, but I'd never met her. Doesn't look like what you'd expect. They call her the Nostalgia Nazi."

"So I heard. Now I know why."

"She's the senior vice president of history and culture," Lyle said. "Which means she's the final word around here on what *really* happened in the '60s and '70s."

"Yeah, but she looks like she was born in the '90s."

"Doesn't matter. She's a hotshot academic, *and* she's related to Maxwell. At least she has a '60s name. How many people do you know named *Drenda*?"

"That's pretty cool, really. And you look pretty retro yourself there, Mr. Deming, bow tie and all." Williams made a face.

"What's the matter with a bow tie? It's part of my cabbie outfit. Hey, lots of famous Americans wore bow ties. Harry Truman, Humphrey Bogart—"

"Pee Wee Herman?"

Lyle searched for an appropriately vulgar response, but before he could say it, Williams held up a hand. He plopped down in his chair and slid over to the microphone.

As Earl announced the next record, Lyle looked out the large picture window that let passersby see the DJ at work. The trailer had been set up near the monorail ride. The track wrapped around the trailer then dropped sharply, almost to street level, before turning toward a straightaway.

"Remember, come by and see us," Earl said into the mic. "We're doing a remote today, right in front of the Soul Train. I call it that. Most folks call it the Nostalgia City Monorail. And now, here's a great one from Rod Stewart." Williams hit a button and set his earphones down.

Lyle took the other chair in the cramped booth. "So you're actually in the park live, in person, not on tape."

"Live from now on. I'm renting a place in Flagstaff. I'm planning to do my national shows from here, too."

"How'd they get you to move to K-BOP?"

"Mostly money. But that's cool. We can hang out."

Lyle nodded. "What'd you do to get Ms. Historically Correct on your back so soon?"

"I sorta dee–viated from the play list."

"You like to deviate. I've seen you."

"All I did was play "A Hazy Shade of Winter.""

"Simon and Garfunkel, 1966."

"Actually I played another version."

"The Bangles?"

"Yeah."

"Earl. That was in the '80s. No wonder she caught you."

"I know, man. It just sounded good."

"Stick with the NC era. Don't you know, you're not only on the air, but you're piped into every building, shed, and parking lot in Nostalgia City?"

"So they tell me."

"Okay, try this one: 'Harper Valley PTA.'"

"Don't kid me. You trying to stump me with that one? Too easy. Jeannie C. Riley, 1968. Okay, Mr. Musical Knowledge, what about, 'The Night Chicago Died.'"

"Oh, I know that." Lyle paused. "Was it...'75?"

"Time's up." Again, Williams held up a hand for silence while he announced a song.

"I give up," Lyle said a moment later.

"You can't beat me. This is my *business*. 'The Night Chicago Died,' Paper Lace, '74."

"Big Earl, you're my hero."

"Fuck you," Williams whispered with a smile then leaned back in his chair and grinned at a family of tourists passing by the studio's picture window.

Lyle was about to return the sentiment when he heard a grinding noise then a high-pitched screech like a buzz saw. One second later, an impact sharper than an earthquake slammed the studio trailer sideways. The picture window shattered. The trailer slid 100 feet then stopped abruptly. Acrid smoke and screams filled the air.

Lyle survived the jolt by hanging onto the console and bracing himself against the wall. Short of breath and gagging on the fumes, he saw his buddy slumped motionless over the control panel. He tried to find something to staunch the blood flowing from the back of Earl's head.

Chapter 10

Kate Sorensen. Is Kate Sorensen here?"
Kate looked up from the rear of the classroom when a young man broke into the orientation session. "Call your office," he said. "There's been an accident."

Kate pulled out her cell phone as she dashed from the room, only to realize that she didn't know the extension to her own office. She found a directory on a desk and was soon listening to her secretary.

"Someone just called from the monorail. It's bad. Lots of people hurt."

Even before she got to the square, Kate could hear children wailing. She jumped out of the cab and dashed around two ambulances, dodging paramedics and firefighters loaded with emergency gear. She froze when she saw the destruction. An entire monorail train had leaped off its track and slid across the open plaza. Passengers lay strewn about the pavement, some moving, some not. Three crumpled cars lay on their sides. People struggled to drag themselves out of side windows now facing skyward. *Like a bad disaster movie*, Kate thought, *only real*.

One of the cars had remained upright as it skidded across the terrazzo square and collided with a small carousel, knocking wooden horses—and children—onto the ground. Kate stumbled forward, stunned. She passed the bright blue and silver monorail engine, its nose buried in a trailer marked with red letters: K-BOP Remote Studio.

She didn't know what to do first. Paramedics were already clambering into the trailer's broken picture window, so Kate sprinted to the carousel where a handful of adults were bending over injured children. She picked her way through the splintered ruins. Children cried while absurdly cheerful calliope music continued to play. The chaos here mirrored the main square. Some children appeared dazed but unhurt, others lay motionless. Kate stopped when she saw a tiny body squirming beneath the chartreuse and purple head of a wooden horse. She dragged the horse to the side and the black-haired girl looked up at her with unexpectedly blue eyes. Kate saw in a moment the girl had a compound fracture. A hint of bone protruded from her left arm.

"Don't move, honey. We're going to take good care of you." The girl moaned and shifted. Kate noticed her T-shirt: *Grandma's Little Angel* in bold script. Unsure of how to treat the injury, Kate followed her instinct and shouted, "Medic. Need help here!"

A paramedic rushed over and soon had the girl's arm immobilized with an air splint. Moments later, a white-haired man, himself injured, coat ripped, a rag soaking up blood from a gash on his head—appeared next to them. "My granddaughter," he said. "Oh, my God. Is she okay?"

The paramedic reassured the grandfather. Kate left the girl in their care and crossed the square where emergency personnel—supplemented by guests pitching in—comforted the injured and helped passengers out of the smashed monorail cars. Crowds of curious tourists started flowing into the plaza. People gasped at the wreckage and injuries. Paramedics were setting up a triage, while men in NC security uniforms tried to direct the onlookers away.

Kate slid to a halt beside the last monorail car and bent to help a dazed and bruised woman who was trying to crawl out of the now-horizontal doorway. As Kate stood and glanced around, she saw a long, damp splash of red across the pavement. She turned away and steadied herself on the edge of the car. She was *not* going to vomit. After a deep breath, she rounded the car and saw the red liquid was ketchup. Next to it lay the shattered frame of a hot dog cart.

Finally, the last of the injured were extricated. Paramedics transported the most serious cases and bandaged those with cuts and bruises as they awaited more ambulances. Kate shifted gears mentally and started looking for the camera people and reporters she knew would start streaming in. She drifted around the chaotic scene trying to get an idea of what happened while trying to anticipate questions the media would throw at her. *Was anyone killed?* she thought suddenly. Maybe "how many?" would be a better question. One or two people on gurneys were unconscious.

Kate spotted a man with a gray crew-cut shouting to the security guards. He was wearing a suit and seemed to be in charge.

"Excuse me," she said. "Do you know if anyone's been killed?"

"No." He looked away from Kate and shouted to two security guards, telling them to move the line of onlookers farther away.

She showed him her ID badge. "I'm Kate Sorensen. I'm the new VP of public relations."

"Congratulations."

Kate looked at the man's ID badge. It said he was Bates, chief of security. "Can you tell me where the injured will be taken?"

"Depends on how bad they're hurt."

"Is there a hospital in Polk? I'm new here. Today's my first day."

"Welcome to Nostalgia City," Bates grunted, then turned away immediately and shouted, "Nelson, I told you to move those people back."

"Any idea what caused this?"

Bates turned back and looked as if he was surprised to see her still there. Kate's only consolation was that she had at least two inches on the security chief, forcing him to look up slightly. "I don't have time to answer questions," he said.

"Maybe not, but we're all going to be answering questions when the media show up. We need to give them at least basic information."

"I wouldn't worry about the media. You want to know what happened? Ask that engineer over there. This is his responsibility."

Kate looked for someone in a uniform, but Bates gestured to a guy with bushy red hair who wore a shirt and tie. He was directing workers as they collected pieces of debris.

"If anyone from the press talks to you, would you please have them see me?" she asked.

"Sure, lady," Bates said with a leer. "I'll send the assholes right over."

Kate formed a quick opinion of Bates, but gave him benefit of the doubt. He was probably as shocked by everything as she was.

Wandering around the perimeter of the disaster, she soon saw what she'd expected—a TV news camera crew. She introduced herself to an eager-looking young man in a tan shirt with his collar open and his tie loosened.

"I'm Mike Lopez, Channel 6 News."

"Looks like you're the first ones here."

"We're the *only* ones here. The guards at the main gate have orders to keep us out. But then you probably know that."

"No, I didn't. I wouldn't—"

"Yeah? You've got this pretty well sealed off. My camera person's boyfriend is a paramedic. If we hadn't come in with the ambulance, we'd still be outside. Guess you like to keep a lid on your accidents, right?"

"A lid on it?" she said, pointing to a man aiming a cell phone camera at the mangled monorail cars. "This is on Twitter already. I'd rather have real newspeople reporting this. I'm not stupid."

Showing her frustration to the media would not improve on a disaster. She took a couple of breaths then explained that it was her first day on the job, that she never ordered the media to be barred, and that she'd let them know whatever she found out.

She left the camera crew and walked over to the supervisor Bates had pointed out. She found him kneeling over a heavy piece of twisted metal near where the monorail must have left the track. Dark slashes of grease decorated his shirtsleeves. He glanced up from his work with a frown and a serious look in his green eyes. Kate bent over to speak.

"Do we know what caused this?"

The man looked at Kate and turned his head, trying to read her ID badge. She straightened the badge and told him who she was. His face was shiny with sweat, his hands coated with black dust. He introduced himself as Dennis Zorn.

"Among other things," he said, "I'm chief safety engineer."

That kind of engineer, Kate thought. "The media will be asking all kinds of questions. I'll have to tell them something." She could only imagine what must be going on in his mind.

Zorn brushed off his hands and stood up. "It jumped the track. Neat trick for a monorail, but it had help. Luckily the track wasn't far off the ground at that point." Kate glanced over at the broken section of track, only a couple of feet in the air.

"We won't know everything for sure 'til I collect all the pieces." Zorn's face had a trace of sadness, or was it guilt? "That may take a while." He gestured toward the smashed cars. Jagged bits of sheet metal and steel parts littered the square.

Kate glanced away and saw the TV crew focusing on two children covered in blood. She knew how that would look on the 6 o'clock news. "We'll have state or federal inspectors out here investigating, right?"

"Nope."

"I don't understand. Who, who…"

"Regulates us?"

"Yes. Safety regulations. Is it federal or state?"

"Neither."

Kate stared at him.

"We're in an unusual position. Theme parks are exempt from federal oversight."

"But what about consumer…something?"

"Consumer Products Safety Commission. But they only regulate rides in carnivals and fairs—the ones that move from place to place. Theme park regulation is left up to the states."

"So Arizona—"

"Doesn't regulate us either. Not yet. We're one of a few states that don't have theme park regs."

Kate slowly shook her head. Before she could say anything, Zorn continued.

"Until Nostalgia City was built, Arizona didn't have a major theme park, so we didn't need regs."

"So who inspects the rides? Who's the final word?"

"We are."

Chapter 11

Lyle insisted on riding in the ambulance with Williams to the emergency room in Polk. Lyle's sole injury was a scratch on his right hand which he received clearing glass and debris off his friend. When they arrived at the hospital, paramedics carted Williams into an examining area, relegating Lyle to the nearly empty waiting room.

He leaned against a wall. "Right in front of me," he said. "I was right there."

A woman at the other end of the room looked up momentarily then went back to her reading.

In a few minutes, other ambulances arrived. Family members and friends of the injured filled up the waiting room, hospital personnel rushed in and out of the ER, and Lyle paced.

After many tours of the room, he stopped in front of a vending machine. "Sodas. Nothing but sodas," he said to no one. "No goddamn beer." He walked outside.

Maxwell had offered him a bonus to investigate the sabotage, but as much as he wanted to help preserve his new job, he didn't want to be a cop again. Now NC's problems had collided with him—and his buddy was in the ER. When he saw Clyde Bates drive up and walk into the ER, he followed him inside.

As a television news crew interviewed a nurse in the admitting area, Lyle stopped at the desk to ask about Earl. Nothing yet. They were swamped. Lyle crossed the hall, looking for Bates.

With anxious people now crowding the waiting room, the air carried the smell of nervous sweat.

"Are you Lyle Deming?" asked a voice behind him. He turned to see a much-too-young doctor in scrubs. "Your friend is going to be okay. He has just a mild concussion and some bruises. We took X-rays. There's no fracture."

"But all the blood?"

"Superficial cuts. Head wounds tend to bleed a lot."

"How long will he have to be here?"

"A day. Just to be sure. He's gonna be fine. We tried calling his family but couldn't locate anyone. Can you help?"

When Lyle came out of Earl's room a few minutes later, having assured himself that his friend—now quiet and disoriented—would be back to normal soon, he looked for Bates. He found him loitering around the admitting desk. He was wearing a black suit and dark glasses and looked as inconspicuous as J. Edgar Hoover in a dress.

"How's Williams doing?" Bates asked.

"Doc says he's okay. You find out what happened?"

"Engine jumped its track. Lots of injuries, a few critical. Thought you didn't want to be involved."

"I changed my mind. Can you fill me in?"

With people everywhere, Lyle and Bates walked outside. This was the third or maybe fourth time Lyle had seen the security chief and each time he was dressed the same. He looked as if he followed the IBM dress code of the '60s: a white shirt and solid, dark tie, plus shiny, black brogans. Lyle had an idea Bates was not just dressing for Nostalgia City.

"There was something over the track. Looked like scaffolding."

"Where'd it come from?"

"Crews were working on a wall next to the spot where the monorail derailed. But the scaffolding and power equipment was supposed to have been put away for the day."

"So, it was intentional?"

Bates uttered a mirthless laugh. "Some of the bolts that held the track in place were taken out."

"Sabotage."

"No. Just an accident. That's our official story. For now."

"Official story?"

"You know, for the press."

"How many people were hurt?"

"Twenty five, maybe twenty six. Some just had cuts and bruises, but more than a dozen had to be hauled away to hospitals. Most of 'em are here. A few serious went to Flagstaff."

"Awful."

"Coulda' been worse."

"Worse?"

"One of the monorail cars hit the carousel, but it was between rides. Only a few kids were hit. Only one or two of 'em look bad."

Lyle leaned on a railing and stared out across the street to a vacant lot dotted with sagebrush. "Do you have any better idea of who's doing this?"

"We pieced some things together."

Lyle waited. Bates was obviously weighing how much to tell him. He fumbled in his pocket for a cigarette, lit it, and exhaled a cloud of smoke. Lyle moved upwind.

"We have descriptions of people," Bates said. "People who were around the yo-yo ride when it was sabotaged. They might match the description of someone who was in the vicinity of that stolen car—before it crashed into the gas station."

"The Torino was stolen?"

"Couple from L.A. rented it. Reported it missing."

"What'd the witnesses see?"

"One witness said she thought it was a Hispanic, but another witness identified the man as Native American—Indian."

"Was it the same person?"

"You know eye-witness descriptions. They're all over the map. Could I make a guess? Yes. I'd say it's one or more Indians. And I'd say they sabotaged the railroad bridge, too."

"Any witnesses today?"

"We're still asking questions."

"You think it was Native Americans because the bridge collapse was on reservation land?"

Bates nodded. "But we have no witnesses there."

"Prints anywhere?"

Bates gave Lyle a look between a frown and a sneer. "On NC rides? Not likely. They handle thousands of people a day." The funny expression stayed on Bates's lips. It made his flat, rectangular face with its gray, guarded eyes look like a gargoyle.

"What about the scaffolding on the track?"

"We checked for prints—where we could. Doubt it'll be helpful. Sheriff is investigating that, too."

"Deputies were here earlier, talking to victims," Lyle said.

"One of them a tall, skinny, Hispanic guy?"

"Yes."

"That's probably Rey Martinez. He's undersheriff, second in command. He's not as big a prick as the sheriff."

"So, we get a lot of cooperation from local law enforcement."

"You should talk to Maxwell about the sheriff."

Chapter 12

Next morning, Kate read the details on the front page of the *Phoenix Standard*: twenty-five people hurt, fourteen hospitalized, a popular DJ injured, one ride destroyed, one damaged. The tearful face of a young child stared out from a photo next to the story. Blood streamed down the girl's cheek as a paramedic cradled her in his arms. The shattered remains of the carousel formed a macabre backdrop. Kate had already seen the same photo on the pages of a dozen online editions of the country's largest papers. Somehow, an Associated Press photographer had slipped past Bates's shock troops.

She set the paper down on her lap and looked over at Maxwell. He stood with his back to her, staring out his office window. When she heard a noise, she turned around to see Lyle, the cab driver, walk in and take a seat next to her in front of Max's desk.

He wore a sport coat and slacks—no bow tie or yellow cap in sight. Kate discovered that he was trim and handsome. Hadn't she noticed before? His thick, light brown hair and dark brown eyes were appealing. For a second she wondered how old he was.

Max walked back to his desk and sat down. "Okay. Just talked to Earl Williams. He's doing fine. Wants to get back on the air. Kate, what'd you think?"

"I think he ought to take it easy for a while. He was unconscious for a few minutes."

"No, I mean about his publicity."

"I think we should let him come back to work quietly, without fanfare. When he's on the air he can tell listeners that he wasn't seriously hurt and that the park is back to normal."

"I suppose you're right. That's why you're here, isn't it? Okay. You've met Lyle, right? He's going to investigate. Find out why the hell this is happening. What about the publicity? How bad will it be?"

"How *bad*?" She held up the Phoenix front page. "*This* is how bad. We were on all the network newscasts last night, plus CNN, Fox, you name it. Today we're on the front page of every major paper in the country.

"We've had phone calls from *The Daily Star* in Toronto, the BBC, Japanese Broadcasting, Russia, Australia—all over the world. Videos of the wreckage already have over a million hits on YouTube."

"But we'll get this behind us, right?"

"We've got fourteen people in the hospital. One of them might die. This is the *second* serious accident in three weeks. Max, this story is *not* going to go away overnight. Count on it."

"What're you going to do?"

"Right this second? Nothing."

"You're going to wait?"

"No, I'm going to be prepared. We'll tell everyone we're shutting down the monorail, inspecting, and rebuilding before we open it again *and* instituting even more strict safety standards. I'll get Dennis Zorn to talk about safety on TV."

"All right. Get started."

"Hold on a second. We have to be careful. We can talk safety, but the more we talk, the more we remind people about the accidents. Reporters will keep asking us if our rides are safe. Sometimes you need to know when to shut up."

"We can't wait. Attendance and hotel reservations are critical. Number one priority." Maxwell shifted uneasily in his chair. "We can't let the numbers dip. Understand?"

"I hope they won't. I also hope you'll let *me* handle media relations."

"What'd you mean?"

"I mean your chief of security locked the press out of the park yesterday."

"But some got in anyway," Max said.

Kate glanced at Lyle, then back at the boss. "Max, hiding stuff from the press always backfires. Always. I had to make excuses and apologies all afternoon. Besides, it was all over the Internet. Ever heard of Twitter?"

"Bates was just trying to keep everything quiet."

"Sure he was. It looked like we were trying to pull a cover-up. And Max, did you know our rides aren't regulated by the state? We can't say we conform to government standards because there aren't any."

"Nothing wrong with our safety standards. Our insurance carrier mandates regular inspections. Zorn's people check every ride every day."

"I know. I've been telling the press that ever since the crash. God help us if something else happens."

"That's where Lyle here comes in." Maxwell turned to Lyle. "You've got to get started right away. But stay low key."

"Sure, okay."

"Ask questions, but don't tell anyone what we know. We'll try to keep the details to ourselves."

"What about Bates?" Lyle asked.

"Of course. He knows what's going on. He's working on it, too."

"Where do I start?"

"Wherever you want. Told Clyde to give you copies of the files on all the incidents. Do whatever's necessary. Clyde's conducting the 'official' investigation. You're our backup."

"And I report directly to you?"

"Right."

"Sounds as if Indians are Bates's prime suspects for everything. I've heard some of them aren't happy with the railroad going through their territory."

"That's an angle all right. Tribe stands to make a mint on this, but one band is upset about the whole thing."

"We're lucky," Kate said. "None of the stories today mentioned the reservation bridge collapse. But some reporter is going to remember it. Then it's going to look as if everything's been intentional."

Lyle looked at Kate then over at Max. Neither man spoke. Kate had a sinking feeling in her stomach. "What? Something I don't know?"

Lyle looked uncomfortable. Max was annoyingly unperturbed.

"Turns out, these weren't accidents," Max said. He nodded at Lyle. "You tell her."

"The gas station thing was deliberate," Lyle said. "Someone stole the Ford and sent it crashing down the street. We don't know who did it. And the railroad bridge was pulled down one night after work was finished. It didn't just fall over."

"What's going on, Max?" Kate's voice rose. "Was the monorail sabotaged, too? Is someone trying to destroy the park? Is that it?"

"We don't know what's going on," Lyle said, "except the 'accidents' weren't accidents."

"If the car crash was on purpose," Kate said, the magnitude of their troubles sinking in, "that guy under the awning was *murdered*." The last word gave her a sudden, oppressed feeling. "And now the monorail. All those people. What next?"

"Nothing," Max boomed. "We're going to find who's doing this, and you're going to contain this goddamn publicity."

Kate wanted to throw up her hands and shout, or just spend five minutes berating Max. But she wouldn't do it in front of someone. She forced herself to think before she spoke. "You could have *told* me about this. If I'm the spokesperson and I'm trying to put the vandalism or alleged accidents into perspective—" She sighed. "Shit, Max, what a mess."

Max's indifference was infuriating, yet not out of character. She knew what she was getting into when she went back to work for him. "I don't know what's worse, admitting the park is being sabotaged, or having people think we're careless."

Kate got out of her chair.

ᏋᎧᏋᎧ

In the elevator, Kate stood next to Lyle, her arms folded across her chest. They both stared up at the lighted floor numbers above the door.

"You didn't know the gas station crash was intentional when you said you'd come to work here," Lyle ventured. "Did you?"

"No. I didn't. I read about the accident, but that's how it was treated, as an accident. There wasn't even any speculation. It probably wouldn't have made a big difference, but..." She wanted to tell him how, in the past, Max deliberately forgot to tell her something when the news was bad. "I should have guessed there was more involved when Max made me the offer."

"Guess he's tough to work for."

Kate put her chin down slightly and glared at Lyle.

"Hmm. 'Course he is." Lyle grinned wryly. "Least I have a grasp of the obvious."

Kate let out a breath and relaxed against the back of the elevator. "Could you do me a favor? If anything *else* happens, or if you uncover a plot to drop a neutron bomb on Nostalgia City, tell me."

"I think that can be arranged. Although I don't know what I'm likely to uncover."

"Let's just keep in touch, okay?"

Chapter 13

The day after his meeting with Max and Kate, Lyle got in his Mustang and headed for Polk. His previous statements to the contrary, he was not at all sure Clyde Bates had a handle on what was going on. Lyle had a sense he would do best by starting from scratch on his own. Whoever was trying to sabotage the park had killed one person, injured dozens more, and put Earl in the hospital. The sooner Lyle found out who was doing this, the sooner he could get back in his cab full time. Max had suggested he cut back his hours in the cab, as necessary, to accommodate his investigation.

On the car radio, Tommy Roe sang, "Dizzy," as Lyle slowed his silver convertible and pointed it down the main street of Polk. Until the coming of Nostalgia City, Polk was a dusty Southwest town that relied on its scenic railroad and its proximity to old Route 66 to lure tourists.

When Maxwell's project was far enough along to persuade the locals the park would become a reality, it was as if gold had been discovered. Opportunists rushed into town. Some arrived in search of a job; others had different ideas of how to make money from the millions of tourists who would be flocking to this high-desert Disneyland. Speculators and developers bought up land. Existing merchants adopted '60s- or '70s-oriented names and sold rock-and-roll souvenirs.

Lyle found the San Navarro County Sheriff's Office on a commercial street, a few blocks from the main drag. It looked as if *it* was left over from the '60s. The black ceiling fans and battered desks made Lyle think of scenes from *The Fugitive* TV show. Although the sheriff, Jeb Wisniewski, didn't seem to understand why Lyle wanted to speak with him, he had nonetheless agreed to a meeting.

"So you're the guy who's gonna stop all the accidents and

malicious mischief in Nostalgia City," Wisniewski said. "That right?"

He was a heavyset man with long, jet-black hair that flowed down his back. Dark eyebrows, like stocky caterpillars, inclined over each eye.

He sat behind a dark mahogany desk. The words *Sheriff Wisniewski* were displayed in bronze letters frozen in a fat acrylic nameplate. Next to it, a scorpion and a large stone arrowhead were also sealed in acrylic. Wisniewski hadn't stood up when Lyle walked in, just pointed to a seat. He introduced Lyle to his assistant, Rey Martinez, who leaned against a cabinet. The sheriff wore a suit, the tall Martinez a tan uniform.

"They're not just accidents, are they?" Lyle said. "That's why I wanted to talk to you."

"That place where you work is pretty important to this town," the sheriff said. "Half the people in Polk work there. We don't like it when someone tries to trash it. Ya know what I mean?"

"Do you have any theories about the accidents or whatever you want to call them?"

"You're asking me? Why don't you ask Clyde Bates? He's got all the answers out there. Don't you work for him?"

"No."

"But you're the ex-cop from Phoenix, right?"

Word got around. "Right now I'm just a civilian."

"Well, if Bates doesn't know what's going on, I suggest you do some police work on your own and find out. We'd like to know, too."

Lyle was ready with a smart remark but remained silent for a moment. He tilted his head to one side.

"What the sheriff means," Martinez began, "is that we don't get any cooperation out there. Bates is ex-FBI and—"

"He thinks he runs everything," Wisniewski said.

"What do you mean?" Lyle said. "I thought—"

"What did you think? That since I'm the sheriff of San Navarro County I might have jurisdiction in the county? That's what I thought, too. But your buddies out there think they're in another world. We go out there to investigate an accident or a theft. We get crap from the guards at the gate. So I tell them they have to give us immediate access. Through employee entrances, or whatever. Finally, we get that straightened out. Then there's the gas station crash. That guy from Texas is killed. But by the time we get the call, everything's been cleaned up. We don't even see the car until it's been towed to the body shop. Now your attorneys are trying to settle with the family. Wonder how much that will cost?

"And now you got a dozen people in the hospital, your monorail is all smashed up, and you come in here and ask *me* what *I* think is going on. I don't have a theory. I don't have a clue. I don't know shit. Does that clear things up for you?"

Lyle could see why Bates and the sheriff got along so well. It was obvious that Bates had Maxwell's approval to handle some crimes on an in-house basis. Understandable, but not the best way to deal with local authorities.

"One more thing. My name's Wisniewski, but I'm a quarter Native American. So don't give me any of that shit about the tribes being involved in this. That's what Bates thinks. If there's any problem on the reservation, I can handle it. Or anything else. Some of my ancestors may have been peaceful, but that doesn't mean I am."

The sheriff looked as if he might be remembering something else to throw at Lyle, but a deputy stuck his head in the office and motioned to Wisniewski. The sheriff looked at his watch then got up and left without another word.

After several seconds passed, Martinez spoke. "The sheriff and I really want to find out what's going on at the park."

"I would, too."

Martinez took a step forward and put one elaborately stitched cowboy boot on the other wooden chair in front of the sheriff's desk. He leaned toward Lyle. "But we need help. We can't solve crimes if we're called to the scene a few hours or a few days later."

Martinez had a tall face and light skin that only hinted at his Latino heritage. Lyle noticed the distance between his nose and upper lip seemed unusually long, as if he had just shaved off a moustache making the empty space seem vast.

"I didn't know anything about your disputes with Bates," Lyle said. "Talking to the local sheriff was the logical first step, but I can do this on my own."

"No. You need to cooperate with us." Martinez made eye contact with Lyle. "The sheriff is just a little upset about this."

"A *little* upset? What happens when he's really mad?"

"You know what's it's like, trying to solve cases, getting shit from superiors and no help from anyone else."

"I have an idea, yes."

"If I can help, I will. We decided the gas station death was just a freak accident, so that's what the papers reported. Any talk about sabotage would have been bad for business. Bad all around. Besides, we didn't have evidence, remember? Maybe it *was* an accident."

"So…"

"So you can see we're on the same side, but you need to keep us informed. First we heard about the monorail crash the other day was when someone called paramedics. Who knows when Bates would have called us? He's being foolish. We *have* to know what's happening out there."

"If I find out who's doing this, I promise to let you know before I do anything. But I can't guarantee that Bates will be any more cooperative. I don't work for him."

"How's that work? Weren't you involved in both big crashes?"

"By accident. Literally. I just happened to be in the wrong places. Earl Williams is a friend of mine. That's why I was at the mobile studio. The president of NC asked me to nose around, see if I can find out anything. I said okay."

"Are you going out to the reservation?"

"Some members of the tribe don't want the railroad to cross part of the reservation property, even though the tribe has already signed off on it."

"I talked to them myself, and the tribal police work with us. George Brown is the chief. He's hiring lots of people for the casino. *He* thinks the tribe'll be rich over this."

"And you don't?"

"I don't know. Not all Native Americans support the idea of gambling. Slot machine money doesn't always mean better schools or better jobs for the people on the reservation."

"I understand someone named Johnny Cooper is the leader of the band that's against the railroad." This was one of the few useful items Lyle had learned from Bates. "Is that right?"

"They say the casino shuttle will violate sacred grounds."

"But you don't have any evidence against Cooper?"

"Not really. I already talked to him."
"Can you tell me what he's like?"
"A hothead."

Chapter 14

For days you've focused on injuries and damage. Do you think you could give us a chance to talk about safety? Yes, I said your news crew is welcome any time. My suggestion was that you have someone interview Dennis, our chief safety engineer."

Kate was on the phone, trying to get the news director of a Phoenix TV station to listen to reason. "Yes, I know people are still in the hospital. I *know* it was a horrible crash. But we're doing everything we can to assure our guests' safety. We've hired additional safety inspectors."

The news director's station always spiced up its newscasts with the latest murders or rapes. A spectacular crash at Nostalgia City was their kind of story. They could milk it for weeks. "No, Andy, it's too early to tell if our attendance has been affected. We've got a lot of visitors here today." That's all I need to do, Kate thought, tell Impact News that all our business has been scared away.

"And you're supposed to be fair and balanced," she said after she hung up.

She looked up at two young employees, Matt and Amanda, who had just seated themselves in front of her desk.

Kate started reading the news release stories they'd brought in. After one paragraph, she wanted to crumple the pages.

"We can't keep promoting the *rollercoaster*," Kate said, failing to keep the annoyance out of her voice.

"But it's the fastest in the west," Matt said. "It's awesome." His short, moussed hair formed random spikes.

"Now's not a great time to emphasize the speed of our rides. Know what I mean?" Really! What kind of people did she have working for her? "And besides, fast rides are not why our prime visitors come here. And who *are* our prime visitors?"

"Old people?"

"Old*er* people, yes. Our prime market is baby boomers. Seventy two *million* of them. So, therefore, we don't focus on the rollercoaster." Kate paused. "How about the drive-in?"

"The drive-in?" her employees said in unison.

"Either of you ever been to a drive-in movie?"

Both shook their heads.

"So go see ours, then write about it. Boomers like it. People can go there even if they don't have a car. The drive-in has empty cars parked and waiting. Some of the cars are just for show with retro-dressed mannequins in them. It'll make a great story."

Both staffers looked puzzled.

"Nostalgia City is all about realism. *That's* what makes us unique. If we're going to build our image back up, we've got to focus on authenticity, not speed. Now, go check out the drive-in." Kate paused and looked up to see someone in her office doorway.

"Drenda—Dr. Adair—come in. I'm ready." Kate introduced her to the two PR staffers. "If you have questions about NC era history, this is the person to talk to. She's our expert."

ↄ∕ↄↄ∕ↄ

As she offered her visitor a seat at the worktable in a corner of her office, Kate wondered how her young employees would hold up if more sabotage assaulted the park.

"I just saw the latest attendance numbers," Drenda said as they settled into their chairs. Her short hair curled under her ears. Delicate features, coupled with her petite stature, made her look more like a school girl than an executive. "Attendance today is off about 25 percent."

"Glad I didn't know that when I talked to Impact News."

"I hope this is just temporary."

"So do I. Sometimes stuff like this can actually boost attendance. It attracts morbid curiosity. But if anything else happens…"

"This isn't all coincidence—or is it?"

Kate shrugged. "You have any ideas?"

"None. My parents and I were talking about this last night. Is it bad luck?"

"No. I don't believe that. We still have a chance to get the park back on its feet."

"From what you were saying to your writers, it sounds as if you're getting back to the original concept of NC. It's just what we envisioned."

"It's what you and I talked about the other day. It makes sense. Isn't realism the main thing we have to sell?"

Drenda leaned forward on her elbows. "Yes, it is. I wish everyone here had the same attitude you do."

"Don't they?"

"I don't know. It's just that—" Drenda took a deep breath and Kate wondered what might be coming. "Sometimes I feel like I am always the bad guy around here, the resident persecutor."

"Persecutor?"

"You haven't been here long enough to know. Before the park opened, I was involved in everything. I brainstormed with the architects and the ride engineers.

"I even identified vendors who were willing to modify their retail strategies to conform to our historical framework. Now, I'm the one who has to spend hours and hours enforcing the rules and restrictions.

"Am I the only one who cares?"

"You're the historian behind all this."

"Yes, a historian. I should probably be back at the university instead of a theme park."

"You're not married, are you?"

"I was for a short time; then Mr. Adair and I went our separate ways."

"So you can do what you want, can't you?"

"This *is* what I want. Or I did, before Max made me the enforcer."

"Max *made* you?"

"He's not just the boss, he's my uncle."

"I'd heard that."

"He got the idea for Nostalgia City from me. I mean, I didn't conceptualize a theme park, but my specialty is the '60s and '70s. That's what my dissertation was about, the history and popular culture of the period."

"So that's what led you to the idea of the park?"

"Not exactly. After my post-doc, when I started teaching full time, I wrote a paper theorizing what would happen if someone created a town, frozen in time. It was just a hypothesis about the empirical research that could be done in a re-created historical environment."

"And that's how Max got into this?"

"When I was in college, Max was generous. He helped me with tuition. My folks couldn't afford it, especially Ivy League grad school.

"So when my paper was published, I sent Uncle Max a copy. At the time, he had already acquired some of the land and was planning an old west amusement park and hotel complex."

"So he read your paper and liked the idea."

Drenda nodded. "He called me and we talked about how difficult it would be to actually *create* a town from the past and ensure its accuracy. Pretty soon, he threw out his wild west plans and started to construct Nostalgia City."

"And you became what, the technical advisor?"

"In a sense. But there were problems. We envisioned this as a faithful 'slice of life' from the past—differentiated from the average theme park. Naturally, it cost more."

"I've been reading estimates of how much was spent here. It boggles the mind."

"It was the price of authenticity."

"Financing was an issue?"

"A big one. He struggled. Somehow he found the money, but he cut back on the plans, too."

Kate was surprised at the solemn look in Drenda's eyes and the earnestness in her voice. Perhaps Drenda sensed she had found a sympathetic friend or ally, another young, female executive she could trust.

Drenda was still leaning forward across the table as she talked. "You know Max. He's almost impossible to argue with."

"You can't win. I try to plant ideas."

"I should have done that. It's not that I wanted to alter the theme park, I just suggested a little more substantive naturalism—realism."

"I'll bet you wanted to inject the social issues that started boiling up in the '60s."

"Exactly!" Drenda started blinking as her eyes became moist. "Kate, you *know* how I feel. Max eliminated every suggestion of controversy. But controversy was the *paradigm* of the times, the defining attribute."

Kate thought of her first conversation with Lyle. "We're not as realistic as we say we are."

"Max once told me I was trying to set up NC as my own experiment." Drenda shook her head. "That wasn't it."

"But Max wanted it bland, right?"

"And he appointed me the one-woman censorship board. I despise it." Drenda leaned back in her chair then blotted her eyes with a tissue.

"Don't worry," Kate said. "Maybe the two of us can find a way to maintain authenticity and persuade Max that a little controversy is not a bad thing."

"I'm glad you're here," Drenda said. "I'm really glad you're here."

Chapter 15

Lyle strained for breath as sweat rolled down his face. His feet pounded the dirt trail that led around his housing tract and into the brush. A few minutes before, he'd been chilly. His running shorts and Arizona Diamondbacks T-shirt provided little protection from the cool temperature. At 5,000 feet elevation, it was cold as the sun came up, even in Arizona. Visitors from the East and Midwest were often surprised that the NC area was much cooler than Phoenix, 150 miles to the south. The elevation also meant less oxygen and a more rigorous workout.

Dashing over a small rise, Lyle willed his legs to keep going. When he got to a familiar boulder, he stopped and leaned against it. Extending a leg behind him, he stretched one hamstring, then the other. He had to be cautious about strains and pulled muscles. Being over fifty was a bitch. After jogging for twenty minutes more, Lyle circled back toward his condo. He had not quite returned to the pace he was used to at lower elevations, but close. He enjoyed few things in life more than running. The muscle strength, stamina, and other physical rewards were substantial, but Lyle ran for other reasons. Endorphins reduced stress.

When Lyle approached his patio, his dad was outside, reading the paper and smoking a cigarette. "Don't overdo the exercise, son. You don't want to hurt yourself."

"Yeah." Lyle looked into his father's dull, watery eyes. For someone in Hank's condition, smoking was like playing Russian roulette. Obviously, the latest attempt at quitting hadn't lasted too long. Lyle pointed to the cigarette. "Dad?"

"Lemme alone, Lyle. It's not going to hurt."

Lyle felt a twinge of anger, then guilt—a familiar one-two punch whenever he had a disagreement with his father.

"Oh, your stepdaughter called."

"Sam has a *name*, Dad."

"Sam, Samantha, okay. Your stepdaughter. Something about getting physical therapy. Is that insurance company of yours denying claims again? Maybe you should have gotten it through the government—the national health care program. Could you get it free?"

"It's not free, Dad. You still buy it from an insurance company. And I already *bought* Sam's policy from a company. And now they're not paying off. Bastards..." Lyle's voice trailed off as he wandered inside.

If there was one person in the world Lyle knew he loved, beyond everyone else, it was Samantha. It hadn't happened over night. She was six years old when he and Jan were married. At first, he didn't know how to relate to a child, but Samantha had made it easy. Feeling her tiny hand in his when they went for walks in the desert warmed him in a way he couldn't describe. Samantha's father—Jan's first husband—lived in Tucson. He showed up once in a while, stopped paying child support, and sometimes called Sam on her birthdays. Lyle was the one who went to her school plays, helped her with homework, made her school lunches, and watched her grow up. Now she was 20 years old and a junior at Arizona State. She would probably lose credit in several classes as a result of her accident and hospitalization, but she was back in student housing, still having regular physical and occupational therapy sessions and occasional visits with her neurologist and orthopedist. Lyle was proud of the way she'd fought back from the injuries and tried to stay up with her classes.

After a shower, he settled down at his bedroom desk to pay bills and again go over Samantha's insurance claims. Federal Patrician Insurance had denied a claim for her most recent physical therapy sessions and for a portion of her hospitalization. At first, claim denials had angered and frustrated Lyle. If the company didn't pay, Lyle wasn't sure how he could continue to cover Samantha's expenses. Gradually Lyle learned that denying claims outright was just a part of the company's M.O. Deny it first, regardless, then wait and see what happened. Mercenary tactics.

For the hospital claim, Lyle had wasted no time in contesting the denial and flooding the company with documentation. Now he had to call again. He checked his watch. Federal Patrician Insurance was headquartered in Boston so Lyle always tried to call before noon his time.

"This claim was denied," the voice on the other end of line said. "There was no medical report."

"That's what I was told last time, but I faxed the hospital report directly to you."

"When was it sent? What number was it sent to?"

Lyle was ready for this. He kept records of dates, phone calls, names, and other facts. He gave the phone rep the details.

"I see. I can't—can't find that in the file. It usually takes a week or more for records to get into the system."

These people could give lessons in stalling to North Korea. "This was sent almost *two* weeks ago."

Silence.

"Let me speak to your supervisor."

"Uh, one moment."

Lyle heard new age music for a minute or two. Then momentary static—and a dial tone.

"Shit."

He slammed his hand down on his desk. Immediately he saw the rubber band on his wrist and forced himself to calm down. More tactics. No point getting upset. His anger retreated. His morning exercise helped.

He called back. This time he spoke with a new representative who told him the documentation had been received. A claims review committee decision would be rendered within a week.

When he hung up, Lyle muttered a few obscenities and tried to resign himself to the fact that, although it would take time, the claim would go through. It had to. With a broken leg and minor brain damage, Samantha needed continuing therapy. Lyle wanted her to have the best.

"Calm down, Deming," he said aloud.

He glanced again at the rubber band and snapped it against his wrist. The psychologist he had seen when his marriage was breaking up had recommended the rubber band for anxiety and anger. The sharp, brief pain produced by the snap was supposed to break the pattern of worry and force him to focus on the present. Occasionally, it worked.

Lyle's divorce preceded his exit from the police department. When Jan left him, she moved in with some no-account and, as Lyle discovered, they were not well off. Thus, Lyle became Samantha's financial backstop, an increasing challenge since Lyle's father had moved in. Lyle's brother Bob helped with their father's expenses, but Bob and his wife lived in a small town in Montana, collected Social Security, and were struggling themselves.

Lyle called Samantha and found out she had a medical bill to email to him. She sounded upbeat. Her neurologist had described her brain injury to Lyle as similar to a minor stroke—one from which he expected full recovery within six months. She was such a good kid, Lyle wondered why his father never took an interest in her activities. Because she was Lyle's *step*daughter? But then for years Hank hadn't taken an interest in *Lyle* either, except recently to prod him into going back to the police department. That wasn't going to happen.

Lyle's next call was to the tribal casino to see if Chief George Brown would have time to see him that morning. The Indians were Bates's chief suspects. Lyle wanted to decide for himself.

∾∾∾

Red dust rose in the parking lot as Lyle pulled in, and it mixed with the smell of sawdust and generator exhaust. The open space around the massive new building contained a hodgepodge of heavy equipment, mounds of earth, parked pickups, and construction trailers. Lyle maneuvered his way through the maze.

The Crossroads Casino looked like a smaller version of Hearst Castle. An expanse of Spanish tile roof was supported by stucco walls, accented by multiple archways, and topped by two ornate bell towers. Arms of the building extended out in several directions.

As Lyle walked to the chief's office, he noticed a railroad station under construction west of the casino.

The building that housed the tribal offices was obviously not finished yet, either. Carpenters were building a railing around the porch that surrounded the front entrance. Just inside was a large room that looked complete except for the bare plywood floor and stacks of storage boxes. Lyle found George Brown busy at work in an office off the main room. He was seated at a makeshift desk. The texture of his skin told Lyle he had probably spent more of his sixty-plus years outdoors rather than in an office.

Brown greeted him enthusiastically and Lyle wondered if

the Native American leader had misunderstood the reason for the visit. "Welcome to our new home at the crossroads, Mr. Deming. Do you think it's an appropriate name? The Crossroads Casino marks a crossroads, a milestone in the lives of our people. With the help of Nostalgia City, we will make this an overwhelming success."

Lyle was ambivalent about casinos and gambling, but anything that helped keep NC alive and well was worth supporting. "The building's impressive," he said.

"We were sorry to hear about the accident earlier this week. It's always sad when children are hurt. A tragedy."

The chief wore jeans and a western shirt with a bolo tie around his neck. He met Lyle's gaze with sincere, dark eyes.

"The kids are going to be okay. The only people still hospitalized are adults."

"At least this is good to hear." Brown wandered over to his window and pointed outside. "Did you see the railroad station as you came in? We're proud of it. You know NC City was supposed to pay for construction of the station, but we're so happy to be in partnership with you that we're paying a big share now."

Lyle started to speak but stopped abruptly when a power saw started up just outside the office. Brown's office window lacked glass. The noise made talking impossible.

When the saw stopped, Brown shrugged. "I was supposed to get my windows today but, inevitably, there are delays."

Lyle admired Brown's composure. The noise and confusion could make someone go nuts if he was trying to work. Before the jagged sound started again, Lyle jumped in. "Not everyone in the tribe is as eager as you are to see the railroad finished."

"I'm afraid so. And that's why you're here."

"We're concerned about the damage to the railroad bridge. And you know what else has happened."

"It is a bad situation, but I'll tell you what I told that Mr. Bates and the police. I'm doing everything I can to keep the construction on schedule and keep an eye on my people to the best of my ability."

He walked to the doorway and looked out at the main room. Gesturing toward a handful of people gathered around a large folding table, he said, "You see those men and women? They're our leaders, our brightest people. They don't all agree on everything, but they're trying. This casino will be a blessing to my people. I believe that. But it represents change, and that's upsetting to some."

"I realize I'm not the first person to come out here and ask you about this. Mr. Maxwell is worried. Finishing the rail line and the casino without any more trouble is important to a lot of NC employees as well."

"Agreed."

"I've heard that Johnny Cooper is leading a group that's against the railroad coming through one part of the reservation."

"Yes, and the tribal police and the sheriff have talked to him. Made sure he knew he was a suspect. But we're working on the whole issue now. We've made slight changes in the route of the tracks. We have things under control. There will be no trouble."

The chief paused and looked out his doorway. "Jen Smith, would you come here for a moment?"

A slender young Indian woman with short dark hair and worn suede pants covering the tops of cowboy boots broke away from the others and walked over.

"Jen, this is Mr. Deming. He works for Nostalgia City. He wants to know if our people are against NC and want to vandalize it."

The young woman turned her face toward Lyle with a defiant look in large brown eyes. "We had nothing to do with your monorail crash. The security people over there are paranoid of us *injuns*. They know nothing about tribal customs, laws. They see Native Americans behind anything bad that happens."

"I don't. And I don't work for security *or* Clyde Bates."

"Is that the FBI agent who runs the place?"

"I don't work for him." Lyle held up a hand. "I'm on my own. Someone was killed in the park and Earl Williams, the DJ who was hurt, is a friend of mine. We need to find out why this is happening."

"And so you think *we're* responsible."

"I just want find out what's going on."

"Our people work at the park, too. We're affected by this." She paused and looked at the chief for a moment then back at Lyle. "That's all I can tell you. We talked to security. We talked to the cops." She turned and walked back across the room.

"She is under pressure now—" the chief began.

"It's okay. I understand."

After another few minutes, Lyle had not learned much more, other than clearly understanding Brown's passion for the project. He also understood that Brown was a politician.

Chapter 16

"At least that gives me a couple of ideas," Lyle said in his car as he headed out of the reservation.

He turned on the radio. The Rolling Stones were reminding him, "You Can't Always Get What You Want," but the music faded to background as Lyle thought about his conversations. The chief had defended his tribe against suspected involvement in NC sabotage, but he had *not* denied that Johnny Cooper and his band were responsible for the bridge incident.

Lyle came to an intersection and almost turned the wrong way. He could see why the railroad would be so important to NC. Driving to the casino from the park would take a long time on two-lane roads. The train, traveling a more direct route, could cover the ground in well under an hour.

Lost in thought—and the Stones—Lyle did not immediately notice the motorcycle rapidly gaining on him. As his car rounded a turn and headed out a long straightaway, Lyle saw the biker's image in his mirror. As the bike's reflection grew larger, Lyle slowed to let the motorcycle pass. Instead of passing, the bike pulled up directly behind him and cruised along at fifty miles per hour, just a foot from Lyle's bumper. Then, as Lyle watched, the bike swerved around his rear fender and the rider brought the motorcycle up to the side of the car. With a gloved hand, the biker motioned for Lyle to pull over. He considered flooring it, wondering if his V-8 Mustang could outdistance the speedy bike. Before he could make a decision, the biker flipped up her visor and Lyle saw the face of Jen Smith, the woman he'd talked to at the casino. Her sly smile said she was proud of herself.

"Hope I didn't startle you," she said, dismounting a powerful Japanese dirt bike after she and Lyle had pulled up on the shoulder. She took off her helmet and set it on the bike's seat. Her clear skin was the color of light oak. Her full lips now carried no hint of defiance. Small ears poked through her dark, shiny hair. "I didn't want you to get the wrong impression back there."

"If you're thinking our security people blame members of the tribe, you're right."

"We're used to that."

"The security guys are jumpy right now."

"I guess so. That gas station crash looks like murder, doesn't it?"

Lyle tried his old detective's noncommittal expression. "Officially, an accident."

"I used to work at the park, until recently," she said. "I heard all about the car crash and the damaged ride. And now the monorail wreck in the Fun Zone. Are they related? Is that what this is about?"

Max would be disappointed to know NC's sabotage fears were about as much of a secret as the Watergate break in. Nostalgia City was a small community. Lyle decided nothing he could do would spread the story any farther than it already was.

"We don't know for sure. Frankly, *I* don't know much at all. That's why I'm asking questions." Lyle rested against the side of his car. "What'd you think?"

"I think you're funny. No, don't frown. I heard you talk in the training center when I was first hired. You were funny."

"Is that funny ha-ha, or funny peculiar?"

"That's funny, too. Your jokes. I liked your delivery. That's why I wanted to talk to you. I couldn't tell you this at the office."

"You don't want to get too cozy with the white man."

"Something like that."

"So, what *do* you think is going on?"

"I'm not sure. I've heard rumors. I used to work in accounting. I heard employees saying the tribe was damaging things because they didn't want the casino railroad. Well, there's a few people that don't want it, but most of us are hopeful. There's a lot riding on this."

"You know Johnny Cooper? Could he be involved?"

"Maybe, but he's never worked at NC. I don't think he would be able to get access to the rides and that car that crashed. It doesn't sound like something he'd do, anyway. He's just against the railroad route."

"So he could have wrecked the bridge."

"You know, we're not the only people you should think about. Have you talked to Sean Maxwell?"

"Sean. Is that the—"

"President's brother. He used to work at NC."

"They started the park together, didn't they?"

"That's what I heard. But they split up and the brother went back to his store."

"Store?"

"He runs the Route 66 Emporium and Museum outside of Polk."

"You think he'd do something to harm the park?"

"You're the detective. Find out."

"I'm not a detective. I drive a cab."

"Sure, you're a cab driver. Okay. Whatever."

"Thanks for the suggestion."

Smith smiled and turned to go.

"Hey, you didn't make a bad impression on me before," Lyle said. "And now that I see you're a dirt bike rider—And you're in accounting, too?"

"I'll be a CPA one of these days. I just finished working my way through Northern Arizona University."

"Why'd you quit the park?"

"They wanted me at the casino office. The tribe needs a smart college girl to help them keep an eye on the balance sheet."

"Our loss."

Smith walked with sure steps to her bike and pulled on her helmet decorated with a drawing of a coyote running and the words "Li'l Coyote."

As she swung a leg over the bike, Lyle noticed how her pants were like a second skin and almost the same color. *C'mon, Lyle. She's half your age. Talk about too young for you.*

"If you need to know any more, you can call me at the casino."

"Do I ask for Little Coyote?"

"Jen Smith will do."

Chapter 17

Kate! How *are* you?"

The singer's voice was still strong and rich. Kate noticed his curly hair, broad mouth, and square jaw. From a distance, he looked much as he probably did in the late '60s when Bobby Bostic and the Bombers were one of the most popular groups in the country—for a year at least.

"Bobby, nice to see you," Kate said, accepting a show-biz smack on the cheek and a generous hug that lasted a second too long. She held a sheaf of papers in her hand. She had just stepped out of her department offices into the elevator lobby when Bostic spotted her.

"I heard a rumor you were here," he said. "You work for NC now?"

"Yes. My first week." She pointed to the sign leading to the public relations office.

Up close, Bobby Bostic's hardened features made him look more like Bobby Botox. It was a nasty thought, but Kate was in a hurry and didn't have patience for Bostic. Several years ago, she'd gone out of her way to obtain superstar publicity for him when he played the Vegas hotel where she worked.

In return, Bostic became a querulous pest. He hung around her office, complaining about other stars who got bigger stories and, on one occasion, hitting on her. Uck. What a thought.

"So, how are you doing?" he asked. "Are you still going with the football player?"

"Bruce hasn't played football in years, but yes. We're looking to buy a house in the area."

"Did Max lure you away from Vegas?"

Kate nodded. "Are you going to be appearing here? Is the band still the same?"

"Oh yes. Same guys. Listen, Kate, can I talk to you for a minute? You could really help me. Is there some place we could go?"

"Uh, sure." Kate led him around a corner to a small conference room. She left the door open.

"Kate, Kate, Max is trying to put us out of business. You've got to stop him."

"Hold on a minute, Bobby. Now, *what's* Max doing?"

"He's dumping real groups like mine. Haven't you seen the calendar? Next month, Danny's Review is going to be here. They're not originals. They're kids, Kate, kids who do rip-offs. They copy everybody's material, and they even dress like us."

"Don't they do tributes to the stars of rock and roll?"

"Tributes? Tributes? Know what that means? They steal your songs, they steal your ideas, and they put you out of business. What kind of tribute is that?"

"Aren't they just impressionists?"

"Impressionists? Hell, no. Dana Carvey. He does impressions. He does a good one of me. But he doesn't make a living being Bobby Bostic. See what I mean?" Bostic started to sweat.

"Wait a minute, Bobby."

"I figured a place like Nostalgia City would hire the originals, not fakes. There's another tribute group booked here later. This sucks. I hate it. Somethin's gotta be done."

"Done?" she said, noticing Bostic's momentarily clenched fist.

"Talk to Max. You know him, Kate. Talk to him."

"Max doesn't book talent. He probably isn't even aware there's a problem."

"Yes, he is. Mel Levy said Max told him they had to streamline the budget. Cut talent expenses. I'm booked for this summer—but just a long weekend! Mel says Max likes the idea of fake groups."

As he spoke, his voice rose, but his expression stayed the same. Maybe he really did have Botox shots.

"Take it easy. I'll look into it. And I wouldn't worry. I'm sure you'll be a regular here."

"Maybe. But you know Bif Stevens, from Bif and the Rondos?"

"I think so."

"I saw him in Branson last week. His agent told him Nostal-

Mark S. Bacon

gia City wouldn't hire him 'cause they could hire a rip-off group for half the money. Then he told me there was some trouble here. I read about the accidents."

"What does that have to do with Bif Stevens?"

"Nothing." He patted Kate's arm. "I just don't want you to get a bad name. People won't want to come here."

Kate looked at her watch. "Look, Bobby, four days ago twenty five people were hurt in a crash. We've kind of got our hands full."

"So you don't care about performers?"

"Bobby. That's not fair. I said I'll look into it."

Kate ushered the aging rock star back to the elevator lobby.

"This is serious," Bobby said over his shoulder as he entered the elevator. "We're talking about livelihoods here," he shouted through the closing elevator door. "Somethin's gotta be done."

Kate turned to go and almost bumped into a man behind her.

"Was that Bobby Bostic?"

"The one and only."

"He looks different than on TV. Must be the makeup."

"Could be."

The man paused momentarily, so Kate introduced herself. Kevin Waterman was average height, five inches or so shorter than Kate. His blond hair was thinning prematurely; puffy eyes were the only distinctive characteristic in his bland face. Kate thought he looked like an accountant, an assumption he seemed to confirm when he told her he worked on the fourth floor.

"Finance?" Kate asked.

"No."

"I thought accounting took up the whole floor."

"It does, except for my office. I work for FedPat Corporation."

"A vendor?"

"We're investors, really. My title is liaison officer."

She was just about to ask what that meant, when the nearby door to the public relations office opened and Joann motioned to her. Kate excused herself.

"A tourist just died," Joann said.

Chapter 18

Y'all tryin' to bribe me?" Gayle LeBlanc asked as Lyle set a carton of doughnuts on the counter. "You wouldn't be looking for a car to be ready, would ya?"

LeBlanc eyed the box with mock suspicion. Lyle felt guilty bringing in the deep fried goodies when he saw the manager of the NC garage. She'd never be mistaken for Twiggy. She probably outweighed Lyle by seventy-five, maybe one hundred pounds. But to be charitable, half a pound was makeup.

Gayle's looks, however, weren't the reason she was hired. She ran the sprawling NC repair and body shop as efficiently as a high-priced spa. Fenders, doors, and other body parts were smoothed out, sprayed with a glistening coat of paint, then placed under sunlamps. Gayle's harried crew then followed her thorough directions to make sure the various parts got back to their original vehicles.

Lyle had heard about the NC shop, and that you had to get on the good side of Gayle if you wanted to get your car fixed quickly. Sometimes the shop ran a week or two behind with body work. So on the way back from the reservation, he'd stopped and picked up a dozen Krispy Kremes.

The manager's desk sat on a platform so she could look out at the service bays and stations spread throughout the hangar-sized building. Her perch, Lyle thought, gave LeBlanc the appearance of a well-fed monarch. In a way, she was.

"How many cars you figure we work on a day?" she teased Lyle. "I'll tell you how many. Twenty, sometimes twenty-five. That's a load o' cars. I used to run one of the biggest body shops in Miami. That was nuthin' like this. These old clunkers need constant attention. We're either tuning 'em up, patching 'em up, or restoring 'em. Now don't tell me. You have a cab, right?"

"Yes, ma'am, I do. It only had a smashed bumper and a few

air holes in the trunk lid, but it's been out of commission for a long time."

"It's not a high priority, honey. There's no shortage of cabs. The rental cars, they bring in the big bucks. We have to keep them runnin'."

"I understand. I just prefer driving my own taxi, if possible."

"Wait a sec." LeBlanc's chubby fingers started tapping her keyboard.

"You're Deming, Lyle Deming, right? Oh, Lord. I remember. You're the guy almost got creamed by that runaway."

"That's me. What ever happened to that Torino? I'd like to find out."

"We laid it to rest, ya know? Carlos can tell you."

She stood up and turned toward a row of junked cars that looked as if they'd been sitting in the desert since Liz Taylor played Cleopatra. "Hey, Carlos, you out there?"

Soon, a swarthy man in surprisingly clean work clothes stuck his head up and walked around from behind a rusted Mercury Comet.

"That's Carlos, honey," LeBlanc said. "Go see him for your cab."

"Thanks."

"One good deed deserves 'nuther," Gayle said, popping open the doughnut carton.

Lyle introduced himself to Carlos Ortiz who had his name stitched on his shirt along with the word *supervisor.* Perhaps that explained the spotlessness of the shirt, though Lyle noticed the man's slender fingers were obviously used to work.

Lyle pointed to the Comet. "This one ever going to make it to the streets?"

"Too far gone. We'll use it for spare parts. Are you looking for your car? We'll deliver it when it's ready."

"I know. Just wanted to look around a little. I'm curious how you guys restore these old beauties."

"What's your car?"

"Seventy-three Dodge taxicab."

"Hey, you the guy—"

"I'm him." Lyle wasn't even going to mention the monorail crash.

He and Ortiz wandered slowly down the rows of service

stalls looking at the irregular collection of '60s and '70s cars in various stages of restoration. Many were large American sedans: an Olds Toronado, a Plymouth Fury, and a Buick Riviera. Farther down, they came to several foreign cars.

"That looks like a Renault," Lyle said. "Those things sold new for less than $2,000."

"Close," Ortiz said. "That's a '67 Simca. It's kind of rare. They were imported by Chrysler. It does look like a Renault. And a little like a Corvair."

"Where'd you get all these?" Lyle asked as they walked. "Collectors?"

"No, they charge too much. We look for cars that need work, junkers sometimes. We buy from auctions, but many come from Mexico and other Latin American countries."

"How do you get 'em up here?"

"Mexican brokers send us some, but we've got a guy who travels the Southwest and Mexico, looking for old cars in garages, backyards, farms. Save money that way."

"What happened to the four-door Torino that did all the damage?"

"We went over it for security. It was all smashed up."

"What about the parking brake?"

"Release was worn. Could've slipped."

Lyle stopped walking and turned to Ortiz. "Really? Just an accident, like they said?"

"Maybe an accident. That's what I told the sheriff."

Lyle didn't mention that the transmission was in *neutral* when he saw it after the crash.

"I think the driver's side wind wing was pried open. Did you notice that?"

Ortiz shrugged.

"Did you see the ignition? I wondered if it was—"

"Hotwired? Coulda' been. Some ignition wires were ripped out when the car was brought in. Crash would'na caused that."

"The old models were easy to hotwire. Not like today. What'd you tell the sheriff?"

"Head security guy investigated first. Told me what he thought happened."

"I bet he told you it would be best for everyone if this was just an accident, right?

Ortiz looked at the floor.

Lyle let it drop. He stepped over to a Plymouth with its hood up. "Carlos, this Valiant doesn't have an engine or tranny."

"It's one of the prop cars. From outside they look normal, but they don't have a power train and sometimes the suspension is shot."

"It's one of the cars that are parked on the streets."

"Si, for looks."

"I've seen guys moving them around at night."

"They tow 'em around so they don't sit in the same place all the time."

"Are they locked?"

"We keep 'em locked so people can't get inside. There's a little ring you pull, under the wheel well, to pop the driver's door."

"So your wrecks that are too far gone either become a prop car or a mini spare parts depot."

"That's what happened to the Torino. Spare parts."

Chapter 19

Wrongful death suit?" Kate said. "Don't know anything about it."

That didn't take the Chen family very long, she thought. Monday morning, one week after the monorail catastrophe, Kate was surprised by a phone call from the Associated Press.

Albert Chen, a 68-year-old visitor from San Francisco, had suffered serious head injuries in the monorail crash. He'd lasted four days in the hospital. His death the previous Friday had kept NC's troubles at the top of the news statewide. By the last count, Kate's office had received 137 media calls since the monorail crash, and YouTube hits reached more than 1.5 million.

"The suit's being filed in Phoenix," the reporter said, "by the family of the Houston man killed in the car crash last month."

Kate took a deep breath and was glad she hadn't made some remark about the Chen family. "Obviously I don't have any information on it," she said. "I'll have to find out and get back to you."

Before she could put the phone down and pick it up again, Joann walked in and put the new attendance reports on her desk. Kate turned the report face down as she dialed the phone, looking for information on the lawsuit. No luck. Max was out of the building. Executive VP Brent Pelham was in a meeting.

She wandered out to Joann's desk in time to hear her secretary answer the phone. Joann scribbled on her notepad: *Phoenix Standard – Craig Gibbons.* Kate made an "I'm-not-here" gesture and headed out the door in a rush.

Two minutes later, she stepped off the elevator on the executive level. She found Brent Pelham in the coffee room. The tall man in his late thirties was filling his cup. He turned around when Kate walked in.

"We just got socked with a wrongful death suit by that ego-maniac attorney Craig Gibbons," Kate said, dispensing with pleasantries. "The media want to know our comments. Do we have any?"

"I just heard about it."

And were you going to keep it a secret? Kate thought. She just looked at him, her brows arched.

"I was on my way to call you," Pelham said, forcing a thin smile. "Sorry, I should have known Gibbons would release it to the media immediately."

Kate had met Pelham the week before. As executive vice president of NC, he was second in command, but Kate knew that anyone who was second to Max had as much authority as Napoleon's second in command. Nonetheless, Pelham had an impeccable background, including experience as CFO at another theme park and, Kate remembered, a Stanford advanced degree. Max hired good people. And often, he let them do their jobs.

"I thought we settled with the family," Kate said.

"We were close. We gave them a big offer. But after the monorail thing they changed their minds."

"Gibbons'll make a media circus out of this."

"To force a bigger settlement. Max has good outside counsel. Maybe we can get a quick agreement."

"I'll tell the press we can't comment on the specifics because it's in litigation and then give them ten minutes worth of sound bites on the extraordinary steps we're taking to assure safety. That sound okay?"

Pelham nodded, the light glinting off his glasses. He had a sprinkling of acne scars that gave him a rough look, out of place with his three-piece suit. "I see you're finding your way around here now."

"Haven't taken a breath. I keep trying to stay two steps ahead of the media *and* learn all about this place at the same time."

"If I can help…"

"Yes, you can," she said. "What's a liaison officer?"

Pelham was Kate's height, but he didn't look her directly in the eye. "Like in government service?"

"No. Like in FedPat Corporation."

Kate could see Pelham realized what she was talking about.

"Oh, you mean Kevin Waterman."

"Does he work here?"

"Yes, uh huh."

"What's he do?"

"He's an accountant, a CPA."

"And he's here because FedPat is our biggest investor?" Kate briefly had looked into NC's finances after she'd met Waterman.

"It's not unheard of for large institutional investors to have liaison people in place."

"What is he, a watchdog?"

"Not really. More of a financial consultant. It gives FedPat some input."

"Into corporate decisions?"

"He attends some management meetings. He's concerned with performance standards."

Kate wondered if Brent played poker. He was able to maintain the same expression, no matter what he said. "FedPat is the parent company of Federal Patrician Insurance, right?" she asked.

Pelham nodded.

"What's an insurance company doing investing in a theme park?"

"Insurance companies invest in lots of businesses," he said. "Nostalgia City was a good choice."

Kate still thought it unusual that FedPat had an employee working at NC, but then she was in PR, not finance.

"Why do you ask?" he said.

"Just curious. Like I said, I'm trying to learn my way around."

Chapter 20

Wandering through the brightly lit store, Lyle paused to look at a framed and matted oil company road map that dated from the 1950s. It showed a portion of Route 66 stretching across north-central New Mexico through Tucumcari and Gallup.

Lyle turned over the price tag. "Whoa. Seven hundred for a map? And they're free at the Auto Club."

"That's an original, not a reproduction." The matronly clerk had silently walked up behind Lyle. She smiled eagerly, showing exceptionally white teeth.

"Bet my dad had a map like this. He should have saved it."

Except for Nostalgia City ashtrays and shot glasses, the Route 66 Emporium and Museum was stocked with tasteful gifts and artwork. Lyle picked up an Indian pitcher.

"We get those directly from the local reservation," the clerk said. "No middleman. We have pieces you won't find in Polk or Flagstaff."

"I have a couple of small Santa Clara pots but nothing like this." He set the pitcher down. "I was hoping to see Mr. Maxwell. Is he here?"

"That's Mr. Maxwell over there."

She pointed to a man across the room wearing a western shirt and tailored leather vest. As Lyle approached him, he could see a Maxwell family resemblance.

Though Sean was considerably younger than his brother, and taller, the facial profiles were similar. Sean was leaning against a file cabinet, looking through a three-ring binder. His trim, western clothes and closely cropped brown-and-gray beard made him look like a prosperous rancher in a cowboy movie. He appeared lost in thought.

When Sean looked up, Lyle introduced himself and watched

for a wary look as he explained that he was investigating the accidents at Nostalgia City. "Wonder if you could help me. I'm talking with all the senior NC executives to see if anyone knows why someone might want to damage the park."

"Damage the park? I don't understand. Weren't they accidents?"

Lyle thought Maxwell did understand. "You're an executive of NC. I just thought you might have an idea why these things were happening."

"I'm not an NC executive. More like a consultant, now."

"But you were at the park from the beginning. I just thought you could—"

"In fact, I was here *before* the beginning. And I'm still here. But I don't have any idea about what's going on, or why there've been accidents. I think it's terrible, but I haven't been briefed. Maybe security is not as good as it should be."

"I don't know about security. I don't work for them."

Lyle was glad he'd called Max before driving out to see Sean Maxwell. He didn't call to get permission, just to tell Max what he was doing. He found out Sean was still on the NC payroll but didn't work regularly. The president's brother was a logical person for Lyle to question.

Max's response had been swift and surprising: "Ask him about anything you want. Sean is shifty. See what he says. I'd like to know myself. He's no supporter of Nostalgia City, but I doubt he's involved. Besides, everyone knows him. How could he do anything?"

Lyle had the feeling he might be getting himself in the middle of a family quarrel, but he could hardly avoid talking to Sean. He had to meet all the players. "Do you think the railroad link to the casino will help the park?" he asked.

"Of course. It's absolutely necessary. Why ask me that? Oh yes, the bridge problem." Sean glanced around at nearby customers then shot Lyle an irritated look. He motioned for Lyle to follow him to a quiet corner stocked with Native American blankets.

"You think I had something to do with the bridge?"

"No, but I guess you figured out it wasn't an accident."

"I really don't know. I heard some talk at the park. I attend meetings there every week or so."

Lyle had noticed Sean's uneasiness, but what did it mean?

Everyone at the park had some idea that everything wasn't an accident. "Just wondered if you had any theories."

"I have no idea. My brother runs the park the way he wants to. If he can't get better security, then maybe he ought to fire Bates and get someone who can do the job. I was against Bates in the first place."

"Why?"

"His attitude. Just because he worked for the FBI doesn't make him an expert in theme park security."

"But Bates thought so?"

"He told us security people should carry guns. He was giving orders even before he was hired. I wanted to know why he left the FBI."

"Obviously Max—your brother—approved of him."

"At the time. Being an FBI agent sounded good to him. Now, I don't know. Is that what you're looking for, the security position?"

"No. Bates's job is safe, far as I'm concerned. You could call me a sort of consultant, too. Most of the time I just drive a cab."

Sean looked at him as if Lyle was either kidding or was a suspicious person.

"You and your brother get along okay?"

"Are you joking? Of course, we don't. Everyone in the park knows that."

"They do?"

"I was here for years. Then Archie came in and bought up all the land. He was in the driver's seat."

"You work together when the park was being built?"

"For a while. But Archie controlled the money and had his own ideas about the park. I became his consultant. And that's what I am now. I'm happy back at my museum. He doesn't tell me what to do here."

Sean sounded rightfully indignant, but straightforward, with nothing to hide. A great strategy—if it was a strategy.

Chapter 21

"Are you going to ask Marko to help with the investigation?" Hank Deming asked. "If you're going to be a detective for Max Maxwell, why not be a *real* cop again?"

Early Tuesday morning Lyle was preparing to drive to Phoenix to see Samantha and talk to her doctor. Then he was going to stop in at the Phoenix PD to see his friend and former partner.

"I'm just going to ask Marko to do a little favor for me. I'm not looking to get my job back. You know that."

"Lyle, I don't mean to belabor this. I just hate to see you turn your back on everything you accomplished."

Lyle ignored the comment. "I'm mainly going to see Sam and find out what her doctor says about her progress on recovery. I know she's been really pushing herself in physical therapy. I'm concerned about her condition."

"How long you going to be gone?" asked his father. "I have a condition too, you know."

⌒⌒⌒

Lyle waited in the lounge of Samantha's housing complex at the university. When she came out of the elevator, all thoughts of Nostalgia City and the accidents evaporated. She walked slowly, carefully until she saw Lyle, then she rushed up to him.

He could see she was still moving cautiously with a little less of the unbridled confidence that characterized her, but she was still his Samantha.

After an encouraging visit with Samantha and her doctor—his daughter's rapid progress diminished his fears—he drove to the Phoenix PD headquarters. The station looked the same. No surprise. Lyle had been gone just over a year. He'd arranged to meet his friend Nick Markopoulos in a meeting room away from the investigations bureau where the two used to work together. As Lyle walked down the corridor and heard his footsteps echo, he thought about his ex-wife. Their divorce had become final when Lyle's ongoing battle with Lieutenant Collins escalated into the charges and counter charges that led to Sergeant Lyle Deming's reassignment to shuffling papers.

The smell of the place was the same: a combination of floor cleaner, desert dust, a touch of sweat, and other elements all stirred and distributed by the air conditioning system that ran twenty-four hours a day, year-round. It reminded him of after-work poker games, drinking at cop-friendly bars, and the camaraderie. He missed those things. But as he passed a bulletin board and glanced at a departmental memo, he remembered things he didn't miss: the politics, the occasional racist cop, and, most of all, crime victims' pain. Burdened with a caseload that never diminished, Lyle had been unable to keep in touch with the victims he'd desperately wanted to help.

"Shit," he muttered to himself. He didn't even like being in the building.

When he spotted Marko standing in a doorway down the hall, he picked up his pace. Suddenly, a door opened and someone stepped in front of him. Lyle had to leap aside to avoid a collision.

"Hey! Oh, it's you. What are *you* doing here?" said the man Lyle knew well.

He was number two on the short list of people Lyle hoped never to see again. The dark, beefy man was as surprised to see Lyle as Lyle was to see him. Did his blurted question carry a note of alarm? Or simply animosity?

"Visiting," Lyle said. He continued down the hall. He could feel the man's eyes on his back.

"Marko," Lyle said, slapping his former partner on the shoulder. "Imagine my running into that jerk, Bensen, after I've been here two minutes." Lyle looked over his shoulder.

"Forget him," Marko said as he and Lyle moved into a sterile conference room.

Markopoulos still looked the same: penetrating dark eyes, salt-and-pepper hair, and the trademark space between his two front teeth. Muscular shoulders made him look larger than his

statistically average height and weight. The gregarious detective
of Greek ancestry had been his partner for six years until Lyle's
forced transfer. Marko had helped Lyle through his divorce and
later had been his leading supporter when Lyle needed it.

After a few minutes of reminiscing, Markopoulos said, "I'm
curious about what you said on the phone. You want me to run
some names for you?"

"I'd appreciate it."

"You said you're investigating the crashes at Nostalgia City.
I thought you were driving a cab."

"I am. But Archibald Maxwell has sort of made me his personal private dick. I'm supposed to find out who's been sabotaging the park."

"Sabotage? I thought they were accidents. Aren't you having
safety problems?"

"That's what the news says. But they're *not* accidents."

"Wasn't your buddy Earl Williams hurt?"

"Yeah. I was talking with him when it happened. We had a
wild ride for a few seconds."

Marko looked concerned.

"Relax. I'm okay."

"Who'd want to sabotage a theme park?"

"Marko, that's what I'm trying to find out."

"What can I do?"

"Two things. First, run these names for me." Lyle handed
him a list. "And could you get me motor vehicle info, too? Addresses, vehicles?"

"Easy."

"I don't think you'll find a criminal record for that third
name, but I'd like anything you can find out."

"You looking for something specific?"

"I dunno. I don't think he's from Arizona. I'd just like a little history. And by the way, please don't mention this to anyone."

"Like who 'm I going to tell? The National Tabloid News?"

Lyle held up a hand.

"Speaking of investigations, I've been doing some checking
and—"

"I think I know where this is going," Lyle said.

"Just hear me out, okay? I heard about a case similar to
yours. It happened in California. Ultimately, the guy got reinstat-

ed with back pay, and then some. The city wanted to settle the mess."

"Couldn't have been just like my situation."

"Testimony from the department shrink was involved."

"Where'd you hear this?"

"My sister's husband. You know, the attorney?"

"And I bet he'd like to take my case."

"Nothing like that. Doesn't even practice in Arizona."

"I appreciate your help—and your concern. But I really enjoy what I'm doing now. The cab, I mean. I meet people. I ask them where they want to go. I tell a joke. They're happy. I'm happy. And I don't even want to think about this," he said, gesturing at the room, the building, his former life.

"We know you were set up. If you saw one more shrink, I think you could turn things around, if only for your record."

"Maybe I like being crazy. People don't expect as much from you, and they're not surprised if you do something loony."

"You're not crazy." Marko grinned broadly this time. "You're just confused by all those little voices you hear."

Chapter 22

I don't know if this will come as a surprise to you," Lyle said, "but just about everyone in NC knows it was sabotage."

Kate stared at the colorful Denny's menu in front of her. "I've come to that conclusion."

The day after Lyle's trip to Phoenix, he and Kate were seated in a corner booth in the back of the restaurant. The coffee shop had emptied after the breakfast rush and was an hour away from filling up with lunch guests.

Unlike other theme parks, NC encouraged employees to eat in park restaurants, especially if they were in period costume.

Lyle and Kate, however, were not in costume, nor were they wearing their name badges. They wanted to attract as little attention as possible.

"This diner is really authentic, isn't it?" Kate said, looking around.

"I don't think they needed to change much to have the right retro look. You been to a Denny's recently?"

"Once or twice. I wonder if they had a Grand Slam back in the '70s."

"Or, Moons Over My Hammy."

After the waitress took their order, Kate looked at Lyle with anticipation.

"I haven't come up with much, I'm afraid," he said, "but Maxwell wants a progress report anyway."

"Thanks for getting together with me, first. We'll keep this meeting to ourselves, okay?"

That was fine with Lyle. He wondered about the value of discussing the investigation with Kate. But she was drop-dead gorgeous, and having a coffee-shop lunch with her was the closest thing he'd had to sex in months. Also, Max had said he wanted them to work together, so that's the way it would be. Maybe she could help him sort through possible motives.

"Nobody in the park knows the details," he said, "but there *are* lots of rumors."

"And with something like this, if we tell employees nothing's happening, we're only calling attention to the fact that something must be happening."

"Employees are worried."

"About their jobs, their safety?"

"All of the above."

"I don't blame 'em. Two people killed. Attendance in a nosedive. What are you going to tell Max?"

"I've been wondering that myself. What do you know about Sean Maxwell? I talked with him the other day."

Kate's eyes widened. "What can I tell you? You know he and Max don't get along."

"That's pretty obvious. Were they partners?"

"Not exactly partners. They worked together—at first. I met Sean once when I was working for Max in Vegas. I think he's pretty bright. At the time, he was telling Max what a wonderful place northern Arizona is. So what did you think of him?"

"He seems a touch resentful."

"I wonder if he has reason to be. I don't know if he and Max were ever really close."

"Has Sean been in the area a long time? I should have asked him that."

"Oh yes. He's run his little store and museum in Polk longer than Max was in Vegas."

"How long did they work together?"

"Max brought him into the project early on. But it didn't last. Guess they didn't agree on the direction for the park. At the time, Max was having financing problems."

"As in, not enough money?"

"Only by a billion or two, according to what I've read. I don't know how or why he and Sean split up. Max never talks about it in front of me. Obviously he found the financing he needed, and Sean faded to the background."

"But he still works for NC. Says he's a consultant."

"Must be some deal with Max. I never heard about it, and the press didn't mention it. If you think it's important, I'll ask Max."

"It's only important if Sean's been sabotaging rides and rolling empty cars down the hill at gas stations. How likely is that?"

The waitress appeared and set heaping plates in front of Lyle and Kate.

"So where does that leave us?" Kate asked.

"The reservation, I guess. I found out the name of the angry individual who's against the railroad--Johnny Cooper. He's stirred up his followers against the train."

"Think he was involved in damaging the bridge?"

"Could be. I can see why he's on Bates's hit list. He's got a history."

"History?"

"Couple minor scrapes."

That morning, Lyle had learned from Marko that Cooper was arrested a year ago for disturbing the peace, and again for simple assault. He'd never been charged. Lyle decided to keep the details to himself, for the time being.

"I talked to the tribal chief," he said. "Seems like a reasonable guy. Says he's committed to making the casino successful and wants the rail line completed ASAP."

"Are you going to tell Max about Cooper?"

"I should, though he's probably heard plenty of dirt on the tribe from Bates already. Bates has been out to the reservation asking questions. I wouldn't say he was equipped to do PR for the park."

"That winning personality."

Lyle smiled. "George Brown—that's the chief—told me he worked out a compromise with Cooper. Maybe that will settle things."

"We can hope."

They ate in silence for a few minutes, then Lyle said, "That's all I've come up with. You have any suspects?"

"Me?" She started to shake her head then stopped. "Ever heard of Bobby Bostic?"

"Are you kidding? 'Stompin' Down My Heart!' One of the big hits of '72. What about him?"

"He's pissed off at Max. Really furious."

Kate explained her encounter with Bostic and told Lyle about Bif Stevens.

"Let me ask Earl about them. Big Earl knows everyone in the music business. If Bostic has a skeleton in the closet, Earl will know. He's back on the air and sounds good."

Kate picked up the lunch bill from the table and held up a hand when Lyle pulled out his wallet. "My treat. You can get the next one." She reached for her purse. "How did you happen to switch from the police to a theme park? Get tired of it?"

"That's the short version. Tired, burned out, ready for a change. Long story."

Lyle reached into his shirt pocket, pulled out his NC badge, and set it on the table. His first name in large letters was just above the NC logo. Below that, in small type, was his department and his full name, Lyle S. Deming. Instead of putting it on, he toyed with it absently.

"Amazing how Max persuaded restaurants and stores to locate here," he said. "NC doesn't have to run them, but they're all a part of the place."

"Not too amazing. Disney started the idea of sponsored rides and attractions. It was part of Max's early game plan. It fills the park with attractions and well-known retailers and restaurants, but it keeps the costs down."

"So where *did* Max get his money? I read a little NC history, but finance is not my specialty."

"Are you going toward the offices? Let's go. We'll talk on the way."

As they walked out, Kate glanced at a black-and-white TV in the waiting area. "Shouldn't that be a color set?"

"Not necessarily," Lyle said. "Color televisions didn't start to become popular until the mid-to-late '60s. We didn't get a color set until later than that. I was in junior high."

"Really?"

Chapter 23

S o is a theme park a risky investment these days?" Lyle asked as they walked toward the executive offices.

"Not necessarily. U.S. amusement parks take in more than $13 billion every year."

"That's a lot of thrill rides."

"That thirteen billion includes admission, souvenirs, and meals. But NC's more than a park. That's where Max hopes to make money. We have hotels and attractions in one place. When you add the Indian casino, we'll be like a combination of Disney World and Vegas."

"Sounds hard to beat."

"That's one of the reasons I came to work here. But it turns out, the park is leveraged.

"In debt?"

"Yes. Max didn't pick a great time to start building. As the recession got worse, labor was cheap, but Max had huge problems with his contractors. They grossly underestimated the cost of creating a city from scratch out here. Max stopped construction a couple of times and two of the contractors went out of business in the middle of the work. There were some lawsuits and Max wound up having to pay for a lot of materials he ordered ahead of time, and the stuff just sat and deteriorated in the desert. Of course, he was years behind schedule and was not taking in anything."

"Sounds like a mess."

"That's just part of it."

Kate paused as they passed a clothing store. She glanced up at mini-skirted mannequins in white vinyl go-go boots and matching belts. As Kate looked in the window, Lyle looked up at her.

"How tall are you?"

Kate didn't appear startled by his out-of-the-blue question.

"Six-two and a half."

Surprised, Lyle glanced down at her shoes. Her heels gave her at least another two inches.

"Sometimes I wear flats, but in my size there aren't a lot of choices for work."

When Lyle first met Kate, she struck him as all business. Since then, he'd seen a more complete person. For a woman to be a successful executive, even today, Lyle judged she had to be focused, usually smarter, and more driven than a man in the same job. He knew a police lieutenant who fit that mold. Back in the '60s, and later, Lyle's dad did not expect—nor want—his wife to work. His authoritarian philosophy and seeming inability to compromise was one of the reasons Lyle's mother had divorced him.

"I didn't mean to interrupt the finances," Lyle said, "I just don't know too many women over six feet. Do people call attention to your height?"

"Uh huh. Sometimes it's disparaging."

"Men or women?"

"Either."

Lyle nodded. He could imagine situations where men *and* women could find Kate's height distressing. He found it intriguing. "So you said Max had money problems."

"He was stuck. He could either cancel the whole project—after he'd already acquired the land with his own money—or find more money. It was in the news. Remember?"

"Vaguely. I don't usually read the business section."

"I missed some of the details myself. I knew he found the money he needed, but I didn't remember where it came from. He'd been in predicaments before."

"So where *did* he get the cash?"

"He got money from two wealthy individuals, but the biggest loan came from FedPat, the financial services conglomerate."

"I've heard of that, I think."

"They've got a guy working here, a CPA named Kevin Waterman. His title is liaison officer."

"Liaison for what?"

"That's all I know. He goes to staff meetings. He looks at performance standards. Whatever that means. You think NC investors might figure into this?"

"Big money's always an incentive for crime. But what's the motive for sabotaging the park?"

Before Kate could answer, an ambulance, siren wailing, screeched around the corner. The paramedic unit raced down the street, an NC fire engine close behind. Lyle watched as the emergency trucks made a left turn a few blocks away.

He glanced back at Kate. "Maybe somebody tripped."

"I hate to wish for a simple heart attack, but—"

They looked down the street to see an NC security black-and-white tear through an intersection and follow the path of the trucks.

Lyle threw up his hands. "I better check it out."

"I'm not sure I want to know. But you'd better call me when you find out."

He jogged back to his cab, parked in a nearby lot, and was soon chasing after the emergency procession. He followed the sirens to the edge of Centerville near the auto repair garage.

An NC patrol car blocked access to an alley that led to a be-hind-the-scenes work area. Gayle LeBlanc and other employees gathered at the entrance to the alley.

A burly security officer stood guard, arms folded across his chest.

"Is Clyde Bates around?" Lyle asked Gayle.

"He's that security guy, huh? Yeah, he's over there."

Lyle shouted at Bates and motioned for him to tell the guard to let him in. Lyle followed Bates down the alley, which ran behind the Nostalgia City Bowling Lanes.

"Maxwell call you?" Bates asked.

"I heard the sirens. What happened?"

"Take a look."

As Lyle walked around the corner of the building, he saw it. An open-air, canvass-topped tour bus had failed to make a turn in the alley and plowed into a block wall. The rainbow-colored bus was one of several small converted school buses used for guided tours. Painted on the side were the words, "Woodstock or Bust." It appeared to be empty, unless the passengers were on the floor inside.

Lyle walked up to the door. The driver was slumped over the steering wheel and a paramedic was putting an oxygen mask over his face. Next to them, on the floor, an NC employee in a garish orange tour guide uniform lay motionless. A second paramedic was trying to find a pulse.

Lyle shuffled backward and stopped to lean against the ambulance.

"This is lucky," muttered Bates who appeared next to him.

Lyle stared at him. "Lucky?"

"Lucky it happened back here. No tourists involved and we got the area sealed off. This is one accident the press won't find out about."

Chapter 24

A bus crash? What are you saying?"

"This is Rene Reynolds, Impact News, Phoenix. We want to know about the tour bus crash there on Wednesday."

Shit. Kate clenched her teeth as she gripped the phone. "Bus crash?"

"One of those open buses of yours with an awning on top?"

Kate faltered for a second.

"Well, was there a bus crash or not?"

"Yes, there was. No guests were involved. It happened in a service area."

"The pictures we have look pretty bad. Front of the bus is smashed into a wall."

"Pictures? Where did you—"

"I can't divulge our sources, Ms. Sorensen. Was anyone hurt?"

"You doing a story?"

"Yeah."

"Two of our employees were injured. I'll check out the details and get back to you with a comment. When's your deadline?"

Kate hung up and glanced at her watch. Just past 9 a.m., the end of her second week at Nostalgia City. She and her staff, worn out from responding to the media, now faced additional grief. Two employees were hurt in the bus crash, something she couldn't deny, as much as she wished it hadn't happened. Impact News would make this the top story that night. *And how did they get pictures?* She scribbled notes to herself. At least she could say the employees were out of the hospital and suffered no permanent injuries. She had tried to tell the media that little mishaps were not unusual at large theme parks—or small towns for that matter. But now *any* little accident at Nostalgia City made news.

Max wanted magic, wanted the bad news to evaporate. Kate hadn't heard from Lyle since he'd called her Wednesday about the bus crash. That probably meant he was no closer to solving the mystery. How could she continue to explain that the park was safe *and* make excuses for new accidents? She kept asking herself why someone was trying to destroy Nostalgia City.

Joann came in and handed her new phone messages.

"Don't tell me, Joann. More reporters."

"Just one call from the media," Joann said, "plus others."

Kate took the slips from her secretary. The first one said, *Nick Lassiter, president of United Veterans of the Vietnam Conflict, wants to see you soon.* Joann had underlined *soon*.

"Now what?" Kate asked.

"This group has called us before," Joann said. "Your predecessor met with someone once. They wanted to put up a memorial on the grounds."

"What happened?"

"I think Bob brought it up to Mr. Maxwell. Don't know what happened after that."

"I can guess. I'll give this guy a call. Maybe we can interest him in dedicating a crash dummy as a memorial."

Joann wrinkled her nose and gave Kate an I-hope-you're-just-kidding look.

"I know," Kate agreed. "It's bad. Nine o'clock and I'm already tired. After I give Impact News a comment, see if you can distribute the media calls to the rest of the staff for a while. I've got a meeting." Before she got up, she glanced at her other messages. Bruce had called.

"You're on the phone all the time now," Bruce said when he recognized Kate's voice. "I miss you."

"Me too. I wish you could postpone your meeting this weekend. After all, you're going to be quitting pretty soon."

"They don't know that yet, so I couldn't say no. You could have come here."

"Be serious. You know what's going on here. We've been over that," Kate said taking a breath. "What have you been doing? I called last night."

"I know. I went out with Dave and forgot to take my phone with me. That's why I called you back at work."

"Did you find a real estate agent to list the condo yet?"

"No, but I've got a list. I'll settle on someone tomorrow."

Kate wished she and Bruce were settled somewhere nearby, but that would happen when it happened—if she still had a place to work. In a way, she was glad Bruce was not around because she could devote all her time to the continuing disaster.

e/ɔe/ɔ

"It looks bad," Kate said, "but we can't just sit by, stay in one place."

"I know," Drenda agreed. "I'm trying not to let it get to me."

They sat in a small plaza near the edge of Centerville where outdoor tables clustered around a snack bar. An open-air gift shop sold newspapers, magazines, and souvenirs. Few tourists were out. The faint smell of eggs frying mixed with the odor of damp pavement drying in the late spring sun.

"At least we're off the front page."

"Temporarily."

"Anything new?"

Kate shrugged. She didn't even want to *think* about bus crash photos on the evening news.

"It's horrible," Drenda said.

"It is, but right now, the cops and security have to deal with it. We have to do what we can to improve the image around here, no matter what happens." Kate tried to smile. "And you have the ideas we need."

Drenda nodded and unrolled the architectural drawings on the table between them. "This plaza is the best spot. The timeline exhibit can go along here. And we haven't stocked those two shops in the back." She pointed to the rear of the square. "We could change our merchandising and have *something* finished in five or six weeks."

"Wouldn't it take longer than that to remodel the whole square?"

"We wouldn't need to. I've learned a myriad of tricks working with the designers and our construction crews. It wouldn't be difficult to change the ambiance and the visual effect. Here's the look we originally had in mind." She pointed to a rendering.

"This looks great."

"It's completely period-authentic."

"I think the time has come for an update on realism. Don't you?"

Drenda smiled. "It may take a while. Normally something like this has to be reviewed by the senior management committee and integrated into the budget. Then marketing will want to do focus groups. Finally it would be submitted for approval to you-know-who."

"Drenda, this *has* just been approved by Nostalgia City's two-woman executive committee. And I'll take it to the president and *he'll* approve it, too."

"You sound as stubborn as Uncle Max."

"Where do you think I learned it?"

Chapter 25

Kate, tell me the publicity is going away," Max said. "I can't believe this." He held up a printout of a popular Phoenix-area news commentary website. "This asshole says I carried my Nevada jinx with me to Arizona. Listen to this. 'Unless Maxwell can figure out how to make his scary rides a little less scary—and a whole lot safer—he won't get the last laugh on the Vegas crowd.'" He folded up the pages noisily and slapped it on his desk. "This is crap."

Kate nodded her head, but she knew the truth in what the blogger had written. "I know, Max. But you said we were going to get a clean bill of health from the outside safety engineering firm. Then, wham, that bus crashes. But maybe we can start over."

"Start over? May *have* to start over, from scratch. Hotel reservations are down over 30 percent and attendance, ha!"

Kate sat opposite the president's desk listening to the anger and frustration in his voice.

"We've got to do something," he said. "We need to boost attendance."

"We can deal with this. It'll be tough. But we'll make it. We have to stick to the crisis plan. If everything would just stay quiet for a little while, the stories will fade away. I promise. Then we just have to build ourselves up again."

"Hope you brought some miracles there." He gestured to the tablet computer she'd set up on a corner of his desk. "Because if we don't get attendance up soon, it won't matter what happens next."

Kate wasn't always an optimist, but she could summon a positive outlook, something she learned from sports. "We'll bounce back," she said. "I know it."

Max stared at her in icy silence.

"Remember when people put hypodermic needles in Pepsi?" she asked. "You couldn't give the soda away. And the Tylenol scare? Crises pass. We can come back, too. It'll just take a little time."

"We don't *have* a little time."

"We don't?"

Max looked as if he'd said more than he intended. He started to say something but stopped. Then he was silent. His mouth formed a tight, straight line.

"What's the matter? Max, it's me. Kate Sorensen, spin doctor to the rescue." Please, no *more* surprises.

When he finally spoke, he began by repeating that increasing the turnstile figures was paramount. Then, reluctantly, he told her why.

When he finished, Kate asked only a few questions. It was her turn to sit in silence. After the past few weeks, she was almost immune to bad news. Now this.

She tried to focus on the brief presentation she'd rehearsed. As she spoke, she realized that what had started as a pet idea, would become the centerpiece to her strategy to save Nostalgia City. "The plan I have here will grab the media's attention—in a positive way. And get quick results," she added.

Max looked sullen, and she knew what she was about to tell him would not improve his mood.

Ultimately, however, her plan—as she modified it on the fly—would lead to success. "Remember me telling you I persuaded Charles Dumond, a columnist from *NY Town Magazine*, to come out here? His article on us just came out. I have an advance copy."

"Is it good?" Max didn't sound enthusiastic.

"He acknowledged the monorail accident, but really focused on the park itself and our future. Let me read you part of it. He says that our people are friendly and he liked the food. He was intrigued by the re-created TV newscasts in our hotel rooms. But he said the news was, quote, 'a little more cheery than I remembered.'"

"Sounds okay."

"So, far. But here's his conclusion:

"Something is missing in Nostalgia City. It's not

that the cars and buildings are inaccurate. The hardware is perfect, right down to the vintage telephones. What the park lacks is heart.

"As I remember it, the '60s and '70s were about change and a questioning of social, political, and moral values. It was a time of disorder brought on by an undeclared war. It featured civil rights marches, the free speech movement, Timothy Leary, love-ins, hippies. An era of both idealism and skepticism. None of this is evident in Nostalgia City. What you see instead is the Brady Bunch version, a sanitized history."

Max turned away and stared out the window. "Thought you were going to have *good* news."

"I do, Max. Dumond wasn't trying to malign the park. In fact, he loved our rides. He said so. He said our *Night of the Living Dead* ride offered 'campy, scary fun.' But obviously that wasn't his main point. We need to do something *new* to get attention—in a positive way. Get attention from the media *and* the public. What I'm going to show you is not my work but the work of several people. It's our plan to get NC out of the doldrums, attract attention, and boost attendance." She touched a corner of the tablet on Max's desk and a colorful image appeared.

Max, still facing the window, looked over his shoulder at it. "I've seen that before."

"No, you haven't. The art department finished it this morning. It gives you a rough idea of what we're proposing for Centerville."

"Too expensive."

"No, it's not." She clicked to the next drawing. "We can do all this for practically nothing."

Max made a noise between a snort and a sigh. Kate ignored him and clicked through the rest of her renderings, enthusiastically describing the plans, including an idea she'd just thought of for an impressive news media day when the project was ready to be unveiled.

"We'll have this finished—" She hoped. "—so the opening will coincide with the start of the excursion train to the casino on the Fourth of July weekend. And we'll have a special press day. We'll invite everybody. Media, celebrities, bloggers, politicians.

Maybe some politicos from the '60s and '70s. This'll be a new start for Nostalgia City."

"Will you be able to do all this in a month? I *hope* we have that much time left."

"It'll be ready." Kate would have to badger Drenda to shave some time off her projected construction time.

"Leave this stuff here," he said, folding up the tablet's case. "I'll look at it."

Chapter 26

Lyle stepped softly so he wouldn't disturb his dad. It was 5:30 a.m. He walked outside, wearing his usual running shorts and T-shirt with sweatbands on his wrists. He never wore the rubber band when he ran. A good workout was therapeutic enough.

As his feet thumped the trail, he could think about potentially distressing subjects as if he were reading about other peoples' lives in a newspaper. He could consider a story then turn the page with a sense of detachment.

After warming up and stretching, he started on his customary tour with a plodding tempo. After he had jogged away from his condo, his thoughts drifted from the park to his father's condition—and disposition.

Soon, a crunching sound to his left interrupted his dark thoughts. Someone was running toward him. He heard the noise then saw another trail intersecting his.

Suddenly a woman sprinted across the path in front of him. For a second she was just a beautiful flash, then she was Kate.

"Kate, you're out early." Lyle paused a second to catch his breath. "You a jogger, too?"

"Not always. But it helps me relax. Right now I need it."

Lyle nodded. So she ran for some of the same reasons he did.

"This is the earliest I've been out since I moved here." She straightened her Nostalgia City T-shirt. Under it, she wore Spandex shorts and probably an industrial-strength sports bra. She was practically bounceless. Did she sense him checking her out?

She put her hands on her hips and one foot on a large rock. "We need to talk. I was going to call you. Anything new on the bus crash? Good thing our people will be okay."

"I checked the maintenance schedule. That bus had been out

of service for weeks, just sitting in a lot waiting to be tampered with."

"So we don't know when the sabotage took place. Could we get together this morning? Exchange information?"

"I'm on duty in the cab at ten. Want to ride around the park?"

"How about right now?"

"Now?" Lyle said, looking down at his running outfit.

"Okay, when we're finished jogging. Can you meet me at my apartment? It's the high-rise, about a mile down this trail. I'll make coffee."

ᘓᘓᘓ

Lyle could hear the coffee machine hissing as he walked into Kate's kitchen.

It was modern and bright, with white cabinets and a light wood dining set nearby. Working with Kate was starting to make sense, but it wasn't like police work—unless he considered her a partner. *What would that have been like?* He sat at the table and noticed a large, gray cat eyeing him suspiciously from a corner.

"That's Trixie," Kate said. "She'll just stare. She likes to keep her distance until she knows you."

Kate smelled clean. She had her hair up and wore a simple blouse, beige scarf, and dress slacks. Her briefcase full of papers lay open on the counter. She probably wanted him to know she'd invited him over for business.

That was fine with Lyle. What he expected. "Nice place."

"I'm renting by the week. It's one of those furnished executive apartments. Okay for now. My boyfriend Bruce is coming out this weekend and we're going to look for a house in Polk or Flagstaff. But maybe that's optimistic."

"About your relationship?"

"No. The park."

"I know what you mean. But if we can just find out who's doing this—"

"There's more to it, Lyle. I'll explain." She pulled out two mugs, set them on the table, then spun back to the counter to grab the coffee pot. Even in business clothes, she looked athletic.

"Did you play basketball in college?" Lyle asked.

"Yes." A tiny smile replaced her solemn expression. "Good guess. Four-year scholarship. Forward. USC Trojans. Nineteen points per game my senior year."

"Wow. You were good. I suppose people ask you that all the time."

"Not *every* day."

"I've known you for three weeks and I just asked."

"I admire your restraint."

"Maybe it was just slow thinking."

"Basketball was good for me. It got me into USC. I'm not sure my grades would have been enough otherwise, and USC would have been a strain on my parent's finances. Where'd you go?"

"Arizona State, on the GI Bill. I lived at home part of the time. Wasn't great fun."

"Major?"

"English lit. I like to read and I wasn't interested in anything else at the time."

"A lit major. And you became a cop?"

"It did make me a little unusual."

"I'll bet you didn't have too many coworkers who could discuss Henry James."

"No, but they could discuss *LeBron* James."

"Why'd you become a cop?"

"My last two years in the service I was an MP. When I got out, I tried several careers. Nothing seemed to fit. Finally, it was the PD or teach English."

Kate squared the note pad in front of her and glanced down. Time for business. Lyle wasn't too eager.

"Ever find out anything about Bobby Bostic," she said, "or that Bif Stevens guy?"

"Yeah. Earl calls Stevens a second-rate Roy Orbison. He says after the '60s, Stevens got religion and now plays at retreats, that sort of thing. No threat. Bostic, he's another story. Earl's interviewed him a couple of times."

"If Bobby wasn't a sleazy, conceited, pain in the ass," Kate said, "he'd just be a has-been entertainer."

"Earl agrees with you. Said Bostic's ego has an ego. He told me Bostic once got into a fistfight at the Grammy Awards. Earl thinks he could be dangerous."

"There's something about him. He really rubs me the wrong way."

"Literally?"

"He'd like to." She raised her shoulders in a shudder. "So what about the bus crash?"

"The sheriff and security questioned everyone in the bus garage."

"And?"

"Bates is still talking about the tribe. Two Native American mechanics work at the park so Bates is ready to call out the cavalry."

"And it could have been sabotaged at any time?"

"Even before the monorail. The bus was just sitting. Whoever diddled with the brakes did too good a job. The bus was probably meant to run for a few miles before the brakes gave out. Instead, they quit after two blocks—no passengers on board."

"That's the good news," Kate said. "But now we're just waiting to see if something *else* happens. I hate waiting. I want to *do* something."

"How'd the crash photos get on TV? Bates had the thing cleaned up in less than an hour. You should have seen him."

"Some employee with a cell phone camera sold shots to the station."

"Great. I'm sure Maxwell would like to find *that* guy."

"He's got other things on his mind." The tone of Kate's voice dropped sharply.

"Something I don't know?"

Kate made eye contact. "I talked to Max the other day. I'll tell you the whole story."

She poured more coffee. "Years ago Max owned a Vegas hotel. Nice, but off the strip. After a while, he decided to expand, and he started construction of a new hotel called the Subway. The theme was subways of the world. Lots of it was going to be underground."

"Today it's called the World Underground Hotel, right?"

"That's the new name. Back then, it was the Subway Resort. Only it wasn't. After Max announced his plans and dug this giant crater, he ran out of money. He became sort of a laughing stock. Construction stopped and the pit just sat there. It would fill up when it rained. They called it Maxwell's mud hole."

"Eventually he built the hotel, right?"

"Eventually. And he made a bundle. But Max had a hard time getting over being the butt of jokes. He didn't inherit any of his money. He worked for everything, all his life. He took the setback personally." Kate took a quick sip of her coffee and set down the mug. "So then he moved to Arizona and started this huge project, using his own money and looking for investors. Before long, it became obvious he'd need help."

"Is that where Kevin Waterman's corporation came in?"

"Right. Only FedPat drove a hard bargain. Max needed *lots* of money. He didn't want to run short half-way through like he'd done before, so he agreed to a loan with strings attached."

"Strings?"

"NC not only has to make loan payments, we have to meet certain operating criteria. They call it *performance standards* or covenants. In other words, this mega-loan came with minimum attendance requirements. We have to keep enough people coming in or else."

"Or else what?"

"It comes down to this: the corporation has the right to make operating and management changes if we don't keep bringing in more and more guests."

"So, Waterman is here to count our attendance?"

"Looks like it."

"Could they take over if we don't pull in enough people?"

"Ultimately, yes. In the meantime, they could start making management decisions and personnel changes. Max says we don't have much time."

Lyle looked into his coffee, then back up at Kate. "So now we maybe *have* a financial motive. They wreck the park, then take us over. And Waterman is like a...spy."

"Not necessarily. Max is worried, but he thinks FedPat will give us a break. They invested more money than he expected. He's grateful to them for sticking with him. Besides, what good would it do them if Nostalgia City tanks? They'd be losing their own investment."

Lyle thought for a moment. "Not if it was just temporary. They haven't blown up the park, just wrecked some rides."

"That's pretty hard to imagine. Would a big corporation use sabotage to run us out of business?"

"Do big corporations—*banks*, for example—cook their books, flout regulations, and plot hostile takeovers?"

"Sure, but not like this."

"Guess I was a cop too long. It just smells bad."

Kate shook her head. "Okay—just for argument—let's say the motive is plausible, but how could we prove any of this?"

"Prove it? We could, uh… "

"What would you do if you were still a police detective?"

That was an ugly thought, but it gave Lyle an idea. "We could tap his phone. That would give us some evidence."

"Tap Kevin Waterman's phone? You can't do that."

"Sure I can. I've done it before."

"Didn't you have to get a court order?"

"We'll skip that part. The NSA does."

"What if you get caught?"

"Don't you want to know what's going on? I thought you hated waiting." The more Lyle thought about it, the more he liked the idea.

"Break into his office?"

"Wouldn't need to. I know an electronics guy in Phoenix who can tap a phone line with a paper clip and Scotch Tape. I used to get Travis Stringley a lot of work. He'll do it."

"Max'd fire you. No, we need to try something else." She picked up her cat and walked Lyle to the door.

"I'll keep working on it, but Waterman and his company look good for this to me."

Kate turned her cat's head toward her. "What do you think, Trixie?"

Opening the apartment door, Lyle suddenly turned around. "Hey, did you ever think about playing for the WNBA after you got out of college?"

"When I graduated, there was no such thing as the WNBA."

"Really?"

Chapter 27

Kate and Bruce had never been apart for more than a few days at a time before she moved to Arizona. She thought seeing him again would tell her in an instant how strong their bond was. It wasn't that easy. In the first twenty-four hours after he arrived in Flagstaff, and Kate picked him up at the airport, she only learned how much they both wanted each other—physically.

They didn't waste time having dinner in a Flagstaff restaurant but headed directly to Kate's apartment. She'd stocked up on food. She'd had a pretty good idea how they would spend their first day together.

By Saturday morning, their prolonged sex had taken up as much time as sleeping. When Bruce finally awoke, he reached for Kate, but she wasn't there. She was sitting across the bedroom wearing a silky robe and looking through a real estate guide to northern Arizona.

Bruce pulled the sheet back and patted the bed next to him. "Come here."

"In a minute. Our appointment with the real estate agent is in a couple of hours. I want to show you some of the possibilities we're going to look at."

"Bring it over here."

He smiled and Kate saw the broad face, muscular shoulders, and child-like grin that had originally attracted her. He had joined a team in the Arena Football League out of college and played pro two years until an injury made him look for another line of work. He had coached for a few years then tried selling cars. Finally, he decided he was more comfortable working in a gym. He kept in shape and found out he was good at selling memberships.

Kate stood and pulled her robe tightly around her. Doing so covered more skin, but emphasized her hips and breasts. She sat on the bed and set the real estate booklet in her lap.

"Do we really want to buy a house here, now?" Bruce asked. "What about all the accidents and the publicity?"

Kate had the same thoughts but, hearing it from Bruce, she took offense. Didn't he think she could rescue the park? And he didn't even know about FedPat's deadline. Realistically, could she help NC pull out of its downward spiral of fear and financial losses? It was a risk. But she'd taken risks before.

"Yes, we're going to look at houses. Now pay attention."

"Can't we go on some rides today, instead?"

"You think it's safe?"

"I don't know. Is it?"

"How about a little confidence?" She pointed to a photo of a sprawling ranch house. "Here, look at this house."

He reached over and ran two fingers along her neckline, under the robe.

She pushed his hand away playfully. "Here's a house in Polk. You've never been there. Take a look."

He put his hand back where it had been. "Kate how can we really be serious about this? Besides, we haven't even sold the condo."

"We can afford it. Max's giving me a low-cost loan and a bonus."

Bruce pulled his hand away and sat up. "A signing bonus? You didn't tell me about that. And a home loan?"

"Yes."

"Polk is kind of a small town, isn't it?"

"What, are you interested in house hunting all of a sudden?"

"I always was."

"Yes, Polk is a small town. We'll look in Flagstaff first."

"Yes, Flagstaff." Bruce pulled the real estate guide off Kate's lap.

ᴄⲟᴄⲟ

"It's Saturday. Why did you have to work all day today?" Hank Deming looked up from his chair in the family room.

"Can't you speak to somebody? You shouldn't have to be a *cab-bie* when you're doing this detective work."

Lyle had just returned from work. He had walked in the door, twirling his hat with two fingers. His father's expression stopped him. "Dad, I've always worked Saturdays. It's fun. You know I like the cab."

He and his father had had this conversation before. Lyle sighed to himself and walked to his bedroom to change. When he was dressed in comfortable jeans and a knit shirt, he glanced at his desk to see if his father had brought in the mail.

In a corner was the stack of Federal Patrician Insurance forms and letters. He had not looked at the mail from the Boston company in a couple of days; NC problems crowded insurance out of his mind.

"May as well get to it," he said. He slid into his chair and pulled the stack of loathsome papers toward him. He opened the first envelope and started reading a message about which lab tests were covered by Sam's policy. Halfway through, he stopped, mid-sentence. He let go of it and the letter seemed to float on the top of his desk. He stared at the logo in the upper left corner. "Son of a bitch." He grabbed the letter, stood up, and for a moment didn't know what to do. "Dad—" he started to say, but his dad wouldn't care. "Son of a bitch."

In a few seconds, he'd decided. He grabbed his car keys, muttered a few words to his father, and was gone.

It took him barely four minutes to reach the building and another four before he was up the elevator and rapping on the door. No answer. He knocked again.

"Just a minute." The voice sounded a long way away.

Lyle looked at his feet, then at the letter clutched in his hand. Finally, the door opened.

Kate was barefoot and wearing shorts and a blouse. The top buttons of the blouse were unfastened. She straightened her collar and looked as if she couldn't decide whether or not to fasten the buttons. Lyle took this in, but barely.

"Those bastards at FedPat," he said. "It's them. Look at this."

Kate opened the door wide enough for him to step into the entryway. He held out the insurance letter.

"I've been fighting this company for months," he said, waving the letter. "FedPat stands for Federal Patrician Insurance."

"I know."

"They're snakes. They sell you insurance, but they don't pay claims." Lyle realized he was breathing hard. He paused to calm down. It was only then he understood Kate was not alone. "Sorry to bust in. I forgot."

"That's okay." She closed the door and he walked into her kitchen. "Now, what's happening? What about Patrician Insurance?"

"It hit me all at once. I should have realized it was the same company."

Kate's expression told him she still didn't understand.

"This is the same company that's my daughter's insurance. Those bastards. I'll bet FedPat *is* behind this. We talked about it, remember?"

"We didn't decide anything. We don't have any evidence."

"We'll *get* evidence. You don't know what kind of people these are. They don't want to destroy the park, just take it over. They know all the percentages. Delay, deny, wait till the customer gives up."

"But, Lyle—"

She stopped talking when someone entered the room. Lyle turned to see a guy as tall as Kate and more muscular than Jack LaLanne.

"Everything okay?"

"Sure," she said. "Bruce, this is Lyle Deming. Lyle works at the park."

Lyle started to shake hands while holding the letter. He shifted it to his left, shook hands with the bruiser, then turned back to Kate.

"We've got to do something. We *have* to get evidence. Stop them. Who knows what they'll do next."

"Okay. We'll talk about it."

Lyle folded up the letter and stuffed it into his back pocket. "We're going to get them. We're going to stop this."

"Okay, Lyle, okay."

Chapter 28

Lyle's morning in the cab dragged on. He should have told his supervisor he needed more time off to do the president's bidding. As soon as he could take a lunch break, he parked the cab in a lot and headed toward the Maxwell Building. A block down the street he passed the NC Cinema. *True Grit* and *The Sting* were on the marquee.

He remembered seeing both pictures. Those were the days. In the Maxwell Building lobby, he asked the guard how to find the office of Kevin Waterman.

The liaison officer's door was open when Lyle walked up. Waterman sat at his desk with a soda can and what appeared to be a hardback novel open in front of him.

Busy day.

Lyle tapped on the door and stepped in. He wore a white shirt, tie, and name badge. He'd left his hat in the cab.

"May I help you?" Kevin looked up at Lyle momentarily, then glanced back at his book.

Lyle explained he was investigating the accidents at NC.

That got Kevin's attention. "Are you with park security?"

"I'm working with them."

"And you're trying to find out…"

"Why we're having serious accidents."

"People are careless. They're making mistakes."

"Is that what you think?"

"I don't know, but it's not helping the park."

"No kidding."

Kate was right. Kevin Waterman did look like an accountant. His suit was expensive, but the man wearing it was nondescript, his round face—except for the puffy eyes—as expressive as a blank ledger page. His wore his light hair cut short. If he ever lifted anything heavier than a pencil, it didn't show. His voice, however, was more complex. It carried a note of suspicion mixed with—what was it—conceit?

"My duties here involve financial analysis. I don't have that much contact with other employees. Technically, I don't work for NC."

Was he defensive? Lyle played dumb. "You don't?"

Kevin pushed his book aside. "I work for FedPat Corporation. I'm their liaison officer here."

"Liaison?"

"My corporation is one of the major backers of this project. I work with NC management." Kevin was lecturing.

"Your company invested in Nostalgia City, so you're keeping an eye on us."

"What's this got to do with your investigation? Where do you work again?"

"With security. We're trying to keep the park peaceful. Know what I mean?"

"Okay."

"You're not taking this very seriously. I think your company would want to *make sure* nothing else happens."

"Of course."

"But what if the park goes broke? Who wins?"

"What do you mean?"

Lyle was losing patience. "You're just here to keep track of how well we do, aren't you?"

"Part of my responsibilities are to look after the terms of our agreement."

"Why did your company invest in the park?"

"A business decision. Do you really want a pro forma? Our return-on-investment expectations? Would that be much use to you?"

"Doesn't look like a good investment now, does it?"

"I don't think I'm going to be able to help you any further."

"Yes you are," Lyle spat out. "Have you heard anything suspicious around the park?"

"I told you, I don't have much contact with employees."

"You know what's going on around here. You're being *paid* to pay attention. Who do you report to anyway?"

Kevin put his hands flat on his desk and tried to rally his self-importance.

"I'm trying to be helpful, but I don't have to put up with this or answer anything more."

"I don't know why not. We're all in the same boat, aren't we? You have any other ideas?"

"This is ridiculous. Are you really with security? Let's call them." He picked up his phone.

"Ask for Bates. Maybe he'll want to know what you do here, too. I'll come back and we can talk some more."

Lyle left the office, knowing that soon Waterman would be telling him all he needed to know about his "liaison" duties. And Waterman would have no idea he was doing it. Clearly, the accountant was not the type to hot wire a car or do the heavy work necessary to derail a ride. But he worked for FedPat, and that was enough.

Chapter 29

"So, what do we have to do?" Kate asked. "We can't break in."

"Not necessary at all," Travis Stringley said. "This shouldn't take long."

Stringley looked more like a golf pro than a high-tech nerd. He was a preppie-dressed young man, athletic, and carrying a leather briefcase. Nonetheless, Lyle knew him to be a high-tech genius, even if Stringley never owned a pocket protector. Lyle also knew Stringley rarely let the technicalities of wiretap and invasion-privacy laws interfere with his work.

Stringley had met Lyle and Kate outside the Maxwell Building just before seven o'clock Monday morning. Anyone entering the building before or after business hours or on holidays had to register. They signed Stringley into the building as a vendor, which technically he was. The security guard paid little attention even though the trio arrived to work early on Memorial Day when most of the office staff had the day off.

Lyle was glad Kate agreed to come along, though she'd hardly spoken since he picked her up. Without her help, his plan wouldn't work. As they rode the elevator to the fourth floor, Kate shifted her feet and kept stealing glances at him. Lyle couldn't tell if she was nervous, angry, or something else.

"I appreciate your coming up here on a holiday, Travis," Lyle said. "Thought it would be easier since no one is working today."

"I owed you one. Besides, I brought my girlfriend with me. We're going to spend the day here."

Lyle stepped out of the elevator first and looked both ways, seeing no one. Kate and Stringley followed.

Stringley looked at Kate. "We need to find the IDF closet."

"The what?"

"It's the little room where the phone and computer lines come into this floor," Lyle said. "I forgot to ask you if you knew where it was."

Kate just stared at Lyle.

"No problem," Stringley said, "They're usually easy to find. Let's look over here."

Down a hallway, a short distance from the elevators, Stringley investigated a door near the rest rooms. "This must be it. Sometimes they're unlocked."

He pulled the knob. It didn't open.

Kate's expression was a combination of lowered brows and pursed lips. Lyle motioned for her to step back. Stringley reached into his briefcase, pulled out a small tool, and inserted it into the lock. In seconds, the door was open.

Lyle saw a confusion of wires along one wall of the booth-size room.

Kate glanced nervously over her shoulder, then back at Lyle. "So what do we do?"

Stringley set his briefcase down inside the tiny room. "I'm going to go in here for about a minute and hook everything up. Should be no problem."

The Ralph Lauren-dressed wire tapper pulled out a slip of paper on which he had Kevin Waterman's name, phone extension, and office number. As soon as Stringley went into the little room and closed the door, Lyle heard the elevator door. Kate heard it, too. She gestured toward the closet, asking if she and Lyle should duck inside.

Lyle shook his head. He listened. No voices echoed down the hallway, so he assumed that just one person had gotten off the elevator. Footsteps sounded in the hall, but Lyle couldn't determine the direction. Were they getting louder?

He looked at Kate then saw a figure in the corner of his vision. The skinny woman was as surprised to see them, as they were to see her.

"You startled me," the woman said. "I didn't expect to see anyone." She wore a loose fitting dress and a sour expression.

Kate flashed a smile. "We're getting started early today, too. I hate to work on holidays."

As Kate talked to the woman, Lyle realized that Stringley could come out of the closet at any second. He took a slow step back toward the closet and put a foot tight against the bottom of the door.

"I got way behind last week," said the unhappy-looking woman. "I thought if I came in for a few hours today I could catch up. Don't tell anyone you saw me, will you?"

Kate smiled again and promised secrecy.

"Smooth," Lyle whispered when the woman walked away.

Stringley opened the door. "All set. Take a look."

Kate and Lyle squeezed inside. Light filtered down from a small fluorescent tube fixture above. Dust hung in the air.

"Sergeant—I mean Lyle—said he didn't want a transmitter or anything complicated. This should do the trick." Stringley pointed to a small device tucked into a corner shelf. "It's a low-tech solution, and they work great. Hard to trace."

"Looks like an answering machine," Kate said.

"Basically that's right, but this digital guy works harder. It'll record every conversation on the Waterman line and it's voice activated so it only records when he's talking."

"The only thing we have to do," Lyle said, "is come in here and exchange memory cards so we can take them home and listen."

"I have a good idea who's going to have to replace the memory cards," Kate said.

"It's easy." Stringley demonstrated. "Just flip this and pull out the card. I put a label on the bottom of the machine. It says, 'Property of Nostalgia City.' I even copied the logo. Looks official. If anyone finds it, they'll think it's supposed to be here. I'll give you a little unit you can use to play the recordings."

"Travis is very resourceful," Lyle said.

Chapter 30

Lyle tried to relax. Seated in a coach aisle seat bound for Boston Logan International Airport, he had no place to go. He'd read the first page of the book in his lap several times. He'd gotten further with cocktails. He was on his second. His dad had been angry at first when Lyle told him he was going to the East Coast for a few days. Later he appeared to withdraw. Lyle made sure that a neighbor would look in on his dad at least once a day. He told Kate and Earl that his dad would be alone and he left Earl's phone number with Hank, just in case.

Before he'd told his dad he was leaving, he had to persuade Maxwell to let him go. When Lyle walked into Maxwell's office, he didn't know how he would explain it. He didn't have anything to go on. He just knew he had to go to Boston, had to see the headquarters of Federal Patrician Insurance.

At first, Max refused. "Are you trying to antagonize one of the few allies we have?"

"Allies?"

"Yes, FedPat. First, you grill Kevin Waterman, now you want to go there and piss off the whole corporation? And what good would it do? They're not involved. Anyway, you're supposed to be looking for suspects with *motives*."

Lyle, of course, was forced to explain he knew about the loan. That had not gone well, either.

Although Max seemed resigned to Lyle's knowing how involved NC was with FedPat, he still defended the corporation. "Hate to admit it, but if it wasn't for FedPat there might not *be* a Nostalgia City. They're still behind us all the way," he said. "No, we want you *here*, not stirring up trouble."

The possibility of quitting or watching NC go down the drain had drifted through Lyle's mind.

Ultimately, Max gave in but with conditions. "Don't let anyone know who you are. It's a touchy situation right now. Looks like we'll have to ask them for forbearance. You can hang around, play detective, that's okay. But keep a low profile."

NC was figuratively on fire and Max didn't seem to know if Lyle would fan the flames or douse them. Lyle had left Nostalgia City with anything but carte blanche. But he didn't care.

When the flight attendant offered another drink refill, Lyle declined and focused on the present. A good place to stay. He looked at his rubber band then watched the flight attendant walk down the aisle. She was an attractive, middle-aged woman, but nothing like the slinky stewardesses of the late '60s and '70s—who'd sported miniskirts and sultry smiles. Lyle had been a teen-ager when he'd taken his first flight and had fallen in love with a Hughes Air West stewardess. He only saw her the one time, but the memory lingered. At least his musings were now turning to women instead of his hostility toward Patrician Insurance.

After he landed, retrieved his bag, and rented a car, he head-ed north, straight for FedPat Corporation's offices in the Boston suburb of Peabody. Two-story glass and steel buildings spread out in two directions. By the time he arrived, it was past 5 p.m. East Coast time and the offices were closed. He watched as strag-glers came out of the buildings and got into their cars. Lyle won-dered if any of them were people he'd spoken to on the phone during his many attempts to straighten out his daughter's claims.

He left the offices to check into a nearby hotel. As he headed back toward Interstate 95, he spun through the car radio dial look-ing for an oldies station. He stopped when he heard a familiar voice singing about "Suspicious Minds." Lyle nodded. *The King* understood.

Lyle had a piece of fish for dinner, called to see that his dad was okay, talked to Samantha, and went to bed early.

∾∾∾

His first stop the next morning was the Peabody Library. The public library, housed in a 150-year-old brick building, didn't look promising. But inside Lyle found computers and he quickly logged onto the Internet. He started searching for background on FedPat Corporation and Federal Patrician Insurance. The research could have been done from the comfort of his home before he left. Now it cost him ten cents a page. He printed out a stack of articles on FedPat for later reading. He also discovered that insurance companies in Massachusetts were regulated by the state's Insurance Division, and he noted the division's Boston street address.

When he walked out of the library at midmorning, it was already getting warm. Not like Arizona, but humid. He felt surrounded by a hot, invisible fog. By the time he drove the few miles to the FedPat headquarters, the back of his shirt was wet and sticking to the car seat. He had the air conditioner on in the Ford Focus, but he was still sweating.

The FedPat investor relations office was housed with several other departments including Consumer Affairs. That was a laugh. Consumer Affairs existed only so the company could show the government that they really cared about policyholders.

Inside the door, Lyle had to sign in and obtain a visitor's badge from the receptionist. He asked where he could find an annual report and she directed him around a corner and down a corridor. His other objective was to check out FedPat's security measures, so when he was done, he pretended to get lost so he could look around. He left the building by another door and kept his visitor's badge.

Back in his car, he started the engine and ran the air conditioning as he flipped through the annual report, looking for names of mid-level managers. Using a search engine on his phone he quickly found phone numbers and started calling executives, looking for people who were out of the office. It took three calls.

"I'm sorry. Ms. Burgess is out of the office today. May someone else help you?"

Ms. Burgess was one of the corporate attorneys. Lyle thought the legal department would be a good place to hang out and eavesdrop so he tucked his cell phone in his pocket, picked up his small briefcase, and headed back inside. A few clouds took up space in the blue sky, but none blocked the sun. It beat down, reflecting off the mirrored office windows.

The reception area was larger than he imagined. Federal Patrician Insurance must generate lots of lawsuits. The room, with a combination of upholstered couches, chairs, and glossy wooden tables, looked like a furniture showroom, except that several people in suits were sitting and waiting. Lyle asked a receptionist with bleached hair for Ms. Burgess, saying he had an appointment for 11 o'clock.

"I'm sorry. I think she's out today."

Lyle looked puzzled. "Not here?"

"I don't think so. Um, her administrative assistant is on break."

"Anne—Ms. Burgess—told me she was going to be out of the office this morning but would be back about now. Said I should wait if she wasn't here."

"Okay. Can I have your name?"

Lyle gave a phony name, took a seat near the front of the room, and settled in to wait. He wasn't waiting for anything in particular—certainly not the absent Ms. Burgess—just sitting, watching, and listening.

After lunch, he repeated the process in another department. Then he modified the visitor badge to make it look like he worked there and hung out for a time in two employee lounges, listening and making note of what he heard. Unfortunately, after several hours, he'd not collected any intelligence he thought would be useful. But there were still a couple of hours left in the day.

Chapter 31

Looks like we made a mistake with our friend Lyle. He was discharged from the Phoenix police for mental illness."

"Lyle, mentally ill?" Kate said.

Max had come to see Kate in her office, a rare occasion that meant he was mad, that he wanted something, or both. This looked like the third option.

He made himself comfortable in one of her padded aluminum visitor chairs and glared at her.

"Clyde Bates told me he checked Lyle's background."

"And they fired him because he was mentally ill?" Kate said. "I don't think they can do that, can they? Wouldn't he have to get treatment, disability, something?"

"Yup, that's what I thought. Bates didn't have all the details. Obviously, it would be in private personnel files. Don't know whether he took disability or what. But Bates was sure on the mental illness part. I called Deming. Must have his phone turned off."

Kate's immediate instinct was to defend Lyle, but she didn't know why. The other evening he had burst into her apartment, insisting that because the company had denied his daughter's insurance claims, FedPat must be the evil force behind the park's troubles. He hadn't said it exactly that way, but that's what it sounded like. Still, she didn't have enough information. "You going to ask him about his mental health on the phone?"

"I want to know what he's doing. He could really screw things up. We made a big mistake with him."

Max reminded her of a basketball coach who called the wrong plays then tried to blame it on the team's execution. "Why don't we wait for his side of the story?" she asked.

"You shouldn't have told him about our financial relationship with FedPat."

"Max, it's done. Let's see what he has to report."

"Well, doesn't he seem, you know, a little crazy?"

"He's different," she heard herself say, "maybe even excitable at times, and anxious." Some other words occurred to her but she didn't say them. "He's been questioning people, running down leads, everything you told him to do. And, he's been keeping me up to date, something Bates hasn't done."

"He doesn't seem strange at all?"

"Because he wears that cab driver's outfit?"

"No. The way he behaves. What about his running into the gas station with all that gasoline spewing out? That sounds wacky."

Or brave, Kate thought. Was Lyle wacky? Had he recruited her into his delusion? Earlier that morning, Kate's curiosity had led her to check the memory card on the telephone listening device. Little had been recorded. Waterman had evidently not talked on the phone much the day before. She listened for a moment then slipped the card back into the recorder and slipped herself out of the electrical closet. This was definitely not a good time to tell Max about the wiretap. She was pretty sure there never would be such a time.

"So why did Bates wait until now to tell you this stuff about Lyle?"

"Said he just found out. Told me when Lyle started investigating for us, he checked Lyle's personnel file here and it looked okay. But recently, one of his contacts came up with the story about Lyle's condition. We've got to get a hold of him," Max continued, "pin him down. I want to know what he's up to in Boston. I told him he couldn't interrogate anyone. I'm going to keep calling, but I was wondering…"

"If I could wheedle some information out of him?"

"Ask directly. Pump him. I don't care. See what you can find out. Only we need to get him the hell *out* of there."

꩜꩜꩜

Having temporarily run out of ideas, Lyle realized there was one more office he could haunt—legitimately: the customer service department where policyholders congregated to inquire about claims. Unlike the other offices he'd been in, the waiting room provided people with styleless, utilitarian furniture. It reminded Lyle of the waiting rooms at HMO clinics or tire stores. At the front of the room was a long, low counter separated by partitions into small, half-height booths.

He had to take a number and wait. It took thirty-seven minutes.

"How may I help you?"

Many of the customer service reps in the room were young. The guy Lyle sat down opposite wasn't. His wide-set eyes and the curl of his lips reminded Lyle of Strother Martin, the actor who played the warden in *Cool Hand Luke*. Lyle wondered if he too would suffer from a failure to communicate. "I have a policy for my daughter and I have several claims pending. One is more than two months old."

"Let me have your daughter's name and social security number."

Lyle gave him the information, and the clerk entered it in his computer terminal then looked over the results.

"I can explain the situation to you. It's fairly common." Strother Martin smiled and sounded as if he might be interested in Lyle's problem.

Lyle relaxed slightly. "Tell me about the claim for physical therapy sessions first."

"It looks as if—" The clerk paused, squinting at the computer screen. "—as if it hasn't been resolved. There was a request for complete treatment records from the clinic."

"They were sent in a month ago and I was told they never got there. So I had the clinic fax them directly to the claims department. This was weeks ago."

"We have no record of them being received. Let me look one other place." He clicked more buttons. "No. Nothing."

Lyle was ticked off but he was prepared for this one. He reached into his briefcase and pulled out a copy of the entire clinic record he'd obtained prior to his trip. "Okay. Here's the report."

The clerk gave the stack of paper a cursory look. "I can submit this for you and the committee will consider it."

"Just a minute, please." Lyle added the word *please* because he was controlling himself. "I'd like you to sign this receipt. It says that I'm giving you my daughter's medical records."

Eyeing Lyle suspiciously, the clerk quickly scrawled his name on the paper and handed it back to Lyle. "Was there something *else*?" Now he was starting to *sound* like Strother Martin.

Lyle pulled out more paperwork. "You denied a claim for some tests."

The clerk punched his computer again. "Oh, these were disapproved because your policy requires prior authorization. We always ask for prior approval for these."

"I did get approval." Lyle pointed to his records. "Back on this date I called and talked to Lucy Lomax and she said Samantha could have the tests."

"There must have been a misunderstanding. We don't give approval over the phone to relatives. Only to health care providers."

"Misunderstanding? Does that mean that you're not going to pay that claim, period?"

"I'm afraid it does."

"I'm afraid I want to talk to your supervisor."

Cool Hand Luke's warden got a fixed look on his face, stood up, and walked off without a word. Several minutes later, he returned with a supervisor: a bony, younger woman with straight hair. Lyle could tell by her expression that she was primarily paid to say "No." She stood behind the low counter and glanced over the papers. Looking down at Lyle over her nose, she confirmed what the clerk had told him.

"Look, my daughter is recovering very well. She really had me scared. But hospitalization and therapy is so expensive. I bought this insurance specifically to cover her if this kind of accident happened. Your agent assured me this policy was comprehensive."

"The policy *does* cover a variety of circumstances," the supervisor said, still standing, looking down at the counter. "Have you *read* your policy and the exclusions?"

"Yes, I read the policy. That's why I made the claims. Okay. I have one more question." Lyle stood up, reached in his jacket pocket, and pulled out a letter he'd received the week before. The letter was crumpled and damp. "How is it that you can deny my claims," he said in a resounding voice, "and then *raise* the premiums?" Lyle slapped the wrinkled letter down hard on the counter.

His quick movements startled the woman. She took a step

back. Lyle glared at her then realized people in the other booths were staring at him. He sat down on the edge of his seat. The supervisor scanned the letter then looked down at Lyle. "We must keep up with rising medical costs. We had to re-underwrite your daughter's policy."

"Re-underwrite, huh?" Lyle said, almost to himself. "Re-underwrite *this*."

He said it under his breath, but the two employees heard him. The clerk smirked, but the supervisor's expression turned from dour to assertive. "Sir. I don't think—"

"That's obvious," Lyle growled as he stood up again. "You guys don't think. You just say, 'no'." He grabbed his papers and shoved them into his briefcase. Everyone in the office was watching him now.

For the first time, Lyle noticed surveillance cameras around the room, especially the one in the ceiling facing him. He stood, staring into the camera. He wasn't smiling. He pointed at it with his index finger like it was a gun barrel and took aim. Then he brought his thumb down as if it were the gun's hammer. One person a few booths away clapped his hands. A few people gasped. Lyle clutched the handle of his briefcase and stalked out.

"You really told them, didn't you, Deming?" he said as he headed to his car. "What the fuck were you doing? How are you going to get insurance now?"

He had parked in so many places at FedPat that day he momentarily forgot where his rental car was. As he wandered down one aisle, dangling his keys and shaking his head, he noticed someone out of the corner of his eye. It was a security guard following him from thirty yards away.

As the guard approached, he said something that sounded like, "Excuse me, sir."

At that moment, Lyle saw where he'd parked his Ford. With few wasted movements, he got in, started it up, and pulled out of the lot. He watched the security guard in the rearview mirror.

Chapter 32

Lyle debated about having a third gin and tonic. He decided against it and just had a couple of beers with his dinner hamburger. Maxwell had called him just after he left Fed-Pat. He sounded funny. He wanted to know if everything was going okay. He asked if Lyle had found out anything yet. Lyle told him the truth—that he'd learned very little. Max told him to pack it in and return to Arizona.

Lyle finished his burger, drained his beer, and headed out of the sports bar to walk back to his hotel. The sun had gone down, but it hadn't cooled off much. He hadn't been back to his room and wore the same clothes he'd put on that morning. His shirt was still damp and his feet hot. So was his face, but that was probably the alcohol. The air smelled of exhaust from the nearby freeway.

He hated to admit defeat, but he readily admitted stupidity. "You blew it, Deming," he said aloud. He crossed the street and walked diagonally through the hotel parking lot. He retrieved his briefcase from his car and found the safety of his room. Dropping his briefcase and jacket on a chair, he adjusted the air conditioning then flopped on the bed. He started to replay the scene in the claims office again.

"You're not going to confront anyone there," Max had said on the phone. "We really don't have evidence."

Why the hell did Max say that? *No, I didn't confront anyone. I just pretended to shoot them.*

Kate had urged him to delay his trip a week until they heard Kevin Waterman's conversations with his superiors in Boston, but he hadn't done that. He had thought more sabotage was on the way. He had to go to Boston, immediately.

What was it the shrink had told him? It wasn't reality or the world out there that had the power to influence how we felt—to make us upset—it was only our *reactions* to the world. We made our own reality. That had made sense at the time. No two people saw the world in the same way. You could choose.

Lyle's hotel was not fancy enough to have an honor bar. Just one more drink would have been perfect. He turned on the television.

ৎৣৣ৶

He awoke at 7:14 a.m., later than usual. But as a hazy reality slowly formed around him, he realized he didn't have anything pressing to do anyway.

First priority was coffee and a shower. He called room service. A dull ache in his head accompanied the churning in his stomach. His tolerance for alcohol seemed to have decreased as he'd gotten older. As the hot water flowed over his face, details of the previous afternoon flooded back. He pushed them away.

By the time he toweled off, a bellboy arrived with Danish and coffee. After a half cup, slurped between swipes at his face with a razor, he still felt woozy. He swallowed two aspirin. '*Why trade a headache for an upset stomach?*' The old TV ad slogan jumped into his head from nowhere. Why did his brain store such a pile of crap?

A half hour later, dressed in fresh clothes, he felt a little better. He looked at his watch and saw it was still too early in Arizona to check in with his dad. He'd forgotten to call last night and saw in the morning that he'd switched off the phone after Maxwell called.

On the desk in his room, he spread out the stack of corporate literature he'd picked up and the copies of newspaper articles he'd meant to read the night before. Everything could be read on a computer screen today, but he preferred paper. He leafed through the stories until one from a Boston paper caught his attention. The headline read: *Will CEO Retirement Prompt FedPat Power Struggle?* The writer speculated who would be the successor to Stanley Shaw, the president /CEO of FedPat, who planned to retire before Christmas. The story named three people who were considered likely candidates to succeed Shaw. Lyle underlined the names. He wondered if Maxwell had dealt with Shaw, with one of his lieutenants, or someone else.

After skimming all the articles, reading some, Lyle pulled

out his pad of paper. He'd made a few notes the day before, during, and after his hours of loitering and listening. It looked as if he'd collected a handful of nothing. He'd learned that:

~ New parking assignments, based on seniority, were irking some employees.

~ Many departments would need help from temp agencies as the summer wore on, due to vacations and increased workloads.

~ Ashley in the travel department was having an affair with a married guy in sales administration.

~ Tuesday's mystery meat in the FedPat cafeteria was dangerous to your health.

~ Sandy something—it began with a T—an investigator trainee, was being promoted ahead of others because he was a department manager's nephew.

More useless information, like the trivia that clogged his brain. Absently, he flipped through the FedPat annual report and noticed the addresses on the back. One was in Peabody, but the other was in Boston. He skimmed back through the book and discovered FedPat had its "Executive Offices" in downtown Boston. Consulting his map, he found that FedPat was not far from the state offices. How convenient. After a visit to the state, Lyle could play "loiter and listen" one more time. Then he'd have to follow Max's order and fly back to Arizona.

Chapter 33

Locating the Massachusetts State Insurance Division was the first challenge. Having been to Boston only once before, Lyle had difficulty finding his way around a downtown where few streets ran parallel and drivers seemed to use their horns as often as their brakes.

The visit to the state building yielded little. Files, facts, and figures filled the state insurance offices, but nothing seemed useful. After talking with several people, he discovered the regulatory agency was most interested in keeping tabs on the financial condition of insurance companies. He'd read in the paper that FedPat's profits were down, but he doubted that an insurance company—especially one as greedy as FedPat—could be in financial jeopardy. He learned, however, that FedPat's profits and reserves were below average. Before he left, Lyle checked out the Insurance Division's Consumer Service Department. FedPat had a record of policyholder complaints. Big surprise.

Next stop was the nondescript stone and glass FedPat building on Franklin Street in the financial district. From the street, Lyle looked up and saw the FedPat logo. It would forever be as familiar to him as Coke's or Nike's.

FedPat took up the top six floors. The main reception area was on the twenty-third. When he got out of the elevator, he saw marble floors and wood paneling—a quieter, more refined atmosphere than at the Peabody center. To the right, double glass doors opened into a lobby area with a reception counter. He wanted to walk in and ask to speak to the CEO then grill him for all he was worth. Shaw was going to retire anyway. What did he care? He probably had his hand on the ripcord of his golden parachute. But he had promised Max he wouldn't alert anyone to their problems or suspicions and, after yesterday, Lyle needed to be Mr. Cool.

He rode the elevators and scoped out all the floors. They

were filled with corridors and doors with executive names on them. He tried his loitering and listening technique, but the secretaries and receptionists downtown were sharper than those in Peabody. That was executive efficiency. By the time he traveled back to the ground floor, the elevators were crowded. It was almost lunchtime. The small restaurant on the street level was packed and noisy so Lyle squeezed his way in to get a coffee and listen. He was just starting to feel normal again. Anything over two drinks and he felt it for hours the next day.

He sipped coffee and eavesdropped. Even though the word FedPat came up every once in a while, as did executives' names he recognized, all Lyle heard was useless gossip. The coffee didn't help his head, nor did the noise level in the tiny restaurant. He was ready to quit. He should not have come to Boston until he had more to go on. He'd accomplished almost nothing, except likely getting his face on FedPat security's Scary Customer of the Month Show.

On his way out, Lyle eased through the clutch of people waiting to get into elevators. As he passed by, a large man in a brown suit spoke to the person next to him. "Not as hot as it is in Phoenix."

The word got Lyle's attention. He looked at the man as he moved past. He recognized him—he thought. Lyle turned and followed the man into the elevator. Four other people were in the car. The man Lyle thought he recognized was standing behind him. Did the guy recognize Lyle? Lyle took a chance and moved to the side, pushing an elevator button that was lit already. He glanced at the guy and the man looked directly at him. No recognition.

Lyle glimpsed the man with him, but was more interested in the guy who had mentioned Phoenix. He stood about six-three with broad shoulders, long, dirty blond hair, and a thick neck. He looked out of place in a suit. Lyle decided he knew him from somewhere—jail, court, the PD? After so many years of suspects and perps, it was difficult to keep them all straight. But this guy was no insurance man. As the two men got off the elevator, Lyle noted the floor number and saw one of them glance at his watch. They must have an appointment.

Back in the lobby, Lyle shoved his hands in his pockets and walked toward the door. He wanted to follow them when they came out, but how could he? His car was in the garage and the men might have come by cab or even the subway. Heading back to the garage, he realized he would need to move his car to the lowest level possible. Luckily, Lyle found a parking space near the ramp and backed in. Next, he walked outside. When he reached the sidewalk, he'd decided: If the two guys came out and headed his way, he'd gamble they were going into the garage. If they crossed the street, or headed the other direction, he'd improvise.

Lyle didn't have to wait long. The muscular blond and his companion, also athletically built, came out of the FedPat building and walked toward the garage.

Lyle reached his car and waited. Soon he saw the two heads and shoulders go past him in a black Chrysler. Traffic in the garage wasn't heavy. Lyle fell in behind them.

The black car turned left out of the garage and Lyle followed, letting one car get between him and his quarry. The Chrysler headed northwest, leaving the downtown area. Lyle followed them as they skirted Boston Common. He was confident that a green Ford Focus was not going to stand out in anyone's rearview mirror, but he didn't want to push his luck. In a minute, however, he had dropped almost a block behind the Chrysler and he started to get antsy.

He pressed the accelerator to close the gap. Just as he was catching up, a giant ship on wheels suddenly lurched in front of him. He slammed on his brakes as the ungainly vehicle lumbered out from a side street. It looked like a Navy landing craft turned into a carnival bus. Was Bozo the Clown driving?

In reality, it was a military amphibious duck fitted out for city tours. Lyle swerved around it. Now, where was the Chrysler?

He found it in the next block and hoped it would not make too many more turns before it got to its destination. The black Chrysler crossed the Charles River and headed through Cambridge. After a few miles, it made two quick turns and stopped in front of a two-story office building. Lyle passed the building, made a left turn, and parked where he could see the car. The men got out and went inside.

Lyle sat with his car running and the A/C turned on low. He was hoping his suspects might be coming out soon. But ten minutes passed and the Chrysler sat unattended. Lyle switched off the ignition and rolled down the window. Warm, humid air rushed in. He took off his coat and loosened his already loose tie. Now he wished he hadn't had so much coffee. Solo stakeouts were murder on the bladder.

After a while, he decided either the two guys were not coming out soon, or they went out the rear. Before he drove off, Lyle got out and walked up to the front of the building. He saw no name on the outside, but when he got close enough he could see through the building's glass doors. On a wall inside was the corporate name in stylized letters: Topaz Investigations.

He got back in his car and had just started the engine, when he saw the two men come out of the building and head for the Chrysler. The driver had taken off his coat and tie and rolled up his sleeves. He swaggered rather than walked, swinging powerful arms. His hair was cut military short, in contrast to the dirty blond who had a small pony tail. They headed back toward downtown, almost reversing the route they'd taken out of the financial district. They stopped at a downtown hotel. Lyle saw them shake hands and then the dirty blond went inside.

If he was staying in a hotel, he *could* be from Arizona. Lyle broke off the tail and headed for a restaurant and a men's room.

Chapter 34

Kate flinched when the whistle blew. The train jerked forward, stopped, then started to inch ahead. The NC railroad operations manager sat opposite her in the first car. The gray-haired man with the bushy moustache and red cheeks gave her a knowing smile when she started at the train's shrill call. Tufted leather seats, polished wood floors, and iron luggage racks gave the full-size, steam-powered train the feeling of a bygone era closer to the 1870s than the 1970s. Seated next to her was Stu Goff, marketing director for Wrangler Resorts, operators of NC's dude ranch.

"The casino train is all ready," she said. "After some road-bed tests, we're finished."

"How long'll the trip take?"

"Thirty-two minutes," said Herb Herndon, the railroad manager. "Saves lots of time over driving."

Kate shifted in her seat and pulled a chart out of a folder. "Along with the other additions we talked about, we expect the train to increase overall visitors to NC by as much as twenty percent the first year. Here's what our projections look like."

As Goff looked at the tables, Kate silently cursed Max and Brent Pelham. Brent promised her that he or Max would accompany them on the train trip, but they were "unavoidably detained."

This left the task of impressing Goff to Kate. A few days before, the president of Wrangler Resorts had told Max they wanted to pull out—unless they could renegotiate their contract. Bad publicity had affected dude-ranch bookings. Kate could see that if one discouraged commercial partner left, others might jump ship. It was up to her to keep Wrangler Resorts in the fold. Goff's severe expression was not encouraging.

"How often is the train going to run?" he asked.

"About every forty five minutes during peak times—" Before she could finish, the train's whistle signaled that it was approaching a crossing at the border of NC. "We'll have two trains, one running in each direction. We're going to announce this stuff at the big media preview."

Was Goff impressed? She glanced at Herndon, who took her cue. "Would you like to see the rest of the train?"

Herndon started his spiel and led Goff toward the rear of the car. Kate sat back in her seat, feeling the quickening rhythmic motion as the train increased its speed, rolling across the arid plain. She glanced out the window at the distant hill then forced her attention to the file of press reports in her lap. Bloggers and columnists continued to savage the park for a sloppy safety record, reviewing the number of people killed and injured in recent "accidents," and liberally quoting attorney Gibbons, who thought the park should be shut down. A local newspaper reporter's story recalled the railroad bridge collapse and questioned the safety of the casino train. A state legislator had called for an investigation.

The waves of publicity caused thousands of visitors to stay away. That led to the NC downturn itself becoming the story. Kate detested how exaggerated media coverage perpetuated the situation, scared people away, then focused on the lack of visitors. Positive publicity tended to feed off itself, but so did the negative.

She needed a big break—and lots of luck—to turn things around.

She jumped again when her cell phone rang. Was she letting the pressure get to her? "Bruce? I'm surprised you could get through. I'm on the casino train."

"I just wanted to know if you're going to come back for the weekend."

"I'd like to, but there's too much to do." What she didn't say was that she wanted to be in NC when Lyle got back from Boston. Max had talked to Lyle briefly and had ordered him to come home.

"I understand how that's important," Bruce said, "but I'm lonely."

Kate wanted to be sympathetic, but Bruce sounded selfish. He was just about to quit his job in preparation for moving, but they had no concrete plans and he had paid scant attention as they toured homes in Flagstaff.

"It won't be too much longer and we'll be together, but we have to find a house," she said. "Has anyone looked at our condo yet?"

"I dunno. Maybe while I was out."

"Didn't the agent tell you?"

"I can manage this, Kate, all right? C'mon, can't you get away for just a day or two?"

e/ɔe/ɔ

Seventy-five minutes after he saw his suspect go into the hotel, Lyle was back. At lunch, he'd considered several ways he might approach a desk clerk. When he walked in and saw a middle-aged woman standing alone at the desk, he decided on Option B. He described the dirty blond and said he was a deadbeat dad who had stolen money from his ex-wife, Lyle's sister. It worked. The sympathetic clerk told Lyle the guy's name was Jones—probably a phony name Lyle told the clerk—and that he was from Mesa, Arizona.

After Lyle thanked her for the information, she told him that Jones had just checked out and that he'd mentioned something about going to the airport.

Lyle went back to his car and headed toward his hotel. No point in trying to locate his man at the airport. Was the guy going back to Phoenix?

On the way to the hotel, Lyle stopped at the Peabody Library. It didn't take him long to discover that Topaz was a private investigation firm, started by a Joseph Renke. It had been operating in Boston for about nine years and had twice come under investigation itself. In the first incident, a Topaz operative was accused of strong-arm tactics when tracking down a suspect in an insurance fraud case. In the second, Topaz personnel were questioned during a federal investigation regarding illegal weapons. It wasn't clear whether the Topaz people were implicated, or simply witnesses. One of the articles carried a grainy mug shot of Renke. It was the same man Lyle had seen with the guy from Arizona.

e/ɔe/ɔ

After a restless night, Lyle wanted to be sure that Topaz worked for FedPat. He called the FedPat accounts payable department and asked to speak to the person who handled invoices from Topaz Investigations. Yes, they had an account there.

What next? He decided to spend his last hours in Boston doing more surveillance. He hung out at Topaz until lunch. Several people came and went, but the athletic dirty blond was not among them. Discouraged, and with just a few hours left before he had to get to the airport, he spent time on Franklin Street and in the elevator lobby of the FedPat building. The day was a tiring dud— like so much police work. His feet were sore and his shoulders drooped as he turned in his rental car and boarded the plane. The only positive from the whole trip was the face of someone he knew from Phoenix. When he got home he'd call Marko and look at mug shots.

Just as the plane touched down at Phoenix Sky Harbor Airport, something jogged Lyle's memory. He realized the guy's name *was* Jones. *Art* Jones. He'd phone Marko and maybe they could find out what Jones was up to. At least he had something to report.

The corridor of the Phoenix terminal was a river of people, even at night, and Lyle drifted with the flow toward the parking garages. He turned on his cell phone and called his dad. No answer. Probably asleep. Lyle rescued his Mustang from the long-term lot and hurried up Interstate 17 toward home. It was late when he arrived. Driving past his condo he saw a figure near his front door. It wasn't his father. Lyle parked and got out. He crept around the outside to the front door. When he saw Earl Williams, he knew something was wrong.

"Earl?"

Lyle's friend took a few, slow steps toward him. "I got bad news, man."

"What is it? Are you—"

"It's your father. He was shot. There was nothing they could do."

Chapter 35

Kate sat in her apartment, staring blankly at the TV. She didn't know any of Lyle's relatives so she had called Earl and told him that someone needed to see Lyle before he walked into his house. She persuaded Earl to be the one, but as the evening wore on, she thought she should have gone, too. She started to call Lyle then changed her mind. Better to leave the two of them alone.

She'd heard about the murder second hand, hours after it was reported to security. Clyde Bates left a message with her secretary that afternoon. The message said there had been a murder in the Timeless Village housing area. The name of the victim was Hank Deming. Even if Kate had not lived in Timeless Village, and even if the victim had not been Lyle's father, she would have wanted to know why in hell Bates waited so long to tell her. And then he took the chicken way out and left a message. Bates's people had finally started to give Kate regular security updates, but this was the kind of news she should have heard immediately.

When she got the message, she rushed across the park to the security headquarters, marched into Bates's office, and sat in front of him as he explained the crime in detail. NC security had been first on the scene and later, the San Navarro Sheriff's Office had been notified. Hank Deming was shot twice with a handgun. There were no suspects and few leads. The sheriff was treating the case as a daytime burglary gone wrong.

Kate briefed her media-relations manager and told her to call if they got any press inquiries. Then she went to Max's office and tried to reassure him and Brent Pelham that this would not be a disastrous blow, though she felt it could be. By 10 p.m. that evening, they had received no media calls.

❧❧❧

When Lyle woke up the next morning, he didn't know where he was. It wasn't a hotel room, but it didn't look familiar. He looked around then remembered he'd gone to Earl's place in Flagstaff. His father was dead. Not another heart attack but murder. Lyle tensed. He wanted to see his father, wanted to know where they'd taken him. He'd seen bodies before. He just needed to know.

"How you doing, bro?" Earl asked, his voice a soft rumble as he stepped into the bedroom holding a cup of coffee.

Lyle hoped it was as strong as Earl usually made. He wanted to think clearly, knew there were things he was supposed to do. "What time is it?"

"After nine."

Lyle groaned.

"Wanted to let you sleep."

"I need to do…something."

"You're welcome to stay here as long as you want. I've gotta leave in a few minutes. I have to tape a program."

"Thanks, Earl. I'll be fine."

Earl put a note down on the nightstand. "One of the guys from the sheriff's department wants to talk to you."

"Rey Martinez. I know him."

"Here's the key to my car. Someone's picking me up. Catch up with you later."

When Earl left, Lyle lay in bed, staring at the ceiling. His mind churned with a variety of thoughts, among them guilt for leaving his father alone and guilt for the feeling of being released from having to look after him. After a while, Lyle rolled over and picked up the note from Martinez.

⸙⸙⸙

Two hours later, Lyle met Martinez at the condo. Lyle got there a few minutes early and looked around. Obviously, a fight had taken place in the family room. An ashtray was knocked over. Several butts lay on the floor. A small end table had been tipped over and the cops hadn't bothered to straighten it. Preserving the crime scene.

Lyle had been at crime scenes—murders—but never one in his own home. He felt as if he were standing in a movie set for an unfinished drama. Martinez had told Lyle on the phone that the condo had already been checked over by the county's criminalists for fingerprints and other evidence, yet he still was reluctant to touch anything. Was it the ex-cop afraid to disturb evidence or the son not wanting to concede the reality of his father's death?

The undersheriff of San Navarro County arrived, dressed in a suit. His eyes met Lyle's.

"Nothing prepares you for this, does it?" Lyle asked. "You can be a cop for years and see murder, but when it's in your own house…"

Martinez said he was sorry then began his explanation. "As usual," he said, "my men were called *after* NC security was already on the scene."

"How'd that happen?" Lyle asked. "I don't have an alarm. NC residential security only responds to alarms, don't they?"

"One of your neighbors called security to report gunshots. She was scared. An NC security cruiser happened to be nearby. The rent-a-cop was armed so he decided to check it out and—"

"But the perps had gone," Lyle broke in, "and so they called the sheriff."

"I guess that's what happened. Security guard said your father wasn't breathing when he got here."

Lyle ran a hand through his hair and roamed around the room. Martinez had questions for Lyle, as he'd expected. Did he and his father live here alone? Where was Lyle at the time? What was his father's physical condition? What valuables did Lyle keep at home?

"Only thing I can think of is a small collection of 45 rpm records. But they're probably too scratchy to be worth anything. C'mon on Rey. I was a cop. My dad's been retired. You think we can afford *valuables*?"

"What about guns?"

Lyle hadn't checked. He kept two handguns at home: a 9mm semi-auto and a .38 revolver. Guns were always a target for burglars, but who would break into his condo in daylight, considering he had nothing of value and didn't advertise the fact that he owned guns? He rooted around in his closet where he kept the revolver and in the kitchen where he kept the 9 mm. Both were there and hadn't been fired.

"This doesn't make sense. My father was shot in a daylight burglary? How many burglars do you know who carry guns?"

"You were a cop for a long time. We do make enemies."

"Yeah, I have plenty of enemies. And not all of them are crooks, either. I've busted some pretty stupid guys, but not too many would break into my house to shoot me when I'm out of state."

Lyle wanted to ask as many questions as Martinez. They sparred, exchanging information.

"We think your father must have surprised him—we don't know for sure if there was more than one—soon after he effected entry."

"How'd he get away?"

"Ran out the back after the shots. Must have had a car stashed somewhere."

Martinez walked across the family room. "I'm telling you this because you are—were—a cop. Right now the only other thing we have to go on is another burglary a couple of weeks ago, two blocks from here. You have any ideas?"

Lyle had ideas. Plenty of 'em. Somehow, this was connected to Nostalgia City. But how? He couldn't even get evidence against the bastards at FedPat. How could he link them to his father's murder?

"Right now, I don't know. Maybe there's a connection to the sabotage at Nostalgia City. I've been talking to people, asking questions."

"You think someone might have been trying to get to you?"

"No. Maybe. I dunno."

If FedPat was involved, Lyle thought, they could have known he was not in town. "Rey, I don't know. It's just a suspicion. Why would they kill my dad to stop me from investigating? That's stupid." He said again, slowly, "Why did they kill my dad?" Turning toward a wall, he struck it with the side of his fist.

Chapter 36

Lyle was glad the day was over. This was only the second time he'd ever made arrangements for a funeral. At least he knew his dad wanted to be cremated. Lyle's brother, Tom, would be coming down from Montana. Lyle's elderly mother had lived out of state for many years and couldn't make the trip. The modest service would be in Phoenix where Hank still had a few friends. Lyle would have to drive south the next day to complete the details for the service and cremation.

He pondered all this as he refilled his glass with ice, tonic, and gin. His stereo played in the background.

"So, what do you do now, Deming?" he said to no one but himself.

Dropping onto his couch, careful not to spill his drink, he saw the chair his father usually sat in and felt guilt creeping in. He grabbed the remote to the CD player and boosted the volume to the level of the first row at a rock concert. Elton John was rolling through "Crocodile Rock."

As the drums banged out a beat, Lyle vaguely heard something else banging.

"Can I join the party?" said the low-pitched voice of the large, casually dressed visitor who wandered into the room.

Lyle wasn't sure what he'd said, but he welcomed him nonetheless. "Earl, fix yourself a drink," Lyle shouted. "I hate drinking alone."

"Looks to me like you're pretty cool with it."

"What'd you say?"

"Like the song, man, but we can't talk."

Lyle fingered the remote. "Sorry. That better? You know it's too bad we didn't have remotes for our stereos back when we were kids."

"I didn't even have a remote for the TV."

"Didn't have that many channels."

"Times change."

"Got that right," Lyle said, "whether you're ready or not."

"So what'd you do today, man?"

"Well, today I talked to the cops. Then I saw my dad's remains. Then I arranged for a funeral. Top o' that, I practiced my mental hygiene." Lyle plucked lightly at his rubber band.

"You still wearing that?"

"You bet. But you know what? The police shrink told me it was bogus. Did I ever tell you that? He said it was outdated therapy." Lyle paused to take a drink. "I told him a shrink gave it to me, but the cop shrink said it was useless. It was designed for that obsessive/compulsive thing. Said I didn't have that. Said I had adjustment disorder and other conditions that made me *unsuited* to police work. Shit, *now* they tell me."

Earl sat for a moment before he spoke. "What'd the sheriff say?"

"They don't know squat. Burglary? No way."

Lyle explained what Martinez had told him. "This *has* to be tied into the FedPat sabotage. I just dunno why. And all I could find in Boston was a punk from Phoenix."

"Slow down a minute. FedPat? What's that? And why *did* you go to Boston?"

"You know I've been investigating the 'accidents.' They're all sabotage and it's tied into the FedPat Corporation, an insurance company conglomerate."

"You think they did it?"

"*Know* they did it. They put you in the hospital and they killed my dad. I gotta *do* something."

"You didn't like him much, did you?"

"No, I didn't. Hated him sometimes. Crazy, huh? But he depended on me." Lyle took a deep breath and blinked his eyes several times. He wiped them with the back of his hand. "Know what they did? They shot him. First shot didn't kill him. Looks like he fought back. Then they shot him again." He looked at Earl then turned away.

"You don't have to do this."

"Yeah, I do…" His voice trailed off and he stared into his glass. "It was my fault."

"No man, give yourself a break."

"When I'm done."

"Why're they doing this?"

Lyle tipped up his glass, emptied it, and set it down with an unsteady hand. "Long story. Bottom line is, if NC goes belly up, the FedPat Corporation gets richer."

"This is all a corporate game?"

"It's no game. You should know that." Lyle put his hand to the back of his neck in the area where Earl had been hit.

"I hear you. And I'm getting it from both sides now. My agent called today. Says NC wants to take another look at my contract. Says they can't afford to pay me everything. Want to spread my salary out over more years. Cash flow problems, he says. Pisses me off. I have cash flow problems too, like alimony."

"But you have a national program."

"Yeah, once a week. But I quit my Phoenix job to come here."

"The park is hurting."

"So am I if I don't have a home station to work from. Know what I'm saying?"

"We have to find the bastards who are doing this." Lyle went to take a drink, forgetting the glass was empty.

"So how do you *know* that your father's death is connected to all this? Is it really one big conspiracy?"

Chapter 37

W hy didn't you tell me you were going to Boston?" Nick Markopoulos asked Lyle several days later as they walked into the Spanish style stucco house in an older Phoenix neighborhood where Hank's reception was being held. Friends of Hank's had agreed to be the hosts after the memorial service.

"So now I told you. I went to Boston."

"What I mean is, Steve Travanti works there. You remember him. He's an old friend of mine from the sheriff's department."

"'Course I remember Steve. We worked on the same task force for six months. That was years ago."

"Now he works for Boston PD. Just got promoted. He's a top guy there now. He could of helped you."

"I didn't need help. I screwed things up on my own."

Lyle and Marko were the first people in the house. They wandered into the kitchen where the hosts offered them drinks. Only iced tea and lemonade were being served, but Lyle didn't mind. He'd had enough alcohol. As he and Marko walked back to the family room, mourners filed in. Lyle nodded to people but stuck with his friend.

He explained to Marko how his investigation had led to the FedPat Corporation. He skipped over the details but said that FedPat would benefit if the park suffered.

"So what did you find out in Boston?"

"Not a hellava lot. I lost my temper. This company has been hassling me about Samantha for months. Now, all this…" Lyle stared blankly across the room. "Anyway, I did find out something. They're working with a PI company called Topaz. They probably investigate fraud cases. When I was there, I saw a guy I knew from Phoenix. Badass punk. Rambo type. I'm sure he's been busted, done time, or something."

"What's his name?"

"Art Jones."

"Doesn't ring a bell. Common name."

"I know. That's a problem. But could you check? I wasn't in on an arrest involving him, but I've seen him around. At the station maybe four, five years ago."

"I'll run his name and see."

"Thanks. It's too much of a coincidence for some Phoenix gorilla to be working at FedPat when this happens. He's white, between 30 and 35, 6-3, 230, dirty blond hair."

Marko pulled out a slip of paper and made a note. "I got a little info for you on your guy Bates."

"Oh?"

"Left the bureau a few years ago for a senior position with a California security firm. He was there for a couple of years when a headhunter contacted him about the job for Maxwell. At the FBI Bates was respected, had some commendations, but—"

Marko stopped mid-sentence as a tall, attractive woman walked into the house. "Ooh, who's the blonde? I saw her at the service."

"That's Kate, Kate Sorensen. We work together. She's in PR."

"Must be nice."

"Just business."

"Sure, Lyle."

☙☙☙☙

Kate was standing in a corner of the living room when Lyle caught up with her. She wore a gray dress with black trim.

"Thanks for coming. You didn't have to. Long drive from NC."

"I wanted to, Lyle. And I got a chance to meet Samantha at the service." She looked at him for a moment then reached over and put a hand on his arm. "I can't imagine how you feel. I'm so sorry."

Mixed with the hushed conversations in the room, Lyle could hear the air conditioning humming. He stared at the wall. "Now that this is all over, we've got to save Nostalgia City."

"You going to stick with it?"

"My job? Hell, yes. I like it. Dad didn't want me driving a cab or working funny hours. He didn't like being alone. I picked NC before my dad had his heart attacks. I'm staying."

"I'm glad. What about the police department?"

"Go back to being a cop? No chance." All day Lyle had felt light headed. He kept thinking he was at a crossroads, that everything ahead of him would be different from his life before. He fought the feeling of relief his father's death seemed to give him. *Not yet.* "I think I'm finding out what I should be doing in life," Lyle started to say.

Then a friend of his father's patted him on the back and mumbled condolences. When the man wandered off, Lyle said, "Let's fill up our drinks and go outside."

As Kate and Lyle passed through the kitchen, he smelled Mexican food. Someone had made enchiladas. He opened the back door for Kate. Only people who had lived a long time in the Southwest could imagine going outside to talk when it was over 100 degrees. Kate and Lyle were used to it.

After they had taken a few steps into the backyard rock garden, he spoke. "I'll never go back to the police department. Some people still see me as a cop, but I'm out of it now and I wish it had happened sooner."

She looked as if she were going to say something, but he continued. "I got forced out. Disagreement, you could call it, with a couple of other detectives. One of them was a lieutenant. Wanted me to look the other way when they manufactured evidence. I wouldn't. I didn't rat them out, but that didn't matter."

Sweat started forming on his upper lip. He brushed it away with his free hand then took a swallow of lemonade. "These two cops decided they'd get even with me. And they did. It was my fault, too. I'd been on the force for more than fifteen years and I didn't want to do it anymore."

"Couldn't you quit?"

"Quit? Demings aren't quitters." Lyle looked into Kate's blue eyes then glanced away. "That's what my dad used to tell me. He worked for the same company for 35 years. Probably hated every day of it, but he never quit, by God. He was afraid to leave. Afraid to try something new. I was that way for a while. Then I knew I had to find something else. But Dad wanted me to stick with being a cop. It would have been a disgrace to quit."

Kate sat down on a concrete bench next to a spiny ocotillo, its tall, thin stalks topped with red-orange blossoms. She looked up at Lyle. "Was it being a cop or not being a quitter that was most important?"

"Never knew for sure. It was hard to argue with him, so I gave up."

"But you found a way out."

Lyle raised his glass. "Right. I screwed up on a couple of cases. I made stupid mistakes—not really on purpose. One day I fired my weapon into the ground at the department range. It wasn't dangerous, but someone told Collins and Bensen."

"Who?"

"They're the two cops who had it in for me. They were everywhere. They started rumors. Told people I was burned out. Crazy. Finally, they got witnesses who said I talked to imaginary friends."

"You fight back?"

"At first. Eventually they made me see the department shrink. Frankly, I didn't care." Lyle stopped and looked around. Through the kitchen window, he could see people still eating and drinking. "I'm sorry to burden you with all this. I don't know why—"

"It's okay. I understand."

"You can't really understand it. I don't. What happened is, the department reassigned me. Sent me to an office where I'd be sort of a clerk. I told them I didn't want to do it. Next thing I knew, I was bounced. My dad wants—wanted—me to fight it. My friend Marko does, too. Wants me to prove I wasn't crazy."

"But you're doing detective work now, anyway."

"Yeah." Lyle stared off into space. "This is different. Someone killed my father and almost killed Earl. And they're trying to take over the park; spoil my new life and—"

The conversation was interrupted by Lyle's brother who stepped outside. "Lyle, can you come in for a moment? We need to talk about getting me to the airport."

Lyle waved to his brother then turned to Kate. "I'm going to prove FedPat's behind this."

He wandered back toward the house. Kate hadn't said much. Was she just being polite? If he just had something more against

FedPat. Before he reached the back door, he stopped and turned around. "Kate. What about the phone tap?"

Chapter 38

Kate studied Lyle as he walked into her apartment late that evening. He still wore his dark suit, but his tie was undone. He moved slowly.

"Sorry for bending your ear this afternoon," he said.

He sounded embarrassed. A good sign?

On the long drive back from Phoenix, she had wondered about his state of mind. Did his story of how he left the PD sound reasonable?

Did it explain what Max had told her about Lyle's background? What about his fixation on FedPat? Did that make sense?

He was, after all, an experienced detective whose instincts must count for something.

Given everything he'd been through—or said he'd been through—with his father, his police job and his stepdaughter's accident, it was no surprise that he seemed rattled at times. His father's death, coupled with the NC crisis—well, she was getting pretty near the edge, too. Something had to be done.

"Sure you want to get into this tonight?" she asked.

"Positive." He pointed to the small digital player sitting on the coffee table. "Is that it?"

She lifted up the machine. "We can use this player or upload the recordings to my computer. I listened to the whole thing."

"Eight hours you said?"

"Kevin's great company when I'm having breakfast, brushing my teeth, doing dishes. I even listened for a while at work."

Lyle glanced at the table. "I see you took notes."

"I used the digital counter and took note of everything that sounded relevant. You won't have to listen to eight hours—unless you want to. Most of this is just garbage. Kevin likes to talk. And gossip."

"What's he say that's incriminating?"

"He doesn't admit to killing the tourist from Houston or derailing the monorail if that's what you mean. In fact, there's nothing conclusive."

"Nothing?"

"Interesting stuff here, all right. He even mentions you. But let me play it so you can hear for yourself. First I felt kind of funny listening to it, then it became boring. Kevin's got a girlfriend back East. Her name's Nicole. They talk a lot."

She sat at one end of the sofa. He took a chair. "There's a lot of stuff to skip over," she said. "When we're done, maybe you could tell me what you found out in Boston."

Kate pushed a button and adjusted the volume. "This first part is him talking to his boss."

"Attendance is still dropping. Honestly. They haven't given me any new figures, but I've heard people talking. You can tell by looking at the parking lot in the afternoon. People are just not coming here. I wasn't working here then, but I'm sure it's less than last summer."

"What about the hotels?" another voice said.

"I tried to see the reservation records for the past week, like you asked, but they said they weren't complete yet. It's just a ruse. They don't want us to know how bad it is."

Kate stopped the recording. "He doesn't sound sympathetic, does he?"

"He's a rat."

Kate nodded for Lyle to pay attention to the next exchange.

"So," the other voice asked, "are they doing anything else about the accidents?"

"They don't know what's going on," Kevin's voice said. "They keep talking about safety, but there's been lots of bad news on TV. I saw a report the other day on one of those kids who was hurt. The publicity is so bad—one more crash and who knows? Most of the employees here are jumpy."

"All the more reason," the other voice said, "why we should be getting attendance and income figures more frequently during the crisis."

"Crisis?" Lyle said, raising his voice.

Kate stopped the machine. Trixie the cat looked up from the end of the sofa.

"Yes, he called it a crisis," Kate said.

Lyle leaned forward. "They know we're hurting and they call it a crisis."

"It *is* a crisis, Lyle."

"I know. FedPat's winning."

"We are doing everything we can with publicity to boost—"

"I—I didn't mean *that*." Lyle sputtered. "I mean we have to stop *FedPat*."

Kate focused on her notes. "Listen to this next part. See what you think. There's politics going on." She started and stopped the recording then found what she was looking for. "This time Kevin's talking to his girlfriend."

She pushed *Play* and Kevin's voice leaped out. "Mr. Bedrosian called me again a few days ago. It was the day after I sent you those flowers, remember? He reminded me how critical my work is here. He calls me FedPat's 'guardian,' but that's not *really* what I've been doing. He said I'll have a pivotal place with the corporation when Nostalgia City defaults on its obligations."

"What does that mean?" his girlfriend asked.

"It means, if we take over managing this place it will be a huge break for me. Honestly, I think Mr. Bedrosian likes me and, well, he's going to be CEO pretty soon and then maybe I could get a vice presidency."

"I don't understand."

"Look, honey, everybody knows that Shaw is going to retire. Remember? I heard from a friend in Boston that at least two of the FedPat board members are already supporting Bedrosian. Now he needs to show the directors he'll do a good job and make lots of money for the corporation."

Lyle motioned for Kate to stop. "Thought you said you didn't have anything conclusive? This is what we need. He's talking about taking us over."

"I dunno. He'd be saying that regardless, wouldn't he?"

"He knows what's going on. And what he says about Bedrosian is right. I read about it. The CEO's retiring and the board'll have to pick a replacement. This Bedrosian character is one of the people in the running. He's FedPat's chief operating officer."

"Why's he giving Kevin so much attention?" Kate asked. "Kevin's a glorified bean counter. He wouldn't report directly to the COO. But listen to this next bit. Bedrosian called Kevin last week. Here's the main part." Kate pushed *play*.

A strong male voice Lyle had not heard before began: "According to these latest figures of yours, attendance has continued to slip. Any reaction from the brass?"

"Pelham doesn't talk to me, unless he has to," Kevin said. "I talked to him about missing their loan payment. He just said they had an accounting problem and that we'd get the money. And as far as Maxwell is concerned—"

"Never mind about him. Has anyone questioned you again? I mean about the accidents."

"No. I told you all about that guy Deming, but I haven't seen him since."

"No one else from security talk to you either?"

"No."

She stopped the player. "That's about all that's worth listening to."

"That's enough, isn't it? Sounds like Kevin's in this up to his neck."

Kate wasn't ready to agree. "They seem to know your name at FedPat, but that doesn't mean Kevin's involved in the violence. You interrogated him. It's not surprising he'd report it."

"He knows more than my name. He and Bedrosian talked about the accidents. Kevin's *involved*."

"They *talked about it*, but they didn't say they *did it*."

"Maybe Kevin hires it done."

Kate shook her head. "He doesn't seem the type. Besides—" She flipped through her notes. "—he never says anything about hiring people."

"He's involved. FedPat's pulling the strings."

"But if Kevin were involved in the sabotage, wouldn't he report on it when he's talking to them back East?"

"Hell, I don't know. You've got eight hours here. Isn't there anything else?"

"Not really. He uses a cell phone too, so we don't hear everything."

"Must be *something* else."

Kate pushed the player toward Lyle. "Here. You can wade through this yourself."

"No. Keep it. We'll get more on the next card."

Lyle sat back and looked at the floor for a minute. "Next time maybe we'll hear him talk about my dad's murder."

"Think so?"

"We're lucky there wasn't much in the papers about my dad. I thought this might really destroy us."

"It looked bad at first, but we only got one routine media call. There's no connection between your father and NC's problems."

"No connection? What do you mean?" Lyle frowned. "Of course, there's a connection."

"*Everything's* not related to the sabotage."

"It's not?"

Kate heard an inflection in Lyle's voice she didn't like. "For the *media*, Lyle. For them it was just the death of a resident in the area. A burglary, that's all. No real relation to the park, so we're safe."

"Safe? What do you mean we're safe? My dad wasn't safe. Who knows what they're going to do next? Is that all you're thinking about, good publicity?"

"Of course not. I just meant that it won't hurt *the park*. You *know* I'm sorry your father was killed."

"And if we don't find out who killed him," Lyle said, his voice rising, "something else is going to happen." He stood up. Trixie jumped off the couch and darted away. "Something much worse. This is the third murder, Kate."

"I know, Lyle. I'm sorry. I'm just trying to put things in the right context." She patted his shoulder as he walked out of the apartment

Even before Lyle closed the door, Kate knew she'd made a mistake. Lyle was agitated, overwrought. She should never have discussed this with him right after the funeral.

She walked back to the living room looking for Trixie. Obviously she had to avoid any comments to the media that might link the murder to Nostalgia City. Obvious. Had nothing to do with how she felt. Couldn't he see that? Even if she were completely persuaded—and she wasn't—that FedPat killed Hank Deming and was trying to kill NC, she wouldn't tell the press that.

Lyle was really convinced that FedPat was behind everything—even his dad's death. Kate sat down, flipped her notebook pages over, and set the voice player on top of it. She thought for a moment about what he'd told her after the funeral. He left the police department because he'd been persecuted by other police officers. Now FedPat. It was hard not to see a comparison. But how could she judge someone on the basis of his reactions the day he buried his father?

She glanced at the digital player again. Regardless of his up-and-down emotional state, she was committed to working with Lyle. She had to find a way. Or get help from someone else.

Chapter 39

"Okay," Max said, "What'd you find out?"

Bates reached into his suit coat pocket and pulled out a tiny black box with a wire coming out of it. He set it on the table.

Kate looked at the object then glanced toward Max who sat between her and Bates at the end of the conference room table.

The morning after the funeral Kate had been summoned to a staff meeting. So far, only the three of them were in the room.

"Well?" Max asked sharply.

Bates's gray-blue eyes were expressionless. "Not much to report on this, I'm afraid. It's good high-tech gear but not unique. Fairly expensive, about $500."

Max reached over and picked up the device. "Well? Did you get a finger print or find out where it came from?"

"It was clean. No prints. And they could've bought it anywhere. I've even seen it on the Internet."

"Dammit." Max hit the table with his fist.

"My Washington contacts will—"

"Screw your Washington contacts. What are *you* doing?"

"What's going on?" Kate interrupted. "What is that thing?"

Max glared at Bates, who spoke. "It's a wireless transmitter. Some people call it a bug. One of my men found it on the floor in the Deming residence."

"Deming? That's Lyle and his father. You found a bug in their condo?"

"On the floor, next to a chair. Not far from the body. We think it's the reason someone broke into the house."

Kate frowned. "But the sheriff said it was a burglary. If they broke in to plant a bug—The sheriff doesn't know about this, does he?"

Bates shook his head.

"You kept this from the sheriff? It might have meant the murder was tied to Nostalgia City and you didn't want the sheriff to know."

"Did I know this for sure?" Bates said. "Of course not. Everybody in the park knows Deming has been asking questions about the accidents. He talked to the chief at the reservation and then he went to Boston. I'm not sure why."

"Clyde told me about it," Max said, "and we thought it best to hang on to it temporarily. See what we could find out. Apparently we didn't find out anything." He looked at Clyde through narrowed eyes.

"We're working on all the evidence. I hope to have something soon."

"You'd better be more than hopeful. One more disaster, one more *accident*, and we're outta business."

"Here's what we know," Bates said. "The device is battery powered, so it would only be good for a limited time. Whoever was going to plant it wanted to find out something soon."

"But what?" Max slid his chair back and got up. He walked slowly to the end of the room with his hands behind him, one on either hip. He didn't turn around.

Kate reached over and picked up the bug. It didn't look sinister. She waved it at Bates. "Are you saying that whoever is responsible for the sabotage tried to bug Lyle's condo and then killed his father?"

"It's a good possibility, unless it's related to a case that Deming worked on when he was a cop."

"They murdered Lyle's father," Kate said.

"It was a mistake. They probably didn't know anyone was home during the day. The whole point of bugging a house is secrecy."

"So you withheld this from the sheriff's department to keep it out of the media. That's against the law, isn't it? Withholding evidence? Anyone who knows about this could be guilty of obstruction of justice. But after we covered up one murder, the next one was easier."

"We didn't know for sure about the car crash," Max said without conviction.

Kate barely heard him. She leaned back and stared at her note pad. If the sheriff had said the murderer tried to bug Lyle's condo, that could have linked it to the park. In his own devious way, Clyde had saved Kate and NC more dreadful publicity. But what about Lyle? Did he know why his father was killed? Did this mean he wasn't just *imagining* the FedPat conspiracy? *Conspiracy is right*, she thought. No matter who was doing it.

She slid the bug back across the table to Clyde. "These people are murderers and we're covering it up."

"Maybe," Max said, turning around and leaning on the table. "But we're using this information to find out who's wrecking the park." He looked at Bates. "Time's running out. Maybe I'll call an investigations company I know in Vegas. They're ex-federal agents, too. Or maybe we should just give up and call the FBI."

"My Washington contacts will come though, Max. I know it. They're checking out the FedPat Corporation and several other leads."

"I still don't see how FedPat could be behind all this," Max said. "But I guess we have to cover all the bases."

Bates nodded knowingly. "We're not sure, either. We'll see."

"So while we're checking this out," Kate said, "they could be listening to us. Maybe they have bugs in other places, too."

Bates grunted. "The grounds here are secure. We sweep the offices regularly."

Max stared at Bates.

"Okay," Bates said, "we'll check the executive offices again this week."

Kate suddenly thought about their tap on Kevin Waterman's phone, then something else occurred to her. "What about other homes, like mine?" She pushed her chair back from the table.

"No one knows you're working on this, do they?" Bates said. Before Max could say anything, Bates held up a hand. "We'll do a sweep of your residence, too. Right away."

"And these guys with guns?" Kate said, looking at Bates. "Are they going to kill anyone else?"

"I said it was a mistake, an accident. They didn't know Deming's father was there."

"That's reassuring."

"Kate lives in the Timeless Tower," Max said. "Be sure we have a guard downstairs."

"I'll be okay. That's not what I meant."

"We have someone there occasionally at night," Bates said. "It'll be expensive to add a full shift."

"Do it," Max said.

Kate slumped in her chair.

"We'll track down whoever's doing this, Kate," Max said. "You just have to drum up good publicity for us. Pump up our attendance."

We're in big trouble, Kate thought, *if we have to wait for Clyde to solve anything.* "I can handle the PR," she said.

"Then do it. What do you have planned?"

She was about to ask if they were having a regular staff meeting that morning when Brent Pelham walked in. A minute later Drenda Adair and several others came in and took seats.

Looking at the faces of the others, Kate forced herself to relax and concentrate on her job. Her press blitz, she told everyone, was just over four weeks away. Soon, invitations to representatives of local and national media would be sent out. The media-day extravaganza, set for the July Fourth weekend, would combine the inaugural run of the train to the Indian casino *and* the opening of a new themed plaza.

"Obviously, this event has to be a huge hit," she said.

No one in the room, not even Max or Clyde, she thought, really knew all the elements of the terror campaign going on against them. Kate was quickly realizing its scope and brutality. She didn't say it, but her publicity program would be successful only if no fearful event intervened.

As the meeting broke up, Kate hurried to follow Bates out the door, but Max pulled her aside.

"Seen Deming since he got back? I want to know what he found out in Boston."

"I saw him at the funeral. We didn't talk about the trip."

"Find out anything about his background? You know, with the cops?"

"It's not exactly like Bates told you. Lyle left the police over a dispute about assignments. I don't think Clyde knows all the details or maybe he only told you part of it."

"Where'd you get this?"

"From Lyle."

"You believe him?"

"Yes." With that, Kate excused herself and hurried out.

She caught up with Clyde Bates in the elevator lobby and rode down to the ground floor with him. She made eye contact as they stepped out. "Why'd you wait until last week to tell Max that stuff about Lyle Deming's record?"

She said it fast and it caught Clyde off guard. "Why? I just found out. Max said Deming was in Boston nosing around so I checked him out more thoroughly. I thought he was supposed to be a hotshot detective."

Kate stood staring at him but said nothing, waiting for Clyde to fill the silence.

He obliged. "Before he was hired I'm sure his previous employment was checked, so I had no reason to doubt him."

"You didn't know he was discharged from the police department?"

"You know, I'm doing what I think is best for the park, just like you. We don't have to be adversaries. I'm pushing my staff to keep Nostalgia City as safe as possible. We're working 'round the clock on this. I know you're busy too—and doing a good job. God, I hate the media." He offered Kate a weak smile. "But then you know that."

That's not all I know, she thought.

"We can work together. We have to," Bates said. "Too much at stake. What do you say?"

"What about Lyle Deming and his father's murder?"

"Like I told Max, I'm going to investigate every possibility. I *have* resources. As for Deming, I'd be careful. He's a loose cannon."

Chapter 40

Lyle tried to sort things out. He'd been trying since he woke up. He remembered the cemetery, the funeral, saying goodbye to his brother, an argument with Kate. He knew he and Nostalgia City were targets, but that's where his logic ended. His thoughts were as piercing and jumbled as the lyrics to a rock song sung too loud in a club too small. At least one thing was clear: keeping busy was his best ally. Endlessly speculating and analyzing the situation was crazy. He knew that.

Thankfully, his taxi shift had started early that morning. He reported for duty at the transportation center before 8 a.m. His venerable Dodge was waiting for him outside the car-washing station.

Before he hit the streets, he called Maxwell's office for an appointment. Max had already left five increasingly virulent messages for him over the previous few days. The president wanted to know what Lyle knew about FedPat, or anything else.

Next, as he gulped a cup of coffee, Lyle called the Phoenix police. Marko wasn't in yet, so he left a message. The person who took the message apparently didn't recognize Lyle's name, so he escaped without needless small talk. He made a mental note to see Kate and apologize—and thank her for helping him.

Sitting in his cab was calming. He headed down the main drag in Centerville and noticed the new features at the cinema: *Dirty Harry* and *In Cold Blood*. Couldn't someone have picked a comedy?

After a couple of hours of ferrying guests around, Lyle's cab was idling at a taxi stand when he heard his cell phone buzz. It made him think of his father. Luckily, Lyle was alone in his cab. He really had no excuse now for carrying around a twenty-first-century phone, except it let him stay in closer touch with Samantha.

"Lyle, I got the information for you on Jones," Marko said. "His name *is* Art Jones, but he has a couple of aliases. One is *Kingman*. That's his prison name."

"Prison?"

"Yeah. Just as you thought, he did time. A couple of years for robbery. He was paroled, but that's over."

"Other arrests?"

"Oh yeah. He was in the Army. Had Special Forces training. When he got out he thought he could beat up people for a living. He was arrested a couple of times in connection with shakedowns. For the past several years he's been clean, far as we know."

"What about his PO?"

"Knew you'd ask. His parole officer was Stan Dickman. I talked to him yesterday. He said Jones fancies himself as a soldier of fortune. Last job was working security for a trucking company."

"Thanks. Appreciate the help."

"You okay?"

"Yeah. I'm in my cab."

"What are you planning to do?

"I dunno."

As he hung up, he glanced at his outside mirror and watched a cab pull up a few car lengths behind him. A woman got out and walked toward him in the street. When she got closer, Lyle realized it was Kate.

"Kate, last night, I—"

"You don't need to say anything." She placed a hand on the sill of his cab's window. "Just listen."

❧❧❧

Lyle called his dispatcher, told her he was taking lunch, drove to the Security Department building, and found his way to Clyde Bates's office. All in just eight minutes.

Bates wasn't surprised to see him. He tossed the bug on his desk as Lyle walked in. "Here it is. Who told you, Max or Ms. Sorensen?"

Lyle's hand shook as he picked up the tiny electronic ear. His voice was flat. "One of your men found this on the floor?"

"I was going to tell you about this."

"When, next year?"

"The decision was made to retain this, for now. I was going to tell you about it today. There was a chance that it either belonged to you or that the break-in was connected to an unrelated perp with a grudge against you."

"Sure."

"Okay. What do you want?"

Lyle wanted to punch him in the mouth. "Tell me about this."

"It's the only thing we found that didn't belong at your place. It's a good one. Good range. Expensive. Most casual users would buy something cheaper."

"Was it working?"

"Uh huh. It had a battery."

Lyle realized it was a stupid question. "Prints?"

"Not even a partial."

Lyle threw the little black box onto Bates's desk. It bounced and landed on the floor. He turned and walked toward the open door.

Bates hurried from around his desk, walked up behind Lyle, and put a hand on his shoulder. "Look, Deming, if you know anything about this, you have to tell me."

That was it. Bates withheld the truth about his father and now he was telling him what to do? In a flash, Lyle turned on Bates and cocked his right fist, ready to swing. The former FBI agent still had good reactions. He saw Lyle's move and jerked his head back.

Lyle held his clenched fist chest high. "Don't touch me again." He let his arm drop.

In the outer office, a security officer looked up and started to get out of his chair.

"We're supposed to be working for the park, *Clyyde*—" Lyle dragged out Bates's first name and made it an obscenity. "—but you're just working for yourself." He brushed past the security guard and left.

Maybe he shouldn't have started to swing at Bates, Lyle told himself as he sat in the Maxwell Building executive reception area. Didn't matter. Now he had other plans.

The moment he walked into Max's office Lyle could see the

boss's eyes on him. Although Max offered his condolences before he had taken a seat, Lyle noticed an expectant look on the president's face. Lyle could see he wanted to start firing questions at him but was working to keep his usual obtrusive nature under control.

Lyle glanced at the Spam painting on the wall then acknowledged Max's expressions of sympathy. "Let's get to it, all right? I'll tell you what I know about the attacks on the park. My dad's death was part of it, but you know that by now. Bates showed you the bug."

"We know someone tried to bug your home. Just assumption beyond that, isn't it?"

"Maybe. But why else would someone want to bug my condo? My life's not that exciting. My guess is they were afraid to bug the offices here for fear the bugs would be found."

Max remained silent.

"So they decided to bug my place instead, since I'd been checking out FedPat."

"Can you *prove* FedPat's involved in the sabotage?"

"Not yet. I need to go back to Boston and—"

"What did you find out the *last* time you were there?"

"I mostly hung around the offices. They have an operations center in Peabody and executive offices downtown."

Max nodded. "Been there, downtown."

"I saw a guy at FedPat I remembered from Phoenix, a hired thug." Lyle explained Art Jones's criminal record and his possible connection to Topaz Investigations.

"So what do you want to do now?"

"Go back to Boston and get evidence to connect FedPat Corporation with Topaz and whoever else has been sabotaging the park."

Max shook his head. "This is delicate. FedPat is our friend." He lapsed into silence for a few moments then said, "Clyde Bates tells me you had a disagreement with the Phoenix police."

"Did he tell you they said I was crazy?"

"Not in those words."

"I had a disagreement with them, yes. More accurately with a couple of other officers. In the end, I left because I didn't want to be a cop any more. I told you as much when you asked me to investigate for you."

"*Are* you crazy?"

"What do you think?"

"You *really* think FedPat is behind this?"

"Absolutely. Tell me, who negotiated the loan for FedPat?"

Max frowned. "Several people were involved."

"Was Jason Bedrosian one of them?"

"Jason? Yup. He's the COO now. He pushed the loan through. You suspect *him*?"

"He's one of the people in line to take over FedPat when the CEO retires next year."

"Could be a real fight for that position, from what I've heard." Max paused, toying with a fountain pen. "We'd have to be very careful. We couldn't accuse them of anything—"

"Without proof."

"Right. Bates is trying to check out FedPat and their executives with his FBI contacts in Washington."

"He can talk on the phone all he wants. I want to go to Boston and find out for myself. I'll be careful, but we've got to move fast. I'd like to leave tomorrow."

Max said nothing.

"You could always call the sheriff," Lyle said.

"Okay. But stay in touch. I want to know everything you find out. Call me *every* day."

Lyle's plans for Boston filled his head as he left Maxwell's office. When he stepped from the elevator on the ground floor, he caught a flash of someone going up in another elevator. Clyde Bates may have been able to see a punch coming, but he couldn't keep from whining to the boss. Bastard.

A few minutes after Lyle got home, his phone rang. Max told him to postpone the trip.

Chapter 41

"Marko says you're the best partner he ever had," the heavyset Boston police administrator said.

"Best I ever had, too," Lyle said.

Although Steve Travanti had gained weight since he moved to Boston, Lyle remembered him immediately. A sweep of light hair across his forehead and a hint of dimples gave him a boyish look, contrasting with his size—and the size of his office. Lyle glanced around the room and realized the guy actually was a big cheese.

"He gave you a big build up," Travanti said, "but I told him it wouldn't do any good because I used to know you."

"That's what my ex-wife says."

Travanti was not part of the detectives, but he was responsible for a division that included the crime lab. He surely could help Lyle dig up a little information.

Lyle had arrived in Boston in the evening and had called Travanti first thing the next morning. In spite of Max's admonition to sit tight, Lyle had immediately used his well-worn MasterCard to buy an airline ticket.

"Marko tell you what I was doing?" Lyle asked Travanti.

"Said you were working for that new amusement park, Nostalgia City."

"We've had a series of sabotage incidents, maybe you read about them."

"I think so. Didn't you have a fatal crash?"

"Two of 'em."

"Marko said your father was also killed. Sorry to hear that." Travanti's resonant voice had power, something that probably helped him climb the chain of command.

"That's right. I think it's connected." Lyle saw that Marko must have told him everything, or at least as much as Marko knew. That was okay. If Travanti knew how serious this was, perhaps he'd be more willing to help.

"You working with law enforcement?"

"To an extent. San Navarro County Sheriff investigated the sabotage incidents. But they're not equipped for something this broad or complex. I need to collect more information. Then we can decide if it should go to the feds, the state, or whomever. Indian reservation land is also involved, so it's complicated."

"You're investigating the FedPat Corporation, right?"

"Yeah, and I'm not supposed to agitate anyone there until we have proof. You know the company?"

"I know of them."

"They have a financial relationship with Nostalgia City that may be relevant."

"FedPat is one of Boston's big corporations. They're very involved in the community."

"I read that the current CEO is quite the philanthropist."

"Donates to a lot to worthy causes. I think my wife met him once at a charity event. She's human resources VP for a high tech company. Diane and I have lived in Boston for more than six years now. We're trying to be a part of the community."

"So here I am to investigate this fine, community-oriented company that I think is involved in corporate blackmail and murder."

Travanti leaned forward, his arms on his desk. "What can I do?"

Lyle wondered what the transplanted Arizonan would *want* to do. "I'd appreciate any kind of information you can provide. I already checked with the state insurance division. Not too helpful. Could you find out if these FedPat executives have any kind of a record?"

Lyle handed him a list of six names and titles he'd copied out of FedPat materials. Travanti took the list and stared at it without saying anything.

"I'm not looking for the usual criminal records. Probably none of these people have any. But maybe you could ask around. See if the company has been involved in strong-arm tactics. Insurance companies hire PI firms to work fraud cases. Maybe someone FedPat hired has a history of assault complaints. One of the firms that works for them is Topaz Investigations. I'd like to know anything you can find out about them, too."

Travanti made a note. "I'll see what I can do. You'll have to give me a few days."

"Sure, whatever you can do."

Lyle had debated about mentioning Topaz. If the company had hired any ex-cops from Boston, Topaz could have good contacts in the BPD. But time was too short. If Travanti could come up with something for him, it was worth any risk.

☙☙☙

After he left Travanti, Lyle found himself driving across the Charles River in the direction of Topaz Investigations. Summer had arrived in Massachusetts with a vengeance. Boston felt like Hawaii without the palm trees.

Lyle parked across the street from Topaz and sat in nearly the same space he had occupied during his first visit to Boston. He spent a boring afternoon that told him practically nothing. Sitting there, however, made him feel he had some measure of control over what was happening—to NC and to himself. He still felt responsible for his father's death. His foolish antics at the customer service office alerted FedPat that he was snooping.

Earlier, Kevin Waterman had told his superiors about Lyle. Those two circumstances, he felt—though he might never be able to prove it—brought the goons to his condo.

When he left Topaz, he drove back toward Peabody and stopped at the library where he logged on to see if anything new had been written about the competition for the FedPat presidency in the past few days. After an hour, he had a collection of recent news reports.

Lyle was focusing on FedPat's Boston headquarters, but wanted to be near the Peabody offices, too. He checked into a hotel just outside Peabody. That evening he sat on his bed going over everything he'd collected on FedPat, including more reports he'd downloaded and printed at home. If Travanti didn't come up with any leads, Lyle would need to generate something on his own. He started reading a story from a Boston newspaper. Apparently Stanley Shaw, the FedPat CEO, was playing it close to the vest as to whom he would support as his successor. The business columnist hinted that Bedrosian was the fair-haired boy, but would not be anointed by Shaw in case one of the other two presidents in waiting came up with dramatic and workable plans to boost FedPat's sagging bottom line. Office politics. It was the same everywhere.

Without any new leads, Lyle was faced with the old problem: Max didn't want him to alert FedPat—or Bedrosian—by asking questions. This might piss them off to the point they wouldn't give NC any slack as attendance figures continued to fall faster than an Apollo capsule on reentry. But if the insurance company was behind everything, no one at FedPat would cut Max slack anyway. On the other hand, if Lyle antagonized FedPat, the company's hit men might respond with a big attack that could get someone else killed. Damned if he did, damned if he didn't. Regardless, Lyle would have to go on the offensive.

Chapter 42

"Kate, you need to get up here. We got a problem."

That was all Max had said, all he needed to say. It was the start of the third day since Lyle had been in Boston and things had been quiet—until now. No one had heard from Lyle since he'd called after his first day to say he hadn't learned anything.

Kate called him back twice and left messages. Bates had started implementing even tighter security all over the park. Max had been restless every time Kate had seen him. Attendance was still down. Now the phone call.

She took a couple of deep breaths and started for the executive floor. When she got into Max's office, he was talking on the phone. Brent Pelham stood over him with an expectant look on his face.

Pelham walked over to Kate and spoke in a low voice, "Something happened at the McHale's Navy ride. We don't have all the details yet. One of the boats went haywire. Guests and employees are in the water."

"This just happen?"

"A few minutes ago. We've got security, fire, paramedics, and engineers at the ride right now."

"I'd better get over there. Don't want to scare any more guests than we have to."

Kate turned to go but stopped when she heard Max slam his phone down.

"Goddamn idiots," Max said. "It was a false alarm. Nobody's hurt."

"What was it?" Pelham asked.

Max got up and walked over. "Some fool tourist decided to stand up in his boat. Tried to step off onto one of the islands and fell in the water. Apparently, his wife started screaming and flailing around. The boat got sideways under the waterfall and she got wet."

"I can see it now," Kate said. "The boat returned to the dock, half full of water with a passenger missing so the supervisor called security."

"That's right. And security pushed the panic button. Look over there." He gestured to the distance where the glow of red and blue flashing lights could be seen through the trees. "They called everyone except the Marines."

"The guest okay?" Pelham asked.

"Son of a bitch is fine. They fished him out of the water and had the ride started again before the fire trucks got there."

Kate looked out the window at the flashing lights. Everyone at the park was jumpy. Many employees had seen one or more of the park's "accidents" in person. And *everyone* had heard about them, talked to other employees, and seen the oppressive news reports. So when an overenthusiastic guest took a plunge, the staff overreacted.

Pelham wandered out of the office, shaking his head.

Kate turned to Max. "What's happening with Clyde? He have any answers?"

"Nope. I'm giving him a week more. That's it."

"Does he know that?"

"Hell, yes. Now, what about Lyle? I tell him to wait for a few days and he flies off to Boston. And then we don't hear from him."

"He's called in. I know he's working. If he had something, he'd call."

Max walked the length of his office in front of the windows. "Well, if we don't come up with something soon, it won't matter anyway. We'll be working for FedPat—if we're working at all."

"You said if my media blitz worked, we'd have time to re-coup."

"But our cash flow has to improve right then and there. We're already in violation of our contract. Legal department says if we can show a positive upward trend, they can fend off court action. For a little while. If it comes to that."

"FedPat doesn't sound so supportive now."

"Bastards are playing hardball. I got another call into them. We just need a few concessions."

"Sounds as if everything *does* depend on making a big splash over July Fourth."

"Not like that splash we had out there." Max waved a hand in the direction of McHale's Navy.

"I'm getting the press invitations back from the printer today. They're beautiful. We're calling it, *Flashback: History Alive!* That should start some buzz.

She turned to go but paused at the door. "I'll call Lyle again."

"I'm inclined to fire his ass," Max said. "Tell him."

On the way back to her office, Kate thought about the tap on Kevin Waterman's phone. She'd put a new memory card in the machine three days before. By now, there must be something—something that she or Lyle could use. She decided she'd replace the card again that afternoon and spend the evening listening.

✐✐✐

It was just after noon and Travanti still hadn't called. Lyle sat in a coffee shop corner booth with his notes and papers spread out in front of him. The dog-eared pages had marks from a highlighter and scribbled annotations, as if a college student had been using the material to cram for an exam. Lyle looked at the pictures of the three FedPat executives who were hoping to grab the CEO's office. Bedrosian's grin reminded him of the character Barnaby from *Dark Shadows*. Any one of the aspiring CEOs—or Shaw himself—could be directing the sabotage at NC. But only one of them, as far as Lyle knew, had been talking to Kevin Waterman.

He pored over all his articles, reports, and notes. His instincts told him he had to grill somebody soon, maybe confront Bedrosian.

He sipped his coffee—then sucked in a quick breath when he realized he was thinking like a cop again: stakeouts and interrogations. Walk in the front door, identify yourself, read 'em their rights, *then* ask questions. But he wasn't a cop anymore. He was free to attack the problem any way he could. And staring down at his old notes, he had an idea. But he'd need Travanti's help. And someone else's.

He reached for his cell phone and dialed Travanti's direct

number. When the captain knew it was Lyle calling, his voice lowered slightly. Lyle knew he didn't find out anything.

"Sorry, Lyle, but I don't have very much for you."

"Were you able to check those names?"

"Yes, but not much came back. Outdated traffic warrant's about all. And as far as the company goes—"

"I don't want to talk about this on a cell phone," Lyle said. "Can I come over? It won't take long, then I'll get out of your hair."

Travanti protested that he didn't have much more to say, but Lyle insisted so the police administrator agreed. Lyle detected a slightly apologetic tone in Travanti's usually strong voice. He thought it meant that Travanti had either not checked up on Fed-Pat or had not done a very thorough job. Either way, it might make the high-ranking Boston cop more receptive to Lyle's idea.

Chapter 43

Glad to be home from work—even if she was two hours late—Kate uploaded the contents of the latest memory card to her iPod. Even before she changed her clothes, she had Kevin's voice for company. She pulled on sweats, grabbed a fruit drink from the fridge, and listened.

The first forty-five minutes were consumed by routine calls. Kevin called someone named Drew who apparently worked in the NC printing department. They talked about baseball, the weather, and exchanged a couple of crude jokes. Like Kevin, Drew seemed to be from the East. He talked about the Phillies as if they were his home team. Obviously, Kevin had made at least one friend in NC. Good for him.

Kate fixed dinner while listening to Kevin and his girlfriend exchange sexual innuendoes. Just when Kate's food was ready, Kevin got a call from Bedrosian. Kate sat with a notepad and pencil next to her dinner plate.

"They're still not close to making their performance standards." Bedrosian was talking. "Maxwell was too optimistic when he started Nostalgia City. So much the better for us. One more accident and they'll be in bankruptcy."

"Looks to me like they're there now," Kevin said.

"They *must* be working on something to attract more visitors. Can't imagine Maxwell sitting still."

"The casino railway is scheduled to open at the beginning of next month. I've also heard talk about them opening a new theme area at the same time."

"On the Fourth of July weekend?"

"Right. Maxwell seems to think this will be the start of a big upswing."

"Fourth of July weekend celebration. Fireworks and fun on the train. Think that'll help them any?"

"Honestly, I don't see how."

Kate stabbed her baked chicken breast mercilessly as she listened. She sliced it in pieces then speared the sections with her fork. "Wait and see, Kevin," she said aloud.

"I've been reading your recent report," Bedrosian said. "It's good. And you have good ideas about ways to cut costs and streamline administration."

"They waste a lot of time and money here."

"What's the atmosphere like? Anything different since the old man was killed?"

"Security is way higher. Like they expect a terrorist attack or something. More guards at the entrance to the employee lot now. They've searched my car twice in the last few days."

"Searched your car? Why didn't you report this?"

"I—was going to."

"Do they search everyone?"

"Not everyone. Maybe it's random."

"File a complaint. Send a memo to security. No. Send it to Maxwell. Tell him you're being harassed. And tell him you want to start getting *daily* reservation reports. First thing every morning."

"Yes, yes. I'll do that."

"Sounds as if they're watching you. We need to be more careful. Do you have a cell phone?"

"Yes, why?"

"From now on, we should talk on your cell. Or I'll call you at home. Don't trust them. They violated their contract with us and now they'll do anything to keep us from exercising our legal rights."

"What do you think they'd do?"

"I don't know. Just a precaution. Has anyone else questioned you?"

"No. Just that one time."

"Well, if you run into Deming again, lemme know."

"Damn," Kate said, dropping her fork so she could write.

Her dinner got cold as she scribbled notes. It sounded to her as if that would be the last conversation they heard between Kevin and Bedrosian.

Before the call ended, Kevin asked Bedrosian if he thought he would be named the new president/CEO when Shaw retired.

Kate wondered if Bedrosian had noticed the patronizing tone in Kevin's voice. Maybe he did. Maybe he liked it.

She didn't know that Clyde had decided to keep a closer eye on Kevin. Searching his car might be a good idea, but it certainly alerted Bedrosian to Kevin's vulnerability—and to the fact that his phone might be bugged. Did Bedrosian sound as if he were planning another "accident?" Kate wanted to call Lyle. She looked at her watch. It was after midnight in Massachusetts.

☙☙☙

Thursday morning, Lyle sat in his hotel room, looking at the telephone, procrastinating. Steven Travanti had just called him to confirm that everything they'd talked about the day before was set.

It had taken Lyle about a half hour the previous afternoon to persuade Travanti to help him. Although he was sympathetic and had no love for insurance companies, Travanti had, in fact, not been very aggressive in digging for information. The information he provided on Topaz was no more than Lyle had already discovered. Lyle let Travanti off the hook. He told him he didn't have to question people about FedPat or find out anything else. He could, however, just help Lyle with one little idea.

Once Travanti agreed, he and Lyle devoted the rest of the afternoon to setting things up. Lyle was surprised at how easy it was. The hard part would be calling Kate for help.

Finally, he punched in her number.

"Kate? It's Lyle."

"I know. How are things in Boston?"

"I found out everything I can without alerting FedPat any further."

"I don't know how important that is anymore."

"What do you mean?"

"I just listened to another phone recording. Bedrosian is suspicious. He told Kevin not to use his office phone to call him any more. Clyde's men searched Kevin's car twice at the employee entrance."

"I need your help." Lyle blurted it out before he could pause to think. He took a chance. Kate's voice sounded considerate, even warm.

"What can I do?"

"Come to Boston."

"What for?"

"I think we can get the evidence we need, if we get inside FedPat."

"I hate to leave right now. Our big press event is two weeks from tomorrow. How long will this take?"

"Not sure."

Kate was silent.

"Sorry for blowing up at you the other night," he said. "I was tired. You probably think I'm crazy. I know your job is to protect the park."

"It's okay, Lyle. I understand. Now, exactly what do you want me to do?"

Chapter 44

"You know some weird people, Lyle," Kate said three days later.

"Fringe benefit of being an ex-cop. Which person do you mean?"

"Lenny Renaldo."

"Oh, he's harmless."

"Harmless? A convicted felon who still counterfeits money?"

"Is he printing again? I warned him about that."

Kate and Lyle were sitting in the crowded bar at a seafood restaurant in downtown Boston waiting for a dinner table. She had spent five hours on the plane from Phoenix and she was ready for a real meal. Lyle was definitely more upbeat than when she had seen him last.

She gave him a hug when he met her at the airport. And he hugged her back.

Sunday night restaurant patrons were causing such a din it was difficult for Kate and Lyle to hear each other so she was not worried about being overheard. "Lenny wanted to know if I was your girlfriend. Is that what you told him?"

"Nope. He's nosy. I told him you were working with me and needed new identification. You were supposed to get a drivers' license, Social Security card, and anything else Lenny could throw in. Did he come on to you?"

"Mostly just teased. He had to take my picture for the license. He kept one for himself. Stuck it up on the wall."

"Did you get a Massachusetts license?"

"Yes. He said you gave him the name and address to put on it."

"I got you an apartment in an extended-stay hotel."

Kate pulled out her phony license and handed it to Lyle."

"Good name, Jennifer Norris. So, you're older than I thought."

She grabbed the license out of his hand. "Lenny let me pick my age. This is close enough. And thanks for the compliment."

"License looks good. We'll get you a local cell phone tomorrow."

"Did you get me a job as a temp, like you said?"

"Yes. Jennifer has an appointment at the temp agency tomorrow morning."

"Why not use my real name?"

"When you start temping at FedPat, it'll be better if you use another name. There are any number of ways that FedPat people might know you. You're on lists of NC executives. Kevin Waterman knows you. It's safer this way."

"How exactly did you manage this?"

Lyle looked up at the bartender mixing drinks. The clink of glasses and the whir of the blender combined with the voices of 150 Bostonians.

Lyle leaned toward Kate so she could hear him. "Last time I was here I found out FedPat was going to need lots of temps this summer. At the time, I thought it was useless information. But I was thinking like a cop. I don't have to follow police procedures. I can do whatever—like try to get on the inside."

"Or get *me* on the inside."

"Right. This guy I know who works for Boston PD—his wife is a big human resources executive. I figured she might know people at temp agencies. To make a long story short, Steve's wife knew the head of one of the agencies that FedPat uses. Steve and his wife just asked her to do them a favor."

"So once I get there, what do I do? I'm not sure I'm spy material."

"Yes you are." Lyle smiled, brows raised, and nodded.

"So you want me to use my charm on these insurance guys."

"It'll work. Believe me."

"You should've told me this before I left Arizona."

"I did."

Kate returned Lyle's smile. "As long as I don't have to sleep with anybody. Anybody I don't like, anyway."

"Let your conscience be your guide."

"'Cuse me. Did I hear you say you were from Arizona?"

said a middle-aged guy sitting next to Kate. He turned so he could get a better look.

Kate glanced over her shoulder and nodded. She could smell scotch on his breath.

"I was in Phoenix once," he said. "Sure hot there."

"It's a dry heat," she said.

Fortunately, at that moment, Lyle and Kate's table was ready and they moved from the bar.

The guy next to Kate swiveled in his seat to watch her walk by—and slipped off his barstool.

"See what I mean," Lyle said. "You're going to be perfect for this."

A part of Kate was nervous about snooping at the insurance company, but the greater part of her was eager to get started. Her biggest worry was that she wouldn't be able to find the evidence they needed in time. She had only a few days. She and Lyle sat at a table and started checking out the menu.

After her conversation with Lyle Thursday morning, she had made plans quickly. She called Max and told him where she was going, but omitted the fake ID and the fact she was going to be working for FedPat. She said simply that Lyle was close to getting critical evidence, but needed her help. Kate told Max she would keep an eye on Lyle, and Max sounded relieved. Then she called Bruce. They hadn't planned to get together that weekend, but Bruce sounded sulky nonetheless. Kate didn't tell him how long she'd be gone.

Finally, she called Drenda and told her she had to go out of town. She impressed upon her the necessity of the new square being finished in time, saying that press invitations were all ready to go. She also asked Drenda to look in on her apartment while she was gone and feed her cat.

After she visited Renaldo for the fake IDs, she had stopped to see Travis Stringley, Lyle's electronics expert. He had several small boxes of gear for her. "Lyle ordered this stuff," he said. "It's exactly what he needs. He'll explain how it works."

"I have all the eavesdropping equipment," Kate now told Lyle after they placed their dinner order. "Am I going to have to 'wear a wire' as they say on cop shows?"

"Maybe. The one I ordered is real easy to use and practically undetectable. It's just a tiny transmitter. We may not need it, but if you find someone who knows about the attacks on NC, a tape—or the digital recording—will be additional evidence."

"What am I looking for?"

"Anything you can get your hands on. See if you can get into Bedrosian's office."

"I doubt he's going to have an NC-sabotage flow chart on his wall. I'll have to go through his files."

"We need to find a solid connection between FedPat and the hired muscle that's doing the dirty work."

"Do we know who that is?"

Lyle told her about Topaz, Renke, and Art Jones. It sounded promising, but Kate had hoped for a little more damning evidence.

The waiter arrived with their salads and asked Lyle again if he wanted a drink. He ordered a soda.

"What're things like at NC now?" Lyle asked.

"Spooky. Everyone's on edge."

"What'd you hear from Kevin's phone?"

"I told you about his car being searched. Bedrosian mentioned your name again."

"My name?"

"Just asked Kevin if he'd seen you."

"They know about *me*, but they won't expect someone checking them out from the inside. What's Max doing?"

"He gave Clyde one more week to come up with evidence."

Chapter 45

J ennifer?"
Kate heard the name but hesitated a second before she turned around. She'd have to start responding faster to her new identity.

"Can you spell me for my breaks tomorrow? Cindy normally does it," said the wide-eyed brunette. "She won't be back 'til next week."

"Sure, Rachel," Kate said, "if Judy says it's okay. She's the boss."

Rachel was the friendly, if slightly ditsy, receptionist Kate had just met in the FedPat Special Investigations Unit office.

Tired after an unrewarding and draining day, Kate walked out of the office and looked for her rental car in the parking lot. That morning she had met with the head of the temp agency, filled out the paper work, and been assigned to work at FedPat. The assignment she received, however, was not what she expected *or* wanted. She wondered how Lyle would react.

೧ഐ೧

"You're not working downtown?" Lyle said when they met at her apartment that evening.

"The head of the agency—that Mrs. Jackson—tried all she could, but FedPat didn't need anyone downtown right away. It was take a temp job in Peabody, or wait a week."

"Not your fault. Trouble is, most of the big shots—especially Bedrosian—work in Boston." Lyle looked disappointed but not angry. His dark eyebrows sagged. "Shit."

"I do have a little good news." Kate saw Lyle look up. "But only just a little. I'm working in the investigations office. I thought if I couldn't get downtown right away, at least I could be in an office that had something to do with investigators."

"Good thought! Did you just land a lucky assignment?"

"Heck no. They had me in data entry. A dead end. But I just had a little conversation with my boss, Mr. Vaughan—" Kate flashed a provocative smile, "—and he was happy to help me transfer."

"I told you you'd be good at this."

"This is the department that hires the private eye companies. At the reception desk I found a list of the companies they work with and their addresses, phone numbers, and account numbers. Topaz is listed."

"We're getting a *little* closer."

"Hope so, but FedPat is really security conscious. Paranoid would be more like it. Everything has a password. To use any computer, copy machine, or even scanner, you need a password. And they change passwords all the time."

"Do they give passwords to temps?"

"That's the funny part. They're so overprotected, lots of people ignore the rules. They swap passwords and write them on machines so you can use them. And they also have surveillance cameras in all the public areas."

"I remember the cameras," Lyle said.

Chapter 46

B y Thursday afternoon, June twenty-third, Lyle was running out of energy and ideas. He knew little more than when he arrived in Boston the second time. He had spent the morning staking out Topaz again and learned nothing. Yesterday Renke had visited Bedrosian downtown, but no sign of Renke today.

After checking in with Kate on the phone, he knew her Thursday wasn't any better than his. She was stuck in another pointless day of clerical work.

For more than three days, she'd been eavesdropping on conversations and probing computer files while constantly looking over her shoulder, all to no avail. The Fourth of July weekend celebrations started in eight days. Kate would need to get back to the park. It was time to talk to Bedrosian. Lyle had no other option. Was he the mastermind behind the sabotage? If not, he surely knew who was. Max wanted Lyle to lay low, but what did they have to lose now?

In his head, Lyle ran through several approaches he might take. Bedrosian wouldn't be expecting him so he'd have surprise on his side. Should he tell Bedrosian they knew all about the hired muscle and were ready to talk to federal prosecutors? Or should he pretend he didn't suspect Bedrosian and try to trick him into saying something about the sabotage that he shouldn't know about?

He could always threaten him later if that didn't work. Sort of a one-man bad-cop, good-cop routine.

✐✐✐

Lyle marched into Jason Bedrosian's sumptuous office suite. A well-dressed secretary at a glass-topped desk offered him an artificially sincere greeting. Her smile looked as if she'd selected it that morning from a Mrs. Potato Head box and stuck it on.

"I'm sorry Mr. Bedrosian is not in today," she said, even before Lyle had told her his name. "He's not expected back until the middle of next week. He's out of town—out of state actually."

Lyle stared for a moment in disbelief. He took the elevator to the president's office. There, another secretary told him that Shaw too, was gone for several days.

Lyle had pumped himself up to wrestle—verbally or otherwise—with Bedrosian and now he had nowhere to direct his energy. He should have been upset, but he wasn't. Had he just exhausted their last chance to nail FedPat before time ran out?

Instead of driving back to meet Kate, he strolled along the streets of Boston. He passed famous buildings—landmarks of freedom—dating back to the Revolution. Our history was a violent one from the beginning. Guns, killing. He thought about the Vietnam War and how his brother had been drafted. On School Street, he stopped in front of a statue of Benjamin Franklin. Where would he find the statue of Robert McNamara, he wondered—or Donald Rumsfeld for that matter. Lyle glanced at the rubber band on his wrist. No need to pluck it. He wasn't anxious, just introspective.

Meandering back to his car, he pulled out his cell phone and called Earl. Gloom had settled over the park. Earl said he was doing his best to keep things upbeat on the air, but employees were jittery or depressed.

Kate called him when she was on the way home and they met at her apartment.

Lyle waited in the living room while Kate changed clothes for dinner. On a table, Kate had several NC file folders. One read: *Plaza Construction: Confidential.* Naturally, he opened it.

∽∾∽

When Kate walked back in the room, Lyle was leaning over the table and saying something to himself.

Before she could say anything, one of her cell phones chimed. She fumbled in her purse and first pulled out her Boston burner phone. It was silent. Then she grabbed the Arizona phone.

"Max, I just got in. Is everything—what's wrong?" She

stood in the center of the room listening and replying mostly in single syllables, the phone plastered to her ear. "That bastard," she said. Long pause. "Maybe he's desperate. What'd you tell him?"

Even from a distance, Lyle could hear Max snapping out his reply, peppered with obscenities.

"That's okay," Kate said. "Yes, he was right. I picked up some stuff on FedPat today. No, never mind how I got it. We'll explain everything soon. Right now, we need to figure out what to do next. Yes, Lyle's right here. We'll call you."

Kate put away her phone and turned to Lyle. "Bedrosian called Max this morning and offered him a deal. He told him if Max agreed to hand over majority control of the park, he'd give Max a mountain of FedPat stock and promise not to lay off any management staff—including Max—for at least six months."

"That shithead. Did he think he could bribe *Max*?"

"I dunno. Max sank all his money into the park. Bedrosian said if Max agreed to a smooth transition, he could save the park any more bad publicity. He didn't *say* he was causing the sabotage, but that was clearly the message "

"I doubt he's bluffing. Guess Max doesn't think FedPat's his ally now."

"Bedrosian told him if there was another *accident* NC wouldn't be quite so valuable. FedPat's attorneys would simply take Nostalgia City away."

"I thought you said Max could stall a takeover," Lyle said.

"If there's another incident—or if anyone else is killed—Nostalgia City would be a ghost town. Then Max'd be broke and Bedrosian could do whatever he wanted."

"I'm guessing he won't do anything else right now. If he sinks the park, it would be worthless to him or anyone. But at least Bedrosian's out in the open. Now if we could just *prove* he hired Renke to wreck the park."

"Did you see Bedrosian today?" Kate asked.

"No."

಄಄಄

A half hour later, they were walking to a table at a Mexican restaurant. As Kate walked in front of him, he admired her hips, her legs, the way she moved. There was something classical about her, in addition to the obvious.

When they got their drinks—Lyle had iced tea—Kate took a sip of her Margarita, licking the salt on the rim. "I snooped in a lot of computers and files today, but I couldn't find our link. Nobody in investigations seems to communicate with Bedrosian. Too many rungs up the ladder. I'll keep snooping tomorrow."

"We don't have much time left, do we? You'll have to fly home soon."

"The grand opening's in just a week, but tomorrow could be promising."

"Yeah?"

"I'm working with Mary Fish, the assistant to Rich Kovak, an executive VP. He's one of the top two or three people in Peabody. Half the departments, including investigations, report to him. I'll poke around his office and see what I can find."

"Be careful, okay?"

"It's not dangerous. What's the worst they can do, fire me for looking at files I'm not supposed to see?"

"Somebody besides Bedrosian may be involved in this."

"That's what we're trying to find out, isn't it?" Kate paused. "Okay, I see that look. I'll be careful. You sound more worried about me than Bruce is. Of course, he doesn't know everything that's going on. When I call him tonight, I'll spare him the details."

When she mentioned Bruce's name, Lyle got a mental picture of the weight-room Romeo. Was he jealous of Kate's boyfriend? How stupid was that?

"I found someone *you* can talk to tomorrow," Kate said.

"Who?"

"Name's Jeff Innis. He's an insurance investigator. He used to work for FedPat, but was fired. After he left, he got a job working for our friend Joe Renke. But when FedPat found out Innis had gone to work at Topaz, shit hit the fan."

Lyle perked up when he heard the name Renke.

"Topaz was told," Kate said, "that Innis couldn't work on anything related to FedPat. A short time later, Innis was fired from Topaz. This all happened about two months ago."

"That would be before the first sabotage."

"Innis is threatening to sue FedPat for getting him fired at Topaz."

"So how do I find him?"

"I copied down his address and phone number. I saw an old case file of his today and somebody made a joke about him. I just played dumb and asked questions."

"Was that difficult, playing dumb?"

"'Course not. I'm a blonde."

"I noticed."

"Oh, something else. Senior officers are going to be gone for several days at a retreat. That's probably why you missed Bedrosian."

"A retreat?"

"Every year the senior execs get together with the board members for a planning session. They're meeting out in the boondocks. Some remote lodge in northern Maine."

"How long are they gone?"

"The meeting starts sometime Saturday. They don't get back in the office until next Tuesday or Wednesday."

"If all the execs are gone, it could be an opening. Can you make an excuse to visit headquarters?"

"Maybe, but—"

"You have to get back to Arizona."

Kate nodded.

Lyle silently munched a tortilla chip. He reached for another then stopped. "That's why Bedrosian called Max. He's going to this big corporate retreat. He wanted to be able to tell the board that he had Nostalgia City in his pocket."

"Could be. He's probably playing politics, trying to win over more board members.

"Oh, I forgot to tell you," Kate said as they walked out of the restaurant. "On the phone Max said you were right about FedPat."

"Was he surprised?"

"Maybe. But he said he knew he was right to bring you into this. Says he trusts your experience and your judgment."

"Sure he does."

Chapter 47

I really appreciate your help," Mary Fish told Kate Friday morning. "Rachel helps me sometimes, when she can."

Mary Fish, administrative assistant to the FedPat executive vice president, was in her fifties. She had frizzy brown hair streaked with gray and large brown eyes—her best feature.

"These special reports always take time," Mary said. "He likes hard copies to supplement his Power Point presentations." She lowered her voice, though her boss, Rich Kovak, couldn't possibly hear her from the far end of his large, adjoining office. "And usually he decides he wants other articles or statistics at the last minute."

"So he's going off to Maine, too?" Kate asked. She and Mary stood at opposite ends of a long counter in Mary's office, collating reports and inserting them into binders. Mary was attired for the executive suite with a stylish dress and jacket that nearly camouflaged her middle-age spread.

"All senior VPs and above go every year. I think." She kept her voice low. "It's an excuse to get away from the office, to drink, and go fishing. But this time may be different."

"Oh?"

"The CEO is going to retire next year and the board'll have to pick a successor. Mr. Kovak says the people in line for president will be showing off for the board members."

"Is he one of them? Is that what these are for?" Kate asked, indicating the notebooks.

"Oh, no. The three top people work at corporate."

"I've heard people talking. One of them is Bedrosian. Is that his name?"

Mary made a face. "Yes, he's one of them. We all hope he doesn't get it."

"Why's that?"

Mary leaned close to Kate. "He pits people against each other. They brought him in here to help the company boost profits. He started encouraging people to make anonymous reports on employees who wasted company money."

Kate shook her head. "Scary to think of him as CEO."

As they finished assembling the binders, Mary slid the last one into a box. "We're done. I'll tell Mr. K the books are ready. Then I'm going home."

"Going home early?"

Kate was surprised. Mary had been with her virtually every minute that morning and she had not had time to spy.

"Mr. K will be off for Maine now. He gives me a day or two off when he leaves for these meetings. I don't have to come back 'til Tuesday." Mary arranged a stack of papers and folders on the counter. "These have to be organized and re-filed. I'll do it next week."

"I can do it for you. I told them in investigations that I'd probably be here all morning."

"That's sweet of you."

After a few minutes, Kovak picked up his binders and left. Kate wished Mary a good weekend as she walked out.

"Just turn out the lights and close my door when you go, okay?" Mary said.

With Mary gone, the office was still. Kate listened. She could make out the sound of far-off voices and the low hum of Mary's computer. She didn't know whether to shut the door or not. She decided to leave it open, for the time being, as she searched Mary's files.

At the back of the office, at a right angle to the work counter, stood a tall lateral file cabinet. Kate started with the top drawer first so she didn't have to bend down. Mary didn't exactly keep her tightly packed files neatly organized. Kate couldn't discern any order to the arrangement and she had to stick her fingers inside and spread the folders apart to scan the contents. After several days of searching through, files she'd become an efficient office sleuth. She worked quickly, looking for correspondence files or anything else that might relate to outside PI firms.

She found nothing promising in the top file so she pushed it closed with a thud and pulled open the next drawer. It was no better organized than the previous one. When she pulled open the last drawer she had to squat down to comb through the folders. She found a file labeled "Contractors – Legal." When she yanked it out of the drawer, pages popped out and slid across the floor.

She reached out to gather them up and suddenly realized someone was in the room with her. She glanced around and saw shoes right behind her. Someone was looking over her shoulder.

☙❧☙

Jeff Innis opened the door to his apartment as if he was expecting trouble. He jerked it open and stood so the door hid most of his body. Lyle almost reached for his nonexistent holster.

"You Lyle Deming?" Innis asked.

Lyle nodded and Innis stepped back, opening the door wider.

Earlier that morning Lyle had called Innis and told him that he was an investigator and wanted to ask him some questions about FedPat. Without giving away too much, he'd been able to arouse Innis's curiosity.

Innis offered Lyle the couch while he sat on the edge of a chair opposite. He wore a sport shirt tucked into casual slacks. He didn't appear to have a gun, something Lyle unconsciously looked for.

In his late thirties or early forties, Innis was thin, but looked able to handle himself. He had an almost gaunt face and close-cropped hair.

"So, why're you investigating FedPat?"

"Long story. I represent a corporate client that's interested in FedPat and its relationship with Topaz Investigations."

"Why ask me?"

"Since you worked for both companies, I thought you might be able to give me a little insight, especially about Topaz."

Innis had not relaxed his body. "How'd you find me?"

"I'm a good investigator."

"You a cop?"

Lyle chuckled and shook his head. "Nope. Not any more, thank God. You're pretty good, too."

Innis leaned back in his chair. "Look, I'm suing the assholes at FedPat. I'm not supposed to be talking to anyone about this."

"This has nothing to do with your being fired. I'm working for an out-of-state corporation that's getting screwed by FedPat.

We think they're using Topaz to help them. Can you tell me something about Topaz?

"What do you want to know?"

"What kind of work does Topaz do for FedPat?"

"Investigate claims looking for fraud."

"Individuals?"

"Sometimes, and businesses. Say someone is injured in an accident at work. They tell the company they're disabled. Can't work. So we follow them around for a while, watch them play golf or go bowling. People're stupid. They think we can't check up on them."

Innis had an accent Lyle couldn't place. Boston, but with a rough edge to it.

"What else do they do?"

"Surveillance, background checks, whatever. When I worked at FedPat we used to use Topaz—and other companies— to help out when we got swamped. FedPat managed the cases. Topaz did legwork."

"How about *breaking* legs?"

"You think Topaz does that?"

Lyle just looked at Innis. He noticed two large brown moles below his left ear.

"I didn't have nothin' to do with that. I just worked on legal evidence. Joe liked his guys to do whatever was necessary, but I never did that. And I didn't know he was like that when I went to work there. You working for him?"

"No. I'm working for a corporation, like I told you."

"Well, you know what? I don't care if Joe sent you here. He already knows what I think of him. He fired me because FedPat told him to. He's a lying son of a bitch." Innis got up.

"Mr. Innis, take it easy." Lyle raised a hand. "I'm sorry, but I'm not checking up on your personal situation. Keep all that to yourself. I just want to know a little more about Topaz and Joe Renke."

Innis walked toward the front door. Lyle stood up but didn't move. He had a hunch. "Were you a cop, too?"

Innis turned around. "Yeah. Long time ago. In Worcester." He walked slowly toward the kitchen. "You want some coffee?"

Chapter 48

W hat're you doing in here?"
Kate looked up to see who was standing over her. When she saw Rachel's smile, she grinned back at the receptionist, gathered up the folder she was reaching for, and stood up. "I'm finishing up some filing for Mary. We did notebooks for Mr. K."

"That's right, Mary told me. I was too busy." Rachel wore a dress that was a little slinky for the office. Maybe the investigators liked it. She had an engaging smile. "I'm on break now. Can you cover the desk for me?"

"Uh, sure." Kate didn't want to tell Rachel that Mary was gone. She might lose the chance to dig into Mary's and Rich Kovak's computers. She stuffed the file she was holding into the drawer, pushed it shut with a foot, and followed Rachel out of Mary's office.

"Mr. K's lights are off," Rachel said. "Is he gone already?"

"Not sure."

Kate didn't like this line of conversation. Fortunately, she didn't have to pursue it because Rachel headed down the hall and Kate stopped at the reception desk. As the minutes ticked away, Kate hoped her boss didn't happen by to ask if she was finished helping Mary. To her relief, in fifteen minutes, Rachel rushed back into the office and Kate headed back down the hall.

Mary's door was still open. It looked as if the executive vice president's assistant was still at work. Kate quickly retrieved the contractors file she'd found and started going through the pages. It contained lists of companies that did business with FedPat, the present status of each company, and reports of complaints and lawsuits. She noticed the name Topaz. This could be useful, but she'd have to copy the file, and the nearest copy machine was around the corner.

She put the file on the desk and sat in front of Mary's computer. Mary had showed her the drawer where she kept the current passwords.

"It's so damn confusing," Mary had said. "Some passwords change monthly, some don't. You're always being reminded to change your password. I write them all down here."

Mary used the last names of old movie stars for her passwords and she kept track of them all, using names over again in a regular pattern. This month's password was *Bogart*.

Kate hurried to click the search function. She punched in her search words, *Topaz*, *Renke*, and *Bedrosian*. She felt slightly nervous, but not as much as she would be when she sat in front of Kovak's computer. That was next.

The search yielded several documents with Bedrosian's name on them, a few with *Topaz*, none with *Renke*. She pulled out a flash drive, stuck it in a USB port and quickly copied all the files. She sent two of the most promising looking files to the printer. Without wasting time, she pulled out the flash drive, let the documents print, and walked into Kovak's office, flipping on the light. Fortunately, anyone passing Mary's office would have to lean inside to see if Kovak's light was on.

Kate was glad that Mary also kept written track of Kovak's passwords, and she opened his computer files as easily as if they were her own. This time her search routine paid dividends. She found more than two dozen documents with Bedrosian's name, a few with Topaz, and two with Bedrosian *and* Renke.

She felt her heart beat faster. She could easily have been afraid, but she told herself the feeling wasn't fear, just excitement. It was a technique she'd used before college basketball games, and it still kicked in when she needed it. She glanced up through the open door into Mary's office, then back to the computer screen. Using her flash drive again, she copied the files. Unplugging the flash drive, she was about to log off the computer. But she couldn't resist reading the documents that had both Bedrosian's *and* Renke's names. A few clicks and the email memo appeared on the screen.

Kate read rapidly, disappointed at first, then—there it was. She read it again to be sure. "Yes," she said, banging the mouse on the desk.

The noise echoed in the empty room. Then another noise

came from Mary's office. She looked up. A man stood in the doorway.

"Can I help you?" Kate said, congratulating herself on her poise, not knowing how she managed it.

"I'm looking for Mr. Kovak," the young man in a suit said. His voice was measured, his actions precise.

"He's gone for the day."

"He left *already*?"

"The retreat."

"Yes, I know. I needed him to approve something for me."

The young man held sheets of paper in his hand. He raised them up and shook them slightly for emphasis. As they talked, Kate closed the file she'd been looking at and prepared to log off the computer.

The young man took two steps into the office. "I don't see Mary. Is she around?"

"Uh, no."

He took another two steps into the office and the pleasant look faded from his face.

"Pardon me, but who are you and why are you into Mr. K's computer?"

❧❧❧

Lyle picked up a hot cup of coffee in Jeff Innis's kitchen and headed back to the living room.

"So, about Renke's strong-arm tactics," Lyle said. "He's been using them on my client's people, big time, with serious injuries."

"He's been investigated for that kind of shit."

"Was he working for FedPat at the time?"

"Yeah, but it wasn't a FedPat case. We never suggested violence. Least I never did. No reason for it."

"What's his background?"

"Army. Special Forces. He always brought that up. Never told anyone his rank or even if he was honorably discharged."

"You suspect something?"

"Didn't at first, but one day two of us were doing surveillance. You know how that is. You spend hours and hours with nothing to do, so you talk. This other guy was telling me how he and Renke and some others did overseas work for a U.S. corporation."

Innis ran a hand over the back of his neck and touched his moles with a finger. "Can't remember the name of the company. They were competing to get a contract with a Latin-American government. Renke and his guys went down there to discourage competition."

"What'd they do?"

"Guy who told me this was full of shit, but if even half of what he said was true, it means Renke's men took out a few people and blamed it on local insurgents. Renke's client got the contract."

Lyle shook his head. "That kind of work pays pretty well, doesn't it?"

"Renke's saving up his dough. He talked about retiring to some island."

"Out of reach of the U.S. Government."

"Guess so."

"If Renke's such a bad dude, aren't you lucky you're out of there?"

Innis shrugged. "Yeah. That guy has a bad temper and he's unpredictable."

"Great combination."

Innis let out a string of obscenities until his voice trailed off.

❧❧❧

"I'm Jennifer," Kate said. "Jennifer Norris. I'm helping Mary on a project."

She stood, casually putting her hand—and the flash drive—into her pocket. Then she walked toward the man who now stood in the middle of Kovak's office.

"Where do you work," he asked, "administration? I haven't seen you before."

"I'm in SIU." She used the company shorthand for Special Investigations Unit and tried to make it sound as if that explained everything.

"You were using Mr. Kovak's computer."

"Yes."

"That violates our security. He doesn't let anybody work on his computer."

"Yes, he does. Mary sometimes gets information from it. Mary and I are collating reports. I needed the last page." Kate pegged the young man as an aggressive corporate ladder-climber ready to step on her if it helped get him ahead.

"But—"

Kate walked past him into Mary's office. She hoped she had the upper hand and could bully her way through if necessary. She paused next to Mary's desk. The documents she had printed were sitting in the tray and the contractors' file folder sat on the desk.

"Everybody is supposed to follow security procedures," the young man said. "I don't know who you are. I'm going to report—"

Just then, Kate's boss walked by.

"Are you about done in here, Jennifer?" she asked.

"Just got a couple of things and I'm finished. I'll be back before lunch."

Kate's boss obviously recognized her would-be accuser. "Hey Paul," she said. "How you doin'?"

Paul glanced at Kate. "Okay, Judy. I just missed Mr. Kovak. I needed his signature."

As her boss left, Kate turned her back on the young man. She busied herself at the counter. After a minute, she turned around. He was gone.

Immediately, Kate collected the documents she'd printed from Mary's computer, then photocopied the file-cabinet pages she'd set aside.

She turned off the lights and followed a zigzag course through the labyrinth of offices and corridors. She wanted to get to the parking lot and her car without passing by the SIU office. She locked the flash drive and stack of memos in her glove box. She could hardly wait to show Lyle.

Chapter 49

Lyle sat in his car outside the copy shop, waiting for Kate to show up. He'd suggested they visit a copy place near downtown. It was Saturday morning June twenty-fifth, and he figured the horrendous Boston traffic would be slightly abated during the weekend. He wanted to have lunch in an historic part of town and show Kate where the FedPat building was.

On the phone, Kate had told him only that she "had the link" they were looking for and that she needed to scan, print, and burn a CD.

When Kate pulled up next to Lyle's car, he looked over and tried to read her expression. She looked solemn. Then she winked at him and a broad smile transformed her face. She dangled her thumb drive from its chain as she got out of the car. "This is it," she said. "Wish I had a portable printer. I'd like paper copies of some of this, but we'd still have to come here to scan the documents."

A few minutes later—their heads side by side in front of a computer screen—they stared at a FedPat email. It was written by Rich Kovak, executive vice president, Peabody Operations, to Jason Bedrosian, Chief Operating Officer. Dated about three months before, the memo began by acknowledging Bedrosian's request for a recommendation for a private investigation firm that was "willing to undertake unusual assignments" and do so with the "utmost confidentiality."

The copy shop was empty except for a woman laboriously clicking a computer keyboard in another corner of the room. Lyle saw Kate glance over her shoulder anyway as they read. The essential portion of the memo said:

In response to your request, I have asked our investigation staff and they recommend Topaz Investiga-

*tions. This is a local firm that has done considerable
work for us before and I'm told would be able to handle
an extended out-of-state assignment.*

*Topaz is a small firm and apparently its president,
Joe Renke, does work for us himself. He's handled difficult situations in the past, including the Summit, New
Jersey case, so it seems he's quite versatile. You should
call Renke himself. His number is listed below.*

"Looks good. Where'd you get it?"

"I copied it right off Rich Kovak's computer. It ties Bedrosian to Renke. It's our missing link, right?"

"I've seen Renke and *he* looks more like the missing link. I
wish Kovak had been more specific."

"I guess 'out of state' could mean Connecticut or New
York."

"Or Arizona. What else do you have?"

"There's another email later than the first one." Kate clicked
the mouse and another inter-office message appeared on the
screen.

Jason,

*I'm going to be at corporate on Wednesday and
would like to stop in and see you. I have recently heard
about some problems with the investigations firm I referred you to in March.*

*I have serious concerns about this firm and its re-
lationship with FedPat. We need to discuss Mr. Renke's
tactics and his current projects immediately.*

Rich

"So, Kovak figured out that Renke's a thug," Lyle said.
"According to Innis, violence is one of Renke's regular services."

"I wonder what Kovak said to Bedrosian."

"Sounds like he was trying to warn him. Maybe he found out
what Renke's been doing."

"Regardless, these memos tie Bedrosian to Topaz."

"They're perfect. You did a great job."

"I've also got memos and reports about Topaz." She showed
Lyle the printed copies. "We need to scan these. One of the re-

ports mentions that New Jersey case. I think Joe may have used, shall we say, unconventional means to persuade a policy holder to settle a case out of court."

"That's Renke."

"I want to print out copies of the emails, scan the reports, and then make a backup CD of everything."

⍦⍦⍦

A half hour later they were sauntering along a broad side-walk in Quincy Market, an open-air shopping and dining area near the harbor. The air carried the scent of mustard, suntan lo-tion, and the sea. "What's our next move?" Kate asked.

"I'd like to confront Bedrosian right now with the evidence we have."

"That'd be a little difficult."

"I know. He's in...where?"

"The middle of the north woods in Maine."

"The retreat."

"They go every year to this isolated lodge. Apparently, you have to fly a puddle jumper then drive for an hour or so. There's no phone service in the cabins and cell phones don't even work up there."

"We can't wait for them to come back. There must be some-thing we can do." He stared at the crowd of wandering vacation-ers carrying shopping bags, cameras, cold drinks, and children. "If we just had a little more proof," he said, "we could go to the Feds or the district attorney."

"We ought to talk to Max. Maybe we already have enough for his attorneys to deal with."

"At least we emailed a copy of the evidence back to Arizo-na. Just in case."

"I need to get back there myself."

Lyle didn't want to think about that. He and Kate flowed with the crowds toward the waterfront where sailboats glided across the bay. He stopped to take a picture for a Japanese family posed in front of a boat. When he finished, he turned and looked at Kate. She was leaning against a piling and trying in vain to keep her hair from blowing. A golden cascade of hair caressed the side of her face. They walked to the end of Boston's famous Long

Wharf then headed back. Lyle glanced at the sleek catamaran excursion boat moored at the dock. *Beantown to P-town* said a sign on the ticket booth. A few steps farther along he saw a street vendor and bought two ice cream bars.

"You don't have your rubber band today," Kate said, pointing her ice cream at Lyle's wrist. "What's it for?"

"To help me relax, get rid of stress. It broke yesterday. I'm living dangerously."

"Speaking of stress…'

"Hmm?"

"You ought to cut yourself some slack. Look at all the things that have happened in your life in the last year—in the last two weeks. You'd score really high on those stress quizzes you see in magazines."

"Enough for a rubber room?"

"I'm serious, Lyle. Give yourself a break."

He started to make a remark. Instead, he put his arm around Kate's waist and gave her a squeeze. "Thanks."

They meandered back to the center of Quincy Market and paused to watch jugglers perform in the sunny square. As he stood there, an idea jumped into his head, like the juggler's ball flying through the air. The idea might not work, and it could be dangerous—it *would* be dangerous. But with luck, he and Kate could pull it off and be back in Arizona with the evidence to convict Bedrosian and Renke and put FedPat out of business.

Chapter 50

Kate woke up Sunday morning in her apartment, wishing Lyle was closer by. He had calmed down on Saturday and she had seen a Lyle who was more like the man she'd met when she first started at NC and less like the frantic person who threw around accusations. After a week pretending to be Jennifer Norris, she had unwound, too. A surprisingly enjoyable afternoon, Kate thought, considering their unfinished business.

She called Bruce several times during the evening, the last time just before she went to sleep. It was early Las Vegas time, but her conversations were only with Bruce's voicemail. If Bruce wanted to talk to her now—he had the number.

Kate stretched and welcomed the sun that was streaming in through the window. She knew she'd have to fly back to Arizona, but the day before, an idea had come to her. She'd thought about it as she fell asleep. Everything she'd learned about FedPat would help her pull it off. It might not be possible, but if it were, their case against FedPat would be tight as a straitjacket.

❧❧❧

"Okay, Lyle. You go first," she said later in the morning when her espionage partner came over to tell her he had an idea.

They were sitting in the dining area of her extended-stay suite.

"Let's look at what we know—what we can prove," Lyle said. "NC's been sabotaged. An Arizona ex-con with a history of violence is working with Topaz. Topaz and its president, Joe Renke, also have a history of violence. Jason Bedrosian hired Renke. Bedrosian told Kevin Waterman that after one more accident, he'd take over the park. Then Bedrosian threatened Max and tried to buy him out. It sounds convincing to us, but it's all circumstantial. If that idiot Bates had been able to find any evidence—fingerprints or whatever—then we could have connected Renke to the park."

Kate nodded. She'd had the same thoughts, but this time she was more convinced than Lyle that the evidence was compelling.

"So, to really wrap up the case," Lyle continued, "and stop the sabotage, we need to get someone to confess. Fat chance of that, right? What's the next best thing?"

"We trick someone into telling us the whole story?"

"Hold on. Listen to my idea."

"Okay," Kate said. "Go ahead."

"We trick someone into telling us the whole story."

Kate laughed. "Joe Renke, right?"

"He's the only one in town—we hope he's in town."

"So I think you should tape him while I try to pull the secrets out of him," she said.

"And how are you going to do that?"

"With finesse and subtlety."

"I don't think Renke does subtlety."

"Well then, maybe I'll try…getting to know him."

"Too dangerous. Besides, you're the FedPat employee. You have to introduce him to me."

"But I don't know him."

"You will. We both will, if we're lucky."

Lyle opened up the box he brought with him and pulled out a small desk calculator. "I don't know if Travis showed you any of this, but this little gem here works perfectly." He added two plus two. The display read: Four. "Who says I can't do math? This device is also a microphone and transmitter. We set this on the desk, like so, and you can be in the next room recording everything. We could just use a miniature recorder instead, but this way you can listen and be a backup witness as it happens."

"How are you going to get Renke to—as they say—spill it?"

"I'm smarter than he is," Lyle said.

"I suspect that's not a difficult statement to make."

"Let's not underestimate him. This is not going to be easy." He pulled out a small receiver and digital recorder and started to show Kate how they worked.

"I think I can figure it out," she said defensively. "I had to disconnect our recorder on Kevin's phone line."

"You did? Why?"

"Max ordered Bates to do a sweep of the building looking for bugs. Don't worry. They didn't find it. And when they were done, I hooked it back up. We're still recording."

***

They spent the rest of the afternoon hashing out their plan, playing devil's advocate until they thought they'd covered every dire possibility.

"Once we get the evidence, we'll have to move fast," Lyle said after they'd killed their second pot of coffee.

"We head for home?"

"Yes. But if we get Renke to cop to everything, we could talk to Boston PD first."

"Max'll want us back there."

"Speaking of Max…"

"I know. It's time to give him an update. Here." She handed him her cell phone. "Why don't *you* call him? You were supposed to be keeping in touch with him, anyway."

"Guess he didn't fire me."

"Ask him and see."

Lyle took the cell phone and pretended to fiddle with a knob. "Open channel D," he said with a smirk.

"That's not *Star Trek*, is it?"

"Heck no. It's from *The Man from U.N.C.L.E.*"

"The what?"

"A spy program on TV."

"Lyle, you know way too much trivia."

"No kidding. I can't get it out of my head. I can't remember the license plate on my cab, but I can remember who played Jethro on *The Beverly Hillbillies*."

"Don't tell me. I don't want to know."

Chapter 51

Kate was at her FedPat cubicle early Monday morning. She'd rehearsed the call as she drove to work. She used the phone on her desk.

If Renke had caller ID, he'd see she was calling from Fed-Pat.

"Is Mr. Renke in?" She took a breath and hoped.

"Who shall I say is calling?"

Kate was relieved but excited. She reminded herself that the feeling was excitement—nothing more—and she waited for Renke to come on the line.

"Mr. Renke? This is Jennifer Norris with FedPat. I'm calling for Mr. Rich Kovak. He'd like to see you this morning. As soon as possible."

"This morning?"

"I know it's short notice, but he said it was urgent."

"I've heard of Mr. Kovak, but I don't know him."

That was just what Kate was waiting to hear. Renke didn't know Kovak. "He's executive vice president for Peabody operations." She tried to put a touch of arrogance into her voice as if she wouldn't even be making a call for someone lower than executive VP.

"Can you tell me what it's about?" Renke sounded annoyed.

"He didn't say. He just said to tell you Mr. Bedrosian told him to set up the meeting."

"Bedrosian, huh? All right. I can be there about 10 o'clock. That okay?"

"That'll be fine. Mr. Kovak's office can be difficult to find. Just come to the Special Investigations reception desk and someone will direct you."

When he hung up, Kate called Lyle. "It worked," she said. "He'll be here at ten."

"That's great. On such short notice he won't have time to think about it or try to check out Kovak."

"And if he tries to call Bedrosian, he won't get him."

"So far, so good. Meet you there at 9:45. That's cutting it close, but I don't want to loiter in the office too long."

ഇരുഇ

When Kate stepped out a side door to the office complex, Lyle was just getting out of his car. She smiled to herself as she watched him approach. He wore a gray suit and looked the part of a corporate executive but, for a split second, she imagined him with his cabbie hat perched on the back of his head.

"Good timing," she said. "We're all set. I put the calculator on the table in Kovak's office and I have the receiver set up in a conference room across the hall."

It was only about a thirty-five-yard walk, down a hallway and past a small cubicle maze, to get to Kovak's office. As they passed a surveillance camera, Kate saw Lyle turn his head away. He looked uncomfortable.

"There's something I haven't told you," he said as they approached Kovak's office.

"Something I have to know, now?"

"Renke saw me once."

"Where?"

"FedPat elevator. Downtown."

Kate and Lyle reached Mary Fish's desk and Kate led him through to Kovak's office. She turned on the light and Lyle looked around the room. Kate told him the door at the back of the office led to a hallway. A round table sat in one corner, ringed by four chairs. Kate pointed to the calculator sitting on the table next to a stack of papers.

"We should test the equipment before you go," he said.

"Okay. Give me a minute, then sit down and start mumbling to yourself."

"I'm good at that."

Kate walked across the corridor and into a seldom-used meeting room. At one end of a conference table, away from the door, she had her briefcase, a pad of paper, and a couple of files. The files were just for show. In the briefcase were the receiver and recorder. She held an earphone up to one ear, flipped on the receiver, and listened.

Lyle, indeed, was mumbling, but the sound was as loud as if he were sitting next to her. Kate switched off the receiver, stepped across the hall, and leaned into the office. She gave Lyle a "thumbs-up" sign, started to leave, then paused. "If Renke remembers you, it'll help. It makes sense you would be downtown sometimes."

Lyle nodded and waved a hand.

Kate looked at her watch. Five minutes to go. She had to be at the reception desk before Renke arrived. She ducked out of Mary Fish's office, grateful not to see anyone she knew, and headed toward reception. When she got there, she chatted with Rachel.

In less than two minutes, a brawny man she'd never seen before entered the reception area. Kate had helped publicize many prizefights in Vegas and she knew a boxer's nose when she saw one. In spite of his business suit, Kate could see he was powerfully built. Only her heels gave her a height advantage. He made no pretext about looking her over. Then he looked past Kate and spoke to Rachel. "I'm Renke. I've got an appointment with Rich Kovak."

"I'm not sure," Rachel said. "I don't know if—"

"I can take you back," Kate said. She looked at Rachel. "He's here. I saw him." She asked Renke to follow her.

When they had taken a few steps down the hallway, Renke spoke. "Kovak's not supposed to be here today. He was at a conference in Maine."

"Yes, I know." Kate was startled but tried to sound only marginally interested. "There's a management retreat every year."

"I called before I came over," Renke said. "They told me Kovak was expected back this morning sometime."

Kovak coming back? Now what? Kate had but a few seconds to think. How could she warn Lyle about Kovak without alerting Renke? She decided she couldn't. "Here's the office," she said.

Renke stood in the doorway while Kate took two steps toward Lyle. He sat behind the desk holding a pen and looking busy.

"Mr. Kovak, Mr. Renke is here to see you."

"Show him in."

Kate backed away as Lyle got up from behind his desk to shake Renke's hand.

"Why don't we sit over here?" Lyle said, motioning toward the table and chairs. "It's more comfortable."

Kate left the office and moved swiftly to the conference room. She clicked on the receiver and recorder then slid the briefcase and her papers to the other end of the table so she could see the entrance to Mary's office. If Kovak showed up, she'd jump up and catch his attention, maybe lure him into the conference room. She'd think of something.

When she picked up the earphone, she could hear Lyle talking.

"I was at a retreat. I came back so I could talk to you about this."

"What's the hurry?"

"Well, Jason—Mr. Bedrosian—is concerned about the next steps you're going to take at Nostalgia City. Wanted me to talk to you right away."

Kate waited, listening to the silence. Would Renke acknowledge Nostalgia City?

Finally, he spoke. "I been working directly for Bedrosian. This is not just another company matter."

"I know," Lyle said. "Obviously the fewer people involved, the better."

"I've only dealt with him. Now you're telling me I'm working for you, too?"

"Of course, you're still working for him. He couldn't get away, and he was concerned that someone go over the details with you once more, before it's too late."

Kate could hear a trace of exasperation in Lyle's last statement. He was applying just the right pressure to get Renke to open up. Again, silence.

"Okay, we can go over this, but let's get some coffee."

"Uh, sure." Lyle's voice lost a little of its assurance. "I'll call Jennifer."

"No. I want some espresso. The espresso bar in the cafeteria here's pretty good. We can talk over there."

"I suppose we can find a corner somewhere. We have to be careful."

It took Kate only a moment to realize Lyle probably didn't know how to get to the employee cafeteria.

Chapter 52

Lyle stood up, wondering where in hell he was going to go. As he walked out of the office, he forced himself not to glance back at the calculator. Lyle had recognized Renke as the guy he'd seen with Art Jones. He motioned for Renke to lead the way, hoping he could simply follow. As they stepped into the hallway, Renke held back.

Suddenly, Kate was right in front of them. She caught Lyle's eye then looked to the right. Lyle took the hint and directed Renke down the hall.

"Are you going for coffee?" she asked. "I'm going on break. I could bring you something from the cafeteria."

Renke was just ahead of Lyle. He didn't turn around or respond to Kate's offer.

Lyle gave Kate a long look then shrugged. "Thanks. We'll get it on our own."

Kate made brief eye contact with Lyle again then, swinging her briefcase, took brisk steps past Lyle and Renke. Lyle saw that she would lead him to the cafeteria.

He didn't realize until Kate led them the length of the building, then through one of the enclosed walkways, that the cafeteria was in the adjoining building. When they entered the cafeteria, they were greeted by an aroma like boiled chicken. Lyle figured he could find the way on his own, but then he saw the sprawling facility—a sea of tables and chairs, a serpentine buffet counter, and several service islands. Where was the coffee bar? Just follow Kate.

She ordered plain coffee, nodded to Lyle and Renke, and then disappeared.

"Nice ass," Renke said.

He ordered something that looked like motor oil. Lyle got a latte.

Two dozen employees were scattered around the room talking and sipping coffee. Lyle saw an isolated table for two in front of a window. As he led the way, he wondered if Renke had insisted on the cafeteria because he was worried about being recorded. No way to tell. If Renke was nervous in Kovak's office, maybe he'd loosen up in the cafeteria.

When they were seated across the table from each other, Renke sat in silence. So much for loosening up. In the light from the window, Lyle took in Renke's face. He'd seen the expression before: eyes that held, not defiance, just latent antagonism toward what, everything? Dense stubble darkened his heavy jaw. He probably needed a shave twenty minutes after he'd put down a razor. His lips were more insolent than Mick Jagger's.

"What you've done up to now at Nostalgia City has been okay," Lyle ventured. "But we're coming to a crucial decision soon. In other words, things are coming to a head." Lyle sounded as wishy-washy as a bureaucrat, and he meant to. He didn't want to lead Renke too much. A holdover from hearing defense attorneys cry entrapment. "We want to be careful."

"So what's this have to do with wrecking the steam train?"

"Steam train?"

"Bedrosian said the new railroad would start this week."

"That's the information we have."

"Well, I'm supposed to be ready to disable the train if necessary."

Lyle just stared.

"Well, do you want us to stop it or not? Bedrosian said to be ready. Said he'd call us in Arizona if he wanted us to do it."

Lyle responded with the first thing he thought of. "We think it might be too dangerous now."

"Too dangerous?" Renke put his cup down on the table with a crack. "What is this shit? He didn't think it was too dangerous when we trashed that monorail or the gas station."

Renke was talking too loud. Obviously, he had lost his apprehensions about discussing his dirty work. Lyle needed to keep him from alerting everyone in the cafeteria.

"Keep it down will you." As Lyle spoke, he noticed Renke had attracted the attention of a few men sitting several tables away. When one of the employees turned around, Lyle saw the familiar face of Strother Martin—the claims clerk. Did he recognize Lyle? Maybe not, but if Renke kept raising his voice…

Lyle looked back at Renke and glared.

"Okay. I'll keep it down. But I want to know if Bedrosian wants us to stop the train or not, dammit."

"Well, is there another way?"

"Another way to do what? Look, Bedrosian wasn't upset before, even when we whacked that old man."

Lyle's stomach twisted into a knot.

"Bedrosian told me someone here was getting suspicious," Renke said, "worried about what we were doing. That's not *you*, is it?" Renke looked menacing.

Lyle worked to keep his voice steady. "Hell no. You want to know why I'm concerned—why Jason is concerned? We don't want to scare everyone off. We don't want to destroy the park, *and* we don't want anyone to know we're doing it."

"That's what Bedrosian said. And we done a good job 'til now. Better than those Indians you hired. They almost got caught."

"I wasn't involved with that."

"They were amateurs. We know how to handle ourselves."

"Except…"

"Except we screwed up when we tried to bug Deming's place. I know. Guys who did it didn't know the old man was there. Look, I explained everything to Bedrosian. He was okay with it."

"You never did plant any bugs."

"Why'd Bedrosian need bugs anyway? He's got a guy on the inside. What more's he want?"

"Do you understand why we're doing this?"

"Bedrosian didn't say, but I have an idea. I've heard talk. Bedrosian wants to be the next president of FedPat. Must tie in someplace."

Lyle nodded. "So we *don't* want to trash the park. No more damage."

"We done okay. Messed up some rides like Bedrosian wanted."

Lyle had heard enough. Clearly, Bedrosian knew what Renke was doing. Bedrosian paid him for sabotage and murder. Lyle wanted to ask about Kevin Waterman, then he'd end their talk.

As he started to ask Renke a question, he saw the nearby employees finish their coffee and get up. Strother Martin turned around and looked directly at Lyle. Instinctively, Lyle shaded his face with his hand, belatedly making it look as if he were scratching his forehead. He silently cursed himself for the awkward move. The squinty-eyed clerk elbowed the guy next to him. He pointed toward Lyle and said something. The other man laughed. The group stood talking for a moment. Lyle decided it was a good time to leave.

He put down his latte and looked at his watch. "Can we go? I've got a meeting."

Renke got up when Lyle did, and the two walked slowly back the way they'd come in. "You still didn't answer my question," Renke said. "What the *fuck* do you want me to do?"

Lyle looked over his shoulder at the FedPat employees. They seemed to be headed out the same exit. "Okay," Lyle said. "Just sit tight. Wait for more instructions."

"We had a deal and I got half in advance." Renke's words escaped through clenched teeth.

"We'll pay you the full amount. Just call off your men in Arizona."

"Okay." Renke shook his head slowly and took a few steps toward the outside door. "I know my way around here," he said and walked off.

Lyle walked to the nearest outside entrance lobby. There was no one around. "Kate," he said, "I hope you're still listening. I think it's time to go. I hope you got everything. I'm standing at the cafeteria exit on the south side. I'm going to find my car. Are you close by? Someone recognized me."

Chapter 53

Kate emerged from the cafeteria and caught up with Lyle in the parking lot.

"Got it all," she said. "Good thing you decided to wear the microphone as a backup."

"Just being careful." Lyle looked over his shoulder. "Were you nearby?"

"In the ladies room with my briefcase on my lap—if you get the picture."

"You're a regular Agent 99."

"Sounds like a cleaning solution."

Lyle shook his head.

"Get going," Kate said. "I'll go back and grab the calculator in Kovak's office. We got what we needed. I should bail out of here today. I didn't get a chance to tell you, but Renke called here this morning and found out that Kovak is really coming in today."

"*Now* you tell me."

"I didn't have time."

"In that case, you *should* leave."

"Let me retrieve the calculator and my purse. What's the next step? I need to get back to the park."

"Not sure. That recording is strong evidence. We can get Renke arrested and maybe get the Boston PD to detain Bedrosian when he returns. We could deal with FedPat later from Arizona. We'll talk about it, decide what to do."

Kate crossed the parking lot and headed for Kovak's office. She wondered how she'd recover the calculator-transmitter if the executive vice president was back. When she was nearing the administration area, she heard her name—her assumed name.

"Jennifer!"

Rachel stopped Kate in her tracks. "Jennifer, where've you been? Judy's really mad. I told her I thought you were on break, but it's been over a half hour. She says you didn't finish the reports."

As Rachel talked, Kate looked far down the hall. She saw Joe Renke come out of Kovak's office. He looked up and down but didn't notice her. He headed out, hastily, in the other direction.

"Are you listening, Jennifer?" Rachel said.

"Uh, yeah. I'm listening." Kate's first thought was to get out of there, but she needed her purse.

"So where've you been?"

"In the bathroom. Over at the cafeteria."

"Are you sick?"

"Yes. It's...my stomach. Bad cramps." Kate pulled a face. "I think I got a bug."

"Oh, sorry. You should go tell Judy."

"I will."

Kate headed down the hall. Instead of going into Kovak's office, she walked into the conference room to grab her purse. Then with her briefcase in her left hand, her purse in the other, she walked across the hall. She paused at Mary's desk. The lights were still on in Kovak's office. Hoping against hope he wasn't there, she walked in.

At first, she didn't see him, and she felt relieved. Then she gagged and almost threw up. Sprawled across the floor behind his desk, Kovak lay motionless. A red volcano had erupted in the top of his head. Blood flowed down the side of his face. The object that caused the crater was an obelisk sculpture Kate had noticed before. It lay on the desk, part of Kovak's scalp stuck to the top. Obviously, he was not alive.

Kate turned sharply to look around the room. Empty. As if on autopilot, she walked a few steps to the table and picked up the calculator. She dropped it in her purse. Then she froze.

"No, Rich's back. Let's ask him," a female voice said from the hallway. "C'mon."

In a second, Kate made a decision. She had to get out. She raced to the back door of Kovak's office and slipped through. As she closed the door, she heard footsteps. Someone screamed. Kate walked briskly down a corridor that led back to investigations. Conflicting anxieties pecked at her. Why did Renke kill Kovak? Was he out of the building already? She'd seen him come out of the office and look around suspiciously. She could prove he did it. The recording would help. *Shit*! She'd meant to give it to Lyle. If police questioned her now, they'd confiscate the recorder.

She needed time to think. She found the nearest exit, shut the door behind her, and took a deep breath. She'd parked her car on the other side of the offices. To get to it, she took a roundabout route, keeping space between her and the building. With every step, she imagined people inside watching her. She got in her car and pulled out of the lot. A siren wailed in the distance.

She looked in her rearview mirror again and again on the way back to her apartment. When she was safely inside, she called Lyle.

"Joe Renke killed Kovak. He bashed his head in with that crystal sculpture." Kate half gagged and caught herself.

"Kovak?"

"Yes. He came back early, like I said."

"You see it happen?"

"No, but I saw Renke sneak out of the office. Then I went to get the calculator and found Kovak dead."

"What did you do?"

"People were coming. I ducked out the back door just before someone screamed."

"Where are you now?"

"My apartment."

"You have the recorder?"

"Of course."

"Get out of there, fast. Don't check out. Grab what you can and leave. Get in the car and come over here."

"I heard sirens as I left FedPat."

"Kate. Get out. Hang up, now."

Randomly, Kate stuffed things into her carry-on, shoved her laptop into her briefcase, and left.

By the time she neared Lyle's hotel, she'd gone through enough adrenalin for a whole basketball season, but she was thinking more clearly. She pulled out her phone and dialed the main number for the investigations office. Rachel answered.

"Jennifer, where are you?"

"I came home. My stomach."

"Mr. Kovak was murdered. It was awful. I saw his body."

"Did you call the police? Do they know who did it?"

"Someone killed Mr. Kovak and pretended to be him." Rachel paused. She started up again more slowly. "You told me this morning you saw Mr. K."

"Saw him?"

"Jennifer, the police want to talk to you. I think they know who did it."

"Who, Rachel?"

"I dunno. Somebody that was here."

"Are the police still there?"

"Oh, yeah. All over."

Kate realized Lyle's fingerprints would be on Kovak's desk. So would hers. "Joe Renke, is he still there? The police need to hold him."

"Yes. The police are talking to him. He knows the whole story."

Chapter 54

Lyle was waiting outside, scanning the street in front of his hotel, and talking to himself when Kate drove up.

"You okay? See anyone at your apartment?" he asked.

"Anyone, like police? No."

On the way up to Lyle's room, Kate explained her conversation with Rachel and told him about finding Kovak's body. "It was—" She shuddered momentarily. "—hideous."

Lyle put an arm around her shoulder. He had to reach up. Once inside his room, Kate put her cases on the bed and sat down.

"That Renke is a dirty son of a bitch," he said. "You saw him come out of Kovak's office when you went back in the building?"

Kate nodded.

"He must have discovered the real Kovak and gone ballistic. Bedrosian told him someone at FedPat was suspicious. It was probably Kovak."

"Maybe they argued."

"Could be. I wonder if Renke killed him just to blame it on me."

"Or maybe he thought about that later."

"Fast thinking, but we'll nail him with the recording."

Lyle got up and walked to the desk. "I thought this'd be easy," he said. "We'd take our evidence to Boston PD and let them collar Bedrosian and Renke. Now we have to deal with different jurisdictions."

"Shouldn't we just take this stuff back to Arizona?"

"We can't do that."

"But they think you killed Kovak. Your fingerprints are all over the desk—along with mine."

"If we run, it looks like we're guilty. We can *prove* Renke did it. It's just that now we have the Peabody police to deal with."

"I think they want to deal with *us*."

"That's because Kovak's murder happened in Peabody."

"Yes, and they're going to say you did it."

"We'll get over that. We've got evidence. But the trouble is, the Peabody authorities will confiscate the recording and the memos. The evidence could be tied up—or even tainted—before we can use it on Bedrosian."

"Max needs that evidence to stop FedPat."

"Damn." Lyle reached for the rubber band that wasn't there. "Look, I need to call Steve Travanti and see if we can work out a deal."

"But won't they arrest us?"

"Renke thinks it's just his word against mine, but we have evidence to back us up. It'll take time, but eventually we'll sort everything out. And Renke'll be in the slammer right next to Bedrosian."

"O—kay," she said slowly. "You're the ex-cop."

It took Lyle twenty minutes on the phone to explain the situation to Travanti.

"Yes, Joe Renke killed Kovak," Lyle said for the third time. "I don't *know* why exactly. He went off the deep end. We think Kovak may have been ready to blow the whistle on him. And Renke knew he had just admitted killing my father and sabotaging the park."

"He did?"

"Sure did. We recorded it. I've got all the evidence we'll need. And the woman I told you about, the one who got the job through the temp agency, she saw Renke come out of Kovak's office after he killed him. She *saw* him."

"Jesus, Lyle, I thought this was going to be a routine investigation, looking for a paper trail. Now there's a murder. I have to talk to Peabody and get back to you."

"But remember, Bedrosian and FedPat are *your* jurisdiction. Boston PD needs to be involved. And, we've got crimes in Arizona."

"Sounds like a mess, Lyle."

"Don't worry, Steve. I'll explain everything."

"Okay. Where are you? I'll call you back."

"He wasn't pleased," Kate said when Lyle hung up, "was he?"

"That's an understatement."

☙❧

An hour later, Lyle had not heard from Travanti. He and Kate used the time to transfer the recording of Renke onto Kate's laptop.

Then they copied the file to Kate's flash drive *and* sent a copy to Kate's NC email address as they had done Saturday with the FedPat memos and emails. Kate hooked the flash drive to a chain around her neck and Lyle watched as it disappeared down the front of her blouse.

When they were done, they went down to the hotel coffee shop and had sandwiches as time dragged on.

"Maybe they're looking for us," Kate said.

"They have my cell number. They'd just call. They're probably trying to sort out who has the best case to prosecute. It takes time." Lyle wondered if the PD would have thought to put Renke on ice temporarily. "I'll call Steve back. I have his cell number."

"Lyle, it's all set," Steve said. "I'm on my way to Peabody. They're going to handle the murder and we'll check out the evidence against FedPat Corporation. We're all going to meet at the Peabody PD. You know where the office is?"

"Have they detained Joe Renke?"

"They talked to him all morning. I think he's at the station now."

"Did they find Renke's prints on the murder weapon or Kovak's desk?"

"I didn't go through everything with them. We'll review the evidence when you get there. Where're you at?"

"Near Peabody. I'll be there soon."

"Jennifer Norris with you?"

"Uh huh.'

"Good. Bring her along."

Lyle put down his phone and picked up his jacket. "It's all set. They have Renke at the police station."

"So we take in the recorder and everything?"

"But we'll leave copies of everything here."

Riding down to the lobby, Lyle felt like his stomach was dropping faster than the elevator. But sorting out a case at the police station—even a complicated one like this—was something he'd done dozens of times. He knew what to do.

They decided to take Lyle's car. Kate carried her briefcase with the recorder and other evidence. Lyle located the police station on the GPS on his phone. Just as he started the car, the phone rang. "Marko, what's going on?"

"What the hell's goin' on with *you*? I heard you're wanted for murder."

"How'd you hear that in Phoenix? Is it on the news?"

"Never mind. I heard your name mentioned in the office so I did some eavesdropping. They said you killed an executive at Federal Patrician Insurance."

"Hell, no. Guy named Joe Renke did. He's the person I came out here to investigate."

"Well, police in Massachusetts think *you* did it. They asked for your picture. Somebody called here and wound up talking to your old boss, Lieutenant Collins. Don't know exactly what he told 'em, but basically they got the message that you're a head case and can't be trusted."

"Steve told me he had it all fixed up. We're leaving for the Peabody PD right now. It's close by."

"I talked to Steve a few minutes ago. They're going to arrest you when you get there. That tall lady friend of yours, too."

"We can sort it out. We've got evidence on Renke. Besides, you know what it'll look like if we don't show up, if we run."

Markopoulos paused for a second. "Lyle, did you impersonate the guy that was killed?"

"Well, yeah."

"They have a witness who places you at the employee cafeteria. And they have a video tape of you pretending to shoot at a surveillance camera. Collins thought that was a riot."

"Shit. Now what do we do?"

"Get outta there."

As Lyle hung up, Kate looked imploringly at him.

"Marko said they're going to arrest us for murder."

"I told you."

"Okay, get on the phone. Call the airline. See if you can get us out of here."

Chapter 55

At Logan International Airport, they stopped in a parking structure and headed for the terminal. As they walked inside, Lyle wondered if he should tell Kate about his videotaped outburst at FedPat customer service.

Before they reached the right ticket counter, Lyle's phone rang.

"Lyle. Where are you? We had a deal."

"Steve. We got delayed. We'll be there soon."

"I hope so. We're all waiting for you. Let's get this cleared up."

He sounded as reassuring as the computer voice in *2001: A Space Odyssey.*

Lyle switched off the phone then immediately scanned the terminal. "They know we're here. They traced my phone. I should have thought of it."

"Can they do that?"

"Yes." Looking left and right, Lyle steered Kate outside. "I'm sure cops are all over the place. They're looking for two people. Let's split up."

A cab was just depositing someone at the curb. Lyle held the door then tossed Kate's bags inside. "Tell the cab driver to take you to the harbor where we were the other day. The Long Wharf."

"What're you going to do?"

"I'll be a few minutes behind you. Meet me at the gate for the ferry to Provincetown."

"Provincetown. Where's that?"

"Cape Cod. We'll hide out. Do you have any money?"

"Over a hundred."

"We'll need more. Do you have an ATM card? Let me have it, and the password."

"What if you're late? We don't know what time the ferry leaves."

"Give me your disposable phone. Keep the Arizona one. I'll call you if I have to. Now go."

He watched the street as Kate's cab pulled out. No one followed her. When she was safely away, Lyle relaxed and felt a little less conspicuous. All he needed to do was get as much cash as he could then meet Kate. He knew Logan security was normally tight anyway. Ever since two of the four 9/11 hijacked flights took off from Logan, it had become the most security-conscious airport in the nation. And as Steve Travanti tracked them heading to Logan, he would have called out a bunch of cars *and* alerted airport security. Officers in police cruisers must be monitoring the airport access routes. Of course, he wouldn't be in this situation if he hadn't called Travanti after Kovak's murder and they had just left town—forget it.

The nearest ATM was tantalizingly close—just inside the terminal. But that was crazy—or was it? Lyle walked inside, his eyes constantly moving. The building hummed with a crush of travelers. He found the ATM, withdrew as much cash as possible from both their accounts, and headed for the exit. Glancing at his watch, he hoped he'd be on time for the ferry.

Just as he reached the door, a man in a suit passed close by. A hand grabbed Lyle's arm. "Stop."

Lyle spun around and shoved his wheeled suitcase into the man's legs. The man fell forward over the case and had to release his grip on Lyle to cushion his fall. Lyle dashed outside, madly looking for a cab.

Twenty yards ahead and two lanes over from the curb was an empty taxi. As he sprinted toward the cab, Lyle glanced over his shoulder and saw the plain-clothes policeman—security guard, or whoever it was—close behind. The crowd forced Lyle's pursuer to dodge in and out.

Lyle just had time to dive into the back seat of the cab and say, "Go. Now. Step on it."

Looking out the back window of the cab, Lyle saw the man pull out a cell phone. He could read the guy's angry lips. Soon the cab was too far away.

"Circle the airport and come back to another terminal," Lyle said.

"What airline?" the cabbie asked. He had an eastern European accent.

"Doesn't matter. Keep going. I'm trying to get away from a jealous husband."

"Ooo, you're a bad guy," the cabbie said. He turned briefly to Lyle and smiled.

The Boston cops stationed outside the airport would now have a description of the cab.

"I drive a cab, too," Lyle said to the driver.

"You do? Where is this?"

"St. Louis." No sense in leaving behind any more clues than he already had.

"You like it?" Did the cabbie sound less suspicious?

"Sometimes. What I hate is fares who give you a lousy tip or stiff you."

The driver's head nodded up and down. "Me, too."

After a couple of minutes, while they were still on airport property, Lyle pointed to a road on the right. "Where does that go?"

"Over there is the water shuttle and the Hyatt Hotel."

"Let's try the hotel."

When they pulled up, Lyle thanked the driver and gave him a good tip. Although everything in him wanted to get away from the airport, Lyle took his time and walked into the hotel. In the gift shop, he bought a baseball cap. Then he walked back out to the street to catch another cab. He waited for one that didn't look like the first one. As he got in, he glanced up and down the street then pulled the cap low over his eyes.

Chapter 56

Kate stood next to her two bags, holding her ferry ticket in her left hand. Crew members of the large catamaran were shuffling a crowd on board, obviously getting ready to shove off. Kate could hear the rumble of the ship's powerful engines and smell the exhaust. She'd been standing on the dock for about twenty minutes. At first, she expected to see police pull up at any moment, but the one policeman she saw paid no attention to her. Later, she started looking for Lyle.

"Do you have a ticket for Provincetown?" a uniformed crew member asked her. "Time to board."

She shifted her feet around her bags and looked down the pier. A block away, Lyle was jogging toward the boat.

He bought a ticket just in time and leaped aboard.

In less than a minute, the ship started to move. Kate and Lyle stood by the rail and looked back at the wharf. There were no screeching sirens, no policemen running toward the boat, arms waving in the air. Only two children waved at them from the dock. Kate waved back.

"Have any trouble at the airport."

"Not much. I maxed out both our cards and got cash. It took longer to get here because I switched cabs a couple of times and walked the last mile."

"Where's your suitcase?"

"Decided to travel light."

As the boat sped away from the harbor, they headed inside.

"It's best if we don't sit together," Lyle said under his breath. "Just in case."

Kate and Lyle sat two rows apart in the air-conditioned cabin. The rows of airline-style seats were filled with people in casual clothes, from tank tops and shorts to short, flimsy dresses. That morning Kate and Lyle had changed clothes at the hotel so they blended in, except that Kate's only shoes were the high-heeled ones she'd worn at work. She'd left her room in such a hurry she'd forgotten her running shoes. Kate wondered if anyone on the boat was looking for them. She eyed a man in slacks and a sport shirt who pretended to read a paper—while actually scanning the crowd.

e/ɔe/ɔ

Low clouds hung over the tip of Cape Cod as the commuter catamaran motored into the dock at Provincetown. Kate didn't think it would be hot and humid, but when she left the cabin and walked ashore, the sticky, moist air wrapped around her like a wet towel.

Lyle joined her when they were well away from the boat.

"You think Renke will have people looking for us?" she asked.

"Good thought. He might prefer that his men get to us before the cops. Or maybe he'll just wait for the cops to get us. I'm a nut case, remember. No one would believe me."

"What do we do now?"

"Find a place to stay. The police won't have given up on us. But at least I ditched my phone. I tossed it in the back of a delivery truck. Good luck for Travanti if he follows that. If we pay cash for everything here and are careful, we should be able to get a plane from somewhere—not Boston—back to Arizona."

"Then what? We'll still be wanted for murder." Kate lowered her voice for the last few words, glancing over her shoulder to make sure no one was nearby.

"We'll get help. I'm not worried. Should be, but I'm not. Funny, huh?"

"Hilarious."

They picked up a Provincetown map in a gift shop and asked a young, curly-haired clerk if she could recommend places to stay.

"Yah don't have ah reservation?"

Kate shook her head.

The clerk chuckled. She pointed out a couple of places on the map they could try.

Provincetown looked out on a narrow, hook-shaped tip of

land at the end of the much larger hook shape that was Cape Cod itself. The town spread out along the bay. Blocks of gift shops, restaurants, espresso shops, and bars sat on either side of Commercial Street, the main drag. The town was a few miles long but only blocks wide.

After she and Lyle found no vacancies at two B and Bs and two motels, even the wheels on Kate's suitcase seemed to roll with more difficulty. Finally, they found themselves in front of Captain McDougal's, a weathered house just off Commercial Street that had been converted to a B and B. A row of flags hung off the porch. A motionless U.S. flag and a nautical pennant were flanked by two rainbow banners.

"Colorful," Lyle said, pointing to the banners. "You see lots of those here."

"We'd be less conspicuous checking in if we were the same sex."

"And you were a foot shorter," Lyle said as they walked inside and up to a bar that served as the front desk.

"My turn to ask," Kate said.

She looked at the stocky man behind the counter. He wore a Hawaiian shirt that was slightly too small and had an earring in each ear.

"We're looking for a room."

"Reservation?"

Kate shook her head.

"I got one. It's not our best. Around back. You get to it from the rear porch."

"We'll take it," Lyle said. "Sign us in, honey."

Kate picked up the pen on the counter and created new personas for them. They were from Seattle, she decided. They had already agreed they would settle for one room for the two of them—and be happy to find that. She thought Lyle seemed pleased with the idea.

"You're a long way from home," the clerk said. "You get a lot of rain there?"

"Oh yes. Buckets."

Lyle paid cash for the night and they carried Kate's bags to their room.

Eclectic, Kate thought, would be a generous way to describe the irregularly shaped room with an alcove near the door, a fireplace in the corner, and a hodgepodge of furniture. The room smelled of lavender—and Lysol. On the wall across from the bed hung a tired-looking, framed print of a sailboat, the kind you saw in ads for art schools.

Kate hung up blouses and slacks from her suitcase, hoping they would lose a few of their wrinkles by morning.

"I need to buy a razor and toothbrush," Lyle said, "but first, let's eat."

๛๛๛

Commerce Street was packed with pedestrians who spilled over the curbs and on to the pavement. Kate was uneasy. The Mardi Gras atmosphere—the music, the aroma of frying fish, the crowd—seemed to offer them cover, but she felt conspicuous, especially in casual clothes with her stacked-heel pumps. Everyone seemed to be looking at everyone else. Gay or straight, you came to P-town to see and be seen.

Lyle obviously had similar thoughts. "We need to blend in here. We've got to find you some flat shoes."

"I'd like to get out of these, too," she said raising a foot, "but I don't see any shoe stores."

"How about flip-flops?"

Chapter 57

Two hours later, they were back in their room. Kate had bought men's tennis shoes in a clothing store and a Cape Cod T-shirt—a souvenir, she said. For dinner, they both devoured plates of fish and chips while each kept an eye over the other's shoulder.

"Tomorrow," Lyle said, "we either have to rent a car or get public transportation—maybe a cab—to Hyannis. There's a small airport there. Maybe we can make connections out of Massachusetts. But if we rent a car we'd have to use a credit card."

"They can trace us that way, right?"

Lyle nodded. "A cab might be better. I'll check the phone book—if we have one in the room."

"But first," Kate said, "Let's check in with Max. Is it safe to use my disposable Boston phone?"

"Sure. It's a dumb burner phone, prepaid, untraceable. Doesn't even have GPS."

Max answered on the first ring. "What the hell's happening out there? You're in the news."

"You might ask if we're okay."

"I know you're okay. You're calling me. Aren't you all right?"

"Thanks for the sympathy, Max."

"Where are you?"

"We're hiding out in Provincetown on Cape Cod. We have the evidence we need against FedPat. I have memos that show Bedrosian hired a private eye named Renke to attack the park. One of his men killed Lyle's father. They're responsible for everything. We can prove it."

"You'd better, because the cops are looking for Lyle. They say he killed someone at FedPat."

"*Renke* killed him. I saw him come out of the office."

"You were there?"

"Yes. Before that we got Renke to confess to all the trouble at the park."

"You sure of all this?"

"We have proof. Lyle's with me and we're on our way back."

"If your evidence is that good, we can void the agreement with FedPat."

"We'll also get Bedrosian arrested. Oh, Max, talk to the sheriff's office. Tell them to check out the train. This guy that Bedrosian hired said he was going to disable our steam engine."

Max swore. "Good thing the train's not running yet. I'll get security right on it."

Kate told him she had used an alias and said she hoped she could put the finishing touches on the press day at NC before she had to talk to the police.

"What'd he say?" Lyle asked when she hung up.

"He's going to call out his legal attack dogs for us. They'll cancel the FedPat agreement. We just have to get back to NC with our evidence."

"He mention the police?"

"They're looking for you. Apparently they talked to Brent Pelham and our friend Clyde."

"I thought Max was going to fire Bates."

"So did I."

"Obviously, the sheriff will be waiting for me at my house when we get back. Lemme call Earl and see if he can get me a place to stay. We should get with the attorneys and work out our case before we talk to the sheriff or anyone."

She gave Lyle a hopeful smile. "I also need to call Drenda and see how the plans are coming—and see if my cat's okay."

℮◌℮◌

Kate's muscles ached, particularly in her neck. Looking over her shoulder ever since the airport had worn her out. Lyle looked tired, too. When they checked in, she had noticed the room had but one queen-size bed. When they finished their calls, Lyle sprawled out on the bed, staring into space. Raising himself on one elbow, he said, "Did Max ever ask you if you thought I was crazy?"

"Clyde told him about your police record."

"I know. Max told me. Were you worried?"

"For about a minute."

"It was all made up. I was on a stakeout one day. Two other cops relieved me when my shift was over. They swore I was talking to people who weren't there."

"And you were really just talking to yourself."

"Uh-huh."

"Then why weren't you reinstated?"

"Because I'd made mistakes. I told you about that. I didn't really care at that point. It was a way out, and I took it."

"And tomorrow, we'll find our way out of here."

"Right," Lyle said, yawning.

"I'm pretty tired, too," Kate said. "I think we'd better turn in."

Lyle agreed. Kate went into the bathroom—such as it was—untied her new tennis shoes and pulled off her clothes. She decided she'd wear just the Cape Cod T-shirt to bed. After combing her hair, she walked into the bedroom. The light was off but she could make out shadows.

"Lyle?"

"Hmm?"

"You asleep?"

"Not yet."

"Good."

"You want to talk?"

"No."

Kate pulled back the sheet and slid underneath it. Lyle was lying on his back. She reached out to him. The hair on his chest felt soft. He made a noise, then turned to her and put a hand on her waist. She felt it slide around behind her and she arched her back toward him.

She and Lyle had survived the onslaught thus far and proved they made a good team. They'd be ready for whatever the police, Joe Renke, or anyone threw at them. And to Kate, seeking temporary comfort in each other's arms was the most natural thing in the world.

Chapter 58

Kate opened her eyes. For a moment, she didn't know where she was. Then she saw the hackneyed sailboat painting on the wall and knew she was in Provincetown, Massachusetts, in bed with Lyle Deming. He was still asleep, breathing heavily, dead to the world.

Kate knew she would not fall back asleep. Groping for her watch, she saw it was a little before 6 a.m. She got up and dressed, pulling on a pair of jeans and a sweatshirt. She glanced in the mirror and was pleasantly surprised. Her hair needed work but it didn't look half bad in a tousled, casual sort of way. First priority, however, was coffee. There was none in the room, but she vaguely remembered seeing an espresso shop not far away.

On the chance she could find some in the lobby, she walked in and was surprised to see the person who had checked them in sitting reading a paper. He didn't look the type to be up early or to be interested in the newspaper.

She glanced in a corner and saw an empty glass coffee carafe. "Where can I get a paper?"

"There's a box down on the corner to the right." The guy motioned with one arm while barely lifting his head from his paper.

"Isn't there a coffee place just down the street?"

"Yeah, Charlie's. It's that way too. We serve continental breakfast here in the lobby in an hour."

Kate couldn't wait, so she headed out around the front of the house and stopped to listen. After a night of music and drink, P-town slept. The glow of dawn offered only murky rays to light the morning. Ocean dampness cooled the air. Kate walked a block to Commerce Street then down a block to Charlie's Espresso Stop. Two customers were in front of her. Kate ordered two large coffees to go, bought a Boston paper from a news rack, and headed back.

As she turned the corner at the rear of the B and B, she glanced up at the porch. The door to their room stood slightly open. Her senses went on alert. She remembered she had forgotten to take the old fashioned key that was necessary to lock the door from the outside. Setting the coffee and newspaper on the walk, she slowly stepped up on the wooden porch.

She pushed the door open a half inch at a time until she could see inside. Two men with their backs to her were standing over the bed where Lyle was lying. One of them held a gun.

"What else you got around here? Any more files?" the shorter of the two men said. He was muscular and had a large bald spot in the middle of his brown hair. He held a semi-automatic in his right hand.

"You already got the computer and the folders," Lyle said. "Look around again."

"Why don't you put a slug in his leg to help him remember," the taller man said.

"I can make him talk," said the shorter man.

As the men focused their attention on Lyle, Kate stepped slowly into the room. She didn't know what she would do, but she saw that she had to do *something*.

She walked around a corner—formed by an alcove—where she couldn't be seen from the room, though Lyle probably saw her walk in. She prayed that he wouldn't look at her hiding place. Kate held her breath and waited.

"Okay," the first man said, "for the last time, where's the woman. Where's the blonde?"

"She's gone. She went to call the police."

"Ha. Sure. Go look for her, Ned."

"Where?"

"Outside, stupid."

Kate heard footsteps coming toward her. Raising her right arm across her chest, she inched forward. In the next second, the man stepped around the corner.

He saw her—too late. She took a quick step toward him. At the same time she brought her elbow up and across, hitting him in the face. Snap. His nose broke as the bony part of Kate's elbow smashed through the cartilage.

The man fell backward to the floor. Kate heard the other man grunt. Lyle must have hit him. The thud she heard was probably his gun hitting the floor. A moment later, the smaller man ran toward the door, trying to step over his partner on the floor. Kate lunged for him. He was considerably shorter than Kate, but strong. He struggled and managed to free one arm.

He hit Kate across the face as she kicked his legs sideways. He had to reach for the wall to steady himself so his fist just caught Kate's left eye.

"Freeze," Lyle said raising the semi-auto. "Hands up. Against the wall."

As if she were a cop and not a PR person, Kate grabbed the shorter man by the back of his coat and threw him up against the wall. She checked his pockets for weapons.

As she did, she saw Lyle going through the pockets of the man called Ned, still on the floor. He moaned and tried to stop the blood flowing out from the deformed lump between his eyes.

"Let's get them in the chairs," Lyle said.

He pulled Ned off the floor, by gripping the front of his jacket, and pushed him into a heavy rattan chair. The man didn't fight. He was obviously in pain. Lyle pushed a second chair into the center of the room and Kate shoved the smaller man into it. Lyle sat on the bed in his shorts with the gun leveled at the two assailants.

Kate stood next to him. In her right hand she held a revolver that Lyle had pulled from the other man's holster.

"You guys aren't cops, are you?" Lyle said.

Kate sucked in her breath. She hadn't stopped to think of that when she decked the guy. In fact, she hadn't thought of anything except what she supposed was self-preservation. She looked down at the gun in her hand. Was her hand trembling?

"Yeah, we're the FBI," the shorter man said with a scowl. "Good thing you got this woman protecting you, Deming."

"She's pretty handy. Maybe I'll let her give you a nose job, too."

The shorter man with thinning hair had a double chin and a down-turned mouth. His partner groaned. Kate got a damp wash cloth from the bathroom and gave it to him. When he started wiping the blood from his face, Kate snatched it back from him.

"Hold it over your nose like this. Put your head back. It'll stop the swelling."

The man complied without a word. Kate sat on the bed with Lyle.

"Let's see who our guests are," Lyle said, nodding toward the wallet he'd extracted from the wounded man.

Kate picked it up and found a Massachusetts driver's license. "This guy's name is Ned Havlicek. He's thirty-two, five-eleven, and has hazel eyes."

"Ned," Lyle said. "You work for Renke? Does he provide medical and dental? I think you're going to need it."

Havlicek looked at Kate and mumbled something.

"Shut the fuck up," the shorter man said.

"Okay. Let's find out who the boss here is," Lyle said.

The second man was sufficiently cowed to let Kate extract his wallet from his coat pocket. Inside she found a blurry photocopy of a mug shot of Lyle. Folded with the photo was a sheet from a notepad. Written in pen were the words:

Jennifer Norris, over 6 feet

175+ lbs, blonde hair, attractive

The printing at the top of the note paper said "Topaz Investigations." Kate handed it to Lyle.

"So, Jennifer," Lyle said, "Renke's not sure how much you weigh." He turned to the shorter man. "How'd you know where we were?"

"We're the FBI. We know everything."

"We need to figure a way to tie these guys up, Jennifer. I want to get dressed."

"I saw a roll of duct tape under the sink in the bathroom."

"Perfect."

Kate reached under the sink and picked up the tape. Her hands didn't tremble now. In a few minutes, she had bound both assailants to their seats, electric-chair style, with wrists tight to the armrests. Havlicek's nose had stopped bleeding. The clotting blood was turning black. Kate gagged both men, poking holes in the duct tape over Havlicek's mouth as an afterthought. He was having trouble breathing out of what was left of his nose.

Lyle went through their pockets and found money, cell phones, and car keys. One of them had a map of Provincetown.

Lyle set the two handguns down on a dresser and picked up the coffee Kate had retrieved from the lawn. "Damn. It's cold."

Soon Kate and Lyle had dressed and packed. They double checked to see that the goons would not be leaving their seats any time soon. Outside, Lyle suggested they dump the guns. Kate pushed the magazine release on the semi-auto, then pulled back the slide to eject the round in the chamber.

"Smooth," said Lyle. He unloaded the revolver and they threw the guns in the bushes. Lyle hesitated with the thugs' cell phones, then he pulled out the batteries and stomped on the phones.

"That was a nice touch back there," Kate said, "your turning on the TV so they could watch."

"Hey, it was an *I Dream of Jeannie* festival. I knew they'd appreciate it."

"You think we should have kept one of the guns?"

"We'd never get one on a plane. I hope we don't need it before then."

They walked around the front of the house. Kate glanced up and down the street. "Now what?"

Lyle held up Renke's men's car keys.

Chapter 59

The key ring told them that Renke's boys were driving a Ford product. One click of the remote and the lights on a car nearby started to flash. Lyle started it up. He found Highway 6 and they headed out of town and around the long, curved cape.

"That was close," he said. "Thanks for clobbering that guy."

"I don't know where it came from. Guess I was mad. They could have killed us."

"That might have been the plan."

"Renke wants to get to us before the police do."

"Uh-huh."

Kate considered the bigger question of their jeopardy, but let it go. "I wonder if Bedrosian knows by now."

"Could be. Maybe he's bankrolling Renke's search for us. With the money we got from his thugs we have enough to pay cash for airline tickets."

Kate turned around in her seat and looked at the highway behind them. The lanes were empty. "The paper," she said. "I almost forgot." She reached in the back seat and pulled the rolled-up newspaper out of her bag. She found the Kovak story on an inside page.

"It says the police are looking for two people wanted for questioning. It has your name and Jennifer Norris."

"That's a little good news. They don't know who *you* are. I never told Steve your real name."

"I don't suppose we can fly out of Hyannis now, can we?"

"No. They know where we are. At least Renke's people do. The cops may find out soon enough."

"We can always *drive* to Arizona."

"In a stolen car? Besides it would take days."

"How else are we going to get back? Even if we can afford

to pay cash for tickets we'll still have to show ID and go through security."

"Yes, it's a risk, but we'll have to chance it. Maybe they won't have spread the word very far from Boston. I think we should try the airport in Rhode Island—Providence."

"Isn't that a long way?"

"Just a few hours. We could be there before the maids discover the uninvited guests in our room." Lyle glanced in the rear-view mirror.

Kate took out a pad and the cell phone then opened up a map. "Looks like the airport is south of Providence. I wonder if we can fly direct to Phoenix from there. I'll call and check with the airlines."

"Let's fly someplace else first," Lyle said, "then change flights. They'll be looking for us to fly to Phoenix or Flagstaff."

They debated the risks of being tracked down if they made reservations. Kate suggested they make a dozen reservations at several airports. Finally, they decided to drive to Providence and take a chance on getting a flight without a reservation. They'd fly to Chicago, then get a flight to Arizona. It was a risk—they might be identified—but they had little choice.

Kate double checked the map. Providence was not too far. It would take two or three hours, if they were lucky.

Before they reached the end of Cape Cod, Lyle saw a Massachusetts State Police car ahead. It held steady at 55 mph in the right lane. Lyle knew he could legally pass it as they headed down Highway 6, approaching the Cape Cod Canal. Their car couldn't have been reported stolen yet, and the cop in the police cruiser couldn't possibly recognize him. Nevertheless, Lyle just stole a momentary glance at the trooper as he passed him briskly, but not too briskly.

Kate saw the police car, too. She looked at the policeman as they approached, but turned her head away just as they were even with the car.

"Chicken," Lyle said.

"I just didn't want to look at him."

"In that case, why didn't you slouch down in the seat? You look awfully tall sitting there."

"Not too tall for you."

Lyle watched the State Police car in the mirror. It gradually

fell behind and then turned off the highway. "Height has ad-
vantages," he said as he reached over and softly touched the side
of Kate's face. A dark bruise was starting to form where Renke's
thug had hit her.

Chapter 60

Two hours later, they were approaching TF Green Airport south of Providence, Rhode Island.

"I wonder if they have special parking for stolen cars," Lyle said.

They ditched the Ford in a crowded, remote parking lot. Kate had called three airlines and found a flight leaving for Chicago in less than an hour. One had coach seats left.

"Hope there's still space by the time we get there," Lyle said as they walked to the terminal.

"Think they'll be looking for us inside?"

"No way of knowing."

"With these tennis shoes on I'm not *too* tall."

"But you're still blonde."

"I thought about that, but there wasn't time."

"Yeah, and I thought of having you ride in a wheelchair. Great ideas—for next time. Now we split up and take our chances."

They walked into the terminal and headed for the ticket counters. Kate glanced around but tried to look casual. "We can deal with this."

"Wait 'til Max sees our expense accounts," Lyle said.

"Max," Kate said. "Max."

"What about Max?"

"Lyle, we've got to get out of here. We don't need this risk."

Lyle touched her arm. "We're okay so far—"

"No. Let's go. Out of here."

✐✐✐

"How brainless. Why didn't I think of this before?" Kate said when they were sitting on a bench outside. "Max has his own plane. He can fly us home."

Lyle looked skeptical.

"It'll work. NC has a company jet. Max offered to fly me to the park for my job interview before he hired me. We just have to get him to send the plane for us."

She glanced up as a man in a suit and sunglasses walked by, then she looked back at Lyle.

He nodded, slowly. "Okay, call Max. See if they can pick us up. And Kate, tell him not to tell anyone. Not even the pilots. Make up names for us."

In an hour, it was all set. The Nostalgia City plane happened to be in Philadelphia, having ferried some vendors back after an Arizona visit. The pilots could pick up Lyle and Kate by 3 p.m. Eastern time and leave for Flagstaff.

A few hours later, they were settled in comfortable lounge seats aboard the NC jet. When they met the pilots, Kate had not liked the idea of deceiving them with false names. The thought of being grabbed by Renke's men—or the police—however, was sickening. Once they were airborne, Kate and Lyle realized they were hungry. Unfortunately, a search of the cabin turned up only a bag of popcorn and two sodas. They made do.

"We'll have to turn ourselves in pretty soon," Lyle said. "We can't hide for very long."

"I need to check on the media event. Even if we have Bedrosian arrested *and* get Max off the hook with FedPat, we still have to pack in the tourists this summer. To keep the park from going belly up. That's how we started all this, isn't it?"

"Seems like a long time ago."

"I need to get busy as soon as we touch the ground. What do you want to do?"

"At this point I want to stay out of jail, catch Joe Renke, and see Samantha again." He paused and looked out the window. "We have enough to convict Bedrosian and Renke—and keep us out of the slammer—*if* we can spell it all out to someone. We need someone to listen to the recordings, see the memos, and let us explain the whole story. Trying to explain it to Steve Travanti on the phone obviously didn't work."

"Who do we talk to, the police, FBI?"

"I don't know. Trouble is, with a high profile murder like this, the police want to collar somebody fast. Explanations come later."

"Can we wait one day to let me make sure everything at the park is on track?"

"Okay. We'll have to decide where we can get the best break when we surrender. I'll have Earl hide me somewhere. They're still looking for Jennifer Norris so you may be safe in your apartment. But not for long. Pretty soon they'll find out who you are."

"We should talk to Kevin Waterman," she said.

"I forgot about him. Maybe once he knows we have Bedrosian dead to rights, he might consider switching sides—to stay out of jail. I'll persuade him."

"Why don't you let me talk to him? I think he's afraid of you."

"He should be. Okay, let me know what he says."

As the stress of the day merged with drowsiness, Kate leaned back in her seat and tried to calculate what time it would be when they landed. Lyle was polishing off a soda. He set the can down and stifled a yawn.

"Are you glad to be going back?" Kate asked. "Back to our make-believe world."

"It's make-believe, but you're putting more reality into it."

"I hope. Our new theme area is full of reality."

"I know. I saw your plans."

"Plans?"

"They were sitting on the table in your apartment last week."

"And?"

"I like it."

"You do?"

"I've been thinking about it a lot recently."

"The past? NC years?"

"The past in general. You can't do anything about it. It happened. No sense pretending it didn't. That's just crazy. The past is a fact. Period."

"This doesn't sound like the person who said Nostalgia City should be a fantasy world."

"That's not exactly what I said. I just said people should be able to come to the park to have fun and remember the good times. Nothing wrong with that. But you have to *reconcile* the past. Even Vietnam and everything that went with it."

"You couldn't have been in Vietnam."

Lyle frowned. "Not me, my older brother. Just before the U.S. pulled out. He was in the Air Cav. Got shot up bad. Looked like he might die, but he pulled through."

"It was horrible, wasn't it?"

"Ten *times* the GI casualties of Iraq and Afghanistan. It sucked all the energy out of the country. I never understood it, but I know I have to accept it."

"So, realism won't be a problem?"

"Realism will help."

"I hope it's ready. We've got a little over 48 hours until the grand opening and the press arrives, en mass. Do you want to give the details to Max tonight?"

"Tonight?"

"Max wants to talk with us tonight."

"Is Max going to meet us?"

"No, but he's sending somebody to the airport."

"We have to talk to the pilot. Tell him we're not landing in Flagstaff."

Kate felt a chill.

"We don't know who we can trust," Lyle said.

"But *Max*?"

"We need to slip into Nostalgia City as quietly as possible."

"What do I tell him?"

"Tell Max we'll meet with him and the attorneys tomorrow. Tell him he doesn't need to send anyone for us."

"Where do we go?"

"Let's ask the pilot if we can set down somewhere else. Maybe Prescott. We can rent a car or call someone. We'll find a way."

Chapter 61

Kate padded into the lobby of the Maxwell Building early the next morning, waved her badge at a security guard she didn't recognize, and stepped quickly into the elevator. She had come in early so she could hide out and work without anyone in Nostalgia City knowing she was back. Later she would find an empty office somewhere in the park where she could work until everything was resolved.

The hallway outside the PR department was still. Kate listened to the echoes of her steps as she walked. The jingling sound of her keys made her think of a jailer. Once inside, she set her purse and briefcase down and headed for the coffee room.

The night before, tired as they were, she and Lyle downloaded the documents and recordings Kate had emailed to herself. They transcribed critical portions of the Renke recording and made an extra copy of everything for Lyle to keep. Lyle was to stash the originals in a Polk bank safe deposit box that morning. Kate now carried the transcript and document copies in her briefcase. When they had talked briefly to Max on the phone, he'd said nothing unusual had been found on the railroad tracks and security was still checking.

After she started the coffee machine, her attention was drawn to papers and photographs spread out over the department conference table. She first saw the list of media people who had sent in an RSVP for the press day grand opening. She was pleased to see the number of major news outlets that would be represented. Many of the reservations had been made late the day before. She moved to the layout of photographs showing the new theme area and the new Indian casino train depot. She glanced through them and smiled.

The moment she heard the noise behind her, she remembered leaving the door unlocked—as she had in Provincetown.

This flashed through her head as she spun around and nearly knocked over—Bobby Bostic.

The former singing sensation jumped back. "Oh! Kate. Didn't mean to startle you."

"Bobby, what're you doing here?"

"I'm an early riser. I've got a meeting in the entertainment office so I just took a chance you might be here. Oh, Kate, what happened to your eye?"

Kate had tried to use makeup to minimize the large bruise. Obviously, it was still noticeable.

"I'm really busy, Bobby." Kate saw that the once-upon-a-time teen idol *must* be an early riser. He was already dressed in a trendy sport coat with shiny slacks, his dark, curly hair all cemented in place.

Bostic picked up a photograph of an outdoor stage. "Is this where the celebration will be?"

Kate grabbed the photo out of his hand. "We haven't released any of this yet. Not until the grand opening Friday afternoon."

"Do you have any of me?"

"Photographs of you?"

"I'm gonna be one of the featured stars."

"Oh, that's right. I forgot. You're going to be on a float, right?"

"That's what I wanted to talk to you about."

"Yes, Bobby?"

"I was wondering—"

Bostic paused and looked as if he was going to put a hand on Kate's shoulder. She moved slightly along the edge of the table.

"If I was in the first float, then I'd be ready for the show after the parade." Bostic's pleading voice went up an octave. "And I'm still only booked for three days. I'm starting to think Nostalgia City doesn't respect me or the other—"

"Bobby, I don't care where you are in the parade. You stay there. That's how it was planned. And if you're not ready to give us 150 percent when you're on stage, I'll make sure you never get booked here again. For three days or three minutes. Is that clear?"

Kate led Bostic out of the office and held the door for him. When he was gone, she realized she'd summarily ejected the volatile singer. But after decking the homicidal goon in Provincetown, a petulant rock star was nothing. She shrugged and went into her darkened office. Instead of turning on the lights, she drew the shades and let in the early morning, high-desert sun. Joann had made neat piles of mail, phone messages, and printed copies of some e-mail. Kate noticed a phone message from a week earlier near the top of the stack: "Vets group chair says they will boycott NC—and tell the media."

No they won't, she thought. Then her mind returned to Kevin Waterman.

She called his office. No answer. She left a voicemail. She tried to sound casual even though she wanted to get her hands around his neck.

As soon as she hung up, her phone buzzed. It was Max.

"Kate, where the hell's Lyle? What's goin' on?"

"Slow down, Max. What's up?"

"That bastard Bedrosian doesn't know he's licked. Now he's saying that if we don't make good on the contract by the end of the week he's going to file an injunction."

"He's lying. As soon as our attorneys hear what we've got to say, it won't be FedPat that's taking over Nostalgia City. It'll be the other way around."

"Think so? Have you seen the Phoenix paper?"

e/se/s

"Delivery for Lyle Deming. Morning, bro." Earl held out a large coffee and a newspaper. Lyle invited him into his motel room.

"You sleep okay?" Earl asked.

Lyle flopped down on the edge of the bed. "I'm okay."

Earl looked suspiciously at the two rickety-looking motel chairs, finally settling for the one that appeared to be least likely to collapse. "You better have some of the coffee before you see the paper."

"Bad news?"

"Front page of the second section."

A two-column story said Lyle was wanted for murder in Massachusetts. It identified him as an ex-cop discharged from the Phoenix PD because of a history of mental problems. The story didn't connect the murder to Nostalgia City, although it did say Lyle was employed at the park.

"It says my whereabouts are unknown." Lyle said.

"No they're not. Your whereabouts are right here in this cheesy motel."

"Pretty soon Undersheriff Rey Martinez is going to figure you're helping me. You weren't followed were you?

"Little late to ask that now, isn't it? Don't worry. I took your advice coming over here."

"It'll just be a day or so and we'll have the bad guys in the slammer."

"You hope."

Lyle borrowed Earl's phone and called Marko.

"Where are you?"

"Back home."

"Not in your condo!" Marko's voice went up.

"C'mon, gimme a break."

"Sorry. What are you going to do?"

"Talk to Maxwell's attorneys, then maybe see the San Navarro County prosecutor."

"Did you see the Phoenix paper today? The Boston cops are saying you're crazy."

"Uh-huh. The article said I had a history of mental problems."

"You're lucky that's all it said. Somehow the Boston and Peabody cops got parts of your personnel file and they're spreading the details all over."

"They can't do that. How'd they get it?"

"Collins. The Boston papers printed some nasty crap about you."

"Imaginary friends?"

"Uh-huh. It stirred up a lot of trouble here in the department for your old buddies. Collins and Bensen are finally taking some heat. The chief is involved."

"But the damage is done. Now I sound as credible as Daffy Duck."

"Maybe not. You've got strong evidence, right? And witnesses? Didn't your blonde bombshell see the murder?"

"Kate was down the hall. I'm a little short in the witness department. The guy that got killed could have been our star witness. What do you hear from Steve?"

"Travanti? He says they found your prints all over Kovak's office. One of their theories is that you killed Kovak because you think he was involved in your father's death."

"But didn't you explain?"

"I've tried."

"What'd he say?"

"He's pretty freaked out. He helped you, and you got him involved in this. Now his boss is breathing down his back."

"So, I'm a wacko and he doesn't have to cut me any slack."

"Would you?"

"Shit, I don't know. Travanti should have Renke collared. I told him to."

"They were watching Renke."

"Were?"

"Apparently he disappeared."

Chapter 62

Kate found a hiding place. In a vacant office, a block from the Maxwell Building, she caught up on good news and bad. An email from the head of railroad operations told her maintenance on the park's main steam locomotive was a little behind schedule. She made a note to have one of her people check on it. She tried Kevin's line again. This time a clerk in accounting answered. Kevin had not come in yet, but was expected. She left another message.

She called Drenda who sounded enthusiastic. Positively bubbly. She said the new theme area and shops were nearly complete and the speaker's platform was under construction. Drenda said she had been talking up the project for two weeks. She was eager to get Kate's opinion on various final details.

"I'll stop by your office later this afternoon," Kate said, "after I talk with Max."

"All of a sudden, he's developed an interest in our project."

"Max? I thought he was ignoring it. He hasn't mentioned it since he approved our plans."

"He drops by to look at construction," Drenda said. "But he rarely makes comments."

Kate's secretary was her next call. She told Joann only that she had a stressful time in Boston and that she wanted to hide out to avoid interruptions while she did last-minute work on press day. This was her first and only priority, she said, until it was history, so to speak. Joanne—who was proving to be a valuable, circumspect assistant—didn't ask questions but brought Kate up to date on the grand opening and said she would relay phone calls.

"Several of the reporters who made reservations asked about Lyle Deming," Joann said. "They wanted to know if there was any connection between him and the accidents at the park."

What irony, Kate thought.

Next, it was time to call Max again.

"If we can get Engine 43 steamed up," she said, "we'll be ready for the grand opening. The press response is higher than I expected. We'll get tons of TV coverage."

"Good. 'Bout time. The attorneys from Reese, Reese, and Genet will be here at two-thirty."

"I'll come over ahead of time with the evidence. We can talk strategy. Are they civil *and* criminal?"

"Just business. I contacted Slade Foster for the criminal side, but he may not get here until tomorrow."

"I wish we could tie it up all at the same time. It'll be complicated."

"What about Lyle?"

"He'll be there. Wait until you hear everything he did to expose Bedrosian."

"Do you think he's, you know, sane?"

"Max, c'mon. You said you were smart to hire him."

"Just checking, that's all. Did you read the story about him in the paper?"

"I explained to you before about Lyle and the Phoenix police."

"I know."

Kate paused. If it was going to be this difficult to explain things to Max, what would it be like to outsiders? "Max, Kevin Waterman is involved in a lot of this stuff."

"That weasel from FedPat? I told Clyde to check him out, but he didn't come up with much. Thinks he's harmless."

Kate knew otherwise, but was it really time to let Max know about the tap on Kevin's phone? Kevin's phone! She'd forgotten. She would retrieve the memory card and drop by Kevin's office.

She told Max she'd meet him after lunch then headed out to track down Kevin. Walking across the street toward the Maxwell Building, she really hoped she didn't run into anyone. She made it up the elevator to Waterman's floor. The door to his office was ajar. She walked in hoping to catch him off guard. The office was empty.

"Mr. Waterman's not here," a clerk said from outside the office. She told Kate that Kevin had just left. He'd gone out without saying anything.

She'd missed him again.

She thanked the clerk, who went back to her work, then Kate strolled casually back into Waterman's office. The desk was clear save for a telephone, an accordion file holder, and his computer monitor. She bumped the mouse on his desk and his monitor sprang to life. She sat down and started exploring his desktop with the mouse. *Let's see what he's been up to while we were gone*, she thought as she opened his calendar. He had nothing down for June 28, the day before, which was Tuesday. Monday contained a notation, "Mr. Maxwell, 10 a.m." Other notes for the week were routine. Funny that Max hadn't mentioned talking with Kevin. Maybe the meeting hadn't taken place. Before she left the building, she ducked into the electrical closet and retrieved the memory card. Back in her temporary office, Kate plugged the memory card in and started playback on Kevin's last few calls. The first two were unimportant business, the last one, a call to Kevin's girlfriend.

"They're after me, Nicole." He sounded scared. "My cell phone battery is dead. I'm calling from the office. I can't talk. I have to get out of here. I'm going down to Phoenix to stay with Toby. I'll call you soon. I've got to get away."

Chapter 63

Lyle's Mustang was out of reach. He wanted to get his car, but his condo was off limits, so he drove to the reservation in a car Earl rented for him.

He had called Jen Smith at the casino office to ask about Johnny Cooper. The motorcycle-riding-accountant didn't sound surprised to hear from him. "I was going to call you," she said. "You don't really look like a homicidal maniac. What's going on?"

Lyle managed to overcome some of her hesitation and persuaded her to ask Cooper to meet with him. Cooper set the time and place. Jen told Lyle the details.

Lyle turned off the main highway and followed an unpaved road that twisted its way around the edge of a small chaparral-dotted bluff. As the road rose up the hill, it afforded a view of a canyon off to the east. Lyle made another turn, as he was told to do, and the road changed from gravel to dirt, then to two narrow tracks in the red dust. Finally, the path ended at a rock outcropping where two beat-up pickup trucks were parked. Four men in jeans and western shirts were standing near the edge of a cliff.

Lyle stopped his car near the trucks and walked slowly toward the men who talked in muted voices.

"Johnny Cooper? I'm Lyle Deming."

"So you're the ex-cop, huh?" a tall, angular man said. He had long hair the color of the Arizona night and he fixed Lyle with a dark-eyed stare. "The shit at Nostalgia City is bad, bad for everybody. People have been killed. This was not our doing. We had no part in the death of your father."

"I believe you. I have evidence that proves it."

Cooper leaned against a rock worn smooth by millennia of wind and sand. He waited for Lyle to continue.

"I'm glad I finally have the chance to talk to you. With the evidence I have now," Lyle said, "we're going to the police. We know the big insurance company, Federal Patrician, has been behind everything. They've been pulling the strings. I know how you got into this—and why."

After seeing the look in Cooper's eyes, Lyle didn't expect him to deny anything. He was correct. "I also know you were not involved in hurting anyone."

"So what is it you want?"

"I need your help. If you'll testify against the men who did this, I'll do everything I can to see that you get a fair shake. We can help each other."

Did Cooper realize that Lyle needed him more than he needed Lyle?

"The sheriff, the tribal police will come for us."

"Sheriff Wisniewski is sympathetic to your cause. I think you know that. George Brown will help. I'll help too, in any way I can."

One of the other men said something to Cooper that Lyle couldn't hear. They took a few steps away and talked.

As Lyle looked into the canyon, something caught his eye—railroad tracks. Cooper had selected a meeting place overlooking the rugged valley where the NC casino express would soon be chugging through, loaded with tourists. Lyle wondered if Cooper was worried about preserving his past, about long-dead generations of ancestors who probably had roamed these same canyons and mesas. The past could be a powerful force. What sort of hold did it have on Cooper? Lyle would most likely never know.

When Lyle turned his attention back to the men in front of him, Cooper had taken a few steps forward. "We'll call you when we decide."

Chapter 64

Driving back from the reservation, Lyle called Kate on a newly acquired phone.

She heard something in his voice. "You okay?"

"Better than Janet Leigh in the shower scene."

"What's the matter?"

Kate leaned back in her chair. Lyle explained what Marko had told him, then said, "So I was hoping to recruit a witness. I wanted to get the Indians who sabotaged the bridge to testify against FedPat."

"Any luck?"

"They may be leaning our way, but there's no way to tell. Cooper wants to think about it."

"Kevin's on the run."

"What? Why didn't you say so?"

"I just listened to his last phone call. He told his girlfriend we were after him. Said he was going to hide out somewhere in Phoenix," Kate said. "I called him earlier and had to leave messages. Maybe that spooked him."

"Or maybe he heard from Bedrosian. Did you listen to the other recordings?"

"Didn't have time. It would take hours."

"Did he say where in Phoenix he was going?"

"No. He just said he was going to see someone named Toby."

"Do we know who that is?"

"Not that I know of. You coming in? We've got to meet with Max and his attorneys."

"I suppose."

"Max said we can't talk to his hotshot criminal attorney until late today or tomorrow. We're meeting with the civil specialists after lunch."

"Wish we could get our hands on Waterman," Lyle said as they hung up.

Kate looked at her watch. If she skipped lunch, she would have an extra half hour or so to listen to more of Kevin's phone calls.

Toby. The name meant nothing. Kevin had never mentioned anyone—wait. She remembered something. She checked to see that all the FedPat evidence was in her briefcase, then she left her temporary office and took an NC cab to the print shop. She remembered hearing Kevin talk to a friend who worked in printing. Now, what was his name?

When she walked into the printing office, it came to her. Before long, she had as much information as a smile and a touch on the arm could elicit from Drew, the assistant print shop manager.

ℰↃℰↃ

"Lyle, are you back?"

"Just pulling into the parking lot."

"I checked with a friend of Kevin's who works in the print shop."

"Does he know where he is?"

"No. But he said this guy Toby is manager of a restaurant."

"Which one?"

"He doesn't know the name."

"Know how many restaurants there are in Phoenix?"

"Let me finish, Lyle. He said it's a place where they cut people's ties off and stick them on the wall. It's in Scottsdale. That help?"

"Yes. I know it. Cactus Sam's Barbecue."

"So what do we do?"

"You know as much as I do about FedPat and Bedrosian. Why don't you talk to the attorneys? Show them the evidence. I'll try to track down Kevin. We could use him about now; at least *I* could."

ℰↃℰↃ

Two hours later, Kate had twice explained all the evidence she and Lyle had collected. She'd played the Renke recording and outlined the entire case against FedPat, murders, sabotage, and all. Sitting in Max's office, the two attorneys, Roger Reese and Anabel Genet, listened, asked questions, and took notes.

"We'd never have advised you to get into a contract like this one with FedPat in the first place," said Reese, a middle-aged man with gray temples in his otherwise shiny black hair.

"Already done," Max said. "Now we want to bury these bastards."

"We should be able to do that nicely," Genet said, "if all your evidence holds up." Her wardrobe and makeup were expensive but restrained. She had a pleasant smile that probably gave antagonistic witnesses a false sense of security. "Obviously, a lot will depend on the criminal proceedings, but the civil side of this will never get into court," she said. "FedPat will settle. As soon as Mr. Bedrosian is even *questioned* by police, I propose we call the president of FedPat, Mr. Shaw, and make a few suggestions."

"Could make a few damn suggestions to them, myself," Max said, "starting with sticking the whole—"

Genet politely raised a finger to silence Maxwell. "We'll start," she said, "by asking them to forgive the balance of the loan and pay damages of course."

"They won't like *that*," Max said.

"They would like going to court even less," Genet said. "Not to mention the publicity. Nothing like this happens in a corporation without other employees being involved. Perhaps Mr. Shaw knew nothing. Perhaps he was aware of everything. I suggest we push for a quick settlement. I'm assuming you're not interested in having this linger in the media, either."

"Of course," said Reese, "we must report all this to the authorities. Any police investigation will benefit your cause, but it sounds as if Mr. Deming might be a problem."

Genet nodded. "I understand what you've said, Ms. Sorensen, about his being slandered by the police. Nonetheless, he doesn't sound like the kind of person we would want to be deposed—questioned for the record—by FedPat counsel."

"We're on the trail of Kevin Waterman," Kate said. "If we can persuade him to testify, to explain everything he knows—"

"That would improve our position," Genet said.

"And," Reese said, "it would help Deming in criminal court."

"Who is counsel for the criminal charges?" Genet asked.

"Slade Foster," Max answered.

"Good choice. Considering the charges against Mr. Deming, you'll need him."

Max looked at Kate. "Where is Lyle?"

Chapter 65

Cactus Sam's Barbecue was a steak house, popular with tourists and locals alike. Chefs cooked steaks over wood-fired grills behind glass windows so patrons could watch. Two of the restaurant's simulated log walls were decorated with ties allegedly cut from over-dressed patrons. Lyle had finished his New York, cooked rare, and had just ordered coffee when Kevin Waterman walked in.

Waterman didn't see him. He entered with another man Lyle supposed was Toby Hawkins, the restaurant manager. Kevin sat at the bar. Hawkins walked around and poured him a beer. Then he leaned over the bar and patted Kevin on the shoulder. Lyle watched as Toby said something to Kevin then walked into the kitchen. A moment after he'd gone, Waterman swiveled his stool and looked around the restaurant. Lyle turned his head.

Lyle wished he could meet up with Waterman in the parking lot, but it might be hours before he left. Then he thought about waiting until the restaurant emptied out. Again, a long wait, and Waterman might spot him if he was the last customer.

Since Kevin was alone at the bar, Lyle decided to take a chance. He walked over and sat down on the rustic, high-back stool next to him. Kevin jumped. He looked at Lyle for a second then averted his eyes.

Lyle placed a firm hand on Kevin's left arm on the bar. "Stay put."

"You're Deming, aren't you," Kevin sputtered. "Oh, my God. You've got to help me."

This was a new approach.

"They're after me. He said he'd kill me like Rich Kovak if I didn't keep my mouth shut and help them."

"Who said this?"

"I never saw him before. My boss—the big boss—told me I

had to cooperate with them. He's crazy. They all are. He lied to me. I should have known. I *thought* it was too good to be true."

Lyle tried to make sense of Kevin's babbling. "Who's the big boss, Bedrosian?"

"Yes."

"What'd he tell you to do?"

"He said I had to help these, these—" Kevin tightened his grip on the beer glass. "They're following me."

"Settle down. Here, have a drink."

Kevin took two long swallows, choking on the second.

"Who's following you?"

"These *guys*. They said they'd *kill* me, don't you understand?"

"Why didn't you call the police?"

"No. I couldn't."

"Because you helped them sabotage Nostalgia City and kill—"

"No. Never."

"You and Bedrosian talked about it."

"I just kept the books. Yes, I talked to Bedrosian about what was happening. But I didn't have anything to *do* with it."

"You set it up."

"No."

"You knew what was going on."

"I didn't—I didn't know he hired hit men. I thought they were *accidents*." The accountant's shoulders sagged. He took another sip of beer. "I hoped they were."

"So Bedrosian suckered you along, and now his thugs are going to kill you if you talk."

Kevin turned and looked around the restaurant again.

"There's a way out of this," Lyle said.

Kevin shook his head slowly.

"Yes. We already have evidence on Bedrosian and the guys he hired. We know what he did. Someone named Renke killed Kovak, and we can prove it. This is your chance. You can show the police you didn't have anything to do with it."

Kevin looked up. He reminded Lyle of crime victims, people too scared to testify, too scared not to. He didn't think Kevin was faking.

"They'll kill me."

"I'll take care of them."

Kevin finished his beer. He looked around the restaurant again then stared at the wall behind the bar. "What—what can we do?"

Lyle wanted to drag him back to NC, but it was late. "We'll find a place to stay then drive up to Polk in the morning."

Lyle watched as Kevin explained to his friend Toby he was leaving, then they walked out into the hot, dry desert night.

"You have a car?"

"It's at Toby's."

"Good," said Lyle. "You can go with me."

As they drove out of the parking lot, Lyle was mulling the options for spending the night and thinking about which direction to turn. When they paused at a stop sign a few blocks away, a light-colored sedan sped toward them from a side street. It didn't stop. Just before it smashed into the driver's side of Lyle's car, the driver hit the brakes. The sedan skidded and spun up alongside them. Two men were inside. "It's them," Kevin shouted.

The man closest to Lyle pointed a pistol at him. He motioned for Lyle to pull over.

Lyle nodded to the gunman then slowly slipped his car into reverse—and jammed down the accelerator. The Chevy Camaro jerked backward. Lyle spun the wheel, turning the car around abruptly. As he shifted forward and picked up speed, he glanced in his mirror. Traffic was keeping the other car from turning around. From the darkness behind them came a flash. And a gunshot. Almost simultaneously, a bullet slammed into the trunk of Lyle's car.

Damn. Lyle tried to decide if his pursuers were trigger-happy idiots or serious killers. Either way, he was in trouble. Kevin clutched the door handle and Lyle worried he might jump out.

Lyle took a sharp turn and hoped he lost the gunmen. He came to the end of the block and turned again. Headlights spun quickly around the corner behind them. Lyle tried to recall the faces of the two men. He had seen them for only a second or two. Was the driver wearing funny glasses? What was it about his face? He looked familiar.

Lyle slid the Camaro out on to a busy, well-lit commercial street. He kept up his speed, racing through a stop signal on yellow. He looked in the mirror again. The light sedan was a block and a half back. They had a little cushion of space. Before he could relax, traffic suddenly stopped in front of them. A semi-truck was turning into the street from a parking lot.

The signal behind them changed. The light-colored sedan was moving. Lyle couldn't wait. He veered off into the opposing lanes. He had to get around the truck. He swerved back into his lane, just missing an oncoming van. A low cry issued from Kevin's throat. Behind them, the gunmen swerved out of the lanes, too. They were closing. Another flash and another gun report. This time the rental car's taillight shattered.

In a second, another flash lit up the night, only this one came from the beacons on top of a cop car. A police cruiser sped up behind the light sedan. Lyle strained to see behind them. He swerved over a lane to stay ahead of his pursuers and the police.

As the police cruiser closed in on the sedan, a second police car shot across an intersection and blocked the way. The driver of the sedan must have panicked because he turned sharply to the right, jumped a curb, and crashed into parked cars. Lyle made a quick left at a light. He tried to put as much distance as he could between himself and the police cars. His passenger shook as they sped down a side street.

Once clear of the accident scene, and the Scottsdale cops, Lyle realized what he had to do. He needed help. Marko was his only choice. He also remembered where he'd seen the driver of the other car.

Chapter 66

K ate. It's me. I found Waterman."

"What's he say? Did you have him arrested?"

"Not now. He's going to help us."

"Lyle, you didn't—"

"What, beat him up? 'Course not. Matter of fact, I saved his neck."

"What?"

"Some of Renke's men tailed him from the park, but we gave them the slip."

"Are you all right?"

"Yes." Lyle grinned as Marko set a cold soda down in front of him. He was slouched in a big lounge chair in the den of his former partner. "Turns out, Kevin didn't have anything to do with the sabotage."

"He didn't? But the phone calls."

"Guess we heard what we expected to hear. Bedrosian was stringing him along. He used Waterman to find out what was happening at the park, but our friend the bean counter didn't have a clue."

"I don't understand. Why'd he run from us?"

"He wasn't running from *us*. Renke's men paid him a visit and told him they'd kill him if he talked to the police or anyone. Said they'd kill him like they killed Kovak."

"Kevin told you this?"

"Yeah. Talk about naive. He heard everyone talking about a crisis, but he still thought they were accidents. He says he couldn't understand why security searched his car. Maybe he spends too much time on spreadsheets, I don't know."

"Sounds like he's figured it out, now."

"Completely. He's scared shitless of Renke and his men, but he's agreed to testify against Bedrosian. Since his talk with Renke's men, he knows that Bedrosian hired all the murder and sabotage. It all dawned on him and he's overwhelmed. Angry, too."

"Then he's what we need, Lyle. I talked to Slade Foster late this afternoon. He's staying at NC. He thinks we can get the charges dismissed—mine, too. Kevin's testimony will be our insurance."

"Did you ask him about talking to the police or county prosecutor?"

"Yes. He thinks it could work. He's heard of the prosecutor here, but he wants to meet with you first. Can you be here tomorrow morning?"

"I'll bring Kevin with me."

"Where are you?"

"I'm staying with my friend, Sergeant Markopoulos. Waterman's asleep on a couch in another room."

"So we go to the authorities tomorrow."

"Tomorrow's the day. I'm also going to have Kevin call Bedrosian in the morning."

"What for?"

"I'd like to have him repeat the things he told Kevin the other day, only with a real Phoenix police sergeant listening in."

"Couldn't hurt."

For a moment, neither of them said anything.

"Lyle," Kate ventured, "if Kevin wasn't involved, that means someone else —"

"It sure does. We'll talk about that tomorrow too. I have an idea."

⁓⁓⁓

"So you and Kate are quite the team," Markopoulos said when Lyle hung up.

"She saved my bacon in Cape Cod. Guys had a gun on me when I was in bed and she smashed one of them in the face."

"In bed? Where was she?"

"Close enough to flatten that guy's nose. In fact, I think that same guy is the one who was driving the car tonight."

"If so, he got away. I just talked to Scottsdale. They collared the guy with the gun—he had a record—but the driver slipped out somehow. They're still looking."

"Are they going to hold him?"

"You bet. Assault, resisting. They've got plenty until Waterman can substantiate other charges."

"I'll testify too, as soon as I—ahem—clear myself."

"The Scottsdale cops who chased the driver said he had some sort of clear shield over his face."

"He did. I didn't figure it out at first, but it's probably like the kind NBA players wear to protect a broken nose."

Chapter 67

Lyle tried not to be overly optimistic the next afternoon when they met with the county prosecutor. Ross Vincent, present holder of the office, wanted to talk to everyone: Waterman, Kate, Marko, Max. Especially Max. Sheriff Wisniewski and Rey Martinez were also there.

A few hours before, Lyle had met with Slade Foster, the pretentious—but nonetheless overwhelmingly successful—criminal attorney Max retained for him. Foster agreed that Lyle had enough evidence to take to the local prosecutor, but the interstate nature of the various charges pending against him would take time to sort out. The important thing, however, was to act fast to secure murder charges against Bedrosian and his henchmen. Foster said that Vincent could bring the U.S. attorney into it, but he thought the county attorney would be eager to play a leading role in a high-profile case involving giant corporations, murder, and extortion.

As it happened, the San Navarro County attorney already knew half the things Lyle had planned to tell him. Vincent had talked with his counterpart in Boston, with the Boston and Peabody police, Sheriff Wisniewski, the Scottsdale police, and even Clyde Bates, whom Lyle persuaded Max to exclude from Vincent's meeting.

Kevin Waterman explained his conversations with Bedrosian, including one that morning, which Sergeant Markopoulos substantiated. Bedrosian admitted the attacks on Nostalgia City were his idea and warned Waterman that police could consider him an accessory to murder and assault. He told Waterman that Max had finally agreed to his offer to turn over control of Nostalgia City, so Bedrosian had ordered Renke's men to clear out. Kevin was to come back to Massachusetts as soon as possible to avoid questioning by Arizona authorities.

Max explained he agreed to Bedrosian's last offer simply to stop the violence, and that he never intended to go through with it. Kate had proven to him that Bedrosian was behind the sabotage, and Max was certain Lyle and Kate had nothing to do with Kovak's murder, except being in the wrong place. Vincent seemed interested in the evidence and listened closely, taking notes as Kate played portions of Lyle's interview with Renke. Arrest warrants for Bedrosian and Renke, he said, would be issued and would be enforced today in Massachusetts. Phoenix police would pick up Art Jones for questioning, pending charges. They'd also issue an alert for Ned Havlicek. Vincent would do what he could to see that charges against Lyle and Jennifer Norris, aka Kate Sorensen, were dropped.

As the meeting concluded, Lyle asked Vincent if he was free to go, provided he promised to cooperate fully in the investigation and hearings that would result. Vincent was sanguine, but Wisniewski balked.

"If he's still wanted on a warrant, we can't just let him walk out of here," the sheriff said. "There's credible evidence that he's, well, let's say unpredictable."

Vincent persuaded the sheriff to let Lyle go back to his home—with a sheriff's deputy watching him—until the charges were dropped. Waterman agreed to stay in Polk—with the sheriff's protection.

After the meeting, Lyle wandered out of the San Navarro County Building and squinted into the setting sun. He didn't feel the heat as much as the light. The night before he hadn't slept much at Marko's and had driven to NC early that morning. Now he was eager to go home, make a meal for himself, and sleep in his own bed. As he wandered out to his car, he loosened his tie and fumbled for his keys. Kate had driven to the prosecutor's office with him. She was a few steps behind, talking with Undersheriff Martinez.

"So none of your men is going to arrest us, right?" Kate asked.

"Not today. But Lyle will have one of my men watching him."

"You saw the evidence. You know Lyle is innocent."

"Maybe, but you guys are lucky. You should be in jail. But the county attorney's an elected office. I'm sure Vincent is aware how important NC—and Maxwell—are to the county's economy."

"Regardless," Kate said, "the important thing now is to get Bedrosian and Renke put away."

"They'll have to *find* Renke first," Lyle said. "Maybe *he's* hiding out in Cape Cod now.

"He's better off back there," Martinez said. "Massachusetts doesn't have the death penalty."

"You didn't find anything wrong with the train?" Kate asked.

"We checked the engines and the tracks—with the help of your unhelpful security people—and didn't find anything. Your steam engine seems to have a technical problem, but no sabotage."

"So we'll be ready for the opening tomorrow," she said.

Lyle opened his car door. "Right now, I want dinner and a good night's sleep."

ᛒᚱᛒ

"Why didn't you tell Vincent who you think's been tipping off Bedrosian and helping Renke?" Kate said when they were on the road back to NC.

"'Cause I'm not sure. Maybe Vincent knows."

"Or thinks he does."

"I'm going to nose around before the festivities tomorrow. Who knows, I may grab the right person."

"Can I help?"

"I thought you had your hands full."

"I do. It starts tomorrow. I expect the media will be lining up."

"From all over the country, didn't you say?"

"Yup. And hell, I don't even know if our locomotive is going to be working."

"You sound just like Max."

"Thanks for the compliment. But he hired me to pump up publicity and that's what I'm doing. Now that FedPat is out of the way—almost—it's up to me to get money flowing through the gates."

Neither of them said anything for a few miles. Lyle watched the sheriff's car following them.

"Want me to drop you off at your apartment?"

"No," Kate said. "The NC employee entrance. I want to hit the office for an hour or—"

"Several?"

"Stuff to be done."

"There's a guard in the building. Lock your office door anyway, just to be safe."

"Yes, sir."

They drove in silence again for the next few miles. Before she got out of the car, Kate leaned over and kissed Lyle on the mouth.

ↁↄↁↄ

When Lyle turned the corner of his street and his condo came into sight, he looked at it with relief and sadness. He thought of his father, but the thought now rested a little more comfortably in the back of his mind. As he pulled up to the front of his home, the sheriff's patrol car pulled in behind him. Lyle got out and walked back to talk to the uniformed young man.

"This is crappy duty, deputy. I used to have to do some of this when I was at the Phoenix PD."

"It's not so bad. Don't mind night duty." The deputy pointed to the back of Lyle's rental car. "Those look like bullet holes."

"How am I going to explain it to Avis?"

The deputy grinned.

"Can I make you some coffee?" Lyle said.

"No thanks." The deputy held up a thermos. "Good evening, Mr. Deming."

Lyle wandered around his condo. Everything looked the same. He rummaged in the kitchen and determined that his 9 mm was still there. He set it on the counter. He didn't need it, but he felt better with it handy. He assumed his revolver was still safe in the bedroom closet.

He stripped off his suit and pulled on worn jeans, a polo shirt, and a pair of athletic shoes. He sat in front of the TV for a while, clicking the remote. Nothing caught his attention. He was tired but still keyed up. He found a beer in the fridge and sipped it while he cooked dinner.

Later, he was still too wound up to sleep. He lay down on his bed for a moment to relax. He knew he should take a shower before he turned in. He picked up a novel he had started weeks before.

୧୬୧

An hour later, something woke him. He hated falling asleep with his shoes on. It was uncomfortable. He opened his eyes wide then froze. A voice said something. A voice close by.

"Kitchen light's on. Maybe he's awake."

"Shut up. If he was, he'd be out here already. Shhh."

The voices came from the family room. The noise that woke Lyle must have been his patio door being jimmied. He rolled onto the floor putting his bed between him and the door to the bedroom. He crouched just below his window. Why did he leave the semi-automatic in the kitchen? The revolver was many steps away in the bottom of the closet. Did he have time to grab it?

Chapter 68

Kate couldn't reach Herb Herndon or anyone at the railroad operations office on the phone, so she decided to walk down and see for herself. The train station was only a few blocks away. Centerville was quiet. When evening came, most visitors wound up at the Fun Zone.

Kate could see the railroad station's glow from a block away. Spotlights flooded the building with white light. *Casino Route Grand Opening* signs fluttered in the breeze. Kate entered the barn-like waiting room. Rows of empty chairs and benches awaited the crowds that would come with the sun. A door leading to the operations office stood open, and Kate saw someone she thought she recognized. When she walked the length of the station, she knew who it was.

"Drenda, what are you doing here this late?"

"Just wanted to double check that old Engine 43 was ready to roll."

"All great minds," Kate said. "That's what I was doing."

"Herb says they'll start getting steam up about 6 a.m. All's set to go."

"Then I can go home."

Kate, six-two-and-one-half, and Drenda, five-one, wandered slowly down the aisle of the vacant waiting room.

"We get through tomorrow, and I think I can relax for the first time in weeks," Kate said. "I've been through some tough times with Max but *nothing* like this."

"You don't have to tell me anything you're not supposed to," Drenda said, "but are you and Lyle Deming safe now? I mean, they know you didn't have anything to do with that murder in Boston, right?"

"Yes. And I hope the whole thing is over."

"That will make working here easier—and safer."

"We still don't know who ratted us out though."

"Ratted you out?"

"That night I called you. Right after the murder. When we hid in that place in Cape Cod? They found us the next morning."

"The police?"

"No, the guys who've been wrecking the park."

"Who could have told them?"

"I don't know. I talked to Max that night. But I don't think he talked to anyone else. I dunno. Thankfully, we got away. They could have killed us."

Drenda shivered. "Thank God you're safe." She reached up to give Kate a hug. "I'd be lost around here now without you."

Kate leaned over and hugged her back. "You and I are a good team. And thanks for looking after Trixie."

℮ↄℰↄ

Lyle had no doubt the voices in his family room belonged to Topaz employees or its freelancers. And he had no doubt what they were there to do.

"I remember, there's a bedroom here." The hushed, gravelly voice was just around the corner.

No time to get the gun. Lyle stood up quietly. He slid his window open then pushed hard at the base of the screen. It gave—with a scraping sound.

"Hey," said a voice now in the bedroom.

By then, Lyle was out the window and running across the small yard toward his familiar jogging trail.

He expected to hear a shot. He steeled himself for it. Instead, he only heard pounding feet and angry voices. "There he is."

Without a gun and outnumbered at least two to one, Lyle's best move was to run. So he did. For what seemed like a mile, he ran, adrenaline-charged, at full speed. His would-be killers were younger than him. He could still hear their voices. They had enough strength to run *and* talk. Lyle kept on.

Knowing the trail gave Lyle an advantage, but running in the moonlight was still risky. As his initial, fear-driven energy started to wane, he realized he'd have to pace himself. He didn't con-sciously slow down, but found a rhythm. It kept him at least 100

yards ahead of the men behind him without draining all his reserves.

As he started into a broad curve, soft trail dust flew up in his
wake. He considered jumping off to the side and waiting to surprise his pursuers. But something made him think there were
three of them. And Lyle wasn't twenty-five anymore. But damn
it, he could still run. He hated to think what must have happened
to the young deputy on duty in front of his condo. That made him
angry. When the trail straightened out again, Lyle could see the
top of the NC Drive-In movie screen. It stood maybe another two
miles ahead on the twisting trail through the sage and creosote.
For a moment, he couldn't hear anything behind him. He paused
for a breath. The voices were faint but getting louder. The men
swore at each other in guttural tones, reminding Lyle of a pack of
dogs.

He ran on.

Taking a sharp turn, Lyle slipped in the dust. His right leg
skidded out from under him, and he slid into a brittlebush. He got
up as quickly as he could. And then he heard the shot.

They must have missed. Lyle ran on.

He could feel the burning patch on his leg where he scraped
it falling down. And now he felt a strange pain on his left side. He
put his hand to his waist. It hurt like hell. The shot had hit him
after all. But it was just a graze, no more than a burn or a cut.
Lyle looked at his hand as he ran. He couldn't see much blood.

He always thought *runner's high* was a bit exaggerated.
Running a few miles didn't give him a big rush, more of a steady
happiness, calming at the same time. It was a hushed assurance he
was truly alive.

This quiet confidence masked the pain in his side and helped
him sail along the miles ahead. He reached the drive-in theater.
With the pack well behind him now, Lyle had a few moments to
think.

No cell phone when he needed it, just like the NC years. He
glanced across the lot and saw the concession stand and projec-
tion room. He could find a phone there. His pursuers would probably figure that out too. And maybe they'd come flying in, shooting. Innocent people could be killed. Along with him.

Lyle decided to duck out of sight, wait for his attackers to
pass by, and then follow them. He stood for another couple of

minutes until he heard the men approach the drive-in. They climbed over the fence that Lyle had scaled. Lyle crouched beside an empty prop car, one of many sprinkled throughout the drive-in, for NC guests.

The men were panting and swearing. Two of them bent over and braced their hands on their knees as they gulped for breath.

"How can that son of a bitch—run like that?"

Lyle was glad to see the punks couldn't take the elevation. It sapped the strength of these creeps who probably hadn't run this far in a long time. And never at 5,000 feet.

Having quickly recovered his wind, Lyle remained silent and listened. He ducked down and looked under the car. The flickering light of the movie screen illuminated three pairs of feet a few strides away on the other side. The men were still panting hard, but they started to walk down the aisle behind the car. Lyle flattened himself in a shadow against the rear fender. One man walked by, so close that Lyle could have smelled his deodorant, if he'd been wearing any.

"Bet he's in the snack bar," one of them said. "Down there."

"Yeah," another said, and the three men headed off.

Lyle followed at a safe distance. He hovered in the entrance while the men went inside.

In just a few seconds, they were coming out again. Lyle looked around and saw another dummy car, but this one had two mannequins in the front and one in the back.

Reaching into a spot in the car's rear wheel well, Lyle found the hidden door release. Quickly, he jumped into the back seat. But he couldn't get the door to catch. It stood open a few inches.

Out of the corner of his eye, he saw the men emerging from the snack bar ramp. In the back seat, next to Lyle, sat a female mannequin. Slowly, he slid his right arm around behind her. He moved his face close to hers.

The men stopped outside the car.

"He's long gone."

Lyle strained to hear them through the crack in the door.

One of the men stomped his foot into the dirt. "Now what?"

Lyle hugged his new date and didn't move. Someone with his back to Lyle was talking. All Lyle heard was, "Blow the train."

"We'll find Deming later," another voice said. "Let's get the tall bitch. I know where she lives."

Chapter 69

Kate got out of Drenda's car in front of her apartment. She glanced around wondering why the sheriff hadn't had her followed, like he did Lyle. Was she less a threat because she was a woman?

Once inside her apartment she dropped her briefcase on the sofa, kicked off her shoes, and draped her suit coat over a chair. The building was quiet. She felt the soft rush of cool air from the air conditioning duct. She reached down to stroke her cat who appeared at her feet. She and Trixie both jumped when the phone rang.

"Kate. Renke's men are here," Lyle said. "They're coming for you. I heard them."

"Here? How do they know where I am?"

"I don't know. They shot at me."

"You okay?"

"Yeah. I got away."

"Where are you?"

"On a pay phone near the drive-in. I'll be there soon. Get out of your apartment, now. I just borrowed a cab. I'll pick you up."

"Should I call security downstairs?"

"No time. Just get out. There's an activity room at the back of your building. I'll meet you at the rear door in five minutes. Go."

❡❡❡

At the drive-in, when Lyle had figured it was safe, he'd kissed his backseat partner, slipped out of the car, and walked to the street just in time to see an NC cab roll by. Lyle knew the driver.

He told him it was life and death, and unceremoniously took

the cab. Lyle took a back way to Kate's apartment and arrived four minutes later.

She wasn't there.

He threw the gearshift into park and got out. As he stood up, he felt a throbbing pain in his side. Blood from his bullet wound had dried to his shirt. When he moved, it pulled off the scab that had started to form. The wound looked like a singe from the shaft of a hot branding iron. He held his side as he scanned the shadowy parking lot.

Footsteps pounded the concrete. Someone was running toward him. Lyle spun around and saw Kate, dressed in jeans, dash out the back of the building, swinging a large purse. She and Lyle jumped in the cab. Lyle pulled out.

"They're crazy," Lyle said. "They're trying to kill us."

"Killing us won't get them off the hook."

"They obviously don't know that. Or maybe Bedrosian put a price on our heads."

"Where are they?"

"Close by. They chased me out of my condo and I ran down to the drive-in. I heard someone say they were going to blow the train."

"Shit."

Lyle turned on to the main road and headed toward Centerville. He and Kate looked forward, back, and scanned the sidewalk. Few people were out. Several times Lyle imagined he saw suspicious figures lurking, but they turned out to be tourists on a nighttime stroll. Or trees moving in the wind. Before Lyle appropriated the taxi, the cabbie had been listening to the radio, and rock music still drifted from the speakers, like the background score to a retro movie. A throaty female voice was crying out a song.

"Shouldn't we be calling security?" Kate asked. "Or the sheriff?"

Lyle was scanning the road, trying to think, hardly listening. The song on the radio ended and the familiar deep voice said, "That was 'White Rabbit' by Iron Butterfly."

"Lyle, are you listening to me? Shouldn't we *call* somebody."

"Yeah. I suppose. Bates's guys will be useless."

"Then do we call the sheriff?"

"Wisniewski?" Lyle slowed for a car crossing the road ahead then looked in his rearview mirror.

On the radio, Earl Williams said, "Now, here comes a big new hit from Eric Clapton, "American Pie."

"Lyle, should we—"

"Hold it." Lyle held up his right hand. "Listen."

The song came on the radio, and Lyle turned up the volume.

"It's one of Earl's oldies," Kate said. "What's the big deal?"

"Earl's in trouble."

Chapter 70

Lyle and Kate pulled up at the side of the radio station and looked around. Lyle turned off the engine and they sat in the dark. "They're in there. Renke's men are in the studio. And both my weapons are at home."

Kate reached in her purse and pulled out a silvery object. "I started keeping this in my nightstand at the apartment."

"Where'd you get *that*?" Lyle said, looking at the big SIG Sauer .40 caliber semi-automatic.

"I've had it a while. I know how to shoot. My father taught me."

"So that's why you looked so comfortable with the gun in P-town."

Kate handed the gun to Lyle. Although she might have fired it hundreds of times, Lyle thought, she probably never pointed it at anyone.

Assuming the front door would be locked, Kate and Lyle moved cautiously around to a service entrance at the back of the building. Next to a narrow metal roll-up door, a standard door stood ajar and rock music spilled into the alley. Holding the gun low, Lyle stuck his head through the doorway. Kate looked over his shoulder. The room was dark, but they could see light—and hear music—coming from a far doorway. As the evening DJ, Williams was likely the only person on duty.

Lyle and Kate moved up to the next door and looked out into a lighted hallway. After a few paces down the hall, they saw a large workroom Lyle had been in before. Peering into the room, they could see the windows that separated the workroom from two broadcast studios. One of the studios was brightly lit. Inside it, three men stood around the disk jockey's console, with Earl seated in the middle. One of the men was Joe Renke.

The console, stacked with electronic gear and a microphone

boom, blocked their view. Lyle and Kate could see the men only from the waist up and could just see Earl's eyes and the top of his head.

"You'd better get back to the car," Lyle said. "Call the sheriff's department."

"I'm not leaving. Besides, you've got my gun. You have to protect me."

Lyle gave up easily. He ducked down and motioned for Kate to follow him. Together they crawled into the dark workroom and stopped behind a desk, about fifteen feet from the studio window.

"If that guy in there didn't have a gun, Earl would have flattened all of them," Lyle said. He recognized the other two men. Holding a gun on Earl and standing with his back to one of the studio doors was Ned Havlicek, who Kate had smashed in the nose in Provincetown. The other man was Art Jones.

"I recognize the guy with tape over his nose," Kate said.

Lyle crouched behind the desk. "I've been in here before," he whispered. "With those bright lights on in the studio booth you can't see anything out here."

As Kate and Lyle watched, Earl reached up and grabbed a cartridge off the top of the console. A moment later, the voices in the studio filled the workroom.

"Earl must have thrown a switch," Lyle said. "He can see in the dark. He knows we're here."

Instinctively, Kate ducked lower.

"Look, Joe," Art Jones was saying in the booth. "I don't think this guy knows anything. We need to get outta here."

"He's Deming's friend," Renke said. "He knows. Poke him again."

Jones waved a lock-back knife in the air. "Let's get the money and *go*."

"The money's final payment. So we have to blow the tracks and get rid of Deming and the woman first," Renke said.

"Hell, they won't know if they're dead or not," Jones said. "We'll still get the money."

"You're not the one Deming can testify against," Renke growled. "Are you?"

"So what about the explosives?"

"Morgan and I set up the C-4 already," Renke said. "That's done. Now we get Deming." Renke motioned toward Earl.

Jones bent over the DJ's console.

"I told you, I don't know where he is," Earl said. "He's hiding out from the police."

"We have to *do* something," Kate whispered to Lyle. "There're two doors to the studio. Why don't I—"

"Go around over there," Lyle said, finishing her thought, "and distract them from one door while I come crashing in the other."

"Okay, just be careful."

Staying as low as he could, and moving behind furniture, Lyle inched up to the studio door. He stood in a shadow and waited. Kate had to crawl back to the hallway to reach the other door. When she knocked, all three of Earl's tormentors looked up at once. She didn't walk into the room, just stood to the side and pulled the door open slightly.

"Earl?" she said. "Can you come out here for a minute?"

"I'll get her," Renke said.

He took a step toward the door.

Lyle threw open his door hard, hitting someone. Havlicek tumbled forward into a bookcase filled with stacks of CDs. He hit the floor with CD cases spilling over him.

Lyle lunged for him. He grabbed the gun out of the man's hand with his left, at the same time pointing Kate's SIG at Art Jones.

"Everybody freeze," Lyle shouted. "Drop the knife."

As Jones's knife hit the floor, Lyle saw Renke go through the other door. He turned to Jones. "Don't move. Back up."

Lyle shouted the orders and Jones obeyed, raising his hands to shoulder level. Jones had a gun tucked in his waistband.

Lyle kicked Havlicek who was still on the ground and told him to get up against the wall with Jones. Immediately Lyle saw that Earl was tied up, strapped to his chair with electrical cord. Wire also wrapped his right wrist to the arm of the chair. The moment the two assailants were against the wall, Williams stood up, lifting the swivel chair with him. He back handed Jones in the face with his free hand then grabbed Jones's pistol and pointed it at him.

"Kate." Lyle yelled.

No answer.

As he moved past Earl, Lyle hit a wheel of the swivel chair.

It was just high enough to scrape against his bullet wound. He winced but kept moving.

Lyle scrambled out the door—and tripped over Kate lying on the floor.

"He got away," Kate said. "As soon you came crashing in, he ran."

"You okay?"

"Yeah. He knocked me down with the door trying to get past. He didn't even look at me. Just took off. I heard the back door slam."

They stepped back into the studio as Kate brushed herself off.

"You all right, Earl?" Lyle said.

"I'm okay. But these guys won't be." He jabbed Jones hard in the stomach with the pistol.

"Hold on Earl. We'll take care of them."

"Well," Kate said, "our friend from P-town. How's the nose, Ned?"

"These the guys who crashed the monorail into my studio?" Earl asked.

"Think so." Lyle herded the two men into a corner while Kate helped Earl untangle himself from the chair.

"What happened here, Earl?"

"These dudes surprised me. Don't know how they got in. By the time I heard anything, bam, one of them hits me on the head and the other starts tying me up."

"What'd they want?"

"You. They knew you were a friend of mine. They wanted to find you."

"Sorry. I lost them an hour ago. They went after Kate. Must've come right here when we got away."

"I told them if they took me off the air, security would come charging in here. So they left one of my hands free and let me announce records, while this guy jabbed me with his knife." Earl showed Lyle a patch of dried blood on his arm.

Lyle turned to Jones. He resisted a strong temptation to bash Jones in the face. "Neither of these guys look tough to me," he said. "But we have to find Renke and see if he has any other punks running around."

"I know where he went," Earl said. "That guy who left—is

his name Joe?—he called this guy Morgan on his cell phone. He's going to meet him at the Graveyard Grill. They're going to pick up a big cash payment for killing you."

Lyle took a couple of steps back from the thugs. "Watch these guys, huh, Earl? But don't kill them. We've got to get Renke."

"Do I call security?"

"No, call the sheriff. Never mind. I'll call myself."

"Lyle. Thanks for getting my message."

"Lucky I was listening. I knew even you could identify Jefferson Airplane. And Eric Clapton doing 'American Pie'? I'm surprised these idiots didn't catch that one."

Chapter 71

C an you get me in touch with Rey Martinez? It's an emergency." Lyle drove with one hand, holding Kate's cell phone in the other, as they raced the cab toward NC's amusement park. "Rey, I once told you if I found bad guys in the park I'd call you before I did anything. Remember? Well this is your notice. Joe Renke—you know that name—and another guy are about pick up a cash payment for blowing up the train and killing me."

"You're not dead."

"Very perceptive. But the person paying him off doesn't know that."

"Who's doing the payoff?"

"C'mon on over and find out. Ms. Sorensen and I are going to rendezvous for a late night snack at the Graveyard Grill. Know where it is?"

"Right next to the Living Dead ride."

"That's it. But please don't come crashing in there Code 3. You're liable to frighten Renke and his men more than the ride."

Lyle took a turn a little faster than he should have and the cab swerved momentarily.

"So, can we meet you there, Rey? And please, send some men to the radio station on Third Street—right away. Tell them my DJ buddy, Earl Williams, is holding a gun on a couple of Renke's people who tried to kill him."

"Okay, but—"

"One last thing. You might alert your bomb detail, if you have one. Once we grab these guys at the restaurant they're going to have to tell us where they planted explosives to blow up the train."

❧❧❧

Taking a service road, Lyle pulled up twenty yards behind the *Night of the Living Dead* attraction.

"Here's your expensive piece back." He handed Kate the SIG Sauer. "Havlicek had my 9mm in his pocket. The thief." He tucked the gun into his belt behind his back and pulled his shirt over it. "Let's try hard not to use these things, okay?"

He looked at his watch. It was almost 11 o'clock. The rides would be open until 1 a.m.

"I guess Bedrosian didn't call off Renke after all," Lyle said.

"Or maybe he's taking orders from someone else now."

Lyle followed Kate through the crowd of tourists still wandering about in front of the restaurant and adjacent ride. The aroma of barbecue sauce met them as they squeezed their way to the entrance. Lyle looked over at tourists waiting to get into the ride. The line of people snaked up and down in roped-off rows around remnants of a shattered farmhouse and barn. Draped over splintered walls, a few mock corpses moved and moaned in muted agony.

Inside the restaurant, many of the tables were full. The dining area occupied a large patio overlooking a cemetery where the Living Dead ride began. Every few seconds, tourists, seated in small-scale '60s and '70s convertibles, rolled through the cemetery along a winding roadway. Diners could watch passengers on the ride cruise through the graveyard and into a tunnel leading to the scarier portions of the journey.

Above, the high painted ceiling looked like the night sky. Projections of clouds drifted across it. Lyle had loved the place—until now. It was indoors but had the feel of outdoors. The smell of food cooking mixed with an artificial graveyard dampness created by misting nozzles and theatrical fog.

"Do we get a table and wait?" Kate asked.

"Off in a corner."

Kate flashed her NC ID badge and a hostess seated them at the patio edge, the table partially screened by a faux willow. Sitting with their backs to a wall, they scanned the restaurant. Lighting was subdued, like the last few moments of dusk before night took over.

"I don't see them," Kate said.

"Neither do I."

"Who's the inside person?" Kate asked. "Who's going to deliver the cash?"

"Any guesses?"

"Yeah. In fact—" Kate stopped mid-sentence as they both saw Renke and another, larger man with a shaved head walk into the patio from the bar. A hostess led them past Kate and Lyle to a table on the other side of the dining area. They were seated at the edge of the cemetery near the passing parade of visitors on the ride.

The two men scanned the restaurant. Every sixty seconds a low scream arose from inside the ride. Lyle and Kate had heard it enough to ignore it. Renke and his guest flinched the first time.

"That guy reminds me of Hoss Cartright," Lyle said, indicating Renke's bulky associate, "just not as bright."

Kate was about to speak, but she stopped when someone else they knew stood in the patio entrance.

Lyle had never seen Drenda Adair showing anything but crisp professionalism. Now the shoulder of her dress sagged. Strips of torn fabric hung loose. Strands of hair pointed in different directions. She stared, wide-eyed, across the restaurant. When she saw Kate and Lyle, she rushed over.

"Kate, Kate what are you doing here? You've got to get out. Both of you."

"Sit down, Drenda." Kate yanked her into a chair.

"They're going to kill you and I don't even know who they are."

Kate glanced over at Renke. He was looking the other way.

"I'm so sorry Kate," Drenda sobbed. "It's all my fault. Everything. My father, he—he doesn't know what he's doing. He's not well. I tried to stop him from coming here. When I found out, I called the sheriff."

"What are you saying?" Kate said.

Lyle looked at Drenda. "Your father's Sean Maxwell. He's FedPat's inside man. He's been helping the guys who want to destroy the park."

"I didn't know. He and Uncle Max never got along, but I didn't know Father would do something like *this*."

"Where's your father now?" Kate asked.

"He's right there." Lyle pointed to the far patio entrance. Sean Maxwell stood on unsteady legs, staring out at the tables. Sheriff's deputies stood on either side of him.

"Father!" Drenda screamed.

Renke and Hoss Cartwright jumped to their feet. Seeing the closest exit blocked by deputies, they headed in the other direction. Toward Lyle and Kate.

Lyle told Drenda to get down. As he stood up, he pulled out his 9 mm and pointed it at Renke. Joe hesitated for a moment, stuck his hand inside his jacket, and spun around behind a table full of guests.

Two more deputies—one of them Rey Martinez—entered the patio from the other side. Renke unholstered a large-caliber semi-automatic but didn't fire. Instead, he ran for the edge of the cemetery, leaping a low iron fence. His companion followed, pulling out his own gun as he ran. As dozens of astonished diners watched, the two men landed on the simulated highway, dodged around tourists in model convertibles, and disappeared into the tunnel.

Lyle ran after them. "Stop the ride," he shouted back to Kate. "Get people out."

In a moment, he jumped over the fence and ran into the tunnel. Martinez followed close behind. Lyle strained to see in the darkness, but soon the tunnel was illuminated with a muzzle flash.

Kate knew she couldn't stop the ride. That would strand who-knew-how-many tourists inside. But she could stop more people from entering. She ran to the restaurant door and flashed her ID at a deputy. "Come with me. I need your help."

Tourists crowded around trying to watch the commotion. Kate pushed her way through. She hoped they thought it was just part of the NC show. No one seemed overly alarmed.

Once outside, Kate ran up the Living Dead exit ramp, dodging people as she went. The deputy followed closely behind, hand on holstered semi-automatic.

"Excuse me. Sorry. Out of the way," Kate said as she dashed up the darkened ramp.

When she reached the end, she had to jump sideways to avoid three people stepping out of a car. She put one foot in the car then leaped to the loading platform, elbowing a ride attendant

out of the way. In a few long strides, she reached the control panel. The ride supervisor was talking to another employee.

Kate again flashed her ID badge. "Close the ride. Don't let
anyone go in. Police are inside, chasing two men with guns."

The supervisor glanced at the sheriff's deputy, then at the
ride controller who started throwing switches.

"Don't stop it," Kate said. "We've got to get everyone out.
Just close the gates. Tell people it's broken."

 презентация

By the time Lyle's eyes had adjusted to the low light, Renke
and the other man had disappeared. One of them discharged his
gun as he ran. The steady stream of little cars kept rolling by,
each carrying two or three tourists. The visitors stared at Lyle and
Martinez as if they belonged there.

"Been on the ride before?" Lyle asked.

"No. I was going to."

Lyle pointed ahead. "This road goes in a big horseshoe. If
you keep following them, I can take a short cut and come out at
the other end. Maybe we can trap 'em."

Martinez seemed reluctant to let Lyle out of his sight, but he
nodded assent. Martinez walked down the road trying to keep
halfway between the car in front of him and the one behind.

Lyle worked his way to a behind-the-scenes walkway. At
that point, visitors' cars passed into narrow corridors lined with
boarded-up doors and windows. Realistic mechanical ghouls
reached through the boards in continuous, but always unsuccess-
ful, attempts to seize visitors. Groans and low-pitched screams
from the artificial zombies filled the air.

Lyle stood next to a moving ghoul—actually the mechanism
that controlled a head, torso, and one arm—and peered through
the boards. Renke and his partner were groping their way down
the corridor. Renke's companion tripped over the track that controlled the cars. He fell in front of one of the small vehicles. The
two passengers—a teenage couple—thought he was part of the
show. They laughed.

The man stood and took a swing at one of the teens. The
youth screamed. Martinez appeared down the road. He shouted
above the noise, telling the man to freeze. Instead, the gunman

spun around and pointed his pistol at Martinez. As Lyle tried to shove his gun through the boards and take aim, Martinez fired.

Chapter 72

The bald gunman fell to the side, crashing through the false-front scenery. Before Martinez could get to him, he stumbled off, swearing. Lyle ran around to the end of the passageway hoping to cut off Renke, but Renke was nowhere in sight. Lyle moved farther along the ride's path toward the sound of shots in the distance. He knew the shots were sound effects at the end of the ride. The ride mirrored the climax of the movie. The cars were steered down a lane lined with ghouls on one side, an armed sheriff's posse on the other. As the cars approached, the automated lawmen started shooting across the road at the ghouls. Just as the cars were about to enter the line of fire, the road suddenly dipped and passengers sped down a steep chute toward the exit.

Before the riders reached the shoot-out, cars slowed and passed through a farmyard brightly lit from flames that engulfed a smashed-up truck. Natural gas provided the fuel for the flames. Lyle always marveled at the authenticity the blaze lent to the scene.

As he moved around in front of the burning truck, he noticed the cars passing him were empty. Kate had stopped new passengers from entering the ride. Lyle hurried ahead realizing he was backlit by the flames.

"Deming."

He turned and saw Renke twenty feet away, standing on the edge of the road, pointing his gun at him. Renke took a half step back to get out of the way of an empty car as it passed. "Drop it."

Lyle tossed his gun down on a chicken coop.

"Finally asshole, you're gone."

Renke raised his arm, aiming squarely at Lyle's chest. As he did, Lyle dropped flat on the ground behind the chicken coop.

In the same moment—behind Renke—Kate appeared inside

an approaching car where she had been crouching. She held her pistol in her right hand. Renke didn't turn around.

Instead of shooting, Kate swung her gun in a short arc and hit Renke in the neck. His arm jolted to the left as he fired. He fell and the shot went wild. Kate jumped from the car and pinned him down. He'd hit his head on a genuine boulder—not all the props were fiberglass. His grip on the gun relaxed. Kate pulled it out of his hand. He didn't move.

Lyle snatched up his gun and leaped across the road next to Kate. Above the monotonous, make-believe gunfire, the sound of two real gunshots ricocheted through the ride.

"Go ahead," Kate said. "I've got him."

Lyle jumped into an empty car and it took him to the sound of the shots, both real and artificial. As he approached the posse attack on the ghouls, he saw something was wrong. One of the ghouls had a gun and he was shooting at the posse.

As he got closer, Lyle saw the armed ghoul was really the huge gunman Martinez had wounded. With his bald head, crazed expression, and shirt soaked with his own blood, the gunman looked like another artificial zombie. On the other side of the road, Martinez was sprawled on the ground next to an automated, make-believe deputy. Blood covered his right shoulder. His gun was in the dirt, six feet away.

The gunman took slow, staggering steps toward the road, to get an unobstructed shot at Martinez. Lyle leveled his gun at the live ghoul, now just a few feet away. Martinez saw Lyle. So did the gunman. As Lyle squeezed the trigger, his car jerked downward at the exit chute. His shot missed.

He let go of the gun, stepped on the seat, and leaped for the edge of the road. As he flew toward solid ground, his shoulder collided with the gunman's ankles. The man struggled for a second, then pitched, head-first, over Lyle and onto the roadway thirty feet below.

Chapter 73

How'd you do it?" Lyle asked. "I lost track of you when the ambulances arrived. How'd you get Renke to talk?"

"After you left," Kate said, "he started to come around. I could see he wasn't completely conscious so I told him we needed to blow up the train, but I didn't know where the explosives were."

"Renke thought you were on his side?"

"He was delirious."

"You have that effect on people."

"I told him they were coming for us and he had to tell me quickly. I said the explosion would be a distraction. We could get away."

A San Navarro County sheriff's deputy motioned for Lyle and Kate to step farther back. They were standing above a ravine, looking at a flood-lit scene of deputies and a bomb-disposal crew working near a stretch of railroad track.

"Renke should never have come to Arizona," Lyle said.

"Bedrosian offered him more money, plus the chance to get even with us. He couldn't resist."

"With Sean's help, he knew damn near everything there was to know about the park."

"I feel sorry for Drenda. She was close to her father. Saw him almost every day. She didn't know he was working with Bedrosian."

"I wonder how Bedrosian recruited him."

"They must have met when the FedPat loan was negotiated," Kate said. "Sean was still closely involved with NC back then."

"So when Bedrosian learned that Sean and Max had a falling out, he moved in. Maybe bribed him. Maybe stroked his ego, told him he should be running the park instead of Max."

"So Sean started to figure out ways to sabotage the park."

"He'd done business with the Indians through his shop for years," Lyle said. "Maybe he used his contacts to persuade Cooper to wreck the bridge."

"And anything he didn't already know about NC, he got by pumping Drenda."

"That's how he found out we were staying in Province-town."

"Must have been bitter. He couldn't afford Drenda's college tuition, so Max paid for it. Then somehow Max ran him out of Nostalgia City."

"Kate, back there in the ride. Thank you. You saved my bacon. That's twice now."

"Yeah, I did, didn't I?" Kate grinned.

"Is that a superior look I see?"

"What? You want me to say, 'Warn't nuthin'. Just doin' my job'? I think that's a guy thing."

Lyle looked into the ravine and saw Sheriff Jeb Wisniewski making his way up the hill. He wore a uniform shirt and gun belt over jeans.

Wisniewski's cowboy boots dug into the loose soil and he stepped up on the rise next to Lyle and Kate. "So if you two have this whole shit-mess solved, would you mind telling me who's what, and why in hell they've been trying to destroy the park?"

"Like we said in Vincent's office," Lyle said, "FedPat Corporation wanted to take over. They hired Renke and his thugs. Turns out, Sean Maxwell was giving them inside information."

"All that crap was true, huh? Be damned. Well, the little explosive charge is out of the way. They had it so the engine coming by would set it off. You can run your train across now, no problem."

"That deputy..." Kate said.

"Yeah," Lyle said, "the one out in front of my condo. Is he—"

"He's in big trouble. But he's not hurt bad, if that's what you mean. They just knocked him out."

Chapter 74

A nd so ladies and gentlemen, the turmoil, the protests, the discord that was a big part of the country as America lurched from the sixties to the seventies, *that* created the foundation for today's world. The upheaval shocked our society and forced us to look at ourselves in a new light."

Archibald Maxwell stood on the bunting-covered dais and spoke to the hundreds of media representatives, tourists, and employees who crowded into Protest Plaza—the newest theme area at Nostalgia City. At the back of the crowd, listening conscientiously, Lyle and Kate stood in front of a sales cart that displayed tie-dyed shirts and peace-sign medallions.

"Much of the equality and tolerance—and yes, love—that we have today grew out of the protest marches of the past decades," Max intoned. "To truly appreciate the authentic joy of those times that Nostalgia City represents, I realized it was important for us to put *all* the events of the past into perspective. And into our exhibits. Our dedication of this plaza today, the '60s and '70s news gallery plus the civil rights exhibit and the veterans' memorial, symbolize the accomplishments and the heartache that marked the era."

"I didn't know he felt this way," Lyle said. "This is an amazing speech."

"Thanks. I wrote it."

"Then Max doesn't…"

"Oh, he does, in his own way. But it dawned on me, when I was writing this speech, that Max was an adult when the protests were going on. He didn't take time for politics because he was struggling to make a living. But he's come around. He understands what the protests brought about."

"It all depends on your perspective," Lyle said. "Everything does. Remember what I told you about Vietnam?"

"About accepting the past, because you can't change it?"

"It's true for everything in life. My dad, Collins and Bensen at the PD, *everything*. It's past. Gone. My dad pushed me into things, but it was what he thought he had to do. It's done now. Nothing to do but accept it. Everything."

"And so you're moving on?"

"I'm workin' on it." He held up his wrist to display the rubber band.

"You still need that?"

"Keeps me centered."

"Maybe you should try TM."

"I've been thinking about meditation. It'll also help to be back in my comfortable cab, in a nice, *quiet* theme park."

"I don't see your police escort this morning."

"The sheriff decided I was worth a risk."

"I'm glad he agreed to keep the details of last night's shooting under wraps."

"At least until the media go home."

"Your saving Martinez didn't hurt. How's the bullet wound?"

"Mine or his?"

"Yours."

"It was a scratch. I've got it taped up. Martinez is okay, too."

"And Renke's in the hospital and his men are…"

"In jail or, in Morgan's case, the morgue." Lyle looked at the peace-sign medallions, hefting one of the larger ones in his hand. "Rey said they can prove that big guy is the one who killed my dad. They got statements from the others, and a stray fingerprint matched."

"What about Johnny Cooper?"

"He and the sheriff have an agreement. It'll work out."

Kate turned toward Lyle. "You know, I suspected Bates for a while. He knew about your background all along. I thought he brought it up when he did just to divert suspicion from himself."

"I wondered about him, too. He did know my background from the start. The only reason he recommended me to investigate is because he thought I was a nut case who wouldn't threaten his job. Marko told me he earned some commendations at the FBI. Guess Max will keep him around."

"For one second, I was worried about Max. I saw the name

Maxwell on Kevin's calendar. But it was Sean who came to see him. He probably wanted to find out if Kevin suspected anything."

❧❧❧

As Max worked toward the conclusion of his speech, Kate led Lyle around the crowd and behind the platform. "I want you to see the exhibits and shops."

Two sides of the new plaza were lined with displays featuring newspaper front pages, their headlines telling a story of recent history: Martin Luther King's assassination, anti-war protests, Nixon's resignation, and many other events. Kate and Lyle walked past the exhibits to a new store at the back of the square, Mrs. Ashbury's. It offered long, Indian-cotton dresses, fringed vests, beads, necklaces, incense, and posters.

"Cool," Lyle said, "a headshop." He pointed to a window display of three white jars. The small China containers were labeled, *Marijuana, Hash,* and *LSD.*

"There's no drugs for sale here. It's a joke." Kate grinned. "I hope Max is ready for hippie culture."

Lyle looked at his watch. "By now the cops in Boston have rounded up Bedrosian and anyone else who was in on the scam."

"Kevin will be glad to testify against him, especially after Bedrosian sent Renke's men after him."

"And hey, I got an email from FedPat. They're going to cover all of Samantha's expenses."

"That was quick," Kate said.

"Had to be a coincidence. But in the future, I think they'll know who I am."

Kate and Lyle wandered along the square and stopped in front of a coffee house.

"We tried to make this espresso joint look authentic for the period," Kate said. "But it came out looking like a Starbucks."

"Have time for coffee today, or do you have to pick up Bruce?"

"No problem. Bruce is still working on the condo sale."

"Maybe we could go to the movies. There's a new double bill at the NC Cinema. Looks good."

"I know. *The Godfather* and *Easy Rider.*"

eↄeↄ

"As we look to the future," Max boomed, "we see an expanded view of the past. Different directions and different expressions for Nostalgia City."

"What's he mean by that?" Lyle asked.

"Didn't you know? Max wants to widen our market. We're pushing up to the '80s."

"Cool. I'll get out my Blondie albums."

ACKNOWLEDGEMENTS

Many thanks to the editorial team at Black Opal Books for polishing my prose and making this book happen. I'm indebted to Lauri Wellington, Faith, Reyana and the rest of the talented professionals.

I consulted a variety of people for editing assistance and technical details on subjects including insurance, law enforcement, flight scheduling, and music. Many thanks to Christel Hall, Denise Harrison, Gene Michals, Craig Holland, J. David Pincus, Sgt. Jim Mead, Angie White, Gary and Shirley Bria, Jane Gorby and Jacci Wilson. Any errors here are mine not theirs.

Also, I wish to recognize mentors and friends, Arnold Weitzen, Dayle Molen, Jim Tucker, Nathan Heard, Bev Place, Barbara Cloud and David Shaw.

Thanks to my wife, Anne, for her love and support.

About the Author

Mark S. Bacon began his career as a newspaper police reporter in southern California. He later became a copywriter, creating ads and commercials for cars, electronics, and Knott's Berry Farm, the California theme park. He is the author of several business books including one that was named a best business book of the year by the *Library Journal* and printed in four languages. His articles have appeared in *The Washington Post, Cleveland Plain Dealer, Kansas City Star, USAir Magazine,* and many other publications. Most recently, he was a regular contributor for the *San Francisco Chronicle.* Bacon has taught journalism at Cal Poly University – Pomona, the University of Redlands, and the University of Nevada.

His early background, covering a police beat daily and working for a theme park, influenced his creation of Nostalgia City, the setting for his first murder mystery novel. Bacon is also the author of two collections of mystery flash fiction stories. He lives in Reno with his wife, Anne, and their golden retriever.